T0354123

Monmouth in the Morning

Monmouth in the Morning

Book 1—A Gannon Family Trilogy

Richard W. Ellison

iUniverse, Inc.
Bloomington

Monmouth in the Morning
Book 1—A Gannon Family Trilogy

Copyright © 2012 by Richard W. Ellison

All rights reserved. No part of this book may be used or reproduced by any means, graphic, electronic, or mechanical, including photocopying, recording, taping or by any information storage retrieval system without the written permission of the publisher except in the case of brief quotations embodied in critical articles and reviews.

This is a work of fiction. All of the characters, names, incidents, organizations, and dialogue in this novel are either the products of the author's imagination or are used fictitiously.

iUniverse books may be ordered through booksellers or by contacting:

iUniverse
1663 Liberty Drive
Bloomington, IN 47403
www.iuniverse.com
1-800-Authors (1-800-288-4677)

Because of the dynamic nature of the Internet, any web addresses or links contained in this book may have changed since publication and may no longer be valid. The views expressed in this work are solely those of the author and do not necessarily reflect the views of the publisher, and the publisher hereby disclaims any responsibility for them.

Any people depicted in stock imagery provided by Thinkstock are models, and such images are being used for illustrative purposes only.

Certain stock imagery © Thinkstock.

ISBN: 978-1-4759-5617-7 (sc)
ISBN: 978-1-4759-5618-4 (hc)
ISBN: 978-1-4759-5619-1 (e)

Library of Congress Control Number: 2012919116

Printed in the United States of America

iUniverse rev. date: 3/14/2013

Acknowledgments

To: Doyle Hickerson
Sam "Tunney" Liles
... Eylau Eagles; special families – special friends

To: Gladys Ellison Schultze
... whose smile brings sunshine on rainy days

To John "Gannon"
... writer, who counseled life's charge long after he lived this trilogy

To: George Weissman, MD
... for his tremendous knowledge and heart; the man for whom they created the words *brotherhood* and *family*

To: Sidney Offit, NYU Creative Writing Teacher (1975), Novelist, author of *Memoir of the Bookie's Son* ... elegant, touching, and others. Award winning Teacher at NYU and the New School, NY, NY

To: Sol Yurick, NYU Advance Creative Writing Teacher (1976), Novelist, author of *The Warriors*—NY gangs (a popular movie); *Richard A.*—international thriller, and many others

To: Charles W. Gorton, retired US Navy, CWO, Commander in Chief Pacific Fleet, Pearl Harbor, shipmate memories of life with some of the Navy's finest men

To: Dr. William K. Tunnell, friend, decorated Lieutenant, USN—Buckner Bay, Okinawa, WWII

To: Jeff Rankin, Monmouth College executive, for his helpfulness, his historical knowledge of Monmouth, Illinois, and for sharing his historic photographs - one of which graces the cover of this novel

With Special Thanks: to Alvin Granowsky, Ph.D., Dallas-based novelist, educator, friend. Read his work on iUniverse.com.

Reviews By Novelists:

Monmouth in the Morning is nothing less than an American saga, a fictional excursion into the hearts and souls of the Gannon family and their friends as they adventure west to settle in South Dakota.

With a historian's scholarship and a poet's passion, Richard Ellison treats his readers to an engaging narrative, enriched by majestic landscapes, operatic arias, and a cast of characters as complex as they are diverse.

"Make the evening forget the cares of the day," Tom Gannon advises his family. Richard Ellison does just that for bedtime readers.

Sidney Offit
New York based Novelist and
author of: *Memoir of the Bookie's Son*

Richard Ellison has written a compelling, sweeping saga, expansive in both time and place, of a family that represents perhaps the best of America. His characters are complex and engaging, not to be forgotten.

Jim H. Ainsworth, Author of *Follow the Rivers Trilogy, Home Light Burning*, and *Go Down Looking.*

Monmouth in the Morning – a family success story and fascinating page-turner that portrays the friendship of three youths and their families amidst the life and lingering bigotry in the early decades of the 20th Century West.

Richard Ellison is to be commended for the spotlight he turns on his absorbing historic portrait that has so much relevance for American life today.

Alvin Granowsky, Ed.D., textbook author and Educational consultant Readers Comments

Readers' Comments:

Monmouth in the Morning is an exciting novel. While reading with interest and enjoying the excitement, I felt like I was in someone's back pocket along the way! Came away feeling like I was more involved than just someone reading the novel.

Jace Carrington – Dallas, Texas

Your novel, Monmouth, certainly delivers in a tale that could have been many American families in the golden age of discovery. It is written in clear poetic lines that make the reader want to read on.

Bob Nyilas
N.Y., New York

A really good tale: action, history, and environmental concerns well before its time. The excitement stemming from the ladies singing successes in Chicago, Tom's banking adventures; the one room school house charm, the fascinating experiences of John and his friend, Blue Eagle in the Valley of the Moon, Haggerty Woods…with its sad consequences, and other fine adventurous chapters, pulled the story together well, and kept me reading.

Shirley Chiller, O.A.M.;
and national environmental engineer, Ken Chiller
Caulfield North, Australia

I enjoyed reading your historical novel very much as it reminded me of my own life while being raised by my grandparents soon after that period. Traditional values were esteemed, honesty and integrity revered. Work smart, achieve your best, be grateful and hold out your hand to those who need it. We not only understood these values, we lived by them.

Monmouth in the Morning recaptures that era in American history that should be read by youth, relived by adults and emulated in today's cultural morass.

Sheila Liles McCorkle
Shreveport, LA

Richard, Monmouth is a delightful read. Its time and place in our nation's history - the rigors and charms of early 20th Century, are dazzling in their simplicity and adventure opportunities. Hurry up and give us Book 2 & 3.

James Brooks Day, Seattle

I've read the first part of Monmouth. It truly draws you in; escapism to a different place and time at its best. I look forward to reading more and to learning what happens to the Gannon family.

Carol Eagleton,
Singapore

Author's Note

The names of the people in this novel are fictional, as are many of the scenes and events that are portrayed. The Brule, a magical clear river that caresses the town of Chambers, South Dakota, a small fictional town not that different from early Chamberlain, and Cypress Lake, with its improbable cypress trees and swamp inhabitants, are but three of such fictional settings. The principle theme of this trilogy represents, in part, actual lives of friends of the author. While the Dakota and Lakota tribes are real, the characters and the settings are not. The last known remnants of the majestic Mandan Tribe are speculative only for this created setting. The exceptions throughout are well-known historical names and events that grace these pages to mark the time and place of a growing country on the move, shaping a very small segment of people in a way typical of the industrial expansion of our nation, be it in the city or middle America's last frontier.

Foreword

Monmouth had hammered its way into the twentieth century like most Illinois towns—with a hardy people focusing on development and success. Thomas Gannon's young family was perhaps typical for many years of their lives until restlessness and adventure called out this third-generation young man in 1913 to explore a new life. This family story is like so many early American stories, gliding through life's journey with their pioneer spirit, searching for identity, success, and a new kind of happiness.

Tom Gannon, a ruggedly handsome master carpenter and frontiersman at heart, with his beautiful wife, Helen, who possesses an operatic singing voice of exceptional quality, along with their young son and two daughters, set out to explore less populated middle America—Chambers, South Dakota, on the banks of the incredible Brule River. This is Gannon Country, a land cloaked in a setting not unlike the River Missouri, yet vastly more like a huge virgin spring in its clarity, importance to a community still filled with lingering legends of Dakota, Lakota, and Mandan tribes.

There in Chambers, two thirteen-year-old boys, John Gannon and James Blue Eagle, the Mandan Chief's son, bond in a lasting friendship powered by a one-room school, athletics, and unusual frontier adventures. In so doing, they help their small frontier town grow in stature during a time of mistrust and uncertainty, ultimately launching their own destiny.

While the gifted Tom Gannon matures in frontier banking episodes, the Gannon women explode their talents in the world of opera and art, leading them to Chicago and Europe. These strong magnets nearly rupture family unity just as young John prepares to enter high school in Kansas City, Missouri, taking with him Blue Eagle and the amazing newcomer, "Creature"- once again confronting social customs.

Chapter 1

Monmouth in the Morning

June 1913

The Gannon family felt a new exhilaration in their lives. Packing their last possessions for shipment, saying good-bye to their friends, and saying good-bye to Monmouth, the town where they were all born, caused anxiety for some of them but it was devastating to Tom's wife, Helen. Taking a gifted singer like Helen Gannon far from the opera stage of Chicago was nothing short of a death knell for family relations, yet Tom Gannon, this master carpenter, this frustrated frontiersman, was doing exactly that. His plan had never failed him: *make the evenings forget the cares of the day.* He had a young family to raise, a dream to fulfill, and in his mind, it was now or never.

Five-O-One Fifth Street had sheltered the Gannons all their lives, as it had the Gannons before them. They would go back there often in the castles of their minds even as careers developed and pushed them onward in life's myriad endeavors.

"Are you about finished?" Tom Gannon said to his young son.

"Yes, sir," John said as he forked the last vestiges of sausage and biscuit into his mouth. After a swig of milk, he jumped up to join his father, who was heading out the door. The girls, Sallie, eleven, with flowing black hair, and Betty Jean, eight, with dark bangs, stayed with their mother, a beautiful, shapely woman with striking auburn hair, now finishing the final packing.

"I particularly want you to see this," Tom said to his son, now well over twelve. He was eager yet sad to be saying good-bye to this town, leaving his friends behind.

Down the brick road to the red-bricked square, they hurried to catch the sun, now rising over Chicago some 200 miles east. Just as they had done for the past three days, they reached the town square as the sun's brilliant rays lit the horizon. The man and the boy stood there alone except for the early morning Atlas news people opening shop across the square. It was like the other exciting days, except now the drama tightened in its finality.

"Look at that sight. This is the last picture of Monmouth that you will likely remember. I want you to tuck it in your mind. You were born here just like that new sun bursting over the horizon. Mr. Moffet put it right in the Atlas, second page: 'New Carpenter in Town: John Thomas Gannon, 8 pounds, 3 ounces, born to Tom and Helen'. You were a sight. Just like that sun coming up. All red and glowing, screaming to get your day going."

John moved a bit as his father's grip on his shoulder became uncomfortable. He looked up at the strong-shouldered man's tanned face with eyes unusually softened. "Will it last, Papa? Will it last?"

"I think it will, son," Tom assured him. "Each day brings a fantastic new opportunity. It cranks up our dreams and sets us on our way. And tonight—oh my! You be home on time. Tonight we get the sunset I've been promising you. It'll give you a show, all right, a few wisps of clouds hunkering low to set the stage. You'll see, just like yesterday, and just like it will be tomorrow. But if you think this is something, wait until we get to Chambers. The Brule River—oh boy! You've never laid your eyes on anything like it. It's nothing short of a dream. It's the last frontier, and we're going to be right in the middle of it."

They smiled warmly at each other. "We better be getting back home, son. I have a sizeable job to do at the Haynes." With a gentle hand on John's shoulder, the father walked his son back toward home.

As they traveled along Fifth Street, John was filled with a new warmth. *Can this be my father?* he thought to himself. *If it is, then what happened to the strong disciplinarian who kept me at arm's length?* He looked up into his father's eyes and took the measure of a man that he had never known.

Their day saw no end of last-minute chores and good-byes. When everyone finally gathered for dinner, the sautéed chicken smelled incredible. It was accompanied by mashed potatoes, bacon green beans, and upside down pineapple cake. The whole family was ravenous except Betty Jean, pouting under her little-girl bangs and shoulder-length, black hair.

"Mother, you had better comfort our daughter." It wasn't long until everyone was enjoying the cake. And the coffee—that Gannon coffee!

"All right now, everybody, we start a big journey tomorrow. We are going to be in the car for eight hours each day, so you've got to promise your mother and me: no acting up, and no fits of temper. Okay? Everybody understand? We'll have a great trip. Lots of new country to see. South Dakota is a pretty exciting land—spread out and like nothing around here. And Chambers! Wait until you see Chambers there on the Brule River. You've never seen a river until you've seen the Brule. All pristine, clear, and deep."

"I don't like it, Papa" Betty Jean said.

"Oh, you will, darling. I guarantee you," Tom humored his young daughter. "When you see that big fireball sun coming up in the mornings out there in the west, with its big blue sky, it will knock your bonnet off."

"I don't wear a bonnet, Papa."

The children doubled up laughing.

"Come on now, give your mother a hand. John, go recheck your bag. We have to get all our things on the luggage rack."

He continued, to no one in particular, saying, "We'll start at about eight in the morning and we'll swing by downtown for a last salute to Monmouth, then head on out 34 to Des Moines. That's a four-day drive. We may even stop short this first day and stay over in Ottumwa. I laid on an extra can of gasoline so we're set. Our Buick is new—and so are we. If any car can give a good ride on our journey, it's that black and red-trimmed Pathfinder parked at our front door."

"Who are you talking to, anyway?" Helen said.

"Why the captain of the ship, of course!" Betty Jean turned to look at her father in time for a wink and a big smile.

The next morning had an air of excitement. After breakfast, everyone checked and rechecked the entire house. Tom asked, "Mother, did Ralph pick up the keys for Dr. Eckley?"

"Of course," Helen said. Finally, the family assembled out front at their new 1913 Buick. Almost in unison, everyone turned around to look at their home of so many years.

Tom said, "Okay, now, let's all say good-bye to the house and salute." They all did.

Betty Jean started to cry as they got in the car. "Okay," the father said, snuffing out his daughter's emotions, "let's go do the same for Monmouth."

When they reached the red-bricked square, there were a half-dozen families milling around Main Street to see them off. They all hugged and said their good-byes. Mary Jean thrust a bouquet of marigolds in John's hands and ran off to her parents across the street. John waved to young Ralph Eckley who stood at the entry of the Atlas. They all waved as the Gannons drove around the block. They drove past Monmouth

College, then back to the Wyatt Earp home, continuing on west First Street, passing the Bijou Theater, the catholic church with its tall steeple, around past the Monmouth Browns playing field, circling around past several two-story houses with turrets and wraparound banister porches - ending up back at the town square fountain.

Tom parked facing the People's National Bank and the Centennial Building opposite the Monmouth Library. Nearby was The Fair shop, Rogers Feed Store, Diffenbough Grocery, and shops.

"Okay, let's get out here for our last good-bye. Ready? Salute! Good-bye old girl," Tom said.

Betty Jean made a silent crying face, tears ran down Sallie's cheeks, and John waved a final goodbye to his friend, Ralph Eckley. The Rankin family waved from a distance as did the Chapins and Haynes.

The Gannon family slowly pulled away from the square—the town where Tom grew up, where his ancestors had helped lay the brick, where he learned his trades in building a growing Monmouth. "Good-bye, home," he said, barely audible to his family. He choked back his emotions as the Pathfinder slowly pulled away to begin their new life.

This was the fourth time Tom Gannon had escaped his birthplace, but this time he felt as if it were final—for something strong grabbed at his gut.

Helen Gannon's face was as long as Tom had ever seen it. Her battle to move to the big city was beaten down over and over. With three children to care for and the years quickly vanishing, she saw her chances for developing an operatic career slip away. They were driving to Chambers, not Chicago.

Chapter 2

The Journey

The first few miles trapped the Gannons in a somber mood, but the shifting scenery soon brightened up the whole family. Tom knew that a trip like this, 600 miles, was no picnic, and he would be the lone driver. Roads, he had heard, were little more than wagon trails. *Humor the children, console the wife*, he thought.

Shortly after leaving Monmouth, Tom said, "Tell you what we're going to do. Every two hours, we'll stop and walk around a bit. Keep our legs limbered up. We'll see some sights; you just wait. Maybe your mother might even practice some of your favorite songs."

"Oh, would you, Mother?" Sallie said, pushing her hair aside.

"We'll see," came Helen's short reply. They soon passed over the Mississippi River, their family recreation site for so many years.

"Look, look, look!" shouted Betty Jean. "Is that our river, Papa?"

"You bet it is, darling. The grand old Mississippi. I was hoping we could see Huron Island, but it's too far downriver. John, remember the big bass you caught one weekend when we camped out there?"

"Yes, sir. How old was I then? Maybe six?" he asked.

"All of that," Tom said. "I just let you struggle with it. I knew he was a big one by the way he bent your pole. You slipped down in the shallows, but you got right back up and finally pulled him in. I got the biggest kick out of that. So did your Uncle Earl. I've told that story ten times if ever I told it at all. If you think that was exciting, just wait until you see the Brule.

"Don't get me wrong." he continued. "Huron Island was exciting, and it was a great place for outings. Remember those great Fourth of July trips out there? One year, I think Sallie must have been no more than six or seven or so, half the town was out there. We had perhaps the biggest fish fry known to Monmouth. We all stuffed ourselves with fish, and I'll bet a third of that group camped out all weekend just as we did." Tom paused a moment, just long enough for his wife to get in a word.

"I'll bet they have some great fish cookouts in Chicago, too. Right there on the lakefront. Just park your car and fish."

Tom gulped.

"Why don't we go there, Papa?" Betty Jean said.

"Oh, you remind me after supper tonight; we'll talk about Chicago—Billy Sunday, the shootouts the gangsters have. You and I will get right down in the middle of it, shoot some dice, and dance." All the children giggled.

"Oh, for God's sake, Tom, be serious with our children; be serious with me."

"I would, Helen, except we're all heading for the biggest adventure of our lives. Chambers is the last chance to smell air so pure and get a sense of what the real frontier of the Old West was really like. Chambers is small, growing, and unusual. We will, as we would any place, find our own blocks to build our dreams. Still, I'll grant you this much for Chicago: I had a great time there once. And it is a great city, but just like when I was in Panama or San Francisco, I couldn't wait to get back to Monmouth. Chicago is a young person's town. It costs a fortune to raise a family there. We may get to Chicago someday. Who knows? Maybe sooner than—"

"Watch out!" Helen interrupted.

Tom swerved the car, barely missing an oncoming truck with its load overhanging the Buick's path much too tightly. "Pay attention to the road. You could have gotten all of us killed!"

"We're too young to die, Mother," Tom countered immediately and then continued as if nothing happened. "Why, if it turns out that we have a fine singer in our family … well, who knows our future? You want to audition, Betty Jean?"

"What's audition, Papa?"

"You'll have to check with your mother on that one; she's the talent in the family. She can tell you all about auditions. Look at this. What do you know? This is our first rest stop."

Tom Gannon pulled into the drive of a homey looking roadside restaurant.

"Take the ladies with you, Helen. John and I will find the men's room."

"Afraid you and the boy will have to wait," the owner said to Gannon. "We have just the one."

"We're okay. Too early for lunch, so we'll just have some sodas when the ladies come out."

"I hope they hurry," John said. "I've got to go really bad."

"Can you hold out?" his father asked.

"I think so, but I'm also very thirsty."

"Can you drink and wet at the same time?" his father kidded.

"I've never tried that," John said, chuckling at his father's wit.

Then, the ladies came in and settled at a table.

"We'll be right back. Order us two sodas," Gannon said.

Soon everyone had refreshed themselves, and the Gannon family was on the road again.

"You mean we have ten days of these insufferable roads?" Helen asked.

"Ten, maybe twelve at most."

"Twelve! We'll be half dead when we get to South Dakota."

"Well, Helen, where's your adventurous spirit? Look at the children. All excited and ready for the next turn in the road. Aren't you, Betty Jean?"

"Yes, sir."

The roads went from trails to trenches to occasional level ... sort of, and the miles ahead seemed endless. In certain stretches, Gannon dared not to take his eyes off the road. Some roads seemed little more than rough, torn out trails. That's all they were—worn game runs and cattle traces and wagon ruts.

"I listen to our family, excited, doubtful—some full of wonderment. San Francisco comes to mind," Tom said. Then he spoke for almost an hour in retelling the details of his experiences in the Great San Francisco Earthquake and Fire, ending with,

"I'll never forget it. Never."

The Gannon's Pathfinder rolled on down the road in a quiet not heard since they began the trip. The children fell asleep only to be starkly awakened by sudden jolts from the rough road. By the end of the day, their snail's pace got them no further than halfway to Ottumwa.

As they pulled into the little town of Mt. Pleasant, Gannon realized that the roads were rougher and slower than he thought they would be. This was not going to be easy. He pulled into a travel hotel of log cabins.

"Yes, sir, second cabin on the right. Just perfect for your fine family."

"They sure don't pay much attention to the roads do they?" Tom said to the owner.

"Afraid not—regretfully for the traveler. Our city streets are very good, but everyone kinda views traveling cross country as for the rich. We're pretty focused on our own. We got settling to do. Roads have to come later."

Tom shook his head, exclaiming, "Well, there's a job for the government. I guess they'll do something about it when some politician needs a job."

Sleep came swiftly for the Gannons that night. After a hearty breakfast of biscuits, sausages, and eggs, they drove out eagerly for Ottumwa.

"Mother, why don't you lead us in a nice little song that we can all sing," Tom said to Helen.

Not wanting to disappoint the kids, Helen started singing a small song that she learned as a girl, "Here the Small Children." Soon they were all trying their best to get out the words, but the rough roads made singing impossible. Instead, everyone was hiccupping more than singing the words as the big Buick charged along the uncertain, rough path to Ottumwa. Recent rains presented chug holes, ruts, and double ruts. Everyone starting laughing, purposefully mispronouncing the words, and yelling, "Awwww. I bit my tongue." There was more laughter followed by more yelling and more nonsense … which ultimately led to quiet.

"Well, look at this," Tom said. "A smooth patch of road. How in the world did we luck into this, Betty Jean?"

"She's sound asleep, Papa. She's using me for a pillow," John said.

Just at dusk, at the edge of Ottumwa, the road improved to gravel and composite mixed with clay.

"Oh for some tasty dinner and a good bath," Mrs. Gannon said.

The kids were all leaning against one another, asleep and tired.

Tom reached over and took his wife's hand gently in his. "There, Mother. It wasn't that bad was it?"

It took some effort, but Helen managed to squeeze back a bit, asking herself, *How can one warm up to such a disaster? Twelve days? Good God's glory!*

"Awake, awake, you angels of travel!" Tom yelled to his children, opening the back door of their car. He shook John gently at first and then firmly.

"Come on, son, wake up the girls and help your mother with our things. I'll check us in." Everyone was tired, stiff as a new telephone pole, but finally they got moving.

"Now this is more like it," Helen said. "These are nice rooms."

"More to come in all our big-city stops," Tom said.

Helen got the kids settled in the adjoining room. After dinner, everyone got a bath. Exhausted, the children eagerly sought their beds. Helen made the effort, moving beyond the division between herself and her husband over this trip to the west. Bath accommodations, under the circumstances, lent a certain element of tenderness to weary travelers. Tom and Helen shared their bath, washing each other gently, sensually, which soon put behind them everything but the present moment.

Helen, almost as tall as her husband, was goddess-like at 130 pounds. Her small waist accentuated her beautifully curved hips, her full breasts, her flowing auburn hair, and her handsome, full face with its strong chin and dark eyes. She was all that any man could wish for.

She looked at Tom standing before her, ruggedly handsome with brown, neat hair, a strong face with soft brown eyes—a specimen in every way. His natural build, just under six feet, was chiseled in every detail. His 178-pound frame fit him perfectly. His soft eyes sparkled as they stood before each other, exhilarated after their bath. This was their time of day when life came together, washing away any concerns that might still linger. Given his wife's disappointment in their destination, Tom knew that life began right then.

He walked to Helen, smiling, gently taking her in his strong arms. Their kisses started slowly, growing passionate as they pressed their warm bodies together. He touched all the pressure points, taking her by the hand and gently pulling her to the bed. Their embrace was warmed by body heat, soothing hands, honeymoon in its excitement, sending the room spinning, dancing out of control into a night of family passion.

At dawn, rising was not easy for Tom Gannon, but after stretching and washing, he said, "Want to eat in bed this morning or shall we all go over to breakfast?"

"Breakfast in bed! Oh, I want to see that. Did you awaken the children?"

"Shortly," Tom said, and he started their routine of prepacking.

The Buick pulled out on the open road at 8:00 a.m. Five hundred miles lay before them. "It feels like rain," Helen said.

"I was hoping you wouldn't bring that up," Tom said. The smooth city roads soon gave way to the open country, its soothing vistas, its Conestoga dirt roads, its complaints, and its laughter, even if forced at times, giving family adventure a new name.

"Oh, I just love this road," Helen said. "It's enough to make a Billy goat break wind."

"Mother!" The children all giggle for three or four minutes, punching one another in the ribs at times.

"Mother!" Gannon repeated. "How uncouth. How unlike a lady with a devastating smile," he said, trying to liven up their day.

"Owhhh!" everybody yelled in unison.

"What was that?" John yelled.

"Just a twelve-incher straight down to the devil's pit," Gannon said. The children gave good giggles. So went the day until the fifty-fifth mile. A prairie storm, emboldened with rapid crescendos of prairie lightning of incredible proportions, set upon them, sending mighty Thor's anvil strikes across the dark sky and plunging into the earth all around them. Tom knew it was no small matter. Everyone was very quiet, hanging on to one another, glued to their seats.

"Darn! That one was close," Tom said as a huge bolt struck nearby. His heart sank deeply as he read the heavy water up ahead, the torrents racing to the ditches. Mired. Stuck. They sat for at least thirty minutes. Suddenly, a noise came from the road. A man on horseback sized them up as he passed slowly on by.

"Why in the world didn't he stop?" Helen asked.

"I think he saw all he wanted to see," Tom said. "I hope when he gets home that he finds an answer for us. We may just have to spend the night right here."

"Right here?" Helen said.

"Well, yeah, right here in this muddy road—likely stuck up to our axles," Tom reasoned. "Let's be patient and ride out this storm, which looks like it's already giving way over here on the left. Betty Jean, you want to get out and push?"

"No!" came a loud, giggling reply. "Let John do it."

"John is sleeping," came the boy's reply.

"Okay, then; that settles it. We sit and we pray."

"What'll we pray for, Papa?"

"Why, a nice farmer with a pair of strong mules in double-tree harness."

"What's a double-tree, Papa?" asked Betty Jean.

"We're gonna have to wait on that one, darling. When it gets here, I'll point it out to you. All farmers have them for their mules. A farmer can do a lot of plowing with a good team and a double-tree to pull his plow."

They sat silently for the next twenty minutes when suddenly Gannon said, "Look, look, look. See, that fine man on horseback came back to pull us out of this mud hole." Gannon rolled down his window as the man drew near and shouted, "Hello! You sure are a traveler's dream come true."

The farmer didn't reply. Rather, he dismounted and hooked up a heavy chain to the Buick's front frame. Slowly, he urged his big, black mules onward. The high wheels of the Buick took hold, but the back end slid toward the ditch before following their rescuer on to the farmer's house, now visible a hundred yards ahead.

"How fortunate! How fortunate!" Helen mused.

"Let us hope all of our luck on this trip will be this golden," Gannon said. "We must be doing something right," he added.

The farmer pulled the Buick up as close to the front steps as he could, unhitched the chain from the car, and drove the mules to the barn.

His wife, with a coat over her head, came out to the car carrying two coats, one for Helen and the children, and the other for Gannon—who did not take it, as his bounding stride quickly took him to the shelter of the front porch. The rain slowed. The coats and their occupants flowed to the front porch where everyone introduced themselves and gave endless praise for the incredible rescue.

"Welcome to the Power house! I'm Betty, and my husband is Henry. He is almost deaf, but he signs. But don't worry; he reads lips really well," Mrs. Power said as she ushered the Gannons, now in their stockings, into the charming, sparsely furnished living room, a huge room that also functioned as the dining room.

Mr. Power removed his boots on the front porch as all the Gannons gave him their praise. He signed with his wife for a moment, and then Mrs. Power relayed his message and greetings.

"I have cooked a lot of chicken, as I always do. Come eat with us. You can wash up there on the back porch." As the Gannons moved toward the porch, they heard Mrs. Power say to her husband, "What a lovely family you brought us, Henry. You never know what falls from a storm."

When the Gannons reentered the room, both Powers urged them to sit at the dining table. The children were famished. They started to help themselves to the bowls of chicken in front of them when Helen stopped them. Something new to the children preceded dinner. Mr. Power signed a prayer, crossed himself, and motioned for everyone to eat.

"We're from Pennsylvania. And you folks?"

"Monmouth, Illinois," Tom said. "And may I say, Mrs. Power, this is the finest chicken that ever graced a table."

"Being hungry does not hurt a bit," came the reply.

No one spoke for a while, and the mashed potatoes, cream gravy, chicken, tomato salad, and cornbread vanished from the well-used, ancient oak table.

"More milk?" Mrs. Power said to the children and then to Tom and Helen.

"Monmouth—that's near Chicago, isn't it?" Mr. Power signed.

When Mrs. Power spoke his question, Tom immediately answered with, "Oh, no, Chicago is way northeast. At least 200 miles."

Amid much "Oh my!" exclaiming, Mrs. Power presented a vanilla cream pie to the hungry travelers. It did not last, and Mrs. Power beamed a smile to everyone.

"I'm full up," Betty Jean said.

"I think you spoke for all of us," Gannon said.

Mrs. Gannon spoke to her children, "Now what to you say to our lovely host, children?"

Almost in unison, "Thank you for a fine dinner," came the answer.

Mrs. Power smiled, made small talk for a few minutes, and then said, "I know you're all exhausted after your long drive. Come, I'll show you to your rooms."

"Our rooms," said Helen. "Did you hear that, children? You have your own room."

"Really," Gannon said, "I was just hoping there would be plenty of soft hay for us to bed down in your loft."

"No, our kids are away, and we struggle without them. You are our family tonight."

"You are very kind to take us in like this, Mrs. Power," Helen said. "I would be ever so grateful if you would stay with Mr. Power and talk with Tom. The girls and I will do the dishes." There was a lot of wisdom in the offer, so Mrs. Power obliged.

Soon everyone grew weary for bed.

The next morning, Gannon left two gold coins under his pillow.

After breakfast, Helen said to the Powers, "Give me your address, please. I'll send you a surprise."

A giant painter's sun greeted the Gannons as they drove away from the Power farm. Eager shouts were heard among the waving farewells. "Good-bye! Thanks for everything! You'll hear from us before long."

"My oh my! Weren't they hospitable people? What do you plan to send them, Helen?"

"Perhaps a pair of handsome Indian blankets."

"That might be well received," Tom said. "They are colorful, unusual, and warm. That's just right. Indian blankets. But they gotta be well made and nice colors."

"Certainly!" Helen said.

The road bed, such as it was in places, absorbed yesterday's rain sufficiently, smoothing out the large ruts and making the road somewhat easier to navigate.

"When we get to De Moines," Tom said, "I'll find us a nice hotel—though I must say, that rescue and the Power family hospitality could not have been more fortunate."

"I'll say!" Helen agreed.

Tom shook his head slowly as he said, "If you ever lose faith in humanity, you only have to have an experience such as ours. Did you notice how calmly the Powers went about things? It was as if they went through such a routine every day. Right down to a prayer being signed. I think we should find a nice memory of some sort and send it to them at Christmas, as well," Tom said.

Helen nodded her agreement. "What an incredible treat."

They drove on through the prairie with its vistas and fresh air swirling about them, mixing with the warmth extended to them from the simple grace of a quiet people. It was an impressive act of kindness that they would relive in stories for the rest of their lives.

By the end of the day, with his family increasingly more fragile and short of spirits, Tom Gannon studied his maps, his plans, and the remaining miles on their journey.

When they pulled into De Moines, they were behind his imagined itinerary. At dinner in their hotel, Gannon counseled his family. "Look, this is hard on all of us. These roads have beat us to death, so what do you say to staying two nights here in De Moines? Tomorrow, we'll just laze about after breakfast. Then we can stroll the streets as a family. Maybe poke into a few stores just to see what things look like in a big city out here. When we get tired of walking, we can go back for a rest, lunch, perhaps a nap, and do whatever you all want to do. How does that sound?" Everybody was ecstatic. "Then, it's agreed. Two fine days in big De Moines, and, Mother, here's another surprise for you: how about two nights in Sioux Falls as well."

There was so much noise at the Gannon table the waiter came over to offer his assistance.

"No, young man, we are just discovering ourselves on the road, so to speak," Gannon said to the waiter. Tom looked closely at his wife. "What say you, our mother? Two days in Sioux Falls sound agreeable?"

"Sounds fantastic," Helen said.

"Then it's done," Gannon told his family. Dinner, bath, and a long sleep were never more welcomed.

The black Buick pulled the Gannons along measuredly, safely, conquering one town after the other. Tempers flared occasionally as "body met soul" on some of the roughest roads of their trip. On their tenth day, the Gannons rolled into Sioux Falls. The Southern Hotel looked like a palace in an oasis. Soon they were out exploring.

"Darn! Look at these prices. Things are sky high out here," Helen said. "Look at this: Sirloin steak twenty-four cents a pound, pork chops twenty-two cents, eight cents for milk—that's not bad—butter thirty-five cents ... good heavens."

Tom changed the subject. "Come on, let's go across the street. That hardware store might be fun, and we may find something useful in there." Gannon led his family across the street and amused them by perusing most of the stores until hunger pains told everyone they needed to get back to the Southern and dressed for dinner. No sooner had they entered their rooms when Tom realized his exhausted family would be much better served with a short nap.

At dinner, everyone was ravenous. Steak and chicken appealed to everyone, and there was a long dessert list. Betty Jean let out a small scream of delight when she saw the cart of pies being wheeled to their table.

After a half-hour prowl through the town, a yawning, tired Gannon family took little coaching to return to their rooms for a sleep deeper than the Grand Canyon.

Enjoying a full day of leisure, the Gannon family covered at least a dozen stores in Sioux Falls. Brown-Little Shoes had the perfect shoes for the children, and Tom urged Helen to buy a smart, casual shoe for herself.

The next day, they reached Mitchell. Gannon's pulse started racing as the finish line of this unimaginable journey was at hand, fully realizing that one more hard day of pounding the deep rutted road lay before them. *Good Lord,* he thought, *if that magical place has changed much since I first rode through it, I'll never hear the end of it.*

That night, Tom took his wife gently in his arms, brushed back her hair, and kissed the tip of her nose.

"Tomorrow," he said, "I hope our new home greets us with what I once saw as the most beautiful sunset on earth. Helen, I couldn't be more proud of you and our children. You'll see. Chambers is a town where we can grow our talents and grow our children strong and safely. We'll find like-minded people there, and after a short time, our life in Chambers will tell us that we have found a magical place."

"You better be right, Thomas Gannon. You owe me, and you owe our children."

Pulling out of Mitchell the next morning brought a special excitement to the whole family. The prize lay at hand.

"Dad, how far is it?" John asked.

"Chambers? It's a full eight-hour drive. Just right for a Saturday, don't you think? We should get in there late-afternoon."

"But how many miles, Papa?" Sallie wanted to know.

"Roughly fifty, it looks like. Depends on the road, as well."

The Gannons settled back in the Buick. Several more fields of wheat waved in a gentle wind as they steadily moved ahead.

"Look at the wheat out there. Isn't that a great picture?" Tom said. "And you should see it when it takes on its beauty coat later in the year."

Soon they navigated a rickety, wooden bridge, skewed by recent high creek water, and then an agonizing stretch of deep and shallow ruts that jolted the family hard. Finally, a smooth stretch gave relief, only to fade into several miles of fine, hateful dust, covering the car, and filling the occupants' lungs.

"The top soil is all powder," Tom said through constant coughing. "We should be out of this shortly; only about an hour left to go, judging by the sun and our speedometer ... looks like about twelve miles left. Pretty soon we'll be on the outskirts of Chambers and still have good daylight to enjoy our new town. We'll check into the hotel, clean up, and watch the sun hit the Brule River. One thing is for sure—you're in for some sights."

"Oh, Mother, I like it," Betty Jean said.

Helen looked straight ahead as Tom drove his family into the late afternoon sun that lit up the most important venture of his life. The dice were rolling. The hazards that challenged his courage in Cuba with the Spanish, the fires that fueled the disaster of a leveled San Francisco, and the malaria that fell the multitudes in the tropical hell in Panama seemed remote, fleeting, in the hierarchy of his visions.

Was he right? Was this river, this last frontier, `mythical—some mirage of the mind that lured him like a phantom spirit? Or was it truly the little-known universe at the rainbow's edge that existed no other place on earth. Not in Quebec, not in Sault Saint Marie, and not in the fabled histories of the likes of Salt Lake City. Just here, and it lay directly before him at fifteen miles an hour. He heard the words of his children swirl about him, felt the ice in the silence of his wife, felt each mile move under the creeping Buick—suspended, totally unmeasured, until at last he saw the prize.

Chapter 3

Chambers

The Gannons' mud-splattered Buick turned off the graveled road, rumbled with uncertainty across a rough ditch, and stopped at the top of the high embankment at the head of Main Street.

"At last! Chambers!" Gannon said to his family.

The weary, stiff-jointed passengers hobbled from the car, grimacing, and flailing the dust that covered them. The Buick was no longer red trimmed black, but brown with mud and sand. John stood by his father seeking solace, for deep down, he was sick of it. Sick of the long journey, sick of losing his friends, and most of all, the frequent bickering between his parents made him nauseous. Sallie and Betty Jean stretched at the side of their mother.

Tom Gannon, still knocking the dust from his trousers with his black hat, walked a few steps from his family to the edge of the high bluff overlooking the Brule River. A new bridge stretched across the clear water directly ahead of him. Before him lay vast green meadowlands, storied forests across the river; behind him lay the distant crags of the bad lands. A second, much lower bridge lay to the near side of the first structure. Its dark steel-girded pylons were crowned with steel rails that welcomed the cattle drives from neighboring states and sped the herds to the east for market.

Four horsemen, just crossing the main bridge, approached Main Street in a leisurely walk in the late Saturday afternoon sun. Just a few hours before, the daily zephyr had graced those rails, crossing majestically, powered up a long curve of the slow grade that pulled it into the prairie hills toward Kansas City. Further to his left, beyond the tree line of cottonwood and birch, Tom could just make out the Missouri, which swallowed up the Brule as they became one mighty river a mile downstream.

Quickly, Gannon's eyes swept directly to his right. *How like Huron Island it is*, he thought, comparing the island directly across from town. His vision continued upstream, following the Brule and the woodlands curving snakelike to a white speck on the distant horizon, and then to a high, gentle climbing bluff that seemed to jut out into the river. This was the new home of what were perhaps the last remnants of Mandan civilization—a tribe long ago thought decimated by small pox, dating back to contacts with white traders. How this band survived was largely unresolved. Minnesota, perhaps, held the answer.

Helen Gannon stood at the fringe of town with her arms around her daughters. John was attracted by the town activities. Helen turned and looked directly down the long, hard composite road of Main Street. Her heart sank as she saw the rustic one and two-story, faux crowned, red brick buildings that stretched for several blocks. In the soft, late-afternoon sun, she saw the general stores with bags of feed and implements on the front porches; butcher shops with hams, slabs of bacon, and chickens hanging in the windows; stores of ready to wear clothes for ranchers and workmen; and six large saloons that quenched the thirst of tired trail hands and cattle drivers after long, hard days on the trails. From the far end of Main Street came the echoes from blacksmiths' well-cadenced hammers that could be heard peening for a quarter of a mile.

"Helen, bring the children over here and see this sight. It's fantastic, I'll tell you."

"Tom Gannon!" She never called him in that way except when she was angry. "You've got some nerve standing there gawking at the countryside while your family is starving. Look at your father, children," she said, as if Gannon were not present. "Neglecting his family while he indulges himself in his own pleasures. If it isn't carousing, hunting, or fishing, or … or shooting … it's gawking."

An old crone and an older drifter sat in the shade of nearby trees, sharing a pint of wine, perusing all activities. They had been watching the Gannons' every move since they first stepped out of their car. They suddenly livened up and started shouting, "That's right, lady, give it to him. Give it to him good."

Helen shook her finger at them and yelled, "You mind your own business over there." Then she looked back at Tom and said sternly, "Well? Are you coming?" The drifter slapped both thighs and rolled on the ground with much laughter.

Loud shouts a short distance behind Gannon drew everyone's attention. The four horsemen yelled and galloped full-speed forward, scattering the crowd.

"Get out of the road!" Gannon yelled to Helen. "Get the children out of the road!"

Helen froze in her tracks as the girls ran to her side. John, a little way off from his family, ran toward a store.

The four riders, three sheepherders and an Indian called Crazy Dog, were upon Helen and the children in seconds. With pistols drawn, they fired in the air together. Two riders passed at top speed, one on either side of Helen Gannon, who panicked and fainted with her children at her side. Crazy Dog raced ahead and scooped up John by the arm to straddle his horse, and the four riders—teeth glaring and yelling at the top of their lungs—galloped off down Main Street, shooting out the new streetlights and the glass windows of several stores. The Gannons could not know that marauding Main Street, creating such havoc, was nothing new to this raucous group of riders on early Saturday nights. It was tolerated to an extent, but this bunch would soon learn that the new sheriff had other plans for them.

The street was deserted instantly. Tom Gannon's pistols were packed and locked away. Before he could even begin to get to his weapons, the riders were back. Crazy Dog eased John to the ground in front of his father, and with low guttural laughter, he said to Gannon, "You boy very good rider. We fish. I come for you soon. The high fin blues will run." He spun his big Appaloosa stallion around and raced off with a high-pitched yell of, "Eeeeya-ya-ya!"

Gannon, who had raced to his wife when she fainted, helped pick her up in his strong arms and carried her to a level, grassy area nearby. A well-dressed man and his wife helped.

"It's all right, Mr., she just fainted. She'll come around shortly," he said to everyone now gathering around. Tom, while squatting beside his wife, turned to his son. "You're okay, John?" he asked.

"Yes, sir. I think so," John said.

Tom noticed his son's wet pants. He winked at the boy and said, "You're gonna have to dry your pants, aren't you?"

"My sock also," John said, looking down at his right shoe.

Helen Gannon soon revived. John stood directly in front of her. She grabbed her son and started yelling, "That savage, that savage! And my husband couldn't even find his guns."

The well-dressed gentleman, standing alongside the family, came to Gannon's aid, politely saying, "It's a good thing, ma'am. That would cause some serious trouble in this town."

The Gannons all looked at one another.

"I guess it ended up okay after all; no one got hurt," Tom said.

"From the looks of your car, you've been on the road a long time," the gentleman said.

"Twelve days!" Tom said.

The gentleman put out his hand to Gannon and said, "By the way, I'm Jim Bowers."

"Tom Gannon," Tom said, extending his hand. "Can you direct me to the hotel? We could sure use a good cleanup. Just look at us. This 600-mile trek took a bit out of us, I'm afraid."

"Where are you bound for, Pierre?"

"No," Tom answered. "Right here in Chambers," and he grinned pleasantly.

Mr. Bowers, fingering his chin, said, "Look! Your family," his glance swept all of the Gannons, "are mighty tired." He was interrupted by his wife slipping her arm in his.

"Oh, meet my wife, Mrs. Bowers." After Tom introduced his family, Bowers continued, "This is a fine 'how do you do' you just got from our fair city. Now, I don't want any objections to this offer. Mildred and I want you to come up to our house and have dinner. She has cooked enough food for an army, and we'd like to share it with you."

Before Tom Gannon could make a remark, Helen Gannon rushed up to their newfound friends and gushed, "Oh, Mr. Bowers, that is the kindest offer. We accept with pleasure. Don't we, Tom?"

Recovering a bit, Tom said, "It's very kind of you to rescue us like this, sir. I'll do something special for you as soon as we get situated."

"Then it's settled," Bowers said. "See those two white houses up on the hill there?" He pointed to his home. "The first one belongs to Mildred and me. Drive on up, and we will meet you there."

"You're a fine man, Mr. Bowers. See you there shortly," Tom said.

When the Gannons arrived at the Bowers' home, they were led directly through the well-decorated home to the back porch.

"You must be dying to wash up. Help yourselves to the bowls there on the wash stands. If you need more towels—"

"Here are towels," Mrs. Bowers interrupted and presented several to Helen.

After washing themselves, Helen said, "I feel awful to be in your lovely home coming straight off the road."

"Don't you worry. Come, sit at the dining table. It's time to eat," Jim Bowers said. "Mildred and I only went down to town to see if that wild bunch would show up again. They've been creating bedlam almost every Saturday night, but now our new sheriff has their number, I believe. You may have noticed that he saddled up and chased right behind that bunch. They had their fun; now they will have to pay up. Jeb Stuart is a hard-nosed rancher. They've worked for Stuart for several years now. They'll not only pay up, they'll have to do some of the work," Bowers grinned as he explained. "The bigger concern is, of course, that someday those sheep herders are going to hurt somebody riding amidst so many folks so furiously. And, your son here—what's your name, young man?"

"My name, sir? I'm John Thomas Gannon, son of Tom."

Everyone laughed at the formality. "Well said, John Thomas. Your arm okay where that boozed-up Indian yanked you up on his horse?"

"Yes, sir."

"And how about your sisters? Might I know their names?"

"Yes, sir," John said, and he introduced Sallie and Betty Jean.

"Take a seat. Take a seat, everybody," Mr. Bowers urged. Scarcely had they sat down when out came an amazing feast: prime rib roast, mashed potatoes and gravy, and seasoned Italian beans.

"I like it here," Betty Jean piped up. "My house or town?" Mr. Bowers asked, smiling.

Embarrassed, Betty Jean scrunched down low in her chair, smiled, and said rather meekly, "Both of them, sir."

"Betty Jean, you are a charmer," Mr. Bowers said as he picked up the carving knife and fork and carved generous amounts of roast beef for everyone.

"Oh, my," Helen said, "pink in the middle. Couldn't be more perfect."

"Help yourselves to everything," Jim urged. "Just make yourselves at home in our house. Our children are away in college up east, so your family is a special treat for Mildred and me—aren't they, Mildred?" he asked as Mildred reentered the room with salad dressed tomatoes.

"These are from our garden," Mildred said.

"Mrs. Bowers," Tom spoke with enthusiasm, "you are one fine chef. Your dinner is the best I've had." He paused a moment, looked at Helen, and added, "Except when Mrs. Gannon is right on target." Everyone laughed politely.

Soon, out came the chocolate cream pie with lightly browned, whipped egg whites on top. "What a gorgeous pie, and it's absolutely our family favorite," Helen exclaimed. Soon, everyone was satiated.

"Coffee will be served out in the living room to all of you. Mrs. Gannon and I will talk in the kitchen." Sallie and Betty Jean took the handsome, leather-trimmed, red couch. The men chose the wing backed chairs with maroon and white leaf designs. Coffee was poured.

John sat nearby on the floor, facing the men, his back against the wall. Some toys from years before lay nearby—their owner now away at college. He could hear the ladies talking from one side while the men's voices drifted in through his other ear. Propped against the wall, with one leg tucked under him, his ears were still ringing from the Indian's pistol that fired so close to him just an hour earlier. The smell of gun powder lay heavily upon his clothes.

The toys before him were much like his own a half-dozen years earlier. They were intriguing at this moment, especially the Buick replica. It looked exactly like his father's car, but it wasn't. It was his car. "He was in it." As the warm light from the kitchen lit his face like an old master's painting, placing the shadows of the boy and the car on the wall, he heard the voices swirl around him—first the voices of the men, and then from the women in the kitchen.

He looked at the car and heard the powerful sound of the racing engine. He felt the breeze in the air. The light olive-green coating, new just this year, was brilliant in the sun. The white top was down. Eager hands seized the big, high steering wheel. The button-topped brake handle and long, thin gear shift, with its plastic, rainbow-colored round knob, protruded from the floorboard. The huge spare tire swung out with the right front door. He pushed back into the contours of the black leather seats. He saw the huge silver headlamps protrude like massive fireballs, saw the twin spotlights near the windshield. The silvery luggage rack graced the rear. Narrow tires, mounted on wooden wheels, cut through the soft earthen road. Wind whipped the tears from his eyes. Then it was still.

His mother's warm voice was the first he heard. "I certainly hope, Mrs. Bowers, that today isn't indicative of life here in Chambers. Why, we could have all been killed. That savage! If only my husband could have found his guns, he could have put a stop to that escapade."

John saw the soft red sun rush up at the end of the road that morning in Monmouth. Felt the fingers grasp his shoulder in the village square where he stood with his father. Felt them tighten when the sun grew full. Heard the vision of a new frontier.

"Yes, it was a big decision to leave Monmouth, Mr. Bowers," Tom Gannon said. "No, not really, when I think back now. True it's hard to leave the coals of the home fire, the family traditions, the memories, and all that, don't you know. I once passed through your town, and I said then that one day I wanted to live here.

"My wife, Helen, bless her heart, she has her mind more on the big city, but that's not for me. Out here, a man can breathe. Oh, the sight of that river when we drove up. It lifts up your heart. Why, I felt like I could have swum it with my clothes on. Just as important, you have work out here. I'm a master carpenter and a master plumber. There's much I can do in Chambers."

John saw the sadness in Billy and Sarah Barton, saw the hurt on the faces of William, Fred, and Dan. Saw the mass of swirling hands and faces. Heard the shouts of a last farewell. Sarah placed some marigolds in his hands.

Helen's voice came again from the kitchen. "We were going to Chicago. He as much as promised me. I had such a great future in opera; several very knowledgeable people told me as much. To think that I threw it all away for this. It wouldn't be so bad … even in Milwaukee or St. Paul. Our future should be in a city. That's where the country is building. That's where the opportunities are. But no! Not Tom Gannon. All he thinks about is hunting, fishing, and blazing a new trail."

"You're a singer, then?" asked Mrs. Bowers, her face brightening as she smiled at the prospects of good fortune coming to town.

Going back to the beginning, John saw the rivers when he was four, five, and six. Happy days! His father helped him land the big fish. Then he was seven. It was different in the field; over and over, the gun exploded. Closed his eyes—jerked the trigger. Caught the wrath of his father.

"Remember San Jan Hill?" Gannon asked Bowers. "Who would have thought a man of his stature and background would lead us into such a battle. But there we were. I was in the army at the time, and a handful of other white soldiers and I fought alongside thousands of black troops.

"We sent those Spaniards running in short order. I'll never forget Lieutenant's order, 'Hold your fire; wait for my order.' Wait for your order, hell—while a sniper pinned us down for half an hour? Why, I took him out with one shot. They threw my butt in jail for disobedience. Hero one minute, criminal the next. They finally took it off my record, though. I swore then I would never be hemmed in again."

The grey winters came. John was eight and then nine. Saw his father come and go. Saw him stumble. Smelled the whiskey in the air. Heard the arguments shake the air like thunder. Filled the family with despair. Math, math—it beat him back. Caught the wrath of his father. Felt the pull to his mother's side.

"You're an interesting fellow, Mr. Gannon. What else have you done?"

"Well, several things. For a time there, I was raising my family, and there was little or no work to be found in Monmouth. You'll recall that our government had just taken over the Panama Canal project, and they needed people to rebuild the infrastructure. Tens of buildings had rotted practically to the ground in that swampy land. It was great work for me. They paid me well, but I'll tell you, Mr. Bowers, it was a mess. Every chief engineer who went down there thought the canal ought to be dug at sea level—same as engineers from Europe did, as well. But Mr. Roosevelt was impressed with a highly recommended engineer, John Stevens, and put him in charge of the canal. He was the only one who figured it out. He sent the president plans for a lock-based scheme to lift and float ships through those solid rock mountains.

"I could talk for hours about that, but Teddy bought it right from the beginning. As for me, I stuck it out for six months. Our people did a great job rebuilding buildings and quarters, but we had thousands upon thousands of black people doing backbreaking work who died of malaria, dysentery, and God knows what else. After six months, I had enough of it, so I took my money and started home. Little did I know that I was heading right into a disaster beyond my wildest imagination: San Francisco quake and fire. But let's save that for another day, if you will allow me; it will take hours to retell it to you."

John saw the rich farm land fade in the darkness, saw the barren fields with corn in silo, saw the pastures thick with swine. Passed the river so rich to his childhood, where they summered, fished, and played. Passed the trestle with waving trainmen—forty-nine cars swinging free and gay. On they raced to the new frontier.

As the men stood up to say goodnight, in rushed Mrs. Bowers, excited and bubbling over.

"Jim, can you guess who we have among us tonight—an opera singer!" she blurted out.

"An opera singer!" Bowers exclaimed. His face lit up like a lantern.

"My, how fortunate," he said. "We were searching our minds just yesterday and wondering what we were going to do for the Fourth of July. Our singer is indisposed. Will you help us out, Mrs. Gannon?"

"Well, certainly. At least, I'll do my best."

"It's strange how life works out," Bowers said, smiling broadly.

John saw the thunderheads grow dark and angry. Saw the lightning split the sky and heard mighty Thor pound his anvil. Sent the bolts to shake the ground. Saw the rain come in torrents. Felt the wrath of a prairie storm. Felt the peace when it calmed.

"What a stroke of good luck. An opera singer!" Bowers repeated, as he nodded his head. "But come now, we have to get you and your family off to bed. You all have to be dead tired."

"You are very kind and thoughtful," Gannon said, looking around for his children. Sallie and Betty Jean leaned against each other on the couch, sound asleep. Bowers pointed to the boy, sound asleep against the wall, sitting cross-legged with the iron car in the palms of his crossed hands. The kitchen light played softly upon his light brown hair, posed for the master painter.

"Look at that," the host said. "Isn't that a picture?"

Tom Gannon smiled, reached down, and lifted his son in his arms. He turned to Jim Bowers and said, "He's a sensitive young fellow, but he runs like a deer. And you know, today he rode pretty well."

Chapter 4

Fourth of July

Prelude

The Gannons' belongings arrived early at the train station on Monday. This was June the thirtieth. While they were busy settling in their rented, four-bedroom, white house on the hill behind the Bowers' property, a house owned by Bowers, Chambers became a beehive of activity. Six men were building a platform with steps and handrails for their annual Fourth of July rally at the mouth of Main Street. There would be ample food brought by each family, the men would make patriotic speeches, and Mrs. Rochelle, the very talented school teacher, would have sung a selection of songs in her fine soprano voice, starting off the whole affair with the national anthem and the song "America." Then, she would sing two or three songs as the speeches progressed, with the mayor closing the affair.

Usually, a chief of the Lower Brule would speak. Sometimes, even Crazy Dog, the colorful Mandan, would be asked to talk, if for no other reason than to curry good favor. He was not only kind, but also possessed a certain notoriety and charm ... when he was not with bottle. Yet his background of living with the Apache as a young man left his presence one of intrigue and unreliable by white standards.

Nonetheless, all of Chambers looked upon the Fourth as a very special celebration for the entire town. In the midafternoon, Jim Bowers walked up on the Gannons' Victorian, wraparound front porch.

Gannon greeted his new friend and landlord with a warm smile and firm handshake.

"I would invite you inside, but you can see what it looks like from here," Tom said as he gestured to the crates and unpacking of household goods.

"Your family is going to be busy getting your house in order, but I'd like to ask you over to have lunch with me tomorrow. I want to get another opinion from an outsider."

"Thank you, I'll be glad to," Tom said, sensing that he owed Bower far more than an opinion.

At lunch the next day, the two men settled down to some cold roast and coffee. Jim Bowers was noticeably more formal.

"Tom, you can see how small a town Chambers is. It's a fine place to live, too. The only thing is when it comes time to find someone to do a job with any skill, it's not that easy. I haven't mentioned it yet, but I own the bank here in town. Long story short, I've been watching you ever since the auspicious moment you and your family drove into town. I like what I see."

Tom Gannon just sat there, waiting for something more.

"The bottom line is I just happen to need help in my bank. I need a good teller—a man of your stature and presence. Now, I know you told me you have great skills as a builder, and you undoubtedly have plans. But working at the bank will give you cash right away, every week, and there are opportunities for the right man. What do you say to that? Become a banker; be a take-charge man. I can start you out at $40.00 a week. What do you say?"

"I'll say right now this is one heck of a surprise, Mr. Bowers. Oh, I can count money as well as most any man, I suppose, but you seem to be talking about something else. This sounds more like a possible career change. Could we do this: considering I owe you handsomely for rescuing me and my family the other day, and for all of your wonderful hospitality, I'll come work for you for a month. Then let's see where that takes us."

"Then it's settled," Bowers said, knowing how to close a deal quickly. "You won't regret this, Mr. Gannon. I'm not known for misjudging people. I wouldn't last long in this business if I did. I dare say, you have never been in trouble with the civil law, have you?"

"No, sir! You can wire the *Monmouth Star* in Illinois, and they will tell you, 'The Gannons are all known for doing the right thing,' and of course that includes me."

"Good, then, let's shake on it," Bowers said, extending his hand. "I'll expect you in the bank in the morning at eight to go over some procedures before we open at ten. By the way, we wear ties and a hat." They shook hands again, and Tom headed home. He knew that Helen would be ecstatic.

Tom Gannon walked into his busy house and found Helen and the children unpacking their precious belongings. "Anything damaged?" he asked.

"Where in the world did you get off to?" Helen demanded. "Just look at all this—"

"Shhhhhh," Tom said as he put his finger up to his mouth. "Come over here."

Helen came over to her husband, "What's …"

Tom grabbed Helen's waist and pulled her gently toward him, kissing her affectionately on the mouth. Then he said, "Want to know a secret?"

"What? What have you and the banker been up to?"

"How did you know he was a banker? No matter now. How would you like to have a banker for a husband?"

"Tom … he offered you a job."

"More than that; he hired me. See what I told you about providence, Mrs. Gannon?"

"Oh, Tom! I can't believe it."

"What is it, Mama?" the children yelled, running over to hug them both to share in the excitement.

"Your father is going to be a banker," Tom said. "Well, at least a bank teller—and only for a month to see if things work out for Mr. Bowers. He did indicate that he liked me very much and there was more responsibility there for the taking."

"I'm so excited I can hardly contain myself," Helen said. "And they want me to sing at the Fourth of July celebration. Miss Rochelle came down with an awful throat, they said."

"See!" Tom smiled as he pulled Helen close to him. "All the world is a stage," he quoted. "And we are on it. Let's make the most of it, Mother."

"I'll have to get started on a good selection of arias and songs and running a few scales."

"I didn't hear much of that yesterday, but I know you, and scales are on the menu." He grinned and gently kissed his wife.

"Okay, it's back to work. Look at all the mess you children made!" Tom said as he made a funny face at Betty Jean.

That night, beds never beckoned so urgently to the Gannon family.

The next morning, Tom Gannon and Mr. Bowers opened the bank at 8 a.m. and spent the next two hours touring the bank and reviewing Tom's responsibilities as a teller, and as much as anything else, Mr. bowers urged Tom to observe everything that went on in the bank.

"We'll talk more after three, after the bank closes," Bowers said. "Just one more thing, Tom. Tellers are responsible for all the money given them each day. Lose it through carelessness, and you are accountable." Tom nodded his understanding and turned to prepare for opening.

Helen and the children unpacked all day. They enjoyed the luxury of eating at the little restaurant on Main Street soon after Tom got home. The affairs of the day came out excitedly as they talked quietly about their plans and briefly about the Fourth of July.

"Of course they want me to open with the national anthem," Helen said, "but after that, you know what? I hear there is a new song, just out, 'America,' but it's not in print yet. Anyway, I've not even heard it sung yet. Then too, you know how I love singing *Aida*. Perhaps a short aria will work. They might like it. And something from *Turandot* to close the show. The 'Nessun Dorma' will impress anyone who likes music at all, and Puccini always tugs at your heartstrings."

"Did Puccini sing that, Mother?" Betty Jean wanted to know.

"No, darling, he wrote *Turandot*. And so many other wonderful operas. I'll take you to hear them some time. Maybe one day you'll sing them yourself." Helen smiled a mother's smile to her daughter and then turned to Tom. "Do you think a familiar church hymn would work right after the anthem? Then after a speech or two, give them *Aida*, or something like 'O Sole Mio?'"

Tom said, "Darling, you're asking me? But it sounds perfect. Why don't you do that? You have it in you for at least one of your special high Cs?"

"I do now," Helen said. As the family walked slowly home from the restaurant, Tom took his wife's hand, and Betty Jean quickly grabbed the other;

"You know, it's been one of those 'what a day' days. Any of Mrs. Bowers' cake left, Mother?"

"Just a small slice for each of us."

"That will be just the ticket, with a glass of milk in an hour or so. Won't it, Sallie?"

John, who had been quiet the whole evening, spoke up. "Pa, are you going to sing at the Fourth celebration?" Everyone laughed.

"You watch your step there, son. You know what a terrific singer I am. I just don't want to steal the show from your mother." They all laughed and skipped a bit.

Things went well at the bank for Tom Gannon. There were the usual transactions of handling a modest traffic flow of patrons, but one interesting rancher, Frederick Baker, lingered behind and came back to Gannon.

"Seeing as how you're the only teller in the bank, I've got a question for you. I've never borrowed money from your bank." The men talked for twenty minutes about money and if any of it was available to Baker. Suddenly, Bowers appeared.

"Can I help you, Mr. Baker?"

"No, I was just talking loans with your man, Gannon. We're doing fine."

"Let me know if I can help," Bowers said as he returned to his office.

Soon Baker departed the bank, and Jim Bowers motioned for Tom to come into his office. After a lengthy conversation, Bowers sat back in his chair and looked at his new teller, stroked his chin, and said, "Teller, huh. You don't sound much like a teller to me. See that desk over there in the corner? The man that sits there approves our loans. Ranchers and store owners," he hastily explained, "all need loans from time to time. Next to my running this bank, I look upon that job as the most important work in the bank. Make a good loan, and you make me some profit; make a bad loan, a really bad loan, and I'll have to kick you in the butt." He looked at Tom in a special way, and then they spoke of loaning money.

"That desk over there in the corner? In thirty days, I want to see you sitting there representing my bank."

As Bowers got up to leave, he turned to Gannon and said, "Oh, by the way, the wife said to tell you she wants all of us at the table by seven tonight."

As Bowers walked toward his office, Tom spoke firmly to his boss. "Mr. Bowers, thanks for the encouragement. They say a good carpenter always has a sharp saw. I promise you this much, I keep mine very sharp."

Bowers half-smiled. "We'll see. We'll just have to see. Seven o'clock, then."

"Seven sharp," Gannon replied.

Chapter 5

The Gannon Hour

When Tom Gannon reached home, he could hardly contain himself. Helen saw the look on his face and met him at the front door.

"What in the world is happening?" she asked, coming out on the porch as she spoke.

"Honey, you won't believe this," Tom said, shaking his head. "I've been working for one full day, and that man, Mr. Bowers, is already giving me an ultimatum—or sort of. He wants me to be ready to be his loan officer in thirty days."

"Oh, honey! I'm so proud of you."

"Well, it's far from a done deal, as they say in Monmouth, but you know what? For the first time in 'twenty-two minutes,' I can't believe all of this is happening to us. And furthermore, why? Out of this whole town, am I the only prospect? Here's this bank with no one running it but the owner, our accountant, and a new guy named Gannon. Where the devil is everybody?"

"Oh, honey! Relax. Mr. Bowers will sort things out. He's just shorthanded."

"I suppose so," Tom said. "Still, it doesn't make a lot of sense, but, as he said tonight, 'We'll see. We'll just have to see.' We need to be over at the Bowers' for dinner at 6:30, so we had better start laying out our clothes."

"Oh, I already know what I'll wear: my pretty red dress."

"The white collared one. You'll look smashing in that," Tom said. His eyes swept the house. "Where is John?" he asked.

"He asked to go downtown to the grocery store. He should have been back by now. Oh well, speak the prodigal son, what took you so long?" Helen said as John suddenly appeared.

"Pa, Mr. Clay down at the other grocery store has popcorn on the cob."

"So?" Tom asked.

"I'm going to buy some, pop it near train time, and sell it on the train when it comes in."

"Where in the world did you get that idea?" Tom asked.

"Oh, I just noticed. You know how people like to eat stuff when they travel. I asked Mr. Smith down at the station if I could do it."

"You went to the train station by yourself?"

"Yes, sir."

Tom rolled his eyes at Helen. "What do you know about that? We have an entrepreneur in the house. Guess I'll give notice and retire. We'll talk about this later," Tom said. "We've got to get all cleaned up and get ready for dinner with Mr. and Mrs. Bowers."

After dinner, with everyone complimenting Mrs. Bowers on her amazing stuffed chicken and her lavish chocolate cake, the men retired to the living room. The children had books to read. They were well used but interesting. Bowers and Gannon settled in the big chairs and enjoyed the strong, hot coffee that both wives brought to them before returning to the kitchen to talk.

"Mr. Bowers—"

"Please, call me Jim. My friends call me Jim."

Tom continued, "You know, one never looks a gift horse in the mouth, but with all the good fortune that has come our way in the last few days of our trip to Chambers—settling in here, your and Mrs. Bowers' kindness, I have to wonder out loud, how did all this happen?"

Jim threw his head back and laughed. "I guess it has been a bit fast, looking at your side of the equation." Then his face became serious, as he looked directly at Gannon's eyes. "Last week, my teller was shot, and my loan officer left town."

"Good God," Tom blurted out.

"Don't worry. He wasn't shot at the bank. It was a hunting accident. No one really knows for sure. The sheriff thinks two parties were hunting, facing each other when they fired, accidentally killing my teller. It's a shame in more ways than one. He was a darn good man. My loan officer didn't like it out here. He just pulled out and went back to Chicago. Lucky for me that Tom Gannon came into town—poof… just like magic."

Bowers paused a moment and then continued, "No, we've had no bad luck with robberies since I've been here, knock on wood. Anyway, I think the two of us know how to use a gun—you, being in the army, and I'm pretty handy with a pistol, if it ever came down to that. Though, I don't expect you to put your life on the line. But, what I really had in mind for this evening is your adventures in San Francisco. What were you doing out there?"

"Well, sir, after Cuba, I returned to Monmouth, married my gorgeous sweetheart, Helen, and raised a family for three years only to realize there was little work available. They were screaming for carpenters in Panama, so I went down there alone to make money. It was extremely interesting. Chief Engineer John Stevens sold President Teddy Roosevelt on a lock scheme, and it was being installed. The job paid handsomely, but the living conditions in that swamp of a country were abominable; malaria, dysentery, and typhoid killed thousands upon thousands of workers. I gave it six months. Saved my money and came home. The only thing was when we hit San Francisco on April 19, 1905, the entire city was on fire. That was the day after the big quake. When I went ashore, there I was up to my wallet in a fire storm, and I had no place to go. People were running around all over the place, some badly hurt, some on fire. The dead lay everywhere, and there I stood, healthy and strong, so I asked the first policeman, who turned out to be the chief of police, 'How can I help?'

"He pointed and then shoved me in the direction of a rescue party. Everybody was rescuing people all over town, and we did that until we were exhausted. I even went out to Jefferson Square, later to Golden Gate State Park, to show people how to put up tents. The army and navy were out there as well. They really did a fantastic job handling people.

"But the most challenging situations, the work we did helping different groups rescue people who were pinned under debris, getting them to medical stations, etc., placed demands on us like you can't imagine. It was near pandemonium at times, but most of the time it was people out there rising to the occasion, helping others like it was a fire drill, like this was something they were born to do. I just dove into the middle of things like every other rescuer.

"I'll never forget it. It was a devastating disaster, and everyone was too busy to be scared. People just helping people, plain and simple. And I can't say enough about their mayor, a fellow named Schmitz—I believe that's the way he said his name. He was another Teddy Roosevelt. Right away he sent out the order, 'Shoot all looters on the spot where they are looting.' And, a few did get shot. You know, you're standing in front of a fine jewelry store with the front all smashed in. Looked mighty tempting to some, I suppose.

"The army and navy were called out right away by the mayor, and they did a fine job, it seemed to me. Anyway, I couldn't leave those people. We all worked like the devil. Buildings were exploding from gas, and some were dynamited to keep fires from spreading. Amazingly, some buildings withstood a great earthquake like that, such as the grand St. Francis Hotel—only to be razed by fire shortly afterward. I still dream about seeing that city laid to waste like that. Devastating. Just Devastating. April 18, 1905! I won't likely forget that date—not ever. I'm just lucky they unloaded me on the nineteenth.

"Can you imagine if I had been put ashore on the seventeenth? I sometimes wonder if I wear a lucky charm. Anyway, they counted over a hundred fissures left by the quake ... oh, I'm sure you read all of this stuff in the papers," Tom said.

"No, no, keep going! I want to hear about your experiences there."

"Well, that fire was just God awful. Burned for four days before the firemen could put it out—and much of it just burned itself out. They needed cooks worse than anything outside of doctors and nurses, so I cooked. Just trying to help people cope with living in a disaster like that. I saw enough burned and charred people to turn your stomach for the rest of your life. I can still smell them. That odor of burnt human—it's like the sound of a rattlesnake in that it never leaves you. And I think that's true. I still think I smell it.

"Anyway, after a month of rescue work, I noticed a man wearing a blue suit standing behind me a few yards away. Just standing there, watching me work. Finally, he walked over to me and said, 'Hi, my name is Phelan. I've seen you working around here several times. What's your craft? I told him I was a master carpenter. He just laughed and said, 'You are not—you're not old enough.' I told him, 'We start young in Illinois.' He paused a moment. Then he said he needed a good man with my talents and offered me a job. He paid well, so I decided to go to work rebuilding his house—rather, I should say, his mansion. About sixteen rooms. He brought in stone masons as well as other craftsmen. Where he got tools from, I couldn't imagine. Working away there was eerie. I would find yesterday's sights and sounds emblazoned right there in front of me, just like it was happening again. Soldiers all around, thousands of people running toward the wharfs to get away from the fire, tent cities being erected, people scurrying every place. Unbelievable.

"I heard the navy moved nearly 20,000 people out of there—people rushing to the docks. It was said to be the biggest movement of people in the world. Around to Oakland, I guess. You can imagine the plight thrust upon every single person in the city. No food, no water, no sanitation, no communications—and fire and ashes everywhere you turned. The army sent in rations galore and tents, from conical to flat walls to hospital shapes. I slept in a tent with five other men, but that was no hardship for me. Suddenly, the USS *Chicago* came. What a beautiful ship. And others came as well.

"Early on, something strange happened there right before everybody's eyes. A poor section of town, tenements really, just crumbled and burned. I didn't see it, but I talked to several people who did. It was reported that the quake and the heat from the fires caused the earth under those buildings to liquefy. That's beyond me, but that's where the biggest death toll took place. Hundreds of tenement dwellers trapped with no escape. Just burned alive. Earth liquefying; can you imagine that? I find it so hard to believe, yet there it was. Must have been like a burning hell. The poor horses drawing buggies and wagons caught it too." Tom's face was somber as he shook his head slightly.

"You, uh, Jim, my work in Panama had some danger attached to it, and my time in the Cuban war … well, all of that was like sitting down to Sunday lunch compared to what was put on the backs of those people in San Francisco. They all should get medals. And, just think about it, how do you rebuild? You just lost everything. I guess that's what insurance is all about. Well, sir, there isn't much more to that story, but I get a pretty sick feeling just talking about it." Gannon paused and looked away from his host. Finally, Bowers broke the silence.

"What about you, Tom? What brought you way out here? The Brule?"

About that time, the ladies came in. "You gentlemen finished with wars and earthquakes?" Mildred Bowers said.

"Well, Jim learned a lot; I didn't learn a thing," Gannon said. Everyone laughed heartily, concentrating on Tom Gannon.

"Thanks for inviting us, and thanks for another festive meal," Tom said as he gathered his family and moved toward the front door. They all said their goodnights, the Gannons walking casually to their nearby home.

Back in the Bowers' house, Jim was saying, "What's the verdict, Mrs. Bowers? Have we got a prize in our new friends?"

"I should say so," Mildred said. "I can't wait to hear Helen sing on the Fourth. I'd be willing to bet she's going to create some unusual excitement."

Suddenly it was the morning of the Fourth of July. The Gannons busied about the house.

"Your voice warmed up beautifully, Helen," Tom said.

"I feel pretty good, but I've decided not to sing *Aida*."

"No? What then?"

"I'm looking for a warm feeling, something they can connect with. Puccini, Verdi, it doesn't matter, but I've chosen the 'Nessun Dorma.' You may remember; it's from *Turandot*."

"Whatever you feel good about, honey. Just pretend you're in Chicago—you know, the biggest audition in your life. Please yourself, and you'll win the town."

"I'm going to start off with the national anthem first, of course, then follow that with a rouser to loosen them up a bit, like 'The Battle Hymn of the Republic.'"

"Good Lord," Tom said, "that ought to put a fire in the boiler. Look out! Here comes Helen Gannon."

"Then I'll step off stage for the speakers. That's going to take a while. Give me time to rest for my big song. I'd give a pretty penny to know how many in this town have ever heard an opera," Helen said.

"Not too many, I'm sure, but the main idea is for them to like our Helen and like her fine voice. They will if you give them something interesting." Tom paused, looked at Helen, and said, "You know 'The Battle Hymn' is stirring. They're going to respond to that."

"I feel good about just three songs. Look, I'm going to drop the Turandot thing and close with 'The Battle Hymn of the Republic.' It's patriotic, and everyone will love it. I can make it uplifting, exciting, like only a soprano can, get them to sing the last two lines of each stanza, and bingo—we will have enjoyed a good program. By then, lunch will taste fantastic."

"It absolutely will," Tom said. "It's going to be interesting to hear what Crazy Dog is going to talk about. I can't believe they're going to let that character speak, but I guess they feel good about it or they wouldn't ask him. Do you know that Indian can throw a battle axe and stick it in a tree accurately from thirty feet?" Helen let out a yip.

"Well, Mother, if you have your program all set, sit and rest a bit; there will be a lot of standing out there. They put up a canopy over the speaker platform, so at least you can have shade when you're performing. Say, it's awfully quiet back there. Where are the kids?"

"Sallie and Betty Jean are out back catching butterflies, but guess where your son is?"

"In town?" Tom asked.

"Exactly."

"I'm going to have to have a talk with that boy."

"Gone to town, and not a by-your-leave to anybody. Takes after his papa, doesn't he?"

"A little too much, sometimes," Tom said. "Let's plan on strolling down in about an hour. Get a front-row seat," Tom said. "What did you fix for lunch, hon?"

"Don't worry, you won't go hungry."

"Good. Let's relax a bit and then take off."

Later, as the Gannons reached town, they headed toward an area that led to Main Street, where the tree line blocked out most of the sun. People were already gathering there. John was talking to some boys.

"Well, that's a good sign. He seems to have made friends already."

Helen nodded, a bit apprehensively. "Oh, I suppose we have nothing to worry about out here. People are friendly. Considering we never knew where he was in Monmouth, I just don't like his straying off silently just yet."

"We'll see," Tom said.

By 10:00 a.m., the wide area that started at the river bridge, winding gently up to the entrance of Main Street, was filled with people.

"Looks like all of Chambers is here."

"Seems to be; they heard a new celebrity just blew into town," Tom said, smiling at his wife.

At that moment, Tom heard his name called as Jim and Mildred Bowers walked up. Everyone spoke excitedly as they discussed the morning's proceedings. Dr. Joseph Green arrived and addressed Jim as "Mayor." Tom was taken aback by the title as he and Helen had no idea that he was also the mayor of Chambers. A tall, robust man walked up suddenly, looked at Gannon, and said, "Hi, I'm John Mason. Glad to have you folks with us. You must be Mrs. Gannon. We sure look forward to your singing."

Helen extended her hand. "We're pleased to be here, and I'm delighted to sing for us," Helen said as Mason surveyed everyone.

Jim Bowers said, "John Mason, are we all set? It's about ten."

"All of our speakers are here, so I'll go ahead and introduce you, Mr. Mayor."

As John Mason kicked off the program, welcoming the crowd, Tom turned to Helen and said in a whisper, "Don't let his title throw you, honey. Concentrate on your job. Still going for the high C?"

"If I feel good when I get there; otherwise, I'll slide under it with a middle C. Few in this town will know the difference," Helen replied.

"Absolutely." Tom squeezed Helen's hands. "Go get 'em."

Helen's heart started pounding, realizing that she was moments away from a big opportunity to earn her way into a new crowd. Then she heard Tom's warm voice.

"Just pretend you're warming up, getting ready for your Chicago debut. Those are all your friends out there." When Helen heard her name, Tom walked her to the platform stairs and squeezed her hand.

"This is for Chicago," he said.

Helen sang the "Star Spangled Banner" with the ease of a practiced professional. Her mezzo soprano dropped to the lowest notes easily. She worked the crowd with her eyes and gestures as if they were long-time friends. She stylized the vocal only slightly from the traditional. She could see the crowd, hats covering hearts, a few saluting, some with mouths agape, as she pulled up the final charge to the finish, sliding under the high C perfectly. The crowd clapped enthusiastically.

"Thank you. Thank you," Helen said several times, acknowledging the audience graciously, and then departed the platform. Tom met her at the stairway.

"You were great. I'm glad you chose the mid-C. It fit perfectly, and your audience thought you were wonderful."

John Mason introduced the mayor, who spoke at length about Chambers, all the citizens there, patriotism, and finally, he mentioned the newest family in town, pointing them out where they stood.

"And now, let's bring Helen Gannon back for another song."

Helen, more comfortable in *Aida* and other operas than patriotic songs, ascended the stage again, this time perfectly relaxed. Smiling, she covered the audience briefly with her eyes and slight head movements.

She said, "I'd like to ask you to stand for this powerful hymn, 'America.' It's often referred to now as the other national anthem." The audience expressed their enthusiasm as they rose.

"Feel free to sing with me, if you like."

Helen, feeling the moment, put on her best stage presence. She was dressed more for *Aida*, with her auburn hair, not in a bun, but swept back, flowing, and tied with a bright red ribbon—a crown of sorts for her attractive blue and white dress, which she kept simple and with a high neck line for such a patriotic day. Though not at all too heavy, she was full chested, carrying it well, and presented the audience with a well-equipped voice not heard from their own talented singer and school teacher. Helen was tall for a woman, over five feet seven inches, and she moved about gracefully. She positioned herself near the front of the platform where the full sun highlighted her high cheek bones, dark eyes, and ruddy complexion.

The audience quieted, and she began the moving, Kathleen Bates song. Her sound had just the right amount of warmth and temperament, and she dropped, bass-like, with warmth, to pick up the deep-throated emotion in the first four lines.

The crowd responded with pleasure. Tom Gannon just about swallowed his tongue.

Helen gestured, acted a bit of the story line, and sang the remainder in beautiful, standard style. Casually she shifted to a B in "America, America," and then, still in middle range, finished the last three lines of the stanza in deep-throated tones. After only a pause, she became moody and dramatic, speaking the next line, "Oh beautiful for pilgrim feet," before moving higher and higher, saving the best for last. Instead of the deep tones written for the ending, she rocketed up to a low C. The townspeople were ecstatic, the Bowers were bowled over, and Tom Gannon and his children were clapping wildly. Helen took several bows and walked off stage to her family. Everybody nearby moved in closely, praising and clapping loudly to show their appreciation.

Tom released Helen from his arms and said, "Go back out there and take a bow." Helen did so, appreciatively, nodding her "thank you" to the crowd. She walked back to her family where her children engulfed her with big hugs.

"Well, Mother, I guess that settles it. We are shipping you off to the big stage tomorrow."

Betty Jean pulled on her mother's arm for attention and said, "Mother, when I grow up, I want to sing just like you."

Helen smiled, saying, "You will my love; you will."

"Listen to that; they're calling you back."

"I'll do one more before the speakers start," Helen said as she headed back to the platform, smiling broadly and nodding at the loud applause.

Facing the audience, Helen said, "I can't tell you how much I appreciate your welcome. It means so much to my family and me. It's the Fourth of July. Let's celebrate it with the 'Battle Hymn of the Republic.' I'll sing the first four lines and motion you to join me in the refrain."

The Gannon family stood together, looking on admiringly as Helen choked slightly and then easily moved into her lower register to bring out her most beautiful rendition of the song. The whole town knew it by heart. Her voice built up its power quickly as she gestured, smiled, and moved with the music.

Her smile and eyes swept the entire audience, now sitting erect in anticipation of the special entertainment that was unfolding before them. At the refrain, Helen motioned for everyone to join her, and it started an enthusiasm that showed the excitement and pleasure that finally someone special had come to their town.

Each stanza built up to its own special high point. The singer and her audience were one. Helen didn't attempt even a B flat, yet she held them there as a rapt audience—assured, poised, showing just the right amount of emotion, as each refrain followed the last with a participation the town had never experienced before. With her walking about the stage, looking at each small group, directing with her hand, she "threw the singing" to first one group and then another. She had them marching, singing, and shouting the words.

When Helen finished, people rushed the stage, applauding wildly, laughing, and shouting their appreciation. Finally, Tom Gannon pulled people apart just enough to rescue his wife, who left the stage smiling and blowing kisses to her newly won friends.

After heartily congratulating Helen Gannon, John Mason took the stage and introduced the mayor. Jim Bowers, who had been lavishing praise on Helen Gannon, turned and sprang up the stairs to the speaker's platform to a raucous, good-natured booing by the crowd.

"I know, I know; you'd rather be facing a beautiful lady with a glorious voice than hearing about the affairs of our beautiful city. I do want you to meet the entire Gannon family who just moved to Chambers from Illinois."

He motioned for Tom to bring everyone to the stairs so the crowd could see them. "This is Tom and Helen Gannon and their children, John, Sallie, and Betty Jean. Tom is a master carpenter and plumber as well, but you can only have him when he's not in the bank working as my new loan officer. What a talented family. Give them a big Chambers welcome." The crowd exploded again as Tom and Helen both nodded their appreciation to the crowd, and Sallie and Betty Jean both smiled and waved their greetings. John smiled and followed his family to the nearby shade.

Tom Bowers spent the next half hour updating the townspeople on the affairs of the city, its growth, improved city roads and conveniences, the new entrepreneur who had come to town, and how good it was to be celebrating in proud America on the Fourth of July. After thirty-five minutes of town news, the mayor said, "Now, I've selected one of the best speakers in town to talk about what it means to be an American living in America on the Fourth of July. I'd like to introduce a true patriot, Mr. John Mason."

There was much applause when Mason climbed the stairs to the platform. As he turned, waving to everyone, a rider pulled up abruptly at the back of the crowd, which parted enough to allow him through. The white stallion stopped midway to the stage, rearing up as it did so. An Indian slid off the horse and fell to the ground … drunk. There was a hush and then a low "Ohhhh" from the crowd. It was Crazy Horse. He had been scheduled to speak later in the day. No one attempted to help him. Then a young boy ran over to stand by the side of the Indian. It grew quiet.

Crazy Horse, lying there on the ground, supported on his right elbow, first saw the boy's shoes and then looked higher to the youth's face and outstretched hand. Crazy Horse managed a smile. He knew that face. Tom Gannon rushed over to help his son get the Indian to his feet and over to a shady resting space, where Crazy Horse promptly went to sleep. The stallion grazed nearby. As Gannon and his son went back to his family, there was a gentle applause, but underneath the admiration was an equal amount of clucking criticism of the Indian or those who helped him—perhaps both. John noticed a boy his own age, an Indian boy, rush over to Crazy Horse and sit beside him. Two Indian men, dressed in Indian attire, joined him.

Mason seized the moment by loudly shouting, "Happy Fourth of July!" After the applause died down, he launched into his speech, "What America Means to Me." It was given every year, and he delivered it with passion and in the style of an actor. The town loved it. This year, he was suddenly moved to open up differently, spontaneously.

"We are all Americans, are we not? Just now, a strong man fell off his horse, and a boy of twelve ran to his aid. I submit to you, a strong man doesn't fall off his horse; a well liquored-up man falls from his horse. Indians can't buy liquor; that's against the law. It's something we all need to think about."

Then with a special vigor that was pure John Mason, he launched into his own declaration of independence, as some came to call it.

"But right now," Mason continued, "it's the Fourth of July right here in our Chambers, South Dakota. Some, and I'm one of them, have come to call our town Chambers on the Brule." Mason moved about the platform and talked to every person in the crowd. He held them with his self-assurance, his eyes, an undulating baritone voice—with an extraordinary speaker's delivery.

"You know you're in Chambers when you look from her banks into the crystal waters. It has a special voice unlike any other river that I have ever seen, perhaps any that ever flowed. Anyone who has ever witnessed the Brule at sunset or at sunrise knows the power it holds. That river seems to reach out to the sun and waltzes it into the bosom of its depths to form a river's cache of gold. You fishermen know that. You hunters know that. And I heard our newest residents declare the other day that it created a way of life that is free, natural, and exciting. Chambers, the Brule, and its citizens all intertwined in a magic that does not exist in many places on earth. We celebrate that feeling, that gift, every day we wake up, but especially on the Fourth of July. Each Fourth it is like a proud new beginning."

For the next thirty-eight minutes, John Mason quoted Lord Byron, Keats, Teddy Roosevelt, and the Bible, putting his special stamp on this day. When he had finally said it all, while he still held them suspended, he reached into his package for one more verse, one that he had written for this occasion.

"In closing, I want you to know how alike America is to our river, the way it reflects the good that it delivers to each one of us residents: its vast food source, its life-giving water to quench our thirst, the infinite beauty it shares with all who behold it. It is a spiritual land in which we are so blessed to live, to nurture, to share with all good citizens. Thank you. Happy Fourth of July, and may God Bless America." The applause was loud and long.

Jim Bower quickly took the stage to capture the momentum of Mason's speech. He had a problem. Crazy Horse usually spoke for the Indians, but today would be different. Bowers looked out at the small group of Indians where one still lay on the ground. One well-adorned Native American, a leader of men, walked toward the speaker's platform. The mayor recognized him. "Chief, would you like to say a few words? Ladies and gentlemen, let's hear from our friends across the river. Most of you know the chief of the Mandan, Chief Joseph Grey Eagle. The chief and his family recently built a home out there on Huron Island. Chief, give us your feelings on what the Fourth of July means to you."

Chief Grey Eagle was not as articulate as John Mason by any means, but his English was excellent. He turned and faced the townspeople. He stood with stature and grace, his head held high.

"The Fourth of July is a happy day for your people. You won this country by defeating many warriors from many nations. You won this country by defeating many of my people, tribes who lived in peace and war with each other. But my people coexisted. We counseled, we governed, we lived happily in this country … to use your language—for centuries, before the white man came here. Many of my brothers helped you win wars against your enemies. But here we stand today, driven out of our lands, our buffalo taken from us, our freedom, our way of life, taken from us. You enjoy freedom—my people, prison, for that is life on a reservation.

"With your might, you captured our souls. With your being, you brought us disease. Now we are but a few grains in the sand. Our remnants upriver there on the white mountain are weak, and our time with you is short. Yet across the river are the Lakota and the Dakota. They are stronger. If you want to help anybody, help them. Educate them in the white man's ways. Educate my son, James, here with me today. Finally, I will move back to my people before much time passes. Enjoy our island, as you have for many years, as my people did for hundreds of years before you. This is a special river; keep it clean as you would yourselves. I have one plea. I have watched my people die of the white man's disease, so I ask you: if you care about us at all, do not come to visit us. If life were otherwise, I would welcome you anytime."

With that, the chief walked off the platform toward his tribesman, to Crazy Horse, now sitting up and listening to his chief. There was little applause, and the townspeople looked uncomfortable and puzzled.

"Mother, sing something for us," Gannon urged.

Helen moved quickly to the platform and drew everyone's attention with, "Hello, Chambers, I have one more song for you. This is what I have always dreamed of doing for a living. Would you like to hear it?"

The applause was generous but a somewhat more subdued reply.

"I'd like to sing a piece from *Il Trovatore* by Giuseppe Verdi, my favorite opera composer. Since you all speak Italian, you should enjoy this." After the laughter died down, the small Indian group decided to wait and hear this strange sound. Helen's admirers looked on without much change after the chief's sobering speech. Helen moved with the mood for the piece. She started out slowly and captured the soprano qualities, building gently into soft and then with firm expressions of drama. It took several minutes to build, and it gave her a chance to ease gently into the solid core of the piece, acting out the part as if she were on stage in Chicago. Then it came—first the B flat and then a dramatic high C. It came as smoothly as any performance she could have hoped to replicate. She stole a glance at her family where Tom Gannon sat in proud wonderment.

The crowd broke into loud applause. The Indians moved back to their homes as the amazed township gathering milled about, applauding, asking questions, expressing opinions about this unusual Chambers Fourth of July.

Tom Gannon, when he finally was able to tear his wife away from her new admirers, pulled her into his arms and kissed her fully on the mouth. Then he drew back and said, "Mrs. Gannon, you just hung the moon."

"She sure did," a nearby couple said, smiling broadly and clapping.

"We sure hope you will do that again—and soon."

"Perhaps we can," Helen said, and she turned to hug her children.

The Bowers and the Masons came up, all talking at once.

Mildred Bowers broke in with, "Let's all go over to our house; the Masons are coming, and I've got lots of food. Nothing formal, mind you—just sit around and talk." As they all gathered in the Bowers' big living room, the children rushed for their books, and John sat with the adults.

"Well, look who's joining us. That's our new hero—out there taking charge of a big moment today."

"I didn't do anything," John said, turning red-faced from all the attention.

"Well, I sure thought so. You saw someone you knew who was in trouble, and you went out to help him," Jim Bowers said. "That's the way to handle things in life, son. You see something that needs to be done, and if you think you can take care of the situation, you step right up and do it."

Chapter 6

John Boy

"You looked like your father out there," Jim Bowers said.

"Thank you, sir," John said through a faint smile. He felt more grown up there in the company of the adults. His mother's performance stimulated him more than he had ever known. Secretly, he now felt the difference, and he rather liked this new station. Suddenly, he went to his mother.

"Mother, I'll be right back," and he was out the door before anyone could speak. He ran down to the town square off Main Street. Chief Grey Eagle and the Indian boy were tending to Crazy Horse, making sure he could ride his horse back to White Rock Point. John rushed up to Crazy Horse, saying, "Are you all right, sir?" Everyone looked a little shocked.

"I'm fine," Crazy Horse said. "I was glad to see you out here today, little warrior. Not many people come to help an Indian up off the ground."

"I will," John said. Then he turned to the Indian boy. "You coming to school in the fall?"

"Yes," the boy said. "Do you fish?" he asked.

"So long," John said, not hearing the question. Waving, he ran back to the Bowers. He got a stern look from his mother when he returned.

"Where did you have to rush off to?" Tom asked his son.

"I just ran in to town to check on something," John said. "I thought I wanted to say something to Crazy Horse, but I guess it really was to see if the chief's son was still there. When I asked him, he said he would be coming to school in the fall."

"He did, did he?" Bowers said. "You better go slow with that one, son. It won't sit well with most people in this town."

Mildred Bowers called everyone to the table. The ladies put the last of many bowls of steaming food on the table.

After dinner, the children excused themselves, took their plates to the kitchen, and moved to their favorite spots. John sat against the wall and fought off sleep for only a few minutes before it overtook him.

"That's some young man you have there, Mr. Gannon," Jim Bowers said.

"Sure is," Mason said. "How old is he?"

"Thirteen the end of October," Gannon said.

"Can you imagine," Mason continued, "he's practically a stranger in town, thirteen years old, and he's that concerned with the welfare of people—Indians at that."

Gannon laughed. "I was much the same when I was growing up. Curious, helpful."

"It'll be interesting to see how he develops," Bowers said. "And no one, I mean no one, had any idea your wife had a voice like that. You better watch out. Chicago might just come calling."

"That would suit her just fine. She has always hounded me to move there, but I keep telling her that three months out here, and she will have more to do and find more satisfaction in the doing than being one among the tens of thousands in the big city," Tom said.

"I sure agree with that," Mason said.

"What's the background of our schoolmarm? I hear she is a singer, also," Tom said.

"She is," Mason quickly cut in, "but she doesn't match your wife's voice. Your children will love her teaching. She has a fantastic education from the Cincinnati Conservatory of Music, and she is a real gift when it comes to teaching our children. They love her."

"What about my voice?" Helen said as she came into the room, all smiling and flush with success.

"They were just saying how good you were out there today, but you need work," Gannon kidded.

"You had better kid me toward home; I'm exhausted. And look at this bunch—all three sound asleep," Helen said.

They all waved good-bye, and the Gannons walked slowly up the hill to their home.

"What a day!" Helen exclaimed as the family walked in their front door.

"Sure was, sweetheart. You stole the show. Do you realize that you could not buy that kind of exposure to a town for $10,000 or maybe more? Now everybody in town knows the Gannons—especially the new queen of Chambers. Seriously, honey, that was a big day for us. I was so proud of you, I was busting out all over."

"Bursting," Helen corrected.

"Yes, ma'am, bursting," Tom said, smiling and holding his wife's hand. "And we better keep an eye on John boy, here. He's a pretty high-stepping Gannon." Tom smiled and tweaked John's ear as the boy pulled away.

"Mother, I'm sleepy," Betty Jean said.

"Me too," John said as he walked toward his room.

Chapter 7

The Edge of Paradise

The weekend was made especially for the Gannons—house chores and rest. Monday brought a typical work week. The Gannon household busied themselves with breakfast, and everyone seemed to start their day with a special confidence. John said good-bye to his father as the new banker left for town. Then John turned to his mother.

"Mother, I'm going out back to dig some worms. Then I'm going down to the river to fish."

"Oh, are you? You be careful down there. You may run into your new Indian friend. No doubt, he fishes."

John filled a can with big worms and worked his way down through town to the Brule. Button willow trees grew out into the water down toward the bridge. He strolled on a trail that led him to the spot that he judged looked the most inviting, but he canvassed the shore as far as he could see, hoping his new acquaintance might show up.

John caught a few perch but nothing of consequence. He looked and waited; he became familiar with the shore in both directions and then settled his interest on the island in the middle of this pristine river. The clear sheen on the surface was unlike anything he had ever seen. He secretly wondered if it housed demon fish—catfish so large they could swallow a grown man. He had read of such fish in the library, yet he doubted his new, wonderful river would cuddle such monsters in such inviting waters. He was amazed by the clarity of the river and how it gave way like darkened glass as it slipped in the depths dramatically—caused, perhaps, by some ancient ice formation thousands of years ago. Almost without thinking, the boy suddenly realized that he was close to the entry of the bridge. It was safe enough, containing a small walk area for pedestrians. The view of Chambers, the island—especially the island—and the terrain on the other side of the Brule, rising in a long gentle slope to Hagerty Woods, all invited him to his new surroundings. The woodland front line of huge oak and mixed hardwood were powerful to behold, a giant spruce being its centerpiece.

There was much more than considerable attraction there. It excited him in a mysterious way, and he suddenly felt he needed to know more. He strolled to the center of the bridge and looked down into the dark waters. Then his eyes swept outward, taking in the object for which he came to see: the island … and perhaps some semblance of the Eagle family—fishing, or building, or whatever they did out there. Today he was disappointed. It was not a total failure, though, for with a quick scan in the opposite direction, he was astonished by how well he could see what had been described to him as his schoolhouse. It would be closed for the summer, but tomorrow he would have a look at it.

John returned home just in time for lunch. "Did you catch anything?" Betty Jean asked as he entered the house.

"They weren't biting that much, but I caught a few bream. I put them back, as there weren't enough for a meal. Only two were alive and swam off to grow bigger."

"Better come wash up. Lunch is almost ready," his mother said. "Did you see your friend down there fishing?"

"No, but I had a good look around. Mom, it's really beautiful out here. We're so close to the Brule, and I'll bet anything there are some really big fish in this river."

"I'm sure you'll find out soon enough," Helen said.

"I talked to Mr. Hickerson at his store there on Main Street, and he told me he knew where I could buy some ears of popcorn."

"Popcorn? What in the world will you do with that? Oh, of course we could all enjoy it, but you make it sound like you have bigger plans than that," Helen said.

"I was down at the train station the other day, and three people asked me to get them a bottle of soda. No telling what I could sell when those trains pull into our station. Some peanuts, maybe. Everybody likes popcorn, so I'm going to try it pretty soon, just as quick as I can get some supplies," John said.

"My, my, you are a boy with money ideas, aren't you? You are just like your daddy in that respect," Helen said.

The next evening, John came home with his pockets full of dimes.

"What in the world did you sell?"

"I sold everything for ten cents each. I can make a nickel on each item I sell. I started out charging a quarter, and not one person said no—not one. Then a lady said that was way too much to charge, so I started selling for a dime."

"Wait until your daddy hears this story. He's going to be very impressed." John beamed with satisfaction as his mother complimented him so highly.

Tom Gannon walked in, and Betty Jean was at the front door telling all about her brother's "big adventure on the trains today as they pulled into the station."

"Well, what have we here?" Tom asked as he walked into the dining room.

"Look at this," Helen said, motioning to the money on the dining table that represented their son's efforts for the day.

"How did you make so much?" Tom asked.

"Selling my popcorn and peanuts. I could have made more, except I ran out. Then I started fetching sodas for people. I must have had ten customers just for sodas. I mean people had a fit for something to eat. I guess they won't get fed until they get to Kansas City. Man, everybody was looking at me as if I had just fallen off the moon. The thing that concerned me was how the porters took notice, and even two tramp-looking men at the station. They looked me over pretty good when I started for home. They both stood up and took a few steps toward me. I'll have to watch out for those two."

"You sure will," Tom said. "Don't talk to them, and don't let them get near you. They look for easy money. Handouts, easy pickings. So, you're vulnerable if they see how easily a young lad like you can make money, just as you did today. Put distance between you and them, and they can't hurt you. Any comments from the train people or the station attendant?"

"No, sir."

"Likely you'll hear from them sooner rather than later. You know, to sell food, you normally have to have a license."

"Then I'll go get a license."

"May not be that easy, son; we'll see."

They talked awhile about John's ideas and how innovative they were for someone his age. Finally, they were called to dinner.

"How did it go at the bank?" Helen asked.

"Interesting, very interesting. I made a major loan that Jim Bowers was pleased with, and I got a lot of paperwork done. He still hasn't hired a teller. I'm making plans to go out and visit the ranchers. You know, make myself know. Drum up some business for the bank."

"Jim's sending you out in the field?"

"No, this is my idea. Go get the business. Make people want us; don't wait for things to happen before they have to reach out to us."

"Good idea," Helen said.

"Did you meet the new school teacher yet?" Tom asked.

Mildred is going to invite her and me to tea next week when she feels better. I can't wait to meet her. To have someone with her music background to talk with will be a real treat. I hear she has great knowledge and is a very talented singer."

"I told you these things would happen," Tom said, smiling at Helen.

"Yeah, well, we'll just have to give it some time. She is the teacher at our school, and I hear that she excels in music history and music theory. How did she get way out here, do you suppose?" Helen asked.

"Opportunity, excitement. Same as us. And it's here, all you want life to be, but you have to reach out for it. Anyone who has any personality, any talents at all, can be very content in a small town like this, especially if it's set on a river like the Brule," Tom said. "You should go down there with John and take a look at it."

"You and the Brule. One would think that river swallowed the sun and the moon in one big gulp."

"You're not far off track, Mrs. Gannon. I took John down there on the riverbanks soon after we came to town. The Indians have a story about our river: The Brule reaches out every morning and grabs the sun, pulls its fiery red skin into its bosom until it boils a bright red, announcing the day. When it has had its morning dance and it's evening dance—just at the right moment, just as it seems to go to sleep in a big curtain of darkness—brother moon chases the sun out of the water so it can rest there in its place, schooling the fish, dancing on the water until first light. Then that big fireball morning sun comes back over the treetops only to be swallowed up by the Brule once again. The Indians say that one day the sun won't come; it just won't show up. They say it won't happen in their lifetime, but it will happen long after all of us are gone. And without those two, big glowing giants, there will be no river, be no fish. All the people and animals will slowly dance the death dance."

"That would make a pretty good opera, wouldn't it? *Dance of the Brule*."

"There's much more than a frontier town and a magical river out here," Tom said. "Our children, the people out here, hidden opportunities, a way of life. We have only begun to discover the legacy of this place, the future of this city. If we relax, plan ahead, and grab opportunities, our family will grow beautifully, happily."

"I hope you're right. This is not my idea of a life for our family, yet something started here the Fourth of July. So, we'll wait. We'll have to wait and see," Helen said as she turned her thoughts over in her mind and looked away, as if some majestic vista called far beyond them.

"Darling, there's not much waiting to it. On the Fourth, you held Chambers in your hands, and I can tell you this, you have opportunities here, second only to Chicago. I see richness developing here that we have yet to dream about. Just make the most of it, and you will discover the talents in our children—and the children around town are dreams you never contemplated in far-off Monmouth. We have made a remarkable start here. Everybody in town knows us, thanks largely to you and your fantastic voice. And do you see what is happening to our son? That boy is bursting at the seams to get a foothold here. That Indian boy! Did you notice his eyes? Those dark pools that glistened in the light, flashing bright signals of intelligence, wild as an eagle, yet uncommonly at ease around us. I don't know where that is heading. Sure looks positive to me."

He paused for moment and then continued. "When school starts, you can be sure John will do well. Notice how much time he spends at the library? And he asks everybody about life here, how it works, and who the people are. He's pretty unusual. And the girls—I think they are going to blossom out here. Certainly, I hear no complaints. Say, why don't you and the girls come fishing with John and me Saturday morning? We'll have a family outing."

"No, thanks," Helen replied. "I have practice at the church, and the girls are coming along. Perhaps another time. You two go fishing and have your time together. But I know what you're saying about our new venture out here. I'll wait a year, Tom. Then we can talk again."

"That's a deal, Mrs. Gannon. That's a deal. Work on your skills, work on our social life, and a year from now, this conversation will be a distant memory. Now, I want to hear you run your scales every day like you used to do. Stand out there on the back porch and send that beautiful voice of yours echoing out over the Brule. I want the Lakota to start massing up at the edge of town. They already think you're something of a goddess, you know, just from your performance on the Fourth." Helen grinned pleasantly, eyes a bit dreamy.

"All right, Mr. Gannon. If you say so. You cabinet makers and bankers have a talent for making things seem exciting." Tom went to his wife, folded her gently into his arms, kissing the tip of her nose, pulling back just far enough to look deeply into her brown eyes.

"Mrs. Gannon, you were a goddess out there on the Fourth. You were all that I ever dreamed you would be. And you know something else? I think deep down you've found a new stage." His arms tightened Helen in a firm embrace as he kissed her passionately.

"You're my princess," Tom said. He pulled Helen gently forward. "The children are out. Why don't we go relax a bit. A lay back will soothe the cares of the day."

As they walked hand in hand out of the living room, Helen looked at her husband through a warm smile that said, "My God, Tom Gannon, how you have changed."

The night passed with soft shades of lamplight bathing the affairs of a new family life. They were in the frontier with all ten feet—all five Gannons, five minds sorting out their futures and the future of one another. Their daily routines rushed at them—five explorers in a new world of simplicity, beauty, locking in on the hazards and rewards that build steadfast, happy lives. Before them lay a summer to build their stages on which to perform their dramas in this new land, shaping their happiness, their expanding achievements within their swirling lives.

Helen fell asleep secretly marveling at how she had suddenly become a local celebrity. Tom silently thought of the first miracle of becoming a banker of sorts. A cabinet maker a banker? Yet there he was sitting in that loan officer chair, and who knew the future?

John saw fields of peanuts and popcorn growing on a farm across the Brule. He saw the Indian children at play. Children without a school. Who is this James Blue Eagle? There was something wildly exotic about this new friend, the epitome of all things he had read that said Indian.

The edges of wild and the Old West, primitive and modern at once. A teacher of wild domain?

Sallie saw several girls on the Fourth; perhaps they would be friends. Perhaps someday she would go off to college and marry a doctor.

Betty Jean dreamed her big dream before sleep overwhelmed her. If only someday she could sing like her mother and go to Chicago to the big stage.

Saturday morning, John was shaken out of a deep sleep by his father at 6:00 a.m.

"Come on, son, we have to get down to the river. Those fish should be real hungry."

John bounced out of bed, washed his face quickly with cold water, and joined his dad for toast and jelly and milk. Then they walked quickly to the river. He never felt so in tune with life. *To walk to Brule to go fishing with my father*, he thought. *How many boys can do that?*

They passed the willows—everybody probably fished there—and chose the bridge piers instead. They caught two small bass and two crappie pretty quickly, a lull ensued, and then *wham*. Suddenly, John's pole bent double. "Hold him tightly and play him a bit," Tom urged. "Let him run. Tire him out."

John grimaced, clinching his teeth as he fought the fish.

"Try to work him over to your right and bring him in on that low strip of land." Foot at a time, John moved his fish over to the spot and then started to back up, dragging the bass right up on land.

"Hold tight. Hold tight. Grab the line and work your way down." Hand over hand down the line, John went quickly to the big fish.

"Watch those teeth; they're pretty sharp. Hold him down gently with your foot. Atta boy. Now get him by the gills so you can remove the hook."

"Boy, he's heavy," John said as he picked up his exhausted catch and presented it to his father. "What do you guess, Dad?"

Tom took the fish in his left hand. "Five pounds and eight ounces," he said as he winked at his son. "Actually, that is pretty close."

Suddenly John yelled, "Fish on!" and Tom quickly moved to grab his own pole, which was being dragged into the river. He set the hook and began to make the same maneuver his son just had.

"Feels like the twin of the one you're holding." Suddenly the fish broke water in a fierce leap for freedom, but to no avail, as Gannon held the line too tightly for his catch to shake out the hook. Then he landed him in the same path his son had chosen.

"Wow. Looks like a bass."

"It is. I saw what it was when he broke water in his first big leap."

"Boy, oh, boy. He's a beauty, Dad. Look at the head and big gills."

The tired fish opened his gills repeatedly for air. "Look how big his belly is," John said.

"Yeah, he's a big one all right. Probably been feeding on small fish since first light. See what we've done here, son? Just pick your place, get there at the right hour, and be patient. Fishing is fun when they're biting. Let's leave some for another day."

John couldn't wait to get home to show his mother. Helen saw them coming and met them at the front door. "Well look at our fishermen. How many did you catch?"

"Three each!" John yelled to his mother. "Look at my bass, Mom. And Dad's, too. Just look at Dad's big bass. Look at the head on him. What do you think he weighs, Dad?"

"Oh, he might pull down six pounds. We'll have to find a scale."

"I saw one out in the wood shed yesterday," John said as he raced away to get it.

"Well, I was close—five pounds, ten and a half ounces. Mother, I guess we can put these in a cold bucket for holding and invite the Bowers to fish dinner if they are free. That will be fun, and it will pay back one dinner at least," Tom said.

The Gannons dressed the fish out by the shed, and when John threw the head of the bass out some distance, it hardly hit the ground when a blur came from the back of the shed, grabbed the fish head, and sped away. "What in the world was that, Dad?"

"Wasn't a cat, but I've never seen one of those. Tell you what, son, when we go in the house, look it up. My mammal book is in the living room someplace. Let me know what you find. Look there he is again, standing up and watching us. He's not even afraid of us."

"Sure looks like it," John said.

"Maybe a pet; it's hard to tell. Looks like a ferret, perhaps."

Tom and his son put the dressed fish in a large, metal wash bowl.

"Better take those to the house before that rascal out there decides they're his. He'll steal one before your very eyes if you don't watch out."

Chapter 8

Bank Files

The fishermen strode proudly into the house with their dressed catch of the day. "Ready for some eggs and bacon?" Helen asked Tom.

"A bite or two. Not too much, though."

"How about the pike fisherman. Is he hungry?"

"Bass fisherman, and yes, ma'am, two will be fine ... scrambled," John said.

"Scrambled, please," Helen corrected. "Someone get the door!" she shouted.

"I thought I heard a knock," Gannon said as he went to the front.

"Good morning, Jim. What brings you up here so early? Did you see our catch?"

"Yes, I saw you and your 'guide' coming up the hill. Nice catch," Jim Bowers said, adding, "Listen, step out here a minute so we can talk."

"Anything wrong, Mr. Bowers?"

"There are several files missing. Wagner, H. Smith, and Randel. You know anything about them?"

"Well, yes, I have them in there on my desk. I'm studying them."

"Tom, there's one thing about the bank; files are sacred. They are not to leave the bank. It's too risky. Suppose something happened to them? Anything could, you know. What in the world are you doing with them, anyway? Scared me half to death."

"Sorry, I just didn't know," Gannon said. "I plan to ride out to those places this afternoon and have a look at the properties, meet those ranchers. I can't judge a man that I have never met."

"You're planning to do this on your own time?"

"I'm not fishing," Gannon said, "and I'm not hunting … though I might see something during my trip for the future—but really, it will be an adventure. I may take John with me. Get to know these people. Make them want us before they really have to come in for money."

Bowers stepped back a bit and stroked his chin. "You know, Gannon, the minute I saw you come into town, react the way you did to the 'warm welcome' the sheep herders gave your family, I said to myself, 'There is my next teller.' But I was so wrong." Gannon stood up straight. At just under six feet, his strong, stocky build looked imposing.

"I was quite wrong," Bowers repeated. "You are much more than that. Frankly—now I'm kidding—I think you're trying to take over my job, and I like that in a good man. As a matter of fact, maybe I can get out to fish or travel once in a while. So, watch your step, young man, you may have all the worries of a banker before you know it."

"Well, thank you, Jim. I'm flattered you judge me in that way. You had me worried there for a moment. Do you want to take these files back with you? I haven't even opened them yet."

"No, just make darn sure you don't let them get lost, and bring them back in on Monday. Oh, and I'll be interested in your opinions on those ranchers after you meet them."

"I sure will. By the way, if you and Mrs. Bowers are free, come up and have fish with us tonight."

"Sounds good to me. I'll check with Mildred when I get home. If I don't come right back, we will see you, what—6:30, 7:00?"

"Let's say 6:30," Gannon said.

"Good—see you then, Tom."

Chapter 9

Gannon's First Call

Gannon went in his house and immediately looked at the three files on his desk. "My God," he muttered. *No wonder Jim was concerned. Big deals,* he thought. *No wonder he looked so anxious. Good thing he got upset about it.* "Hmmm," he mumbled and then went into their bedroom.

"Helen!" Tom yelled. "I'm going to lie down to rest a bit. Call me in half an hour, okay?"

There was no answer, but he lay down anyway. In five minutes, Tom was snoring. In his dreams, he saw alligators diving out of giant trees. Strangers circled the edge of the woods, and it wasn't longer than a moment that he awakened to the sight of Helen shaking his shoulder, asking, "Aren't you going out to visit some clients?"

Gannon sat up, rubbing his eyes. "Thanks, honey. Yes, I am. Glad you woke me up. Boy, I was out of it." He grabbed the files and put them in his briefcase, a spare that was laying around the bank. He arrived at Charles Randel's ranch first. Randel saw him coming long before the Buick arrived and came out on the front porch.

"Well, if it isn't our new loan officer. What brings you way out here Mr. uh …"

"Gannon. Tom Gannon."

"What can I do for you, Mr. Gannon?"

"Just out getting acquainted, Mr. Randel. I'm a master carpenter—at least I was until a few days ago." They both made a faint effort to laugh.

"Do you have any sweet well water? I'm suddenly dry. Took my boy fishing this morning."

"Sure, come on in. My well will take care of that in no time. And this one's on me," Randel said, amid faint laughter. Walking through the house, Gannon saw a well-made ranch house, neatly kept too, he thought. Furnished above average for a rancher, painted well, floors were superior, wide, ash. Some rooms in oak.

"Your floors are special. I've made fine cabinets out of worse."

Gannon drank from the well-bucket dipper offered him. Long satisfying drinks. "Thanks, Mr. Randel. That sure is sweet water." They exchanged pleasantries around the well, and finally Gannon brought up the point he was interested in—the terms of his loan.

"Wonder if you have time to give me a quick tour. I've never seen your property before."

"Sure," Randel said. "We can saddle up or go in your car. My property roads are pretty good."

"Let's take my car; it'll be quicker for me, and a short drive about will get the job done fine. How many head do you run out here?"

"Usually a thousand, sometimes as little as seven or eight hundred. Depends on the weather. Drought's our big enemy in ranching. And we're not that big," Randel commented.

"What, 1,500 acres?" Tom asked.

"A little more, counting next door."

"You own that? I thought that was the Whorton place," Tom said.

"He got killed, you know. Stupid jerk. Out hunting opposite other hunters. And for what? A buck deer. Darn fool, if you ask me," Randel said.

"A good friend of yours, I imagine?" Gannon asked.

"Kyle Whorton? Friend? He didn't have any friends. I offered to buy his little ole place half a dozen times; it's not big enough to live on.

Who knows? He was just being Kyle Whorton. Just ornery if you ask me. That's why he worked at the bank; he couldn't make a living on that little ranch."

"Let's stop here a moment," Gannon said as he topped the hill that led to an expansive horizon of valleys and rolling hills. "Well, well, what have we here? What a beautiful ranch you have, Mr. Randel."

"This view is why I bought the ranch. It tells a story in itself. When you first see it, you know this is it. That feeling never quits—almost infinite."

"Look at that," Gannon said, pointing straight ahead. "You've got wolves."

Randel picked up the distant movement instantly.

"That pack never learns. They chase that buck all the time, always the same outcome, thinking they can run him till he drops. Watch this. See that ravine up ahead of the deer? Looks little from here, but it's actually about seventeen feet across. It's pretty deep, too—about twelve feet down to my creek. Those wolves can get down in there, but they can't deal with the problems. They don't like water, as I'm sure you know, and secondly, they can't get up the other side, which is almost straight up.

"Watch this. They're getting pretty close. Watch that buck speed up. Boom. There he goes. He just sails over that ravine like it's nothing. Happens every time they chase him."

"Pretty clever deer," Gannon said, laughing softly. "Nature never fails to intrigue if one cares to pay careful attention. You lose many calves to those wolves?"

"Unfortunately, we do. We set out bait, we poison them, and we shoot some, but they keep breeding and coming back for easy calf kills. Sometimes the herd gangs up on 'em, circles around the cow and the calf until the pack leaves. Doesn't work for long, though; they just bide their time, come back, distract the cow, and finally run her off. Poor thing. She just has to stand there and watch her helpless calf be ripped apart. Wolves have to eat—they have babies to feed, too. Usually happens at night, so we can't help much."

"Well, I've got to get back home. Appreciate your showing me around." Gannon dropped the rancher off at his home and headed for Chambers. Too much time was spent on that visit, but he thought it necessary as it played out well. It solved some questions, opened the door to personal ones, but left open some real concerns that he had to settle with Jim Bowers pretty quickly. *Smart man, Randel—so it seemed. But why did he need four "bodyguards" hanging around on his front porch? Why, exactly, did a rancher need that kind of protection? and then there were the "several offers to buy out his neighbor"—who later got killed in a hunting accident. Were any of his men involved in that?* Gannon wondered.

As he drove, Gannon contemplated taking Randel's advice and cut through the thick woods just ahead, just to take a quick look at the Whorton place. After he drove into the woods about a hundred feet, he changed his mind. He stopped and backed up slowly to the fork in the road. As Gannon turned in to the other road, something told him to look back at the Randel house. Riding slowly his way were four horsemen. He drove on, and they came no further. "Hmmm, that's interesting. Where are they going?" he said and drove on back to Chambers. He remembered the Bowers would be arriving pretty soon for a fresh fish dinner.

"Well, how did it go out there on the range?" Helen asked, kidding about the range part.

"Very interesting, very interesting," Tom said as he kissed Helen hello. "Where is everybody?"

"Come, I'll show you," Helen said as she led him into the dining room and waved at the table.

"Why that little hustler," Tom said, breaking out in a broad grin.

"He sold that much from this morning. Came home for lunch, popped corn, roasted his peanuts, and went back to the station an hour ago. I guess he will be home when he gets home," Helen said.

"Honey, as great as this is for John, and for all of us to see, you know it can't go on much longer. They'll call him on it. Either the town—though I don't know who—or the train conductor. He has to have a license to sell food to the public; that's it, pure and simple."

"Well, let's let it play out on its own," Helen said. "Why upset an entrepreneur like that, eh." Both laughed heartily.

"Okay by me. Where are the girls?"

"Here I am, Daddy," Betty Jean said, coming in the back door.

"Sallie is next door visiting with Leland."

"Is she? Nothing like making new friends," Tom said. "Honey, if you don't need me for anything, I'll go clean up a bit and change for tonight."

"No, I'm fine. You go ahead."

"Well, speak of the devil; here comes the super salesman."

"Hi, Dad. Guess what I did?"

"You sold a hundred bags of peanuts and popcorn."

"You're close. I sold fifty-two this morning. I could have sold 152 if I had that many," John said excitedly. "But this afternoon, I was low on peanuts, so I only sold forty. Can you believe it—ninety-two dimes," John said, very pleased with himself.

"Well now, I think I'll just quit work," Tom joked. "So what are you going to do with all this money? Put it in the bank?"

"Yes, sir. I might keep a dollar for … oh I completely forgot. I have to restock."

"Well, you work it out, son. I'm off to clean up. You children had better do the same. Look your best, now. Mr. and Mrs. Bowers are coming."

Tom went off muttering, "Can you imagine, our boy made $9.20 in one day."

"Wow!" John yelled. "I didn't even think about the total yet."

"And don't get too far ahead of yourself on inventory," Gannon cautioned his son.

"No, sir, I won't."

As Tom Gannon prepared himself for the evening with the Bowers, his mind filled with questions about what he saw today. There were big, unusual questions that lingered in the Randel contract, and he yearned for the details of the so-called hunting accident of the previous teller, Kyle Whorton. Then, there was Randel himself. Contract or no, he was a bit too mysterious, bordering on edgy. Charles Randel seemed too defensive when they stood eye to eye, getting acquainted. He was a bit too uneasy. Those four cowpokes hanging around like body guards; they should have been out on the range. Something told Gannon to throw it in Bowers' lap immediately, yet something told him to just go easy. Things would sort themselves out in due time. He settled on the latter. He scarcely had dressed and checked on the family when Jim and Mildred Bower arrived.

Gannon was charming, as was Helen, and the evening played out smoothly, for Bowers frequently glanced at his loan officer, searching for clues that might flush out Tom's experiences in the field that day. It wasn't to be. Business would have to wait, as the entire evening was devoted to music and how the Gannon family was finding Chambers. Much excitement was made over the new business developed out of thin air by young John Boy.

"John's venture turned out very well," Gannon said. "You should have been in Monmouth back when he was not quite nine years old. Helen and I were away over the weekend, so we left John home by himself with a well-stocked pantry and the next-door neighbors agreeing to watch over him. What does he do? Picks up the phone and orders a half truckload of manure for the basement so he could grow mushrooms and sell them." Everyone roared with laughter. John turned scarlet red but laughed along with the crowd.

"I got sick to death from working down there with no air," John said.

"He had high fever for three days," Helen said. "We actually put him in ice to drop his temperature."

"I think your idea of selling to train travelers is much healthier and a lot more lucrative," Tom said. John squirmed in his chair as if he could ward off being the center of so much attention. Finally, Jim Bowers spoke up.

"I don't want to bring you bad news, little man, but be prepared. Likely the railroad or the station manager will have to file a paper warning you to cease and desist. You know why, don't you, son?"

"Because I'm making too much money?" John joked, producing big laughter.

"I wish it were that simple," Tom said. "Yes, we've already discussed the age thing and the serving the public food without a license, even for a young, industrious man like our boy, John," Tom said.

The evening passed pleasantly, and soon the Bowers were strolling down the hill toward home, discussing their evening.

"You know, every time I'm around that family, I come away feeling how fortunate I was to have found Tom Gannon."

"I couldn't agree more," Mildred said, "and I feel the same way about Helen."

"Is it life on the Brule or just luck?" Jim asked.

"Perhaps it's both. Whatever it is, it sure has my vote," Mildred agreed.

Chapter 10

Drifters' Surprise

July passed swiftly and happily for the Gannons. John didn't miss a train. Popcorn flowed, came in short supply, and he worried about finding another source. Friday, August 1, 1913, he marked it on his "action" list that his father taught him to keep and then finished roasting the peanuts. They would still throw off a good aroma to delight his customers on the next zephyr. He must hurry, he thought. When John reached Chambers Station, the two drifters were in their usual spot. That always sent up caution flags, and he felt a bit uneasy with them around.

The train pulled in; it was time to spring into action. Some passengers dismounted to stretch and walk a block or two. He sold five bags of popcorn before getting on the train. Hawking his treats in the last two cars produced quick sales. He moved on through the cars, and in twelve minutes, John, always neatly dressed and wearing a winning smile, easily sold all of his merchandise. This day's haul was fifty-eight dimes, three quarters.

When he exited the train, he was right in front of the two drifters. Now, he was cut off from the station until the train pulled out.

Smiling, acting genial, they approached the boy slowly. "If you ain't the dangest hustler I've ever laid my eyes on. You sell out every day in no time at all. Good for you is all I can say. Why I'll bet you made nine dollars slick as snot on a doorknob. Grab him, Bob."

As if on cue, the dense bushes parted directly behind the drifters, and out stepped Blue Eagle, giving a loud yell, "Yeeeaaah!" Brandishing a six-foot-long, green, hardwood limb, he hit both the drifters multiple times before they ever realized that he was upon them, sending both of them running for the nearby woods.

"You all right?"

"Yes—thanks to you," John said to his friend. "They never even touched me, but in two more steps, I'm afraid they would have. I've seen them here so often. Looks like they thought today would be the day for some easy pickings. How in the world did you happen to be standing over there?" John said, pointing to the nearby bushes.

"I'm there when they are here; they are trouble. I've got to go now. Come fish in the morning," Blue Eagle said as he walked off. "Down by the bridge. I'll be there about six. They start feeding early."

"Okay!" John yelled. "See you there." The train slowly began the last leg of its journey to Kansas City.

When John was at the edge of town, he decided to stop in the bank to see his father.

"What's wrong, son?" Tom said as he saw his son's serious face.

"Nothing much, thanks to Blue Eagle, but maybe a lot. I just wanted you to know."

"What is it—those drifters try to jump you?"

"Just about. They made their move to grab me, but Blue Eagle came out of nowhere. He had a heavy green limb. You should have seen him, Dad. They never knew what hit them. Wham! Bang! All over their backs, butts, heads. He was a fright. Sent those two yelling and running for cover in the woods."

"I was afraid of that happening," Tom said. "They didn't grab your arm or anything?"

"No, sir. One of them said, 'Grab him, Bill,' or maybe it was Bob. That's when Blue Eagle came out of the bushes nearby, whacking them all over. They are going to have some big knots on their heads tomorrow, I'll tell you."

"Why didn't you run?"

"I was blocked by the train, and I didn't think they meant me any harm at first. I should have taken off up the tracks. They certainly can't catch me, even with a pocket full of dimes weighing me down."

"Well, why don't you deposit your money, and we'll talk more about it when I get home, son."

John approached his house with a long face, prompting his mother to stop her work in the kitchen. "What on earth is wrong? Did you get into some kind of trouble?"

He told his mother all the details.

"Oh, my Lord! You could've been killed, and no one would have been the wiser until the train pulled out. Well, that's it. No more doing business at the train station."

"Yes, ma'am. I'm sure that's what Dad is going to say, too. I pretty much figured it out that way coming home."

"Thank heavens your Indian friend was there to look out for you."

"I know," John said. "Do you know he said that he's there every day those drifters are there. I find that incredible. Maybe he's already a good friend, and I just don't know it."

Helen said, "You've got a good point. He had to be there for a reason. Well, you go wash up and get ready for lunch. Put some cold water on your face. That will refresh you."

Tom arrived just as John came back from washing his face.

"You know, son, this means you have to make a decision."

"I know, Dad. As much as I hate to give up a good job, I have to. It's trouble no matter what I do."

"That's right. If we go to the sheriff, you will be forced to quit. Same results if you go to the railroad. What we can do is run those two drifters out of town with a stern warning; see if that works," Tom said. "I'll check the town ordinance just in case," he added. "They don't look that tough; maybe they'll drift on someplace else."

The next morning, John saw Blue Eagle struggling with a fish as he arrived at the bridge. "I wondered if you would come."

"After what you did for me? How could I not show up? Thanks, by the way," John added. "I've seen those two before. I really didn't think they would go so far as to try to rob me. Anyway, you sure gave them a few welts to suffer with for a few days. My dad thinks they might just move on now that they've showed us who they really are."

"Look at that. Pull him in!" Blue Eagle said excitedly.

"Boy oh boy—another nice bass. My dad and I caught two a few days ago, almost six pounds."

"I know," Blue Eagle said.

"You know? Don't tell me you saw us," John said.

"I was standing right up there in the middle of the bridge. I sometimes come out there to see the sun rise. Yesterday took the prize. Big and red. It's, as you say, a thing of beauty," Blue Eagle said.

"I'll go with you sometime."

"Ooooh, got another one." Blue Eagle played it longer than the first and pulled it up through the shallow part of the bank.

"Boy, he *is* a big one," John said. They made a stringer from a willow branch with a fork at the end, securing the fish by plunging the sharp end deep into the bank at water's edge.

"Now what about that bull boat? What did you want to tell me?"

Blue Eagle thought a moment.

"You've never been in one of our 'skins,' have you?"

"No, yours is the first one I've ever seen," John replied.

"That's it then. Meet me down here at that willow tree over there in the morning, and we'll go out in the river. You'll find it interesting."

John was caught off balance. "I don't know," he stalled. "I can't swim."

Blue Eagle stood there looking at John as his new friend moved around uneasily. Finally, he spoke.

"Don't worry; I swim good enough for both of us. I can teach you in ten minutes. You *can* swim; you just don't know it yet. I'll show you how pretty soon. It's as natural as eating food. You'll see."

That made John feel a lot better, and after all, he had seen Blue Eagle swim to and from his island home almost every day.

"Okay, then. What time do you want to meet?"

"About nine in the morning. Dress light, and wear thin shoes," Blue Eagle said.

Chapter 11

The Drifters Make Their Move

John was uneasy all night just thinking about being out in deep water in the bull boat, even with his friend. After an early breakfast with his family, he headed out to the spot Blue Eagle suggested they meet to start their venture out on the Brule. The Indian was sitting by the button willows under the bridge when John walked up. No bull boat was to be seen.

"What happened to the boat?" John asked.

Blue Eagle was sitting on the riverbank looking somewhat disappointed. "I don't know. They had to move a lot of things upriver, so my parents needed all the boats. Don't worry; we will find another day pretty soon. Want to fish instead?"

"Good idea," John replied, somewhat relieved. The boys fished and talked for a while, and then Blue Eagle suddenly stood up and looked behind them.

"You boys catching anythang?" It was the drifters, standing fifty feet behind them.

"What do you want? You've got some nerve coming around us," John said.

"We've come to apologize to you boys. We were desperate and just needed a couple of quarters to tide us over. We haven't et anythang in two days. I apologize to your pa, too. Both of you'ens. Another thang;

when you're through fishin', if you leave your lines right there with a few worms, we could catch ourselves some food. We're starved."

Blue Eagle looked at John for a sign.

"We will on one condition," John said.

"Yea, what's at? Yea, I already guest it: work."

"That's right, work," John said. "There's plenty of work in town."

"That was the other thing I had to tell you," the short one said. "Tell your pa I'm sorry for mistreating you. I truly didn't want your money—just a dollar at most, but it ain't right, the way we gone atcha that way. An here's the thing. Tell him both of us will be downtown at first light to clean the street and all 'at. Then, if they's be good enough to pay something far it, we'd be going on our way 'morrow, late," the short one said.

"Does he talk?" John asked, pointing to the taller man.

"He can, yes sir, a little; he stutters. He took a had lick on the head a few years ago. His speech ain't been no good since, 'cept for me – I get him pretty good.."

"I hope he can fish."

"Oh, he can fish all right, and he's a good cook, too."

"When you get through fishing, you can have one line to keep. Take mine; leave my friend's here on the riverbank. What are your names?" John asked.

"I'm Bob, and he's Bob, too, so's I call 'em Bob II." Bob grinned widely, like he had just said something clever.

"All right, Bob and Bob II, start your fishing while they're still biting. You'll have dinner before an hour passes."

As the boys were leaving, John turned and said loudly, "By the way, I'll be downtown in the morning in case I'm needed. They may not believe you're all that serious. What are you leaving town for? Why don't you stay around for a while. Clean up—make some money for a change? The sheriff might even need a couple of fellows like you for silent lookouts. No telling what you can do here."

"Listen to him talk, Bob II. Ain't he a smart one? We may just do 'at … for a lil' while. We can't be workin' 'round too long like. Seen some good-lookin' freight trains come through 'ere. They have our names on 'em."

"Suit yourselves," John said. "Throw your lines over by that willow." Then he ran to catch up to Blue Eagle just a few yards from the bridge.

Chapter 12

Sunrise, Sunset

"Come on," Blue Eagle said, "I want to show you something." The boys had hardly walked fifty paces out on the bridge when they heard the drifters' loud commotion. "Looks like he's already hooked into a big one. After a bit of struggling, Bob II landed a nice size bass.

"Nice going," John yelled to the fishermen. "There's your dinner." The men waved, and Bob II held up his catch.

"Three or four pounds. That's a nice fish."

"Do you suppose they mean it—about working in the morning?" Blue Eagle asked.

"With those people, if they get hold of some wine or liquor some way, then no. If they don't, then maybe. Dad told me not to count on anything from people like those two. What's up? What's out here?"

Blue Eagle pointed up ahead and said, "Right up here is the perfect place. It starts and ends right here. When the sun sets, it jumps in the river right there." He pointed out the spot. "When the sun rises, it jumps in the river in that exact place. You have to come see it with me some morning or some evening—or both. A big sun or a big moon. You can't really tell someone about it; it's too big."

"I'll come enjoy them with you real soon; I promise," John said. "By the way, your English is very good. Your father, uh, your chief taught you?"

"Yes, he is good at language. He knows five or six tongues of our brothers. Mandan, of course, Dakota, Lakota, Assiniboine, and Apache."

"What was he doing down in Apache country?"

"He didn't go there; he learned from Crazy Dog. He speaks even more, Crow, Nez Pierce, at least."

"This brings up a good point," John said, "I've been thinking about this for days now. You need to be graduated from our Chambers School. We have six or seven weeks before school starts. I'd like you to go with me to the library and study vocabulary—you know, words. I need it; you need it. We have to get ready to get you into school one way or another, and then move on to high school."

Blue Eagle just looked at his friend.

"Our school, yes. Beyond that, I can't make any promises."

" Your chief said it, Blue Eagle. Remember his Fourth of July speech? He expects you to get yourself educated. That means college. At least Indian college."

"You don't understand," Blue Eagle cut off John's argument. "My father needs me. He's waiting for the right time, a sign. Then he and his woman will move back to our people at White Rock Point. Until then, I'll learn all I can in Chambers, but I can't plan beyond that."

"We'll see," John argued. "Time changes a lot of plans." They stood looking at the Brule for several minutes, and then John continued.

"You see this river—your river? There are many Brules in the world. But to you, your people, and especially my dad, this river is it. It is the overriding force as to why my family came here. And as magic as he and your chief find it, your people and your people before them must have gasped for air in the excitement of first looking upon this place, filled with scents of tall grasses and herds of buffalo. They say many battles were fought here among your people. Those who wanted to live here the most, those who had the most braves with the stoutest hearts. they won it all. One thing is for certain, and my dad and I have already talked about this. To live here, you—the future leader of your people—have to leave, study, then come back and build your schools."

They stood silent and looked at the water for a long moment.

"Someday I may leave here without you, but all that means is that I'm waiting for you to pack your things. I'll be back for you. You ask your chief. He'll agree with me and my father."

Blue Eagle looked at his new friend standing there on the bridge and thought to himself, *Is this a white Indian or an Indian Indian?*

"One more thing," John continued. "I need you to go over to the Dakota Reservation with me to talk to the chief. He won't have anything to do with a white boy like me, but he will if you're with me."

"The chief? Are you crazy? What can you say to him? He's a very important man; he doesn't talk to young boys our age."

"Are you willing to try it once?"

"Sure," the Indian said.

"Good, then meet me at the library at nine in the morning. We'll study our English grammar and words for an hour. Then we'll jog over the bridge and talk to the chief."

Blue Eagle looked sternly at his friend.

"You paw the ground like a bull buffalo, you little man. What in the world are you going to say to him?"

"I'm going to quote your chief. 'Education is the answer. Knowledge will make the Dakota strong. Education is the Dakota's future … just like it is mine, yours—all of us,'" John said as he waved up and down the river. "I'm simply going to say, 'Chief, if you will allow it, school starts today. I want all of your children for an hour each morning.'"

"Ha!" Blue Eagle laughed. "What will you use for tools? You have no materials; you have nothing."

"I don't need any materials, except sticks and sand. That long stretch of sand." John pointed out the spot. "That's my blackboard, my Mandan friend. "We are going to play in the sand."

With that, John turned and ran toward home, yelling as he went, "See you at nine tomorrow."

Blue Eagle turned and sprinted across the bridge. The sky grew white as made by fire. His nose burned, and he tasted a drop of salt water that fell from his eyes. When he reached the end of the bridge, his adrenalin subsided. He turned to face his friend, now at the opposite end of the bridge. Cupping his mouth with his hands, he gave the loud scream of an eagle. John slowed momentarily, waving his arm as he ran toward home.

Chapter 13

Learning the Hard Way

After John left Blue Eagle at the bridge, darkness closed fast, and his gallop turned into a sprint for the last two blocks home. His family was sitting at the dining table, virtually finished with their evening meal. They were all quiet. Sallie and Betty Jean left the table, as did their father. Suddenly it hit him. He had violated the family rules, and his parents were worried. Very upset was more to the point.

"Eat your dinner and go in the back to see your father," Helen said in a low voice.

"Yes, ma'am. I'm sorry, Mother, I just didn't realize it was so late." Suddenly, his food didn't taste very good, but he ate it. Swallowing some milk, he took a deep breath, exhaled, and went to see his father. John opened the door to the large bedroom, and stepped tentatively inside.

"Yes, sir?"

Tom was facing the wall that reached the door, but he cocked his head to face his son squarely. The big razor strap he held in one hand was doubled over. Then his left hand pulled the doubled end taut.

"You know the rules your mother and I laid down for you kids."

"Yes, sir, I do, and I'm very sorry I'm late. I was fishing with Blue Eagle, and I guess we just lost track of time."

"What time? What time must you be home?"

"By dark, sir."

"*What* time?" the father demanded.

"By dark—that's what you and Mom said."

"Think again. It's *before* dark," Tom said firmly. "Don't you forget that."

"No, sir, I won't."

"You know there is a penalty for violating important rules?"

"Yes, sir," John said softly.

"Get over here and—good Lord! What have you got stuffed in your back pockets? Pull your trousers down. Keep your drawers on. Now lay across the bed, feet on the floor," Gannon barked the orders.

John had never seen his father like this before. Ever. He had to go pee badly. There was a long silence. He lay across the bed. Looking down at the covers, he could see his father standing there at the bedside. The thick belt would come any moment now. He gritted his teeth. "Are you ready, young man?"

"Yes, sir."

Any minute now it will come. Any minute—the whack, the sting! Maybe ten.

Tom Gannon looked down at his son's naked back. In that instant, he saw himself—long cutting marks from switches from his own father, an act that created a hate in Tom that took him years to remove. A minute passed. Tom lowered the razor strap and walked to the armed chair across the room.

With tears in his eyes, John waited and winced. He heard a step and then two. He looked forward. Through blurry eyes, he saw his father sitting down in the big upholstered chair. The firm command came.

"Pull your pants on and come over here."

"Yes, sir."

John's pants felt like lead weights; his shorts were moist. By the time he reached his father, he was struggling with his jeans. His father grabbed them and buttoned them, pulling the boy toward him.

"Sit on my knee, here." John sat on his father's right knee. "I just didn't dare hit you. Angry. Disappointed. But I tell you again, you scared your ma and me something fierce. You know that, don't you."

"Yes, sir, I think I do. Those drifters and stuff today."

"That's right; anything can happen to a young boy. You just don't want it to happen to your son. You scared the pee out of us. We were imagining all kinds of things happening to you out there. The girls were crying, just listening to us talking about you. Just so you don't think you are getting off too lightly, young man, if you put me through this again, you are not going to like the consequences. Do you understand me?"

"Yes, sir."

Tom took his left hand and turned his son's face, looking into his tearing eyes.

"You better give your father a big hug and make up."

John grabbed his father's neck in both arms and hugged him hard, holding him for a minute.

"I'm sorry, Dad."

Tom pulled his son back to sitting position, taking his face in both hands, and kissed him lightly on the forehead.

"That's just to let you know that you count. Are you all right now?"

"Yes, sir."

"Here's a handkerchief; blow your nose before we go outside."

As they walked out to the living room, John saw his mother and the girls drying the evening's dishes. Tom said to them, "We'll be back in a moment, Mother. John and I are going to pick up some chocolate ice cream at Hickerson's store. See if we can salvage something from this evening." Loud squeals came from the kitchen.

"Hurry, Daddy, I can't wait," Betty Jean said.

Tom and his son walked silently for a minute, and then he drew the boy out.

"So, you and Blue Eagle went fishing. Catch anything worthwhile?"

"Yes, sir. Two very good bass and three crappie. No pike today. We got interrupted."

"Not by those drifters?" Tom asked, rather anxious at the thought.

"You won't believe this ..." John retold the whole drifter incident, complete with their apology.

"You boys! You're growing up pretty fast. See what you're learning out here?"

"Yes, sir. It's fun. It's actually exciting to me. You know, I think I've found a good friend. Blue Eagle is amazing. Since I don't have a job anymore, he's coming with me in the morning to study at the library. I read that if you learn five new words a week, then in just a couple of years, you've added over 1,000 words to your vocabulary. After that, we're going ..." *Wait,* he thought, *let's think a minute.* He didn't know how to approach his father. He wasn't going to lie, yet he had a feeling his dad might not like his idea.

Tom took his son's shoulder gently. "I've never seen our son go speechless before. Come on, now! What's up?"

"Wait until we get out of the store, Dad."

With the ice cream in hand, the Gannons began their walk back home.

"So, what were you trying to tell me back there?"

"It's just that I see all those Indian kids over there playing. They have no school, no one to teach them," John said, and he told his father his entire scheme.

"We have to talk about this before you go over to the reservation, understand?"

"Yes, sir."

Betty Jean met them at the door. "Did you get both of them? Did you?"

"Of course we did. You didn't think this was just a practice walk, did you?" Tom appeased his youngest, and Helen quickly took over.

"Sallie, come help your mother. Everybody sit at the table." The Gannons were soon relishing bowls of chocolate, strawberry, and vanilla ice cream.

"Touché!" Betty Jean shouted.

"Where on earth did you learn that word?" John asked.

"From Leland, next door. I heard him shout it to Sallie."

"Guess what else we have in the family, Mother? A teacher." Tom continued with the story of John's ambition to start teaching English to the Indian children.

"That's a very ambitious project, John. You might be able to sell it to the chief, and you may not. You have to realize that reservations are governed primarily by the US government. But you and the chief may be able to pull it off since you're a boy and you're just making friends as much as—"

John interrupted with, "I only intend to do it one summer, part-summer really," and he went on to tell the whole family his plan, including his speech to Chief Joseph Fox. Tom looked over at Helen, who was smiling and nodding yes.

"Mother is saying yes, so I'll go along with her. Just watch your step over there, especially with the older boys.

"Oh, I plan to. As a matter of fact, I'm hoping some of the older boys can already speak pretty good English and can be my interpreter."

After John was out of earshot, Tom looked at his wife and said, "I'm afraid our son has come down with something powerful. Something called excitement."

Helen laughed and followed her husband out on the front porch to look at the stars.

Chapter 14

Teacher with Ideas

It was not quite nine the next morning when Blue Eagle met John at the library as promised. John already had ample notes on English grammar, but in retrospect, he thought it might be too tedious in their first session, so he kept it interesting by plunging directly into vocabulary.

"Let's just work on learning a lot of key, useful words to start with. Then we can tackle grammar. It's recommended that we learn six or seven words a week—learn to spell them correctly, use them correctly in a sentence, or even two or three sentences. Repeat them several times a day so we will remember them. Blue, you already know a lot of English. Your chief must be good at languages. He spoke very well on the Fourth of July."

"So, little chief, what is our first word? "Shit or stinking Indian?" Blue Eagle said playfully, an acknowledgment of the growth of their friendship as well as his understanding of white humor.

"Both," John said as he grinned broadly, "but since you are already quite well informed for an original American—"

"Original? What is original?"

"There we are. You just originated our first new word. You are original, I am original, your chief is original. Original means the first one, not a copy. This coin is not an original. The original is at the US Mint for safekeeping."

It was a well-chosen word and created several minutes of enthusiastic conversation between the two friends.

"Do you know the differences in these basic family structures: brother, sister, niece, nephew, first and second cousins?"

"Certainly!" Blue Eagle said, and progress became encouraging and rewarding for John. He patiently, carefully chose the other six words and drilled his friend several times on each one of them. The last was the most difficult: austere. It was too abstract, so John chose another: twilight. In two or three weeks, he would include words that benefitted himself as well as Blue Eagle. He reminded his friend to repeat each word several times a day, spell them, and use them in sentences.

After an hour, the boys headed for the Dakota Reservation to try to speak with Chief Joseph Fox. As they drew closer to the largest dwelling among the wigwams, or "wiggi-ups," a term John thought demeaning, a tall, elegant man appeared at the front entrance. John recognized him immediately as the Dakota's Chief Joseph. Amazingly, no one stopped the boys.

"Sir, could we speak with you just a few minutes? You heard my mother sing just before Blue Eagle's chief gave his speech in town on the Fourth of July."

The chief looked rather distracted, and as he walked away, he said, "You boys go home. We have work to do here." He took a few steps and then turned back and said, "That was *your* mother?"

"Yes, sir. My name is John Gannon, and this is my friend Blue Eagle."

"I know your friend and his chief. Why do you come to me? What would interest you here?" the chief asked.

"Education, sir. Chief Grey Eagle mentioned it in his speech. We still talk about it in my home. I see your children playing out here, but they have no school."

The chief looked at the boys a moment. Then he said, "You boys come back in two days. Then we will talk again."

John was ecstatic when his father got home from the bank that evening. He blurted out the entire story.

"Wait just a minute," Tom said. "All you got from him was a promise of a further conversation. He hasn't agreed to anything."

"I know, Dad, but he didn't say, 'Don't bother me; don't come back.'"

"John, all I'm saying is don't you and your friend get your hopes up too high. Let's just keep an open mind about this. The worst he can do, however, is toss you off the reservation, and he might even say, 'Okay, go do it.'"

The next two days, John and Blue Eagle worked on their vocabulary and discussed John's ideas and what he might promise the Dakota chief.

Finally they were standing in front of the main lodge again. John called out the chief's name, and, as if he had an appointment, the chief appeared.

"So, here are the teachers. What is it you boys want?"

"We want your children, sir. We want to teach them English. Just the young children … or any of the older children who need to learn. Just out there in the strips of sand. Draw words, speak them—the same with numbers."

"This is your idea?"

"Yes, sir," John said. "It's my own idea. One day you will have your own schools, my father says, but that likely won't be for a long time. In the meantime, I can give your village the rest of the summer; your older boys can take it from there. My friend and I are already working on our own English and vocabulary. I plan to make learning fun. Let the children have a good time leaning."

"You are the same boy who came back to see if Crazy Dog was hurt, aren't you? Does your father know you are over here talking about this?"

"Yes, sir, to both questions. We will be over here in the morning. How many children should I count on? Twenty?" John asked.

"Twenty will be fine. Come see me when you finish tomorrow."

At supper that night, the Gannons talked about educating children and particularly how noble an idea it was for John to give his time. Maybe it would lead to something, maybe not. There may even be new friendships. Then, too, that wasn't the only idea John had. The library, he found out, was a great source for ideas. Just last week, he read at length about boat racing in Venice. *Italy is colorful. Why not Chambers?* he thought. *Especially with a colorful people like the Dakota and the Lakota? They can't be too happy just sitting around, an occasional hunt for deer and fishing.*

"John's School" had been underway for a week. The chief took notice now and then, as did several adults passing by. Blue Eagle did his part, but something was missing. Was it the young adult who stood in the background each day, or was there something deeper? The Indian youngsters just weren't enthusiastic about this. Maybe it cut into their play time, maybe it ...

"Blue, see that boy other there?" John nodded toward the tall boy standing in the background. "Call him over to join us. Maybe he can get things going."

"I'm John. What's your name?" John said when the boy came over with Blue Eagle.

"I'm Trig. You're not getting much out of them, are you?"

"Is it playing time?" John asked.

"It is playtime," Trig said, nodding agreement.

"Okay, then," John said. "Let's try another method. We study and learn for ten minutes, then we play for ten minutes. It will take a little longer, but we can get more results. Maybe later we can change back as they find out that they actually like to learn English and understand how important it really is. Trig, you must know what they like. What game do you suggest?" John asked.

"Any game," Trig said, "but especially kickball. They love to run and play that game."

That was it exactly. From then on, John's program took off. The kids were learning the alphabet, saying it, singing it, and kicking the ball endlessly. John and Blue Eagle jogged home each day with a good feeling about their project. Now it was time to sell his big idea: regatta. The Venetians excited an entire nation with their regatta, and somewhere he read that boat racing was once very popular among American Indians.

"Trig, would you keep them playing awhile? We have to go see the chief."

"You can't do that," Trig said. "He's not here. Try two days."

When an audience with the chief finally materialized, John was confident. The chief stood looking down on the boys for a long moment. "You boys may have a good idea, but why? What does it matter if some Indian tribe puts on a show like you say? Why are you concerned?" the chief asked.

"Within one or two summers, Chief, you will make a lot of money. The Brule Regatta, it will come to be known. People will come from all over to see a thing like that. Make it a big race. Make it competitive. Make it colorful," John said, getting more excited by the minute with his ideas and what he read about Venice.

"Sir, in a year or two we could have 5,000 paying customers lining the riverbanks eager to see your show. You could make $5,000, and Chambers could make $5,000 after their expenses. We could advertise in papers all around here. Who knows how many will come if you make a big show, a big colorful show. Lots of Dakota color, lots of Lakota color, lots—"

"Lakota!" the chief exclaimed. "What has the Lakota got to do with this race? They have very swift boats and more men than I do."

"Chief, that's a great idea. Big promotion material. It makes a race in itself. Just like Blue Eagle and I running as hard as we can to beat each other. Next summer, you will see us racing, racing for the town of Chambers. We are going to the fair, and we are going to be hard to beat by these other schools."

John paused and watched Chief Joseph's eyes, as he had often seen his own father do when arguing to make a point.

"Sir, how long has it been," John continued, "since any tribes held a war canoe race?"

"Many years! Many years," the chief said. "This library of yours. I must go see it some time. Five thousand dollars, you say?"

"There is no guarantee, Chief," John said. "It might be more or it might be less, but when you make it a big show, look out. People will want to come see it. People on vacation, traveling people. They go out of their way to see something unusual. It'll be a big attraction."

"We will talk later," the chief said, and he left the boys standing in front of his lodge. Blue Eagle and John looked hopefully at each other, grinning as they left for home.

When Tom Gannon arrive home from the bank, he was in no mood to be sidetracked with a wild idea for organizing two reservations of unhappy Indians into a "world-famous" canoe racing extravaganza. But finally his trying day at the bank subsided, as Betty Jean worked her little-girl charm on her father when she met him at the front door. She did a cute but impressive curtsy to her father and said, "Won't you come in, sir?" And in the next breath, "John is going to put on a racing show, Daddy. What's a regatta?"

"Oh, he is, huh. Your brother has been making some mighty big plans lately."

Tom went straight to the wash basin to freshen up and then joined his family. Helen was finishing up dinner, and soon the Gannons were eating and discussing their news. Finally, Tom looked directly at John and drew him out on his regatta ideas, taking up most of the dinner hour.

"Well, it sounds like an incredible idea, doesn't it? The only thing is, it is a huge idea. One that normally requires big people to get involved. You need sponsors, advertising, and the like. It's great that you're thinking about ideas of this nature, son, and who knows, a boy your age might even create just the right spark to get something positive going. Just take it step at a time, and don't try to organize everybody. Let them have a part in it. What did the chief say when you proposed your idea to him?"

"He sort of looked startled for a few minutes, to be honest with you. I could see that it caught his imagination. He said we would talk later."

Tom Gannon worried that his son was pushing past the boundaries of a young boy, new to this frontier town, but at the same time, he felt proud of his son for taking such initiatives. They talked about tribal history and white and Indian conflicts for the rest of the evening.

A week passed, and then two. Then one evening, as the Gannons had just finished their steak dinner, a knock came at the door. When John opened the door, his jaw dropped. There before him stood Chief Joseph Fox.

"I've come to talk. Is your chief at home?"

"Well, uh, well … yes, sir. Won't you come in?"

"No, I haven't—"

"Hello, I'm John's father, Tom Gannon. Can I help you? Won't you come in, Chief? You were so kind to speak with my son about his ideas. He seems to be full of them lately."

Chief Fox, elegant with high cheek bones and a lithe frame, cautiously walked inside, his dark eyes searching, looking at every aspect of the Gannon house, its furnishings and space. Tom led him into the living room and motioned for John to join them. The chief spoke first.

"Your son is just a boy, yet he has a man's ideas. It is no little thing. I remember stories my father used to tell of such races between tribes. It creates tribal loyalties and develops skills. Much like cooperative buffalo hunts. War? Yes. We sometimes fought, for many reasons." The chief turned, looked at John, and spoke directly to the issue.

"War canoes are big and expensive. First you have to find just the right tree. Not an easy job. Then to make one canoe is a another big job. But three canoes? Maybe four or five for the second meet? Who can say the Lakota will meet with us?" the chief asked.

"We sometimes disagree, but we are friends in many ways." The chief paused a minute and then continued.

"My people have nothing to do but fish and hunt. We prepare for the winter season. We have no schools for our children and no work for our men." The chief looked John in the eye and asked, "You call such a white man's race a regatta?"

"Yes, sir, a regatta. In this case, you are the winner just for racing. Same as the Lakota," John said. "And you help put our town on the map. You know, people will come watch you. Nothing but good can come of such a race." He talked on for ten or fifteen minutes about people coming to see the Chambers regatta." With that, Chief Fox stood up.

"We will talk more." He turned to Tom and said, "We need more boys with ideas. Your son grows very strong."

As he left the Gannons' home, John could hear his heart pound a little louder. He looked at his father for his reaction.

"Sometimes big ideas are born in small initiatives," Tom told his son. "It is way too early, but you could see he was interested; otherwise, he would not have troubled himself to come calling. Did you notice, also, how interested he was to see how we live? At any rate, give him some time to think about your idea. He will let us know one way or the other. Then there are the Lakota people. They might not be interested in the slightest."

"I think I know how to get them interested, Dad," John said. "It's like any race. You throw down the challenge, just like we will do at school. You know, our track team. Yes, I know; we probably don't even have a track team, but we will, and Blue Eagle and I intend to be on that team." Gannon looked at his son with pride.

"You just take things one at a time, but as I told you before, out of a number of ideas, likely all of them will not work out the way you plan, if at all," Tom cautioned.

"It pleases me to see your confidence, son. You're doing fine. Listen to your mind and think things through, just as you are doing now."

Chapter 15

Chambers School

August faded into September, and the Gannon family grew in excitement. Life in a one-room schoolhouse was about to begin. On the second Monday morning, everyone was dressed, well fed with breakfast. Tom and Helen ushered their three children out the front door with reminders that they were to be on their best behavior in school and to pay close attention to their teacher.

John led Sallie and Betty Jean through the edge of town, past the Chambers Bridge, the railroad trestle, covering the half mile to Chambers School—a white, wooden, one-room schoolhouse that would accommodate forty students, grades one through nine. Along the trail paralleling the Brule, John searched the riverbanks where he and Blue Eagle commonly fished, but there was no sign of his friend today.

As the Gannon children neared the school, Sallie spoke up.

"Look! There he is over by that bush."

"You girls wait here for me. I'll be right back." John spoke as he came close to Blue Eagle, who was sitting near a lilac tree just twelve yards from an open schoolhouse window. He sat cross-legged before a homemade easel that held a stretched, tanned deerskin and continued painting his tribal history, marking events of the recent past.

Without a greeting, John said, "You are not going to go inside, are you?"

"Don't worry. I can hear everything that is said right from here," Blue Eagle assured his friend.

"Okay, then. That's a good idea. Meet me at the library after school. I have something to discuss with you." His friend nodded his head in agreement, and John led his sisters to the front entrance of the school.

At 8:30 a.m., thirty-six students from town and local ranches filed in and took seats. John chose three seats midway on the aisle, his sisters next to him. Simultaneously, Ruth Rochelle entered the room and wrote her name on the black board. She greeted her classes and called roll, using her fine voice and professional bearings with just the right touch that caused students to pay attention. New students were asked to stand and introduce themselves to the class.

A tall, rugged rancher's boy, Fred Baker, constantly looked at John, who took it as curiosity and faintly nodded his head as he would to a friend. During the roll call, the teacher segregated everyone by class. John was placed in seventh grade, while Sallie went to fifth, and Betty Jean to second grade. Baker, the biggest boy in school, now fifteen years old, was an eighth grader.

Miss Rochelle, in her late twenties, was very much in charge. She pleasantly barked out the assignments, choosing four students to help with the lower grades. Baker was assigned to help third grade, while John, now more and more looking like his father, was assigned to help the five students in the sixth grade. Two other students helped other grades. The ninth grade seats were all empty this year.

Miss Rochelle, exuding confidence, loved her job. In fifteen minutes, she had the entire room humming with activity as she supervised every grade, making sure there were no laggards, no idle minds. During the entire day, eight lessons were lectured, students were taught and supervised by the teacher, who personally taught the seventh and eighth grades.

At noon, the students quickly ate their wrapped lunches and played games of their own choosing. Blue Eagle was nowhere in sight when John and his sisters perused the schoolyard. John and Sallie talked while Betty Jean skipped rope with other girls her age. The day passed without incident from any of the children. Baker left by horseback, as he was over four miles from his father's ranch. John walked with his sisters directly toward home, but when they neared the library, he sent them alone the final four hundred yards to their house.

"Tell Mother I'm at the library. I'll be home by five," John said. As John approached his friend, Blue Eagle, he asked, "How did it go for you?"

"I had no book, but I heard most of the lessons. Let's do new words another time. I need to be home soon," Blue Eagle said.

"I do too, but this won't take ten minutes. Until we find a way to get you inside school or the library, here is what we'll do: you listen as you did today, and then let's spend an hour together at the library, and I'll go over everything we learned in class. It should be fast, and we both can get home pretty early. I nearly got it from Dad a few days ago for being late. I was sure he was going to strap my butt with his leather strap, but he let me off. We eat early, and I promised him I wouldn't be late again."

"He beats you?" Blue Eagle asked. "My chief would never do that."

"It's common with us. Most white families do it, but only when kids don't do what's expected of them. It makes you remember the rules. What does your chief do to you?"

"We talk. He gives me work sometimes. Other times, he just gives me a hard look. It's a look that makes you feel like a child. It hurts just like a slap."

"See you tomorrow," John said as he started for home.

Blue Eagle ran closely past John, bumping him on the shoulder, and turned around as he ran.

"You 'Injins' are strange!" Blue Eagle shouted. "See you tomorrow!"

John grinned at Blue Eagle's big joke. He walked home with a faster pace than usual. He felt good about outsmarting the township's social system, and it gave him a new purpose in life. He was bubbling over with ideas. Now he was a teacher, contributing, learning to organize.

But how am I going to get so far upriver to Lakota country? Oh well, it will work out, he thought. *My God! Wouldn't that just spin a top? If only the Lakota got excited about it? I've got to come up with a real challenge.*

When everyone was settled at the table, Helen said, "This is a regatta celebration dinner. All vegetable—but special with different spices. And try my new, just out of the oven, cornbread with bacon bits."

Tom Gannon spoke softly, "Okay, kids, sounds like a one and a half."

In unison, everyone said excitedly, "Mama, dinner is delicious."

Betty Jean added, "Especially the corn bread." Everyone smiled and enjoyed the spicy vegetables and bread with great gusto. John was very quiet.

"How did you and Miss Rochelle get along in school, John?"

"You know what, Dad? She is an excellent teacher. She has me teaching, or I should say helping the sixth graders, and she has three other students helping other grades during all the various assignments—except one hour a day when we seventh-graders work on our lessons. This learning in one big open room is all new to me, but it really works. It reinforces everything we learn, whether we need it or not." He smiled. Then he added, "But what really gets me is the fact that Blue Eagle has to sit out in the yard next to an open window and try to guess at what he should be learning—all while he's sitting there painting on a skin."

"That's a good point, son. We'll talk about that after dinner. Right now let's enjoy our mother's fine efforts on our table. Hmmm. The corn bread is delicious. And I particularly love your fantastic butter beans, Helen."

"Thank you, my dear. Any seconds?" Helen asked.

"I would," Sallie spoke up. "Mama, may I go over to Leland's to study for a little while after we eat?"

"For an hour. Then you come home. Don't be late," Helen said.

"We'll expect you back in one hour. That's 8 p.m.," Tom added. "We have a lecture going on right here. Eight to nine. The Boys on the Brule, we call it. John, you and your sister clean up the dishes for your mother. We will relax a minute and wait for Sallie, so we can answer your question about socializing with our Indian friends."

Tom bathed his face in cold water after dinner and pored over several bank documents. He had saved a part of the paper to read—an essay on Billy Sunday and his efforts to reach the Chicago mob and the city. Much was being made over this high-profile baseball player turned evangelist. Tom wondered if sophisticates like Chicagoans would embrace such powerful preaching. He didn't know much about Billy Sunday except that his oratory and his magical name were creating a national religious fervor. He was not soon into that story when he heard Sallie open the door. Two minutes later, the kitchen was clean, and his class was about to begin. Everyone got a drink of cool water and gathered around their daddy.

"We're ready, Papa," the smallest spoke up.

"Okay, let's talk about John's question. It grieves John that his good friend, Blue Eagle, is not allowed to attend class in your all-white school. Why? What is the problem here? Well, first of all, people of the same kind, white in this instance, like to live together and work together, sometimes mixing one type of people with another. But when it comes to socializing, we whites do not readily share our activities with people, in this case, who are not white. That includes our schools, our libraries, and other public buildings. Open-air gatherings, like our Fourth of July celebrations, can and are sometimes the exceptions. Such is the case here in Chambers. Those are our libraries, our municipal buildings. We built them with our own money, just like we did our homes. We choose who can enter and enjoy them. We are very selfish, rightly or wrongly so, about these principals. We exclude everyone who isn't our own color. Are we better than those people that we exclude? Certainly not, yet some people think we definitely feel superior.

"We will always have a few people who think they are better than others, even among the white race. Some are poor, some are rich. They have a right to think however they feel. We are a free nation. You enjoy personal rights that aren't allowed in many other countries. But the good book teaches us that is not right. Our constitution says, 'All men are created equal.' But are they? You have to decide.

"The fact of the matter is that we fought many bitter wars with the Indians. They were fighting for their lives. They had this wonderful country all to themselves for hundreds of years before we whites reached these shores by ship, and, seeing that no one legally claimed this land, by our standards, we simply took it over. We made it *our* home, by *our* government's own rules of law.

"The Indians had no such rules. They simply fought one another; the winner lived on the choicest land and enjoyed it. This country is big, and there was plenty of room for all the Indians in America, coast to coast. Then the white man arrived—a few boats at first, and then more, and then many more. Finally, hundreds of thousands of white men and women and their children arrived and took the land from the Indians. It was a life and death struggle. To put it simply, we overpowered the Indians with our numbers and our more advanced civilization—and the whites just kept coming.

"Soon the Indians were all relegated to reservations, just like the two reservations across the Brule right here in Chambers.

"It was their home, and we took it from them. Rightly or wrongly, we fought them and took their land. They are a conquered people. We killed their buffalo, and the Indians starved. Yet, they did the same to one another when they wanted a certain territory. As I said earlier, the stronger Indian tribe or band won whatever territory they felt like fighting for and enjoyed it as their own. The difference is they did not virtually annihilate an entire people. They simply caused a weaker band of Indians to move to a different area of this vast country. And then the white man came.

"We built our cities and spread across the country, pushing the Indians further and deeper into isolation, reducing their numbers through bloody wars until they all surrendered. And this ongoing war only ended fifty to sixty years ago. There is much more to it than that, but what you are looking at here in Chambers today, this quiet and peaceful town, comes to all of us to enjoy only after many years of broken treaties and bloodshed. The hard feelings among the people around here still linger today. No Gannons are a part of that history. We are from Illinois, and our wars with the Indians were settled long, long ago. We are neutral; we feel sympathy toward these interesting, defeated people.

"These people are human beings. They are not dumb by any stretch of the imagination. It's just that their life has always been one with nature. Yet they too were builders of cities, of a sort, as you will learn later, but their main thrust in life was to live as hunters and gatherers, free from oppressive governments. Yet many of them had their own governments. Their tribal chiefs were smart men, and they looked out for their people by making their own strong laws. They lived off this bountiful land. Many farmed as well as hunted for their highly revered buffalo, which roamed these prairie lands by the millions. By the millions! That is why the first act of the white leaders was to kill the buffalo—the food source of the Indian. It hastened the defeat of the Indian tribes, and soon after that, the struggle was over. We gave them vast acres of land, and then when gold was discovered, the country went wild, breaking all our promises to the Indians.

"I'm telling you this briefly, but that is the gist of it. After much fighting with them, we put the surviving Indians on lesser Indian reservations to govern themselves while we, mostly white Americans, walked freely on the rest of this American soil.

"It must sound terrible to you children. But realize this: the human race has always conducted itself much in this manner, ever since it set foot on earth in small bands. It has always been the survival of the fittest. Basically, it is the same rule that lower animals use. That's what the Indians did, and that's what we did. We still do.

"But today we are supposed to be civilized, not unthinking brutes who use muscle to get everything we want. We mature with each decade of living—or that should be our goal. As I look directly at each one of you, I think about your future. Every twenty- and fifty-year period, we humans make incredible strides. Believe it or not, some say we will someday fly to the moon, yet we have not fully succeeded as developed human beings by any stretch of the imagination. We still have senseless wars, but don't get me started on that one.

"We still must answer two basic questions: Are we better than our American Indians? No, of course not, but we are a more advanced society. What will happen to them, and what is their future?

"The simple answer is, we must educate them and bring them up to our speed in the white world. Build schools for them, teach them, and then it is up to each one of them to adapt to the white man's world. Some won't succeed, of course. Many will live out their lives doing the things that they have always done. Their young people have the best chance.

"John's friend, Blue Eagle, for instance! I think he will be a fine citizen and serve in the white community very well. Many others his age will also succeed. One day, before long I hope, the Indians will have their own schools right here in Chambers. They already have a college up north. Any of them can go to Carlyle to get an education right now. Free. So progress is being made, making each one of them responsible for bringing their own skills to the table of life, just like we all have to do. This country is so young, and you children are living in one of the most exciting centuries of all time, in my way of thinking. It is said that our advanced industrial revolution is already at work. New inventions, new materials will make this country grow. We have vast resources. We have a new car, but as you just experienced, there are no roads on which to drive the darn thing. That can't last long. Soon you'll see highways from coast to coast. Then cars will become common. Also, some big event will set progress in motion. Each of you will experience it. So, get yourselves ready. Go to college. Make the most of the time you have here. Your time in this century is golden.

"There is an old saying, 'Take care of today, and tomorrow will take care of you.' Keep that in mind. Do what John is doing. Develop your gifts as you mature.

"All of this I tell you to try to explain why John's friend, Blue Eagle, has to sit outside of our schoolhouse and our library for just awhile longer—for just awhile longer," Gannon repeated, and only then did he look off into the distance beyond his children.

"But what does it all mean, Papa?"

"Betty Jean, it means we all have to wait awhile longer. It will take years, and even then, there will still be reservations for the American Indian. Who really knows their future. Many will go to college, we hope. Many will integrate with whites through marriage. Many will remain dependent upon our government. Some tribes could strike it rich through mineral rights—gold or perhaps oil. Who knows? There is not much being said about that, except by a few people, and they keep it very quiet. Keep in mind that strong men don't always make good governors.

"So what about today? What can you do to help? Be understanding. Be helpful, as John is being helpful. He has developed a good friendship with one Indian boy already, and he has started teaching young Indian children how to speak and write English. Those are things he can do. Perhaps you ladies will find other ways to help them come into the twentieth century. We'll have to wait and see. Just don't expect big gains in a hurry, and don't expect other people to share the same viewpoint as ours. Be patient and keep working with an open mind.

"John has some ideas that will cause quite a stir in this town. But there again, be patient. Let your ideas roll out naturally. You will win over new friends a little bit at a time with your efforts, and your efforts could even help change the attitudes of an entire town. It is too early to know. You will get there with the township helping you. That's the way

I see it, anyway. Maybe it's an Indian boy and a white boy representing this town in track—running against other towns or cities, creating some interest in our children and some pride in our town. Maybe it is something bigger that brings Indians and whites closer together. John came up with a regatta idea that would attract people from miles around, make some money for a lot of people, and put our Indians and our town on the map. That is a big idea, son, and I'm very proud of you for thinking in that way and for promoting it. Whoever thought that a young man your age could get an audience with a tribal chief? You did, and he spoke with you; he even came to your house. Remember, an idea is only an idea until someone brings it to fruition—does something with it, makes it work.

"And there, let's call it a day. Betty Jean's eyes are getting heavy, and I could use a nice glass of cold water. We'll talk about this again. Save up your questions."

"Thanks, Dad," John said. "Now I understand a lot of things much better. Mostly the time factor, but having patience seems awfully hard sometimes, especially when other people seem so stupid."

"You bet it is, but both are powerful motivators. My, it's about bedtime. Let's call it a day."

Chapter 16

The Bully

October arrived quickly. John and Blue Eagle walked at a more hurried pace as the autumn air grew chilly. The leaves along the Brule were dazzling in color, dressing out the river in hues of yellows, reds, magenta, and greens.

Things were noticeably different at school as well. The cooler it became, the lower the open window became to even the temperature inside the schoolroom, and Blue Eagle's access to hearing the classes was increasingly more difficult. John first noticed it in his friend's review of each lesson. Each day, the Indian boy moved closer to the building, nearer to the window, now open barely an inch. The next day, he ventured to the front porch of the school.

On Friday of the following week—the day they later marked as *that Friday*—Blue Eagle realized that he was not adequately dressed to ward off the cold. An idea came to mind. He went to the back of the school to the woodshed, gathered a large armful of chopped wood, and brought it inside the schoolroom, placing it near the warm, wood-burning heater at the rear of the room. Then he added two sticks to the burning fire.

He stood near the heater for a few minutes to warm his hands and body. The entire class was looking at him. He moved nearer to the door but remained standing. Miss Rochelle broke the silence in the room.

"Thank you, young man. That was kind of you."

Blue Eagle nodded his head, acknowledging her thanks, but he stood there by the door. Then he took a seat in the last row in the back of the class.

Miss Rochelle immediately took command of her classes and got the students focused on their lessons. All except one boy, Fred Baker, the fifteen-year-old, who got up and took two steps toward the rear before the loud order came.

"Mr. Baker, sit down!" Baker stopped and then took three quick steps toward the back. "Mr. Baker, I will not tell you again. Get back in your seat."

Baker stopped, glared at Blue Eagle for a long moment, and then took his seat. Blue Eagle remained settled in his chair.

During the next hour before recess, classes progressed in their usual manner—except the temperature rose remarkably higher for Baker, John, and Miss Rochelle over the first fifteen minutes. Younger students gawked about, sensing a disruption. Baker turned to face Blue Eagle numerous times, and then things settled down to a normal routine—almost. It was noticeably different, some felt, with an intruder in their private domain.

Miss Rochelle gave Blue Eagle his cue.

"One final thing before recess," she said. "Copy these topics from the blackboard. Two weeks from today, I want you to write out a speech and be prepared to stand before the class and talk for five minutes on the subject you choose."

Five minutes passed, and then the teacher rang the bell for recess. Everyone put their books aside and walked quickly out the door. Blue Eagle was nowhere in sight. From the front porch, Baker and his followers, eight boys, eight to eleven years of age, crowded the front porch of the building in search of this intruder to their school.

"There he goes!" someone yelled, pointing down the trail that led to the woods and the river beyond. Baker and his gang of boys started following, slowly at first and then faster. They were not unnoticed by Blue Eagle, who glanced over his shoulder from time to time. Suddenly,

Blue Eagle heard a small rock land nearby, and then he felt a sizeable sting on his leg when a rock bounced off his left calf. After a few dozen steps, Baker and his gang started to run. Blue Eagle wasted no time doing the same. In the meantime, John Gannon, who had taken a higher trail in the same direction, ran down the slope at full speed, burst through the surprised Baker gang, and gave chase after his friend, Blue Eagle.

"That-a-boy, Gannon, go get him!" they shouted as they ran. "Hold him for us," Baker yelled.

The other students gawked from the school front porch. John raced ahead. As he caught up with his friend, Blue Eagle showed signs of uneasiness in his face.

"Race you to the river," John shouted to his friend as he pointed straight ahead. They both knew the other could run fast, but they had never tested each other. Each boy knew this was that time. Blue Eagle lunged ahead and set the pace for a moment, and then John bore down hard. He had not run a real race in over a year. A hundred and ten yards lay before them. John, just two steps behind, suddenly felt the surge of new strength empower his body. He glided past Blue Eagle easily, and then the Indian, startled by this move, found his own competitive gear and shifted into it in a great effort. He immediately pulled even with John and was startled that his friend was so swift. They left their pursuers far behind—the tall one, the fat ones, and the little ones.

John and Blue Eagle ran with all the power they could muster, neck and neck, legs churning, arms pumping, teeth clenched as they drew near to the trees along the river. John gained a step and then two as they pulled up slowly before the river. The howling mob was still trying to catch up.

Blue Eagle stopped at the river. He walked back to John, holding out his platted stag deer hide rope. He said, "I've never been beaten in a race. Here! I give you my rope." John took it and watched his friend race to the still warm waters of the Brule, diving in with hardly a splash. He swam out to his father's bull boat twenty yards into the river.

Baker and his followers pulled up just a few yards from John and hooped and hollered. Baker was ecstatic. "Holy shit! John took his dang rope away from that Indian and kicked his ass in the river."

John winced, suddenly surrounded by the jubilant boys. He stood there solemnly, stern in his composure.

"What's the matter?" Baker demanded.

"I didn't take his rope," John said.

"Then how did you get it?" Baker demanded, moving a step closer to John.

The tension welled up in John like a hot boiler. Then he screamed it out in their faces with the strange force that pulsed through his lithe frame, "Because he gave it to me!"

The long moment of quiet there in the woods was a tension unlike anything John had ever experienced in his life. His eyes teared, and the ringing in his ears was fierce. He never lost the tense stare at Barker, though it grew blurry in vision. John saw the big kid before him, but he never saw the quick fist that knocked him to the ground.

Baker stood over the dazed boy for a moment, and then he walked over to his little band of followers who had stood well back from the confrontation.

John stirred, treetops swirling at first, and then he got to his feet, spitting blood from his bleeding lip. The boys stopped in their slow trot out of the woods. Baker yelled back, "Gannon, your mother is a Squaw."

Blue Eagle rose up out of the bull boat, now fifty yards out in the river, filled his lungs to the maximum, and with hands cupped around his mouth, he screamed the cry of the fish eagle louder than he had ever done before.

When John reached the trail to retrieve his books, Leland Warrenheis was standing there holding them.

Leland was startled. "God, you're hurt."

"I got to get home to see about myself,"

"I'll carry your things," Leland said. "I'm sorry I couldn't help you. I had no idea he was going to hit you."

"That's all right. It' not your fight, Leland."

When John reached home, his mother met him at the front door. She almost panicked, seeing her son's condition. No sooner had they reached the kitchen to care for John's wounds when the front door opened with a sudden force. In walked a very stern Tom Gannon.

"Oh, am I glad to see you. John's been hurt," Helen said through a trembling voice.

"I know; Leland came by the bank and told me about it."

Tom washed his hands and then took the fresh washcloth and gently cleaned his son's mouth of coagulated blood. He examined his jaw, moving it side to side to test for any fractures or broken bones. When he was satisfied that John had escaped any serious injuries, he spoke calmly to his son.

"You got into it with some boy at school?"

"Yes, sir. He was going after Blue Eagle, and I chose to help my friend."

"Well, where did it go wrong, son?"

"We ran out of land to run on. Blue Eagle dove in the river to swim out to his boat, and there I was by myself. I had no idea Baker would explode like that."

"Baker?"

"Yes, sir. Frederick Baker. Big kid. He's fifteen. A lot of the little kids look up to him because he's the biggest kid in school. Throws his weight around."

Tom Gannon said, "Now isn't that interesting. Frederick Baker, a rancher," and his voice trailed off as he ran it through his mind.

Tom suddenly turned to face his son and said, "You know, John, there are several ways to confront a bully: head on, or run and keep out of his way, or you can neutralize him—maybe cause him to change. Look, two weeks from this Saturday, I am going to kill two birds with one stone. I am going out to Fred Baker's house, and I am going to take you with me."

"Me!" John exclaimed. "That big oaf nearly killed me, and you want me to go face up to him again?"

"No, that's not what I have in mind at all. We're going to make a pincer move. You know, a smart, surprise maneuver. I'm going out to visit a bank customer, and you're coming along because you go to school with his son. I might be wrong, but I think under those circumstances you will be quite safe, and, who knows, you just might help straighten out the school bully in the process. Besides, the woods are starting to put on their fall colors. It'll be beautiful out there. Okay?"

"Yes, sir. It gives me time to talk to Blue Eagle beforehand."

Chapter 17

The Bull Boat

The October sun painted the canopy of the woodlands across the Brule River. The water's smooth surface reflected the mirror images of stunning, myriad colors of the white barked giants along the shoreline, forming a wash color of a painter's giant canvas. A lush meadow stretched down the far gentle slope to the river, stopping only for the narrow road parting it from the woodlands, known everywhere as Haggerty Woods.

On the Chambers side of the Brule, robins teetered on tall shoots of Johnson grass and high prairie buffalo grass. They ferreted out long, fat earthworms underfoot, taking flight the instant they caught their prey. Mockingbirds perched on high tree branches, fluffing their feathers in the early morning sun. They filled the shoreline with a medley of long warbles, chirps, and shrill songs in a series of countless imitative cries of catbirds, jays, larks, and other feathered brethren.

The cottonwood and willow were the first to show new fall color. Their colorful leaves fluttered like transparent puppets against the sun as they danced in small gusts of morning breeze—first swirling, and then sailing, and now still.

John Gannon observed it all, and it brought a bright smile to his face. Fred Baker would have to wait. Now, in a faster pace, he chose the river trail just feet from the water's edge, pausing occasionally to skip a flat rock on the clear, smooth water. When the tree line ended, he could see the back of James Blue Eagle standing in the long shadow of the gnarled old willow that extended horizontally out into the river. As John approached, he purposely snapped a twig underfoot, causing the Indian boy to turn immediately. They raised their hands to greet each other.

"I'm late. I ran home to change," John volunteered as he walked closer to his friend. "Catch anything?" he added.

"They stopped biting a little while ago," Blue Eagle said. He put aside the long, green pole that he had fashioned from a nearby willow tree. He untied a line that he had secured to a nearby willow branch, pulling it toward himself. A coarse feed bag came to the surface. As Blue Eagle eased the dripping mass to the bank in front of them, a loud thrashing sound of fish caught John's attention. As Blue Eagle opened the bag in front of John, his catch exploded with energy in a last-ditch effort to escape.

"Wow!" John said. "Those are beauties. How many?" The Indian opened the bag fully. "Gollleee!" John continued his excitement. "What a catch. Must be over a dozen."

"Eleven," Blue Eagle said. He reached his right arm into the sack and ran his first two fingers cautiously into the gills of a big pike, lifting it out to show his prize.

"Darn!" John yelped as he moved back a step from the big fish.

"He must weigh seven pounds at least!" John continued excitedly. "Just look at those needle teeth." He put his right first finger up to test the sharpness of the pike's long, thin teeth, withdrawing as he thought better of it. Then John looked at his friend as he spoke. "You redskins! You know how to do everything," They both chuckled a bit.

Blue Eagle smiled and put the big pike back in the sack, setting off another flurry of thrashing fins and tails. Then he spoke excitedly.

"You should have been here when that big devil hit. He was the last one I caught. I was lying out there on that big willow trunk. The warm sun almost put me to sleep. Then, wham! He nearly jerked the pole out of my hand, he hit so hard. He was like a charging buffalo snorting fire. I darn near peed in the river," he laughed. "I fought him for a few minutes—seemed like an hour. I looked at the green willow pole that I made, and it was almost bent double. Finally, he worked us out to that limb in the water—see it out there where I'm pointing?— and wrapped himself around it several times. Luckily it was a green limb and gave enough so that he couldn't get any leverage to shake out the hook. When I saw that he hadn't broken my line, I threw down my pole and belly-slid further out on the tree, quick as a snake after a frog. I rammed my right hand down his throat and grabbed the gills. At first I didn't feel his teeth on my wrist. I yanked the line free and hauled him up in the tree with me. I must have shaken that tree quite a bit. Anyway, I fell right into the water. It's no more than chest-deep out there.

"Some guys were walking on the bridge up there." Blue Eagled motioned to the spot with his head and eyes. "They were as excited as I was, yelling and calling out different things when I was hanging down by my legs to capture my fish, but I couldn't hear much of what they said. When I got to the riverbank, the tall one yelled, 'Boy, he is a beauty!'

"Then they recognized me. They all held their noses and started walking on across the bridge, yelling at me. The tall kid threw a rock right there where I was fishing."

"Let me see your arm," John said. "Damn! Look at those teeth marks. Went pretty deep in your wrist. Did you bleed much?"

"Not much. I bathed it good in the water. It's clean now. Still stings some, but it's okay. Hey, come on—let's get going."

"What about the fish?" John asked, but Blue Eagle was already in motion. The Indian boy picked up a rock the size of both his fists and eased it into the bag with the fish. After securing the top of the bag, Blue Eagle carried it out along the willow tree trunk growing parallel to the water. He eased the bag of fish into the river and walked the long cord that secured the fish back to the riverbank, tying it to a young button willow near the water's edge. He quickly cut a small, bushy tree limb and covered the rope to camouflage it from unwanted eyes.

The boys walked toward the bridge nearby. The two-man bull boat was tied among the small stand of button willow that grew in the shadow of the railway trestle just before the highway bridge. The height of the willows, some three to four feet, hid the boat perfectly. As Blue Eagle pulled the bull boat to shallow water, John looked at it apprehensively.

"I know you don't like 'the skin,' Blue Eagle said, but we have no choice today. "Besides, you might as well get used to it. It's fun; you'll see."

John looked down into the large, round tub of a vessel. *Amazing*, he thought, It was a round, tub-shaped boat of bent willow limbs, tied at every cross-section and then covered with a tough, well oiled, animal skin. In olden days, always of buffalo. He wondered how it came to be. Mandan. But when?

"Sit down," Blue Eagle said. Then he eased the craft out into the river, jumping inside in one agile move as they reached deeper water.

John sat uneasily just a half foot above the water. He wished he could swim. He marveled at his friend's skills. How could a boy his own age know how to do everything at hand—and do them so well? He marveled at Blue Eagle as he picked up the oar, sending it slashing into the water, knife-like, with hardly a noise, moving the boat straight out into the river.

"How long have you known how to do this?" John asked.

"What? Oh, you mean to oar? This skin? My mother used to tease me about that in front of friends. 'My son was born in a bull boat.'" They both laughed a bit, and then James Blue Eagle continued, "I love it out on the river. Still do. Free as a bird. Responsible only for myself and my own good judgment. I swam when I was two years old—like a fish, they said."

The young Mandan set the boat on a straight course directly out to the middle of the crystal clear Brule River. His total command of the oar was dazzling to see. Knife-like entry, whip, whir, pull. Repeat. The boat moved easily at his every command.

A hundred yards out into the river, Blue Eagle powered the skin hard right with deep, twisting hand motions, sending it spinning saucer-like upon the water. He brought the oar in suddenly, slapping it down across his knees.

"Indian shit! Indian shit! Indian shit!" he yelled. The boat spun for a moment there in the silence. Then, as John recovered somewhat from this sudden maneuver, he spoke, trying to understand this strange change in his friend. Then it made sense.

"That's what they yelled at you from the bridge?" John motioned toward it as he spoke.

"Over and over, even as they walked on across the bridge," Blue Eagle said softly as he slumped over his oar. John frowned.

"Do you know them?"

"I think so. I faced the sun, but I think the big one was that Scott kid."

"What did you say to them?" John asked.

"I didn't yell back. I just sat there on the big willow hanging out over the water and watched them disappear across the river."

Both boys sat there in the boat, silently drifting. After a short time had passed, John spoke.

"My father says a man should be quick to listen and slow to act."

They didn't speak again for a short time. Then Blue Eagle took up the oar again, gently this time, moving the bull boat back toward the bridge. John broke the silence. "My father said you really gave Billy Langton a beating last week."

"Your father? How did he find out about that?" Blue Eagle asked.

"He saw it. He was over at Mrs. Mertaugh's fixing her kitchen sink. He still helps people fix some of those things. He heard all the ruckus down below her house, near the river. He said you were all over that boy like a swarm of bees. And when he got a scissor hold on you, you popped out like hot grease. Then you busted the side of his face with a big rock in your hand. My father said Langton went up the road bawling like a baby. I'll bet he won't be pushing you around anymore."

"It wasn't a rock, just a big dried, piece of clay. Hard as a rock, I imagine," James said. Then he looked out over the river and said quietly, "The one I really want is Baker. Langton is just a big pile of fat, but Baker isn't just big—he's quick, and he brings trouble."

"And he's strong as an ox," John quickly cut in, shaking his head slowly. "You must be crazy. You better think on this awhile," he warned.

"There is a way," Blue Eagle said with a quiet confidence. "Next year, I'll be up the river training with Crazy Horse for two months. My test comes soon, my manhood test. I'll be fourteen. When I come in from the valley country from that ten-day test with just three days of food and water, I won't be much. But who is when he first becomes a man? Then give me another month or two to build up—"

"Baker will kill you," John interrupted. "He'll be nearly seventeen. He's big, and he's mean. He'll be six feet tall by then."

"You don't know Crazy Horse," Blue Eagle said firmly. "He lived with the Apache for four years right after their big wars with the soldiers. Some say he even took scalps. Around here, I've seen him take on strong men twice his size. You can't believe how quick he is. And believe me, he knows all the tricks in fighting, especially if his life is on the line. Two months with him, and I'll be ready."

"All right," John argued. "So Baker gave me a beating one day; that's done. Is that any reason for you—"

Blue Eagle cut in sharply. "And he put his marks over your eyes and busted your jaw."

Gannon twisted his lower jaw to the right and felt it with his left hand. The socket still gave him trouble sometimes when chewing food. The scar from the fight was long and thin over his left eye. He saw it every day when he stood at the mirror brushing his teeth. It would soon be gone.

"Every time I look at you," Blue Eagle said, "I see your face wearing my scars. Maybe some belong to you, but mine belong to me. One by one, I will settle with them." He paused and then added, "My chief says that most boys think as their parents think, but in the end, it is up to me to choose. If my life is to be worth anything when I grow up, I have to stand up for myself.

"In the end, we all must die, my chief said, but to know that you stood up and fought for right, for what you believe in, is the difference between living and existing. I'm not sure what existing means, but my chief talked long into the night about waiting and waiting before you act. That's why we're living out there on Huron Island away from our people. My chief is thinking, and when the time is right, we will go back upriver. He will be the chief of what's left of our Mandan Nation. I have to be ready. He expects it."

Blue Eagle looked out over the river. "My father worries about my being friends with you." He paused a second and then turned to John once more. "He said it will tear my heart out one day."

John took only a second to reply. "And you—what does James Blue Eagle think?"

"My chief is brighter than any of my people. All the chiefs around here look up to him. I always count on him. Just like you and your father, my chief does not want anything to happen to his only son. Yet he sets me free. He says, 'Make up your own mind.' Does your father do that?"

"More and more," John said. "Now it's getting to be second nature. I sense he is just waiting—and you know what? Sometimes I feel like I can feel my bones growing inside of me … like I'm six feet tall already. By the way, I'm going out there in the valley with you on your shape-ups, those short trips out and back. I've never been on a five-mile hike, let alone ten."

"You serious?"

"Absolutely, and I mean this: the valley is for seasoned men. Outlaws, wild animals—they know the valley. You're going out there several times before you have your test. They are going to dump your butt a hundred miles out there with two grasshoppers to eat and just dew off the leaves to drink. That's your big test. That's one time in the valley."

John paused a moment before adding, "Now you are talking about going out there six or eight times to practice? Who says I can't go with you on those first get-in-shape hikes?"

Slowly, Blue Eagle put his right hand straight out toward his friend, making it into a fist. John did the same until the fists touched end to end. Then they sat there and drifted.

John broke the silence with, "Back to Baker. I wasn't going to tell you this, but now I will. Just between you and me, my dad is going out to see Baker's father next week on bank business, and he plans to take me with him. He seems to think it will solve some of our problems with that boy. So, you need to do as I will do: just stay out of Baker's way until my dad and I return. We'll find out if it makes any difference."

Blue Eagle sat erect in the bull boat and looked up the river.

John looked at the Indian boy: triceps pinched high, biceps getting round and full, the beginning of strong shoulders and chest, tight gut. Behind the long strands of black hair sat eyes that could be as wild as an eagle at a kill.

Could this be the young Crazy Horse of next year? John thought.

"I see you, Boy John," the Indian said to his friend. "I see a face full of questions."

John chuckled. "There are just two questions. One, I was wondering whether or not I would ever be able to handle an oar like you. And two, what am I doing out here in the middle of the river with a wild-ass Indian like you?"

Blue Eagle coiled like a rattlesnake. Both moccasins flipped from his feet, and the oar came in. In an instant, his right hand flashed past his right hip, capturing his hunting knife. With both hands, he held the long blade high above his head. "Eeee-yaaah!" he screamed, as he plunged the knife down into the bottom of the boat.

John, struck with panic and fear at the thought of gushing water, threw out both arms for some unknown protection above the top rim of the bull boat.

Blue Eagle released the knife instantly, and in another piercing scream, quickly dropped into a squat and flipped backward into the river. He swam underwater. Under the downward pressure of the sudden vanishing weight of the Indian, the bull boat came within an inch of swamping. Then it shot up out of the water like a cork exploding under pressure. A horror seized John. He couldn't breathe; he couldn't move. Then he saw the knife lying flat on the dry floor of the boat. He sank back—limp, spent.

Blue Eagle surfaced a short distance away. He swam a few easy strokes toward the shore that lay beyond them. Otter-like, he turned over on his back, swimming with only his feet. He smiled at his friend in the bull boat and waited.

Slowly, John picked up the oar and knelt down in position to row. The blade of his oar struck the water with a splash, skipped, and sank unevenly. The ill-spent stroke sent the bull boat spinning in a circle. He grimaced and then quickly tried again with the same results.

Blue Eagle roared with laughter and then shouted to his bewildered friend, "You there, you stinking Indian. Don't run over me with that boat."

Chapter 18

The Two Frederick Bakers

Saturday morning at nine, Gannon and his son took their Buick on the road, which was more like a trail, for four rough miles to the Baker ranch. It wasn't a big ranch, but it contained a nice home on an attractive land.

Fred-the-bully was on the front porch when the Gannons drove up. He went inside immediately. Mr. Baker came out to see who had come calling.

"Mr. Baker? Hello, I'm Tom Gannon. I'm from the bank. Just wanted to drop by a few minutes and make your acquaintance, that's all. Oh, this is my son, John."

"I'm Fred Baker. Come on in."

As the Gannons entered the house, Baker barked the orders to his son, "Frederick, you go on out and finish setting those fence posts like I told you."

"We don't have enough nails to finish."

"Certainly you do. There's a box full on the back porch. Left side. Now get to it." Baker frowned, turned, and started out.

"John why don't you go with your friend and help him with his work," Tom said, gently pushing his son's shoulder in Baker's direction.

"I don't know what setting fence posts are all about, but I'll help you any way I can," John said to his schoolmate as he walked with Frederick out to the backyard.

Gannon watched his son as the two boys walked up the fence line talking.

"What's new?" Mr. Baker asked.

"They're just getting acquainted, that's all," Gannon replied. "Looks like you've got a good boy, and he's of an age and size to help you a lot with your ranch."

"What you say is true, but sometimes he can be a handful. Don't tell me you came out here after money, Mr. Gannon, because—"

"Not at all, Fred," Gannon reassured his client. "I haven't been with the bank but three or four months now, and I'm out calling on our clients to let you know that the bank is there for you if you need us. And suddenly it dawned on me that it would be a good idea for my son to spend some time with one of his schoolmates, get a glimpse of what a working ranch looks like. That's why I sent him along to help your son work. Set some fence posts—now that's a darn good starter for John."

The men talked for an hour or so when John and Frederick returned to get fresh water to drink.

"To goof off, mostly," Mr. Baker said to Gannon. "I have to stay on that boy's butt every hour of the day to get any work out of him lately. And he's a good worker when he wants to be. He's strong, and he's learned what needs to be done around a ranch pretty darn well. It's just the getting down to it that's the problem."

"Well," Gannon grinned and said, "he's growing up and feeling his oats most likely."

Suddenly the boys came in the room. "We saw that deer again over near the edge of the woods," Baker's son said. Then John spoke.

"Dad, setting fence posts is a lot harder than selling peanuts on the train." The men laughed as Tom stood up as if to wind up the visit. The Gannons said their good-byes and walked out to the car.

Baker's son stood at the front door and watched the visitors leave—the man with his hand on his son's shoulder and the son talking to his father. He stood motionless, watching the Buick vanishing in the distance.

"Something wrong?" the elder Baker asked.

Frederick raised his voice as he walked toward his father. "Wrong? Is something wrong? Everything is wrong! I'm wrong. You're wrong. See that man going there? His hand on his son's shoulder? Why can't you be a father like that?" The boy's face turned scarlet. He had never spoken so aggressively to his father.

Fred Baker saw the emotion, saw the hurt, and knew it was time.

"I wasn't going to tell you this until you were older." He waited for the boy for a long moment. Frederick, caught up in his emotions, wiped his eyes with his hands.

"Tell me what," he said, looking at his father.

In a calming, low voice, Fred said, pointing to a nearby chair, "Come sit down, Frederick. I have something to tell you."

As the boy settled in, his father continued. "I planned to tell you some things about our family when you were older, perhaps eighteen, but you've grown faster than I thought. That time seems to be now. The first thing you should know is … I'm not your father."

"Not my father? Then who the devil are you?"

"You'll need to listen to this, Frederick. Are you okay?" Frederick nodded yes and wiped his nose on his shirt sleeve.

"Your real father, Dan Davis, was my best friend. We grew up together. Right here: this house, these woods, that river. There was hardly a day that we weren't together. We hunted together, we fished together. If some bully kid picked on one of us, he had two to fight. Neither of us had a brother, so each of us was that brother for the other. We were inseparable. We grew to six feet. We weighed 170, each of us. We set fence posts and worked the ranch night and day. And we were successful. We teased, we wrestled, we got mad, we laughed, we fished.

We spent weekends camping out—happy as young animals being a part of nature. We were joined in a friendship that you couldn't pry apart with a crow bar. Brothers, really.

"Then I met your mother. I fell head-over-teakettle in love with her and married her, right here in Chambers. The next day, my friend—your father—packed his bags and went to Montana. Jane and I were in absolute bliss we were so happy. I can't even describe it. But, as time passed, like a lot of people experience, we saw that we had a problem. We both wanted children badly. In spite of everything we did—changed food, tried new ways, new methods—nothing worked.

"Two years passed, and nothing. We were desperate. In our minds, we blamed each other. We didn't forsake the other, but we just seemed lost under the same roof.

"Days passed like they were hours. Then one day at lunch, I looked up, and my God, it was my friend, your daddy, walking up on the front porch, carrying his bag. I almost turned the table over getting to him. We were like two teenagers greeting each other, giggling, hugging, laughing our heads off. I asked him to stay here with Jane and me for a while until he got settled. I didn't realize how much I missed Dan until that moment. He was the best brother a man could have.

"Just like in the past, we set fence posts by the mile and mended fences. We fished and hunted together. But things changed. I sensed it right away. I saw it happen every day. Both of them were silly, romantic. Then one day not long after that period, Dan and I were working up the line nearly a mile from the house. He got upset when he 'accidentally' knocked over our water bucket. He never knocked over water buckets. He stormed away from the area.

"'Well, I'll just go get some dam water,' he said.

"When he didn't return, I picked up my rifle and headed for home. I looked through the window and saw them. I took my boots off and eased through the house to the bedroom. There they were—my best friend in bed with my wife. I stood there in the doorway for half a minute. When I cocked my rifle, they threw the covers sky high and jumped out of bed buck naked. I just stood there, rifle pointed at Dan. Excuses flew until I yelled, 'Shut the f— up.' Then I very calmly gave them orders.

"I'm going back up to my fence job. I'll be back here in an hour. Both of you: get your shit together and get out. I looked at Dan eye-to-eye and said, 'You come back here again, and I'll kill you. I don't ever want to see you again—both of you.'

"When I came back to the house, they were gone. It rained for a week, yet not a drop of water fell from the sky. For the first time in my life, I felt like turning the rifle on myself. Somehow, one day it stopped. A calm fell over this house like I had never known. My shoulders weren't heavy anymore. I felt like I had just reached the top of a huge mountain.

"After a couple of years passed, I heard a noise out front one day, and there stood your daddy with the cutest little ole boy you ever saw. Not two years old. Of course I put my rifle aside and my feelings with it. A boy. My God, how I wanted a boy.

"'Where's Jane?' I asked, looking around as if she was hiding behind some tree.

"'She didn't make it, Fred. We were twenty miles from town. Her labor started, and we couldn't get this boy un-breeched. Jane suffocated and drowned in her own fluids. We saved the baby, but there was nothing we could do for her. I buried her in Helena.'

"A long while passed while we two grown men were talking baby talk to you, and once Dan and I caught our breath, I established the new ground rules for the three of us. I hired an Indian lady who was just terrific with you, and Dan and I knocked those fence posts in the ground like you cannot believe. We stretched the barbed wire and shaped this place up from stem to stern.

"Yet there was something there holding us apart. Something unforgiving, something so hurtful that it always had the whisper of a deep wound healing. I'd heard from others, perhaps my own father, *a friendship like ours—once it is fractured, once it is torn apart by some powerful force—can never be restored to its original form.*

"Yet, here we were, so willing to forgive and forget. The big motivator, of course, was you. You simply pulled us back together just by being you.

"Nearly a month had passed. It was fall. Those woods over along the south side of my property, just over a hundred yards from our first line of fences going west away from my house, they simply put your eyes out with spectacular color. We'd be up there mending fences or posting or stretching wire, and every day a specimen buck deer came out of the edge of the woods just into the field. He wasn't grazing or anything. He just seemed curious about what we were doing. He would just stand there and look at us. What a rack of horns he had. A sixteen-pointer minimum. Atypical, hunters would tell you. I would reach for my rifle, cock it, and every time he was gone before I could get off a good shot.

"There had to be a better solution. I told Dan, 'I'll get him next time for sure.' Two days later, we were working just feet from that same spot. 'Now, be careful,' I told Dan. 'I'm setting my rifle against this post, and it's loaded and cocked. There'll be no sound to spook him this time.' Twenty minutes passed. I looked up, and he was just stepping out of the woods. He was as golden as those leaves on the trees. His head was up, checking us out. His rack of horns looked four feet wide. 'Dan, ease me my rifle,' I whispered. Dan handed it to me safely enough: stock first, barrel out from himself. I kept my eyes glued on the big buck. My right arm was straight out to receive the cocked rifle. It came to my hand a bit too long. Dan suddenly changed his mind. He yanked the rifle back as he said, 'I'll take him.' As your dad pulled the rifle hard from my hand, my fingers raked across the trigger guard and the trigger. A shot rang out. I stood there dumbstruck as your dad crumpled to the ground, his left hand grasping his chest, blood flowing through his fingers.

"I immediately checked his pulse. There was none. I don't know what came over me. I went into a rage. I walked around him several times, cursing him. 'You damn fool! You fool! You fool!' I shouted. It just poured out. The stupidly of two grown men—two crack shots, two men who could handle any firearms, anywhere. I cursed him. I threw it all in his face. 'Why did you have to do that? Why did you have to come back here?' I yelled over and over. I almost kicked him, I was so out of control.

"Finally, I sat down beside him, my back leaning up against him. It calmed me a great deal. I took his left hand, the warmth fading. I turned and closed his eyes. Finally, I put both his hands over his chest and straightened up his head to look skyward as he lay there on his back. I stood up, a few feet away from where my friend lay. I recited the Lord's Prayer. I took off my jacket and placed it over his face.

"I raced through the field as hard as I could run, more to relieve my own tension and emotion. I saddled up Joe and rode him hard into town to get the sheriff and his deputy. No one had any reason not to believe me, yet a few low-class people will always whisper innuendoes about a revenge killing. I didn't give a damn what people thought. It was a tragic accident—clear and simple. Hell, I would have taken my own life any day before I did any harm to Dan. There was only one Dan.

"I buried him that same day up there near the woods, right where that red deer came out to greet us every day. It just seemed the thing to do."

A minute or so passed. The man and the boy sat silently, contemplating this awful tragedy, each suffering the deep feelings that engulfed them. Finally, the father spoke.

"I raised you with the most love for a son that I possibly could give, and still be a father. By the time you started sprouting up toward manhood, you looked more and more like your dad. It got to where every time I looked at you, I saw Dan. The more we spoke to each other, the more difficult I treated you for the troubles Dan brought into my life. Rightly or wrongly, that's why I've been so aloof, even bitter at times, in raising you these past few years."

Fred reached out and placed his left hand on his son's knee, looking him directly in the eye, his face turning pleasant as he spoke.

"This talk has done me more good than you, Frederick. One thing I can promise you is this: From here on, I will go that extra mile with you. We will be a father and a son. The hand you said you missed being on your shoulder will be there. I promise you. It will be there."

The Bakers arose abruptly, and the boy put both arms around his father's shoulders. He clung there until his young body started to shake with grief, perhaps relief, perhaps both. The father hugged the boy just as firmly, gently patting his back to reassure him.

"We both are starting over, you and me," Fred said to his son.

Finally Frederick pulled back from his father, and said, "Tomorrow after breakfast, let's go up the hill there and visit my father. I'm so glad you kept him nearby. Maybe we could make a place there. You know, a little graveyard, just for him. Someday maybe a place for all of us."

"I think tomorrow morning will be just right," Fred said. "The sun will be out bright. I think what we'll find out there is a new father and a new son taking charge of this land, taking charge of our lives."

Chapter 19

The New Frederick Baker

Monday morning brought a bright new dawn to Chambers school. Miss Rochelle got everyone settled down and prompted them to get ready for their speeches. She asked Sallie Gannon to start off this new assignment. Sallie chose a good topic, "What I Like about My Parents." She gave a good speech, and her schoolmates gave her a warm applause. Others spoke, some very good, and some too plain and boring.

For the last speaker before recess, the teacher chose Frederick Baker, who had been decidedly more likeable right from the beginning of the day.

Baker stood up from the middle of the room and said, "Excuse me a minute." Everyone turned to watch him as he went to open the front door. Frederick looked out to see a very apprehensive Blue Eagle sitting on the porch. "We would like you to come inside and take your seat. Would you?"

Blue Eagle, at first appearing apprehensive, recovered quickly, nodded yes, and took a seat in the back row not far from the heater, now burning low. He seemed very anxious. The children were very quiet, as was their teacher. There was something unfolding here they weren't expecting. Was it more trouble—right there in class?

Baker looked around the room, first at Miss Rochelle and all the kids, and then directly at John Gannon and Blue Eagle. He stretched his neck side to side as if his shirt collar was too tight, and then he begin to address the class, in a good voice and with a confidence that caused the class to sit up and take notice.

"My talk is about growing up. It's as much of an apology as a speech. Last Friday, I did wrong to two fine schoolmates. To one, I insulted very badly. To the other, I physically hurt him. And just as awful—John, Blue Eagle—we threw it in your face by laughing at you. I just want you to know that I'm terribly ashamed of myself, and I ask you to forgive me. I asked my father yesterday what I should say to you, and he said, 'You know what to do as well as I do. You apologize. You ask them to forgive you. You make friends with them if they will accept your apology.'

"All the way to school this morning, I wondered over and over what to say –if I would say it properly. It always came out the same: 'I was terribly wrong. I'm sorry. Forgive me. Can we be friends?' Then I remembered something that my dad said: 'Apologize, but don't wait for an answer. You make the first move by simply showing them that you really do mean it. Don't be a thug; be friends.'

"My apology has taken up most of my time, but let me just say that we have all grown up over this summer, especially me. I want to thank John Gannon and his dad for coming to my house and spending time with us. Someday I'll tell you just what that meant to me. Actually, that visit wound up causing me to grow a foot taller—maybe more, if that's possible. But that's another story.

"Growing up should lead to leadership. I am the oldest and biggest boy in our school, but I know full well I am not the smartest. My dad said, 'Son, just do your best; lead where you can lead, and things will work out for the better.' So from now on, I urge all of us to grow up and do like John and Blue Eagle are doing. Bring your best ideas, be a team, and help our friend, our teacher, feel like she is not wasting her time with us. Finally, I want to ask Miss Rochelle a question. Actually it came from my dad. Why can't Blue Eagle sit in this schoolhouse with all of us and learn, rather than sit out there in the cold?

"If anyone objects, well, Blue Eagle is chief of maintenance, and part of that job is to tend to the stove and firewood. Of course, we can all pitch in as we always have done, and his seat is as he has already made it—there near the stove. Of course, if he has time to take notes, study, and do homework, then that's his business. If he can pass the exams, then he can go on to high school. College, too, if he cares to.

"Well, what do all of you think?" Most of the students broke out instantly in loud applause. The others followed. When it was quiet again, Frederick looked to the back of the room.

"How does that sound to you, Blue Eagle?"

Blue Eagle rose immediately and said, "I am pleased by what you say, and my chief will be even more pleased. He will have much good to say about this day when the time is right. I also want to say that you have one boy in this school that I want to thank now. He cannot yet swim, he cannot row a bull boat, but he can run with the wind, and he has ideas bigger than men. Even the chiefs of our Indian reservations are taking notice." Then he looked at John, smiled, and said, "I am honored. You are my first white friend. Maybe soon I will have a room full of friends."

At recess, all the smaller children wanted Frederick, John, and Blue Eagle to play with them. Frederick stepped right in among them. "Ask Blue Eagle to teach you how to play kickball." So they did.

Frederick and John spent the next part of the hour talking quietly on the side and watching Blue Eagle as he demonstrated how to kick the ball in all directions and how to score. The small children all wanted to touch Blue Eagle's fringed buckskin jacket, his whole outfit.

None of this went unnoticed from the school window. Miss Rochelle smiled and walked over to ring the bell, setting in motion the launch of more good surprises from her students.

At lunchtime, John saw Baker go over to Blue Eagle. He took out some food and gave half of it to the embarrassed Indian boy, who ate it very slowly. Most assuredly, he didn't like it, John thought, but he ate it nevertheless. Some of the other kids did the same, and finally Blue Eagle raised his hand, politely refusing their generosity with a "Thank you."

"See what you started?" John asked as he walked up beside Baker.

"I have no idea what he eats; that's ham and biscuit that I gave him. Anyway, it's filling. What do you think he eats?"

"I think it's fish—deer sometimes, birds, but whatever it is, it sure powers his legs and his brain. We have nothing like him around here," John said. Then he looked Baker directly in the eyes and said, "Frederick, you are the tallest boy in school, but today, up there before God and everybody, in just five minutes you grew another foot taller. I won't ever forget what you did." Baker looked down at the ground for a minute and then directly into Gannon's eyes as he spoke.

"The idea just came to me, and I said it right away. Maybe it's part of that leadership thing. Anyway, John, I apologized to you for the pain I caused you. I was just an angry kid showing his butt. Now, I see what you mean. Blue Eagle really does have something special about him. The truth is, I see the way you two run together, talk so easily with each other, and I feel some envy there." Baker looked down at the ground again and moved a clod of dirt with his right shoe. "I don't have anyone like that. I really don't have *any* friends." He moved the dirt again.

"That's because everybody knows," John said in a very serious voice.

"Knows what?" Frederick said, looking at John rather anxiously.

"They know all about my busting up your jaw out there in the woods a couple of weeks ago." Baker, caught totally off guard, half-doubled up in laughter. Then he stood up, struggling to speak.

"Gawd! What an awful thing for me to do. All I can say is you are one hell of a good sport to joke about it. I really owe you, John. Tell you what. Before it gets too cold, come stay over with Dad and me some Friday night, and I'll take you fishing in our secret place a few miles beyond our ranch. A place called Cypress Lake. I only discovered it last year. It is full of bass. I mean big fighters. And you'll like my dad. He has some great stories, and you impressed him a lot the way you presented yourself. You really did. As a matter of fact, you impressed me."

At that moment, the bell rang, ending lunch. As they headed for class, John answered his new friend's invitation.

"Thanks! I'll let you know in a day or two. Is that all right?"

After lunch, Miss Rochelle announced that there would be one more speaker for the day. "John Gannon," she called out. "Let's hear your talk." John took the floor.

"We've heard several amazing talks today. Mine may seem unimportant compared to them, yet I chose 'Ideas' as my topic because thinking up good ideas is what I like to do. My dad said to me once, 'Son, when you come up with a good idea, it is just an idea until someone takes it and does something with it.' That's what I like to create: a good idea! It's like a lightning bolt; it makes your blood flow a little faster.

"When my family arrived here in Chambers just before the Fourth of July celebration, my mother and my sisters and I had no idea what our town was like. But Dad did, and that's the whole reason we came here. We traveled 600 miles on awful roads. Just trails, really. Little did we know we would find a fine school like this, an exceptional teacher, or kids like all of you. I had no idea you had all this—all to yourselves.

"Right off, I met another boy at the Fourth of July gathering. There he was with the chief, who just happened to be his father. Funny kid! All dressed up in an Indian outfit and wore a blue eagle feather in his hair. Even his name, Blue Eagle, was different. His 'perfume' was different. But you know what? I soon found out that he can do things I only dream of doing. Most days in warm weather he swims half a mile a day—to and from his home out there on Huron Island. I can't even swim. He startled me with how much English he knows. He startled me with how fast he can run. That gave me an idea.

"Likely, few people outside of Chambers even know about our school. We don't go to any fairs or any competitions. A few of us can run, so let's get a coach and train and enter our track team. Put our school and our town on the map. The Chambers Eagles or whatever name you want. You pick one. Here's another idea. We have two fantastic voice teachers now: our teacher and my mother. Couldn't we enter our own singing group—glee club or soloist maybe. We can also teach others.

Younger kids, older kids—just like right here in our very own one-room school. I know my mother would like that.

"Recently, Blue Eagle and I were standing out there on the highway bridge talking, as we sometimes did all summer, and I looked down the river to the edge of the Dakota Reservation. I saw twenty or thirty young Indian children out there playing ball. Having a great time! Immediately, it occurred to me, and I said to my friend, 'But they don't have a school.' Right then I knew I just had to go see their chief about teaching them right where they were playing. I took Blue Eagle with me, and Chief Fox agreed a short time afterward, 'Yes, it would be okay.' I started it, and today an older Indian boy, named Trig, is still teaching them English and simple math.

"While I was down there visiting, I got another idea—an idea to make money for the Dakota, money for our town, and provide a lot of fun for the Indians and for hundreds, thousands perhaps in time. What was that idea? An ancient war canoe race between the two reservations. My dad says that it's a very big idea. But he cautioned me it's just an idea until someone or some group makes it happen. I call it the Chambers Regatta. I got the idea from our library. Every—"

"John, I hate to cut you off. You're doing great, you really are, but your time expired ten minutes ago. Take your seat, and we will recap today's drama. It was, really, a very exciting drama. You speakers did a fine job." A pause came.

John stood up and said, "Miss Rochelle, I need to say one more thing. It's very important. May I, please?"

"Okay, but say it in one minute."

"I think the biggest idea here today belongs to Frederick Baker. When school started recently, everybody on the playground came inside the school—except one. He had to sit outside there and learn his lessons through that open window over there. It hurt me, and I can only imagine how it frustrated my friend, Blue Eagle. It took the cold weather to drive him inside, and that started with a great idea: wood for our stove. Some from this class chased him home.

"Here is a boy whose people have lived in our country for hundreds of years before we white people came here and claimed their land. Rightly or wrongly, that is what happened. But this past weekend, Fred Baker turned from being on the side of most every person in town to being a peacemaker. It is because of Fred Baker that we now have a way to educate James Blue Eagle inside this schoolhouse.

"Finally, and I feel very sure about this: you will not have to worry yourselves about our new classmate's abilities in or out of our school. You will have to worry about your ability to measure up to the standards he brings to our school. When Chambers School starts coming home with trophies and blue ribbons from competitions, I think a lot of people will start to feel just as we do today."

That night after the Gannons finished their evening meal, John heard his mother greet Miss Rochelle at the front door. Soon the entire Gannon family gathered to say hello to this special teacher. When Tom Gannon entered the room, he wore a big, warm smile and spoke in his charming voice.

"Well, Miss Rochelle, to what do we owe such a pleasure?"

"I came into town to buy a surprise for your son for tomorrow's presentations, but I decided to just bring it by your home to show all of his family. John, would you step over here by me, please." When he was in place, Miss Rochelle took out of her bag a blue ribbon medal, inscribed with one word: champion. She pinned it on John's shirt. Then, she looked at everyone as she spoke.

"I was so proud of your son in class today. He got the big idea that today he would be a champion. He had a lot to say to us all, and he spoke in such a way that he won the admiration of every kid in that room. Myself as well. Well done, John.

"Excuse me for just dropping by like this, but I thought it important." Smiling pleasantly, Miss Rochelle turned to leave, focusing on John. "Now, be on time in the morning, John. Don't let this medal go to your head," she warned half-jokingly as she put her hand on her student's shoulder. Then she was gone.

"My, my—champion! That's quite an honor. What all did you talk about?" Tom asked his son.

"Sure sounds impressive! What *did* you talk about," Helen asked.

John was so flustered by all the attention paid to him, he was strangely silent.

"Sallie, get your brother some water. We're smothering him," Tom said.

He told them about Baker, about Blue Eagle being a classmate now, and about how his new home, Chambers, excited him beyond his fondest dreams.

Tom looked at Helen and the girls. They were all smiling, pleased that tonight their boy, John, had indeed put up on the boards a pretty high mark.

John looked at his dad and said, "Dad, if you had seen Baker today, even you would not have believed the way he acted. Something big happened out there on their ranch after we left. Maybe someday he will tell me about it. He even asked me to come stay over sometime soon and fish."

Tom smiled and put his hand on his son's shoulder.

"You never know what helping a guy set a few fence posts will lead to, do you?"

"He was so friendly talking to me during recess. He was like … like a friend. The idea that he came up with—allowing Blue Eagle to come sit inside with the rest of us—it just floored me. Miss Rochelle seemed as surprised as I was, but you could see she was happy about it. Dad, that school is going to be special."

"Sounds like all of you passed a milestone out there today," Tom said.

Chapter 20

Chambers Duet

When Ruth Rochelle arrived at the Gannon home, Helen met her friend on the front porch with a warm smile and hug. Fall was in the air, leaves were continuing to change, and the Gannons' second year in Chambers was equally as promising.

"I am so glad you were free," Helen said, leading the teacher into the living room. "Tom is out calling on clients, and all the children are off on different activities, so we have the house to ourselves to talk or sing. It's taken forever for us to get together. I've heard so much about your extraordinary voice—not to mention all that you do for the children in this town."

"Well, Helen, I feel the same way about you. I still glow when I recall the magnificent job you did filling in for me during the Fourth of July gathering last year. You certainly put on a show for this town. And your family! What an introduction to the Gannon family. The whole town responded with such enthusiasm."

Helen said, "What do you think we should explore today?"

"What about projects for the two of us? Possibly using Town Hall as well as different churches?"

"We are thinking almost alike. Let's follow your plan," Ruth replied. "I think that our opportunities here in Chambers are unlimited. I had no idea when I first came out West that life was going to be so exciting—opportunities to accomplish things would be so vast. When

I graduated from Cincinnati Conservatory of Music, I recalled that my neighbor had graduated from there several years before. She married her true love, Tom Mayo, and moved to east Texas to found a teachers college. The first two buildings were destroyed by fire, but that didn't deter the Mayos. They just went to the community, raised money, and rebuilt. The third time, they made sure it was built of brick. I believe they named it East Texas State Normal College. He taught and ran the college; she sang and taught singing at all levels.

"I thought that was the bravest adventure that I had ever heard of. Yet, I found myself following practically in her footsteps—in a much smaller way, of course. These children here in Chambers are so inquisitive, particularly your children. I just love all three of them. Anyway, I feel like I'm theirs, and they are mine, so to speak'." A brief silence passed, and then Ruth continued.

"Children out here, out West, learn responsibility early in life. They seem to yearn for it more out here. And your oldest—your son! That boy is thinking and organizing all of the time. You can see it in his eyes when he talks. Brown eyes twinkling like stars. Strong sculpted face. You can be sure he will do well in life. He mentioned that he wants to be a writer."

"Thanks, Ruth. You're kind to say those things about our children. Now what about a first project for us? I doubt that the people in Chambers have heard much opera, yet they responded to my singing with great enthusiasm. I don't see how we can miss with Verdi and Puccini, and my Lord, who wouldn't just be swept away by most of their work. The whole world never tires of hearing them. You are a soprano, and I'm a mezzo soprano. Some ideas come to my mind right away, but you are the Conservatory graduate. What ideas do you have for a knock 'em dead Chambers duet?"

"There are several choices in both Verdi and Puccini that we can talk about, but the greatest duets of all time for you and me to consider is Bellini's *Norma*. We can explore that possibility seriously, and let me tell you, if we can work it out to fit our talents, we will give this town some music they can only hear at the Chicago Opera. I have the sheet music, well-used as it is. A poor student can't afford new sheet music, you know."

"I can well imagine," Helen said. "Sounds like a real test for me. I really haven't tried to sing it very much as yet, but I look forward to trying it with you. I've been concentrating on several of the Verdi and Puccini operas, but I need to spend more time elsewhere. This sounds like the time for me do that."

Ruth spoke with enthusiasm. "Warm up with something you like. How about something from Gianni Schicchi, you know, 'O Mio Babbino Caro' or 'Un Bel Di" from *Butterfly*?"

"Now we are talking the same language. Then you will know immediately if we can even sing a duet. Oh, boy! Or, I should say, oh, teacher!" Helen immediately moved into "O Mio Babbino Caro." She was right on pitch and picked up the mood perfectly, as if it was an encore that followed a fine performance to an admiring crowd. It caught Ruth off-guard. The quality of Helen's voice and the power behind it there in the Gannon home. Ruth couldn't contain her enthusiasm.

"Helen! You are fantastic. Did you warm up before I arrived?"

"Not really. That's something I move into around here whenever I feel in the mood to sing."

"Well, not to overreact to our situation, that rendition came right out of Chicago. I've paid good money for far less—and sung by some pretty good singers, I might add. You really do have an interesting voice, my dear."

"Oh, Ruth! People have been saying that about my voice for years. I'm really fed up to here with it." Helen looked away, both with disappointment and satisfaction. "What I really need is opportunity, and I have just about written that off. We keep moving further away from Chicago, not closer to it." Ruth cut in sharply.

"Helen, Chicago just hangs up there in the air. It's the carrot that we all need if we have any talent worth exploiting. Now let's get off of that. I want to hear you sing 'Un Bel Di Vedremo.' To my ears, it's a mood like no other. Women leave the theater with tears running down their faces. Even the men get out their handkerchiefs."

Almost before Helen heard the request, she broke into the soprano role by pitching her deep mezzo up just enough to capture the sensuality of the piece. When she finished, there were tears in her own eyes. Ruth rushed to embrace her.

"My dear Helen! You are not just good—you have talents and potential that I didn't hear at all last July. People are going to say, 'Where have you been hiding this voice?' Sing a couple of more things for me. Your voice screams for *Norma*."

"'In Mia Mano' or 'Ah! Bello a Me Ritorna'?" Helen asked, but not waiting for an answer, she opened right up perfectly with her favorite of the two, "Ah! Bello," and then stumbled, recovered without apology, and left Ruth stunned and nodding approval as she finished.

"I see some areas where you are rusty, but a little practice will take care of that. What are you doing Wednesday afternoon around four-thirty?"

"That doesn't give us much time; we eat early around here. Why don't you come have dinner with us, and when the family gets scattered on their routines, we can work on a few things together."

All the way home and all that night, Ruth Rochelle could only think of one thing: *how did a voice like that get all the way out West without being turned back to Chicago?*

On Wednesday, Tom Gannon entered the front door with a smile and his usual enthusiasm. "Was that my wife I heard singing?"

"Oh, Ruth and I were just practicing a bit," Helen responded.

"Here! Here!" Tom said. "She has quite a voice, doesn't she?"

"I couldn't agree more," Ruth said. After Tom went to the back porch to wash up, she turned to Helen and said, "What if I told you that if we work hard over the next six months, you and I are going to Chicago?"

"What do you mean."

"Helen, I mean we need to find out about the Gannons' future. I'm not sure that even you are aware that your daughter has an excellent voice. It keeps coming across the other children in class. Lately, I hear qualities in it that may be new, just developing, and I mention it to you now. We need to take her with us. I see us going this coming summer."

Ruth continued after a brief pause. "Here is the thing, Helen. You have something magical in your voice. At the Conservatory, my teacher stressed it every day to all of us whom she felt had a singing future. Everyone heard her, of course, but her eyes spoke firmly to several of us in class. It's the way we embellish a note—the appoggiatura. You have it down perfectly. You slide from a note or a phrase into a sharper one or a lower one so easily. It moves an audience; it brings chills, or it brings tears to one's eyes. I can't get my voice to do it as easily, certainly not as attractively as you do. I don't have the timber. By the way, who was your teacher?"

"Janet Mason. She retired from New York. The Met, as I recall. She pushed the devil out of me. I nearly cried one day; by the time I got home from practice, I swore I would never go back to her. Of course I did. There was no one in Monmouth who remotely had her abilities. I studied with her right up to the time we moved here. She's what I called a 'ball buster' of a teacher. I sang solos at church and at several Town Hall recitals that she sponsored. Both went very well, and she gave me lots of encouragement. She thought my *Aida* was topnotch. I even took to wearing my hair in a ball like Aida. When I said good-bye to her and thanked her for pushing me so hard, drawing out qualities I never imagined I had in me, she said, 'I'll miss you and your voice.' Then she said, 'Get to Chicago, Helen.'"

"That is exactly what teaching is all about," Ruth cut in. "A teacher's reputation is built around achievement. Many can teach; a few have that extra quality—that ability to pull your talents out of you. Qualities you have no idea you have inside you, yet those teachers know. And she or he is not about to let you get out of their classes without learning and producing those qualities of sounds. As you said, they 'kick your butt.'"

"That was Janet Mason. It was weeks, perhaps months, before I fully realized what she had accomplished. She pushed me to a higher level. Who knows—perhaps two levels." Then Helen looked away. "Are you serious about Chicago, Ruth?"

Ruth Rochelle, with more enthusiasm than Helen had ever heard, said, "The other day in singing class, I asked a student to sing a solo, and she did. A simple little song. She was very proud of her performance. Then I asked your youngest, Betty Jean, to come up front. 'Betty Jean, sing something you know. Anything at all, something you like.' She smiled and began as if it were some well-known little ballad. An expression come over my face that I know I should not have shown my class, but it was such a surprise. For her age, with so little training, so little effort, she sang and she acted ... almost like you, It almost bowled me over. Helen, she sang your song, 'Oh Mio Babbino Caro.' You must sing Puccini around the house."

"I do, but I had no idea that she had memorized it, or that she could even sing," Helen said, looking down, shaking her head in amazement.

"Oh, you know how perceptive children are," Ruth said. "They learn poems, they learn songs. Anything around them. And sometimes it doesn't even have to be repetitive. Their uncluttered minds just absorb things like a sponge. But that's only the first part. For a moment there, the way she used her hands and body, she was almost a carbon copy of her mother. The third part is even better. Helen, she has talent. Something from her mother's musical qualities rubbed off on that little girl. Are you sure you've not recognized some of this?"

"Not at all. I haven't heard her sing. In church, I am always the one on stage, so I don't know what goes on in our pew. So that's what you are suggesting! The three of us. And my little one is going with us to Chicago for a reason."

Ruth and Helen stood looking at each other for two or three moments. Helen looked away, her expression more worried, and then she spoke with some degree of sadness.

"Ruth, this going to Chicago thing has nearly torn my family apart for three years, at least. As I stand here now, with all this opportunity buzzing around me, I think Tom Gannon will bounce off the ceiling if I even mention it to him. It's that serious. And in many ways, he has been right. We've all done well here. My family has grown stronger out here. John, in particular, is flourishing surprisingly well. As a matter of fact, he is maturing almost too quickly for me."

"We'll keep this to ourselves for the time being, Helen. I want you to see and hear your daughter. I can't wait for you to hear her performance. As a matter of fact, come to school next week. Say, Thursday, just before two p.m. I'll ask Betty Jean to sing around two, or soon after you arrive."

A week had passed since Helen heard her daughter sing at school. As elated as she was about Betty Jean's developing talents, Helen dreaded to disrupt the momentum of her family. Even with all the convincing evidence she needed there in her hands, she still had not broached the subject with Tom Gannon. Tonight seemed to be perfect. With the bank talk completed, Helen turned to John, who spoke readily.

"Oh, Blue Eagle and I worked on vocabulary for an hour outside the library. He is really doing well. When he went home, I did some schoolwork and then got here just in time for dinner. Why? What's up, Mother?

"Nothing really. It's just that Betty Jean and I … and Sallie have a secret. I was at school today to visit with Miss Rochelle, and it was music day. It seems our very own Betty Jean Gannon has something to tell us. Want to tell everybody what happened?" Helen said softly as she turned her smile toward her daughter.

Betty Jean, smiling pleasantly, spoke to everyone as she said, "Papa, I can sing."

"Oh, well, honey, that's not really surprising. Out of the three of you, someone ought to be able to sing almost as well as your mother," Tom said.

Helen saw her opportunity, saying, "Maybe after we finish our bread pudding, we can have some entertainment, as in a song by Betty Jean Gannon." Betty Jean beamed toward her mother and then turned to her dad.

"Miss Rochelle says I'm doing real well, Daddy."

"Well, we are all about through. Why don't you stand out there a few steps away from us and let us hear you sing something," Tom urged.

"Ruth, Miss Rochelle, just put her before the class today and told her to sing something that she knew. Why don't you sing that song again for all of your family, Betty Jean," Helen said.

"Okay, Mama. Papa, this is by Puccini." Then she put on her serious stage face, lifted her arms, and left her family stunned with her voice, her slight movements of acting, and by her professional appearance. By the time she finished, everyone broke into loud applause. Betty Jean moved to her chair, but her daddy called her over to him.

"That's my girl! You have a gift, my lady. When did you learn to do that?"

"I just watched Momma sing it, so I tried it out at school."

"She really is quite good, and I may as well tell you, Tom, we have a problem. Ruth went off like a sky rocket when she told me about Betty Jean. But before that, she went on for half an hour about my skills, pointing out all the details in my voice that she has uncovered as a voice coach and teacher." Then Helen looked away a few seconds.

"And?" Tom said.

Helen looked at Betty Jean and then at Tom. "She wants to take me and Betty Jean to Chicago this summer."

"Oh, Helen! That's wonderful, and why not? You've shown everybody in town that you have a fine voice. I'm thrilled for you. For you both. Two Gannon singers in Chicago. Why, no telling what may come of this. Seriously, Helen, I've been thinking about this very thing ever since your famous Fourth of July grand entrance to Chambers. Everyone talks about it. Now, here is the perfect opportunity to act upon it." Tom got up and came to Helen's chair and kissed her full on the mouth. "Helen, I couldn't mean this more: I have never been more proud of you than right now." Then he turned to Betty Jean. "You were pretty amazing, too, young lady. Are you ready to go to Chicago?"

"I can go with Mother?"

"Sure sounds like that's what Miss Rochelle has planned for this family," Tom said. "This calls for a celebration. John, run down to Hickerson's and get a quart of strawberry ice cream. When you return, all of you have a bowl, clean up the kitchen, and get to bed. You mother and I have some business to finish, and then we are off to sleep."

The Gannons were on a mission. John was already moving out the front door as the girls removed the dinner dishes and began their kitchen chores. Tom held Helen's chair as she rose. She looked into her husband's eyes, now smiling and glistening, as he put her hand in his arm and led Helen to their bedroom. Sallie and Betty heard them talking for a while, and then it was very quiet.

Helen, spoke in a soft voice, audible only to her husband.

"Tom Gannon, ever since we began this journey out of Monmouth, you have change so much. How could I find fault with anything you do now?"

Tom took his wife gently into his arms. Her auburn hair was out of its customary bun and flowed down to her shoulders. Tom sat on the edge of the bed, pulling his wife down beside him as he lay down. There was a long, delicate kiss, followed by another.

"There are lots of lovely ladies who can sing well, but I have the best of the best, and soon everybody in Chicago will know it."

Chapter 21

Chicago, Here We Come

In the spring of the Gannons' third year in Chambers, Helen and Ruth Rochelle began meeting weekly to make plans for their trip to Chicago. They might as well have been going on a safari to a foreign land. They had never traveled to a large city, and likely they would not venture beyond their intended mission—music. The Chicago grand opera house, museums, churches, functions of those, and certainly the advice of their advisors—that was about it. Perfect timing, too; it was not two years earlier when the Big Storm swept massive amounts of tidal waves from the lakes into the city. Helen had declared in earlier conversations that with her daughter in tow, their visit would be highly confined to music first, and anything else would come afterward. There was no dispute about that.

At first, Helen and Ruth meet at the Gannons, but soon it became apparent that they needed more privacy, more time to rehearse, and more time to dream. The school was ideal, and Saturdays seemed to suit them the best. Helen could still return home to prepare the Gannon evening meal, making sure all of the children were accounted for, supportive in their chores and concern for the big trip.

At the school on Saturday, Ruth drew up a brief outline of their agenda.

"The first thing we have to do is find a descent boarding house near the opera house. I'm told we should look at the Mahoney, also the

Valencia. They both are near the opera house, and it's pretty exciting to just walk around there. Betty Jean will be wild eyed since Chicago's skyscrapers will be her first.

"That one is easy," Ruth continued. "Let's take the Mahoney. If we don't like it, we can always move. Now, the most important thing is: what might they ask us to sing? I think we have to be ready for all the Verdi operas, Puccini as well. We already know them; it's just a matter of several practice sessions to get our voices in gear. Then again, they may toss out something from Bellini, or who knows what. What if they want us to sing that incredible duet from *Norma*? We can't be expected to know every opera written."

"No, of course not," Helen replied, "but let's get our bread-and-butter pieces fine-tuned, and surely they will hit one of them while we're auditioning. Betty Jean can stick to her Gianni Schicchi, which she is so cute in doing. They won't believe what they are hearing, and they won't be able to resist her."

"No doubt about that," Ruth said. "Also, I think you and I should be prepared to sing solos, as that's how they're going to judge us."

"I'm just as worried about our safety. And I don't mean out on the streets. You know what cads some of these show people can be. We will just have to stick together, that's all." Helen paused a moment.

"Absolutely," Ruth said. "And we may just take along a heavy jar of cold cream in our purses!" Both the women roared with laughter.

"Oh, Good Lord," Helen said. "See you next Saturday. I've got to get supper on the table. Can you come eat with us?"

"No, not tonight, but thanks. I'd love to—another time perhaps."

"Is he good-looking?" Helen teased.

"I wish," Ruth said. "A stack of papers to read, as well as tomorrow's lessons."

"My Lord, Ruth, how do you do it?"

"I sometimes wonder, myself. Then I see all those bright-eyed faces in my dreams, and the work simply becomes another adventure. As you can imagine, if I didn't find it exciting, I would find another occupation."

The following Saturday, Ruth's new Victrola arrived from Sears. At last she could show off her music collection, but more than anything, she and Helen could practice in real time with her music-without-voice recordings.

"Sorry I'm a bit late," Helen said when she arrived. "Oh, what have we got here?" She rushed over to Ruth's new record player.

"It just came. Isn't it a beauty? Just look at this burled walnut cabinet."

Helen rubbed her hand over the top of the cabinet. "What a beauty! Oh, Ruth, I am so happy for you. You must have paid a fortune for it."

"Well, they aren't cheap, but this one is special. My fantastic brother bought it for me for a teaching aid—a birthday gift. The tag said $300. And look at this. The cabinet is by a special cabinet maker."

"I guess so," Helen replied. "It's chest high and the finest burl walnut I have ever seen. What is that cord?"

"Helen, this is the first electric model Victor made." They both laughed like they were little girls. Then Ruth pulled out several records for them to work with. "I can't wait for us to try these. The voices are missing; we just sing as if we were in performance with a live orchestra."

When Helen arrived home, Tom was right behind her. "I'm off early, and you are working late. You and Ruth are going to be unstoppable with her new Victor."

"Tom, I can't wait for you to see it. You, the master cabinet maker! What an amazing cabinet, and it's electric. The first model out."

The children all arrived, and Helen ushered them to the back porch to wash and help her warm up their dinner. Soon the Gannons enjoyed Helen's chicken and dumplings and white cake with black walnuts in the icing. Miss Rochelle's new Victrola was the topic of the evening until Tom began asking questions about their Chicago plans. "Where are you going to stay?" he asked.

"Ruth says the Mahoney has a good reputation. We likely will stay there. It's a Victorian design and has a home-like environment. We both decided on it immediately." Then Helen turned to Betty Jean, who was standing attentively nearby.

"And the food is good, too."

"I'm already packed, Mama."

"You have your music business to take care of, of course, but you will no doubt have time for sightseeing," Tom said. "Be sure to make several trips to see the Field Museum. It is unbelievable in its displays of mammals of all kinds, natural settings, gemstones, even our ecosystem models. I hear that the city is already planning for a planetarium nearby at some future date. That area is already attractive, as I recall, but someday it will have a major impact on the city." Then John had a comment.

"Daddy, you're likely to find me in one of their suitcases the way you're talking."

"You'll have your chances later on, my boy. You and Blue Eagle have all of your projects right here in Chambers. Besides, you'll have to help me keep house and cook."

Betty Jean rushed over to her brother and looked up with a smile. "I'll teach you how before me and Mom leave."

"You mean, 'before Mom and I leave.'"

"Oh, are you going with us?" Betty Jean giggled. When the family stopped laughing, she added, "Yes, before Mom and I leave."

"Okay, girls, time for homework." John snapped his fingers, and they all put their lessons on the dining room table as Tom led Helen to the kitchen to talk.

"Oh, Mother, aren't we all growing up," Tom said.

"I just hold my breath," Helen replied. "Every day, I understand a little bit better why you insisted that of all the places that we could have moved to, Chambers was it."

Tom took his wife in his arms, kissed her gently, and said, "Now aren't you the perfect wife. Let's have our coffee out here, and you can tell me all about what you and Ruth have in store for yourselves and our daughter. She may be the shadow-star to watch."

"She is pretty amazing," Helen said, "and she is bright as a light beam. But, oh—wait until you to see Ruth's new electric Victrola."

"Electric? Well, well, well." Then Helen talked excitedly about what Ruth hoped to accomplish with it at school, as well as what it would do for both of them in getting their voices shaped up for Chicago.

"As you were speaking, Helen, it occurred to me. What if you three get to Chicago and dazzle the daylights out of that town? Do we split up, do I find a bank job in Chicago, or do I just sit back in Chicago while my ladies keep us in candy and caviar?"

Helen chuckled softly. "Oh, Tom Gannon, you are full of it, aren't you? To tell you the truth, I'm not prepared for miracles, but if they happen, we will just have to deal with them. There is just no way to answer that question right now."

Tom held Helen's hand, rubbing it softly as he spoke. "Whatever comes, it will take a family decision to decide," he said. Helen looked at her husband in a way that almost brought tears. Then she spoke quietly.

"Why don't you and I walk down to the store for some ice cream."

Chapter 22

Chambers School Track Team

John Gannon asked for a few minutes during Tuesday's Speak Out session.

"Okay, but at the end of the period," Miss Rochelle said. "Then in the afternoon, I have a special surprise for all of you." John, of course, knew it must be the fabulous Victrola.

"All right, class," Miss Rochelle said later that afternoon. "Mr. Gannon wants to say a few words to all of us. John, it's all yours."

John came to the front, turned, and faced the class. He wasn't cocky, but everyone could tell that he had something important to say. So they settled down and listened.

"I wonder if each one of you feels the way I do." He swept the room with his eyes, as he had seen the best speakers in town do on occasion. Then he waited a moment before continuing. "I've been here such a short time, but I've come to love Chambers, this wonderful life out here, particularly this school and you." He hesitated and then said, "Especially what Miss Rochelle is doing for all of us.

"But, we are a secret. No one knows we are out here. Go to the Four States Fair, or just read about it. You don't see Chambers mentioned. No one knows we even exist. Well, it occurred to me last night, even though this has been on my mind for weeks, why don't we let them know we are here? When I discussed this with my father, he said, 'How?'

"I said, 'It's very simple. All the schools enter sports teams.' Much of it is track. We don't presently have a baseball team, but we do have a track team. All it takes is a minimum of three runners. One is in the back row, one is speaking, and I see two or three of you who can run. At least you can try. All of you boys can try out. What do you think?"

Baker jumped up, clapping and yelling, and the whole class followed suit.

Miss Rochelle knew that John was eating into her program time, but she was not about to see this opportunity slip away. She smiled politely and waited for her star pupil.

"All we need is a track coach. Any ideas?"

After a moment, two or three names were suggested. "All right then, I'll talk to them. The first one who agrees to do it will be our track coach. We start practice right away—coach or no coach."

Miss Rochelle cleared the floor with her bell. "It's lunchtime already. At 1:00 p.m., we will continue class studies, and then at 2:00 p.m., I have a surprise for you."

John, Blue Eagle, and Baker had lunch together and talked enthusiastically about building the Chambers School track team. Baker had been steadily improving and would be a good third candidate, but could anyone else run?

Baker finally spoke up. "What about Vincent Ball?"

"That little kid?" John asked.

"That's what I thought, too, but the other day, I saw him take off across the schoolyard after someone, and that boy can really move those little legs."

"Fine, then. So there are four right there."

After lunch, everyone settled down for class, still feeling the remnants of excitement set off by John's speech. It was a new kind of eagerness. Miss Rochelle sensed it right away.

At 2:00 p.m., the teacher called for two volunteers. Gannon and Baker came to the front of the room right away. Miss Rochelle escorted them back to her apartment for a moment. When they reappeared, the class set up a hum of "Ohhhs" and "Ahhs" when the boys rolled out the new Victrola.

It was impressive. It was chest high to John and Fred, about two and a half feet wide. The gnarled walnut cabinet was varnished with an elegant sheen, showing off the brown overall body and the darker greys in the natural gnarled markings. After the boys placed the Victrola in the middle of the area in front of the class, they took their seats and waited for Miss Rochelle's comments.

"My brother thought we could get great benefits from this new electric record player. It's the latest model, made this year. With my records, we can have music appreciation, we can sing with the music, and we will learn about music almost as well as if we were seeing a live performance. This is classical music, of course. Some are opera, and some are symphonic pieces. But all of them are beautiful, and you will—I hope—grow to love them as I do. To celebrate owning this new music machine, I have a surprise for you." With that, Ruth went over to the Victrola, opened up the two double doors to the bottom half of the record player, and motioned to the storage area.

"This is where you store your records. These forty records that you see here are the best part of my collection." She reached in the racks and selected a unique choice for the class. "Be very quiet and listen. This song is by the Italian composer, Puccini. He named it, 'O Mio Babbino Caro'—'My Dear Baby,' approximately." Then Miss Rochelle paused a moment. "On second thought, Betty Jean, would you like to sing? It's your favorite song. I'll prompt you each time as the music pauses."

"Why don't you show us how first, Miss Rochelle. May I sing tomorrow?"

"All right then, here we go." The record began. Soon the class was stunned by how powerful and soothing the music was from this new machine. The air was so full of sound. Then, the first pause came in the music. Ruth Rochelle gestured with her hands, looked at the floor, and then at the whole class as she broke into Gianni Schicchi.

When she finished, her students erupted with applause. Miss Rochelle acknowledged them politely and then explained her plan.

"Every Tuesday and Thursday, we are going to have an hour of music appreciation. I think you are going to love it. I know that it will teach you to appreciate classical music far beyond your imagination, or casual listening beyond this school. Her class smiled and applauded vigorously again. Everyone talked at once for a moment until Miss Rochelle spoke over them.

"Today, we are going to dismiss classes an hour early—except, I believe, the members of the new Chambers Track Club. If any of you boys want to try out for the team, get together on the playground with John and Blue Eagle.

John and Blue looked around for possible boys who might be interested or just good candidates. Frederick Baker joined them, and then Blue Eagle yelled for two more boys to join them. Robert Tiller came over. Vincent Ball stood next to Baker. Suddenly Chambers school had six candidates for its first track team.

John assumed control as the boys expected he would. They all shook hands and waited.

"This is great," John said. "One hundred percent more than we thought we might have. The main thing today is to get organized. We've got to find a coach. Someone respected in town, someone who knows enough about track to put us through the paces and look out for us before and after our track meets. It would be great if he could also teach us to run better. We have a couple of names already, but are there any more suggestions?"

Tiller finally spoke up.

"My father used to run. At least I've heard him talk about it now and again when certain men came into our store. I could ask him."

"Good. First, Robert, see if he would be our coach. We could go to your store tomorrow just so he can meet everyone, but then he would have to come to our practices here after school—maybe not every day, but most days. The next thing is shorts and shoes," John continued.

"We think we can run fast in our school clothes, but we can't. Any old shorts and shoes will do for practice. I'll see about getting a sponsor later. Then we can buy running uniforms. Heck, I'll bet Robert's dad can order them for us. We'll have to choose colors. We don't have any of this organized yet. No school colors, no name—nothing. We're the first team ever for this town, so let's do it right. Think about it. Blue and gold trim. Chambers School sounds ideal for a name, or whatever we decide right here tomorrow after practice. You guys want to add anything?"

Blue Eagle quickly spoke. "You left out jock straps."

"You're the only one who has to worry about that," John said, as all the boys howled. John pushed the Indian's shoulder with his fist, and then he added, "Well, you certainly can't run with just that flap hanging down to protect you. If you did, every girl in the state would be out for that track meet." There was more laughing and pushing by everyone.

"Before we go," John said, "I hope all of you feel as strongly as I do about representing our school, as well as Chambers. If we don't go to these meets with winning in mind, then we can better spend our time at the library or helping our parents. When you show up here tomorrow, I'll know we can count on you to do just that."

As the boys strolled up the path toward town, Baker ran to the woods in the rear of the schoolhouse to find his horse, yelling goodbye as he left. Blue Eagle peeled off the trail with John, heading to the library for a short session on a new topic: sewers. Tom Gannon was getting more and more active in the affairs of Chambers, and now seemed the ideal time to focus on a looming problem. For over a week, as John and Blue Eagle fished, they saw signs in this pristine river that were not only disturbing, they were a menace of vast proportions for the whole town.

"It's been getting worse every time we fish," John said. Blue Eagle nodded agreement, and then he looked at his friend seriously.

"My people don't use the river that way; we use the woods. We bury everything. The reservations have their own special places—special tepees that they move when they need to. Everything gets covered up."

"I know," John said, "but our town flushes right into our river—their river. 'Let somebody else worry about it' is what it looks like. You know, my dad was a master plumber. Still is, really. I rather imagine he'll have something to say to the city board. This town—this Brule River—that's why we moved out here. And people are using our river for a toilet?" The boys looked at each other seriously, and then John said, "Come on. Let's run the rest of the way."

When John reached home just before dark, he rushed through the house to wash up on the back porch. Tom Gannon was just drying his hands.

"You've been running."

"Yes, sir. Blue Eagle and I went to the library after the track meeting. Dad, we have a big problem around here, don't we?"

"Like the title of that book you're holding? I should say we do."

"Blue Eagle and I see mess in the river every time we fish. And, you know, he swims in those waters every day. The water is moving, but that's not the point. We can't keep using our river for a toilet. We're the only town on the Brule, but there are many big cities sitting on rivers all over the country from what I read. What do they do, Dad?"

"That's the problem," Gannon said. "Only a few are just facing up to this menace. Europe has struggled with this human nightmare since ancient Greece. London engineers have made some pretty good inroads lately. Other countries as well. Our septic tanks are getting better and better, and I read good things about a new German system, the Imhoff tank. I'll talk to you about this later, but right now I think your mother has dinner ready. Tell us about your track team while we're eating."

The next day, the Chambers School track team gathered around John, eager and supportive. After a short discussion, John said, "Okay, it's settled. We all agree on blue with gold trim uniforms with white letters. Robert reports that his dad, Charles Tiller, will coach us for the first year. And Mr. Chandler at Chandler's Feed Store is going to sponsor us, uniforms and all." The whole team yelled a bit at that good news. John continued.

"Now for some light work. Remember, we have to get in shape before we start any competitive racing. We warm up, we run our sprints or races, and we do cool-down exercises before heading for home each day. School is out at four, and we meet right here immediately afterward. At five, we're on our way home."

Then John turned to Frederick Baker. "Fred, you probably have the biggest workload of any of us on your shoulders. How does this sound so far?"

"I'll handle it. Just means my weekends will be a little busier than usual."

John surveyed the group, dividing the six boys into two lines of three, facing each other, and started the stretching and limbering up exercises. During a pause and stretch session, he turned to Blue Eagle and asked in quick succession, "What are you doing Saturday? Want to go with me to Fred's ranch and help him get caught up on his work? There may be some interesting fishing."

Blue Eagle kept his exercises going but said, "Maybe. I'll know tomorrow."

"Good! We'll get the work done and get over to Cypress Lake. Fred keeps saying the fishing there is unbelievable."

"Wait! Did you say Cypress Lake? You know about that place? Regardless, I'll have to ask about that. You know how special some of those woods are to us. I can't just go wherever I choose out there, but maybe with good reason, my chief will let me go—as long as I'm with you."

"Oh, you mean your burial grounds? I think they're quite a distance from Cypress Lake. It's an incredible place—ancient cypress trees, Spanish moss hanging from every limb. Sunsets there must be fantastic."

"Don't count on me until I get permission."

Suddenly Baker interrupted. "What are you two hatching over here?"

"We're just trying to figure how to light a fire under your shoes."

After a big laugh with Baker, Gannon switched back to running. "Okay, let's run about three-quarters speed to the end of the playground. That's not a hundred yards, but it will do for training. Then we can increase the distance in three days by using the trail to the river."

John lined up the boys and started them with a quick "One, two, three, go." It worked well as a practice session. Everyone ran abreast, and all the runners had decent rhythm and much energy to spare. "Two more times now; hold the same speed."

"You and Blue Eagle run full speed a lot. Why can't we?" Tiller asked.

"We could, but any training that I've read about approaches things by a set program, with degrees of speed. It's just common sense. Work out; don't get sore. Our coach may have different ideas. We'll soon see," John said.

The next day, Charles Tiller was at the school at four when all the students started for their homes. He spoke a moment to Miss Rochelle and then quickly joined the runners. A seventh boy, Harold, had decided to try out, but John knew immediately that the boy's permanent limp was not going to work out. When the boy moved to the sideline during one of their sprints, John called to him to remain during practice. After Mr. Tiller congratulated all the runners, he lectured them about training, urging them to stay away from sweets as much as possible, and to develop a hardnosed attitude of never quitting until they drove past the finish mark. Just as the team was being dismissed, John spoke up.

"Mr. Tiller, I nominate Harold for your assistant. He has a great attitude."

"He sure does. How about it, Harold? Want to be my assistant?" All the team beamed when they saw the big smile that came over Harold's face.

Two weeks went by quickly, and John and Blue Eagle were now relatively even in speed. Baker was improving near the finish line as his long legs came into play. "You'll be a good candidate for the two-twenty," Coach said after taking note of Baker's progress. And just as Baker had remarked earlier, Vincent Ball could run. He was almost comical in size and in the way his motions propelled him down the field. He was a real competitor and ran hard at the finish line. John bragged on him in Baker's presence several times.

At the beginning of the third week, the Chambers School uniforms arrived. The team had never seen anything like them. There was so much excitement, Coach had to settle them down with exercises and sprints. Yet whenever there was a moment of free time, each boy held up his jersey and admired it.

"Okay, men. Your new practice shoes arrived at the store yesterday. Let's knock off and go get fitted. You jog ahead. I'll be along as soon as I speak to Miss Rochelle a moment." At Tiller's Feed Store, the track team tried on their shoes.

"Man, they're almost too pretty to practice in," Baker said. Then he excused himself to start home to help his father at their ranch. All the boys followed suit. John yelled after them.

"Don't forget your shoes in the morning! We'll store them at school."

Coach Tiller arrived just in time to catch John before he started for home. "Well, you men," he said to John. "See what you started?" He smiled. "I see some promise out there in practice. I really do. If it won't blow your head out of shape, John, I'll just say that you've done a fine job pulling this team together."

"Thank you, Coach. It means a lot to me and Blue Eagle." He turned to find his friend, but the Indian had left without notice several minutes before.

"I just want to say that a sport costs everyone a lot of time. We owe you a lot for coming out to coach us. I told our friends to expect to put in a lot of hard work. No team wins without it."

Coach Tiller grinned. "See you tomorrow, John. Tell your dad to come to practice when he gets a chance."

Tiller went to the front door of the store and watched as John jogged toward home. Some of his own memories followed the boy down Main Street. It gave him a new purpose not only for his son, but for this new bunch of boys who would be runners.

During practice for the remainder of the week, Coach Tiller concentrated on working out and building body strength. He lectured the team frequently on muscle formation, building strength, and how it equated to producing winning teams.

John looked at Blue Eagle several times during these talks and wondered about swimming long distances, especially if his friend was in better shape than he was. They ran about the same speed. They both seemed to have stamina, yet he rationalized that since they both ran sizeable distances each day, perhaps they both already had their maximum endurance and speed. Or would they improve with age?

After intermittent workouts of pushups and squats, Coach lined them up for fifty-yard sprints, three-fourths speed at first and then full throttle. John and his friend were usually neck and neck in those contests. The other boys did pretty well. Baker was last in those short sprints, yet he felt confident, knowing that his long legs and power would serve him well.

Coach Tiller was anxious to move past the one hundred into the longer distances, primarily to judge Baker's ability as well as Dan Nix's, a sleeper who was showing remarkable improvement. John noticed Coach talking to Dan more frequently during the latter part of the week, giving him techniques to practice.

The following Monday, Coach Tiller announced that they would start the following day with more trials, running the full one-hundred-yard dash several times during the course of each practice on alternate days, and the strength-build on the other two days. That was when John Gannon saw the wisdom in proper training. It was also the day his father paid a visit to see his son and the track team practice. In the first heat, John beat out teammates for first place, barely fending off Blue Eagle. During the second heat, both finished in a tie, or what looked like a tie. In the third heat, Dan Nix tied John and Blue Eagle as they finished in first place.

While the boys all got their breath, Coach talked about the power of stamina and why condition was, after natural ability, the single most important factor a sprint runner could master in the preparation for a race. Not just the legs—the upper body was very important, as well. Several boys were bent over and breathing through their mouths. Coach Tiller brought that fact to their attention, telling them that the following week would be devoted to strength building. Blue Eagle and Baker seemed to be in the best condition, but no one would be allowed to shun Coach's routines.

As John and his dad walked home, track dominated their discussion: the team, how John was progressing, and how impressed Tom Gannon was with the way the coach worked the team.

"I had no idea he knew so much about track," Tom said to his son.

"We all think he's great," John replied.

"You did quite well out there until that third sprint. When athletes bend over trying to catch their breath after an event, it immediately points out a problem. They're out of shape. Coach Tiller zeroed in on that immediately with several of your teammates. You need more stamina work. Maybe set a few more fence posts?" Tom said, smiling at his son.

"Gee, Dad, that reminds me of something. If it's all right with you and Mom, Blue Eagle and I are going out to fish at Cypress Lake after we help Fred Baker with his work. He can't give us proper time for track and also keep his share of chores caught up."

"That's fine by me, but you ask your mother at dinner. Cypress Lake is quite a place, I'm told. I was hoping that I would introduce you to that special place, but now I guess you'll get to do the honors for me."

John thought a second and then said, "Maybe sometime after that, the five of us can camp out up there."

"Five?" Tom asked.

"Yes, sir. Fred and his father, you and me and Blue Eagle, if he wants to come."

Tom looked at his son and grinned. *This kid is some politician—and sincerely so. Always thinking of other people and his relationship with them.*

"That's a deal, young man. I'm as anxious to see that place as you are. It's something of a wonder. Cypress trees, alligators? Those things belong in the South. These have to be a throwback to ancient times."

"Baker says it's loaded with big bass. I wonder why more people don't go there."

"Oh, there are probably some good reasons. It's pretty spooky according to some around town," Tom said. "Well, here we are—and look who's greeting us at the front door: Sallie and B. J."

Betty Jean ran and grabbed her brother's hand. "Can he run fast, Papa?"

"You bet he can, darling. He's going to be a winner one day soon. Needs a little work just yet, though." Then, Sallie spoke to her father.

"Daddy, Mr. Bowers came by earlier. He said that he would talk to you in the morning. He said it wasn't very important."

"Thanks, my love. Thanks for letting me know."

John washed his face and hands and then sat in one of the stuffed chairs. His stomach was churning, and sweat broke out on his forehead. His color became almost white.

"Sallie, get John a washcloth soaked in cold water. Your brother ran a bit too much out there just now. You boys overrun your stamina, and it will cost you. You need to keep a lot of water in your system, also. You can get in trouble running at top speed too quickly. Stay quiet a bit; your stomach will quiet down shortly."

Sallie quickly returned with a wet cloth and put it on John's neck as he sat bent over his knees. She massaged his shoulders until John asked her to stop. Then he went to the back porch for air and more water. His mother held up dinner for a few minutes.

Tom went to the back porch to see about his son. John was bent over the long, foot-wide shelf that held the wash pan and water bucket.

"You just take it easy there for a while. Go lie down a few minutes if you feel like it. We're going ahead and eating before it gets cold. Take your time. Then come eat a little—some broth and crackers. See how your stomach reacts."

The next day at school, everything went well. All the same, John thought his coach should know.

"It's all about conditioning. We're not going to run you today. Do a light workout, and then we'll resume regular practice tomorrow."

Two weeks of hard work had passed when Coach Tiller announced to his team that he had an invitation for their first meet.

"It's just a small gathering. Two or three schools, but it's a beginning. The big test will be in five weeks. The Four States Fair will be coming up. It will be your first big competition and the most important race Chambers School will face for a while. Many of our people enter cooking contests there, and quite a few townspeople attend to see the livestock and fowl exhibits. We will get our first really big test, as some of the best runners in the state will be competing."

John and Blue Eagle talked a lot about the Four States. Baker did too, but usually he had to hurry home to the ranch to help his dad. Baker worked more and more on running the two-twenty. He showed vast improvement in his overall time. Coach pointed out how it was all won in the final fifty yards, where strength conditioning took natural ability to a higher level. Baker was developing a kick of sorts, and the entire team took pride in seeing it unfold. Dan Nix showed everyone that he meant business in the one hundred, giving Chambers four good entrants for any meet.

The following week, the team grew tense by the time they arrived at the park grounds for the Stanley township race. Centerville entered the race at the last minute, giving them three teams. The track, an overgrown, mowed pasture in actuality, was large enough to accommodate twelve runners. Each team had run sprints the week before to decide who would participate. John, Blue Eagle, Baker, and Nix represented Chambers. Stanley had some big runners, as did Centerville, but Coach Tiller pointed out in a huddle that size did not necessarily mean speed, and they were not to be intimidated by any big team.

"You're ready to run. Just relax, get firmly set in your stance, and listen for the gun. Drive off the mark sharply when it sounds. You'll run a good race when you do that. You may take this race; you may not. It really doesn't matter except to tell us what we have as a team."

Chambers drew center lanes. Visually, they looked sharp, but "uniforms don't make a team," Coach Tiller often reminded them.

Then it was time. Everyone got into line, right knee cocked, left leg straight back. Except Baker. He preferred the reverse. He looked particularly good today, John thought, and he had high hope to see his teammate do well.

"On your mark, set …" *Bang*. Chamber's blue and gold was suddenly flying down the track. Ten yards to go, and Blue Eagle had half a step on John and the rest of the pack. In five yards, John drew even. At the tape, he leaned more than his friend and took the race. Nix tied for third. Stanley school barely edged out Baker for fourth.

Blue Eagle showed disappointment but nevertheless shook hands with John as they all had been taught to do. There were some good runners competing out there, so, first race or not, it was a good tune-up for the fair.

John kept looking at Blue Eagle. "You didn't lean in to the tape."

"Yes, I did."

"You didn't."

"If you had, you'd have won it. You did that on purpose." Blue Eagle looked hard at his friend.

"You're crazy!" he said.

"All right, Chambers, over here. Baker, get ready for the two-twenty. Everybody else, over here where we can support Baker." They had almost an hour to kill.

Four runners entered the two-twenty. Stanley entered two tall, lanky runners, although they were not built as strongly as Baker. The two-twenty was amazing. The starter had to restart the race twice, but Baker managed a strong launch in the third start. He ran his race as Coach Tiller had taught him. He was cruising in third position as they hit the straightaway. The other two schools' runners held their ground until the final thirty yards. Chambers' runners started yelling louder and louder, and Baker put his head down momentarily, calling on all of his extra strength, and passed all the runners with ease. Coach Tiller and his team were going crazy on the sidelines. Then they all ran down to congratulate Baker just past the finish line. Blue Eagle grabbed Baker's right hand and lifted it up, grinning big.

After the brief celebration, the judges gathered everyone around and awarded the ribbons. There were no medals in a meet like this, but a ribbon was just as sought after. Something to take back to school and put on the bulletin board until something more significant could be built. John later announced that he knew just the right father who could build such a display cabinet.

The judges awarded Chambers four ribbons. There were three in the one hundred and a fantastic first place in the two-twenty. After the usual congratulations, the coaches and runners shook hands and left for their homes. Once underway to Chambers, the initial excitement was centered around Baker, who grinned from ear to ear but had little to say. Finally, Coach Tiller, spoke.

"Your training paid off. I was especially proud of each one of you. You ran against some pretty good runners out there today, and we will leave it at that. This coming week, we will be working out lightly and working more on conditioning. Each one of you got a good look at your performance, what you've got in you, so now you know as well as anyone that, while this was exactly what we said it would be—a tune-up for the fair competition—we have some hard work ahead of us. Let's give Baker and John a big hand for winning their races." The boys yelled for a while, pushed and shoved the winners, and laughed their congratulations.

"You all ran good races, but Fred Baker showed us something new out there today. He's been training hard, and this was the first real test on a strong finish. That's what I've been harping on. That was the strongest kick that you've showed us to date. It will likely get stronger in the weeks ahead. And we will need it. We only have three weeks to get ready for the fair. We'll be running sprints every other day. We will rest on Wednesday's, but we will hit strength-building hard for two days, then light one day, hard the final day. We will adjust a little the last week before the fair. I want you to peak just before we race, not sooner.

"We have one major hurdle out there that I'm aware of: Charlie Parker. He's six feet two, a year older than you guys, and he can run. If we train well, we will make a good showing. If we don't really concentrate on our work, then that cool breeze that just passed you in the big race will be Charlie Parker. We are not going to be intimidated though. Excellent runners have bad days, and good runners have excellent days on occasions. Now I will show you my six-steps training, as we called it at Tech."

The next day at school was not hard to predict. The little Chambers one-room schoolhouse literally jumped off its blocks. Each runner got to stand up front and describe how another Chambers runner performed so that the students could enjoy the event to the fullest.

Then it was business as usual. Miss Rochelle set the class lessons in motion and watched the progress. The youngest children always got the most attention. It was a big day for Chambers School.

When the students were dismissed at four, John went over to Blue Eagle and guided him to a spot outside, out of earshot of their friends.

"Coach asked me if I thought you ran your race, meaning, I guess, if you were in shape or if you let up at the end. I told him you just couldn't run very fast. That I could beat you seven days a week." Blue Eagle snapped his head around to see the grin on his friend's face.

"Come on out to practice, and I'll give you a lesson, you slowpoke pale face."

John grinned widely, pushing Blue Eagle out of his way a little, and they both ran over to Coach Tiller. John grinned as he said, "Coach, Blue Eagle here claims he can beat me. We better keep an eye on him. He might be a little overconfident."

"Well, gentlemen, we will know in just a few minutes. First, let's get to work on some exercises."

Later in practice, Blue Eagle did beat John, but just barely.

"See, pale boy, Indian can run. You need work."

"You call that running? When we get over to the fairgrounds, you're going to be eating my dust from start to finish."

"Then Parker boy is going to be choking, isn't he?"

"All right, you two, get over here," Coach said. "I want to talk to you about your shoes and about getting off the line at the gun."

On the way home, John and his friend stopped at the bridge and talked a minute. "I can't make it Saturday to fish with you and Frederick. I have to go with my father—my chief and Crazy Dog. We'll be up at White Rock Point with our people for several days."

"So that's what's worrying you. Anything you want to talk about?"

"Not really. It's tribal business. They don't tell me much about it. Anyway, I told my chief I'd go. It seemed important to him."

"Okay, then. There will be other trips. We can go out to Cypress any time. You go help your family. We'll make that trip in a week or two, you'll see," John said.

Blue Eagle looked at his friend and spoke quietly, seriously. "This name keeps coming up like some picnic playground. But I tell you now, Cypress Lake is much more than strange, giant trees and hanging moss. It's not just a beautiful place; it's spiritual to us. Some would be very upset if a group of people went up there as if it were just any fishing lake—making a lot of noise and being disrespectful of this wild, special place."

John nodded agreement. "Thanks for telling me. I'll see that your feelings are made known around here. That group outing was my plan, anyway. A beautiful place like that can best be enjoyed by two, maybe three at most—family or friends who are just looking for a quiet campout that's special, unusual."

With that, Blue Eagle turned and walked across the bridge.

No "see you tomorrow," no nothing. Strange, John thought. *He usually runs home.*

John didn't move from his spot until his friend was well on his way. When James turned to look back toward Gannon, John put his hand in the air and turned for home. *I sure would like to be a fly on the wall of that island lodge tonight. Is the chief getting ready to move his family back upriver or is this something that he's not going to discuss?* John thought as he jogged home to his family.

Now, with all the hard training, John was loathe to stay up beyond dinner and homework. Sometimes he checked his sisters' lessons, but those sessions took no more than half an hour. Then he was off for nine hours of solid sleep before his mother sent Betty Jean in to shake him awake. She relished the job. She shook him gently at first and then more vigorously, jumping back quickly after doing so in case John's flailing arms caught her off guard and banged into her lip or nose, as she had experienced once before.

Coach Tiller's tactics worked, especially for John. He showed it in the spring of his step, his stamina, and his voracious appetite. Coach Tiller lectured more frequently now, and he was more serious. Lately he seemed to have "Parker-itis." The team joked about it whenever they were out of Coach's earshot. Yet, by and large, everyone was all business. Coach Tiller even gathered the team together to demonstrate their tactics with spikes.

"I'm counting on soft turf, but if we find different, say hard or semi hard turf to run on, we're going with 3mm spikes. If it's soft or normal turf, we're going with 6mm spikes. That's what most will use. I'll have extra spikes in case we need them and wrenches to put them on. Don't forget the wrenches."

Chapter 23

Four Corners Fair

The following week quickly moved to race day. Coach T., as many began to call him, arranged for the team to get to the fairgrounds two hours early to sit, rest, and enjoy several exhibits before moving over to the race track, which was just right for 6mm spikes. Coach made sure all the team was properly spiked.

John caught a motion from the crowd, and a big smile came to his face as he waved to his parents and sisters and Miss Rochelle. The whole team noticed and waved to their teacher.

After Coach Tiller got the team's attention, he moved them into the milk cow exhibit—primarily Jersey, Guernsey, and Holstein, cautioning them that they would be there half an hour before moving a short distance away to stallions and mares. The later would be vastly more interesting to the boys and serve to thoroughly distract them. When several Chambers families tried to say hello or wish the team good luck, Coach Tiller acknowledged them but politely excused themselves, moving his charges on to their next exhibit. Before the team realized the time, Coach Tiller was rounding up everyone and moving them over to the nearby track and stands. A good crowd was already assembled, and there was a steady stream of people pouring in and looking for seats.

Coach Tiller talked to his team. "We've trained hard. I want you to relax and get off the line strongly. Dig in. Move out powerfully. Show your strength. Set your left leg straight back, head down. Catapult yourself down that track the split second your ear hears the gun. Run relaxed, lean forward the first thirty or forty yards, and then run your style. There are other good runners out there, but this is your race to win. We want this Four Corners Fair trophy, so go get it."

Chambers drew the first four lanes, and Parker was in lane five with his teammates. He was all business, shaking his arms and each leg alternately. Coach put Nix in lane one, Baker in lane two, Blue Eagle in lane three, and John in lane four next to Parker. There was no eye contact. But then it started. John could not help thinking about his friend on his left. He worried if he was ready or if he was still distracted by family business.

It was time. "On your mark, get set …" *Bang.* As John and Blue Eagle came off the line, they looked up and saw Charlie Parker already running down the track. The gun fired again, stopping the runners.

"All right, let's try that again. Wait for the gun, gentlemen."

"On your mark, get set …" *Bang.* And there went Charlie Parker again. John looked at Blue Eagle and raised his left eyebrow.

"All right," he said out of the corner of his mouth. "This race is ours; let's take it."

"Gentlemen, you know the rules. A third false start by any runner, and he is disqualified automatically. Okay, have a good race."

"On your mark, get set …" *Bang.* All runners got off. Parker was lightning quick, even when he hung back. The Chambers runners were a foot behind him. John decided to stay on Parker's heels and make his move late. He felt good. He could take this race. He dug in, half a stride behind. Blue Eagle ran on John's left shoulder. Nix was nearly with them. Baker ran hard but fell a step behind. Then it happened.

Gannon's mind took over his race. *Will the Indian chin the tape? Will he lunge? Will they give him the ribbon? Will John stop managing the race?* Thirty feet from the tape, John woke up and dug in. Charlie Parker was a full step out in front. Gannon pulled even in three strides. Blue Eagle matched him. The crowd was screaming in a pitched fury. Arms pumping, teeth clinched, legs churning with full fluid power, the

Chambers team ran hard. John and Blue Eagle, neck and neck, edged passed Parker a full head. The two friends both hit the tape straight up—and Charlie Parker leaned into the tape brilliantly and took the race. Dan Nix took fourth, and Baker was fifth.

John's eyes burned and ran dry. His ears rang like a bell, and his stomach knotted. He couldn't look at Blue Eagle, yet he mumbled under his breath, "Now we'll have to wait for state." *Two piss-ass mistakes in a row,* he thought as he kicked at the track clay.

The winners went over to stand on the platforms. Blue Eagle and John Gannon flanked the highly touted Charlie Parker, now strutting like a peacock. They gave Blue Eagle second place by a nose, and John and Dan Nix took third and fourth respectively. At least Parker's school, Centenary, lost on points. Chambers runners cooled down and then went to Coach Tiller.

"Very good race, men. Well run. You brought home three ribbons and a team ribbon. Now let's see how these next teams run." He said the right words, but there was something in his voice—the tone lacked excitement. He looked at Gannon, who could not hold his stare. John stretched his shoulders, his neck, and turned to face the field, taking deep breaths and exhaling hard.

As Chambers waited for the next race, John and Blue Eagle looked at each other. Each knew, and each knew the other knew. Did it stop there, or was it some smoldering fire in the lightning bolts of pride and friendship within the history of ancient red and white transgressions? *What the hell?* John thought. *Why must I keep falling on that sword?* Yet he wanted Blue Eagle to win that race. *Damn it! Why didn't he lean to the darn tape? For now, just chalk it up as two races in the history of Chambers School, two screw-ups for the school record book.* He would take them both home, knowing full well that next month, state just might offer his redemption.

The days ahead were hard, sometimes exhausting. Vigorous training fell on the Chambers runners at each practice. Coach lectured them, introduced them to new exercises, new techniques in running sprints, and faster, more concentrated methods of getting off the starting line. Baker did drills for his leg strength. He picked up his pace from the start to the three-quarter mark and found something new in his kick, giving him more confidence. The entire team exercised more intensely, longer and more seriously than they had at any other time. They felt like Coach expected them to win state. If they didn't, it was not going to be his fault. A new, more confident team began to emerge. Now Blue Eagle was pushing John. Coach separated them as if they were twins out there practicing to finish at the same time. He called them to his side one day and instructed them.

"We have ten more days of this. It may work out that your times will end up identical, but if they are, I'm going to kick both of you right in the butt. You're good runners. I like you very much personally, but this is Chambers School that you're running for—not a tribe, not a family, not a friendship. As much as I value all of those, they place second in any race. When we race at state, I'm lining you up a lane apart. Dan Nix will be running in the lane between you. If you two run like you did at the fair, then you can go look for another coach. Now, I'm serious about that. You both can win this race. If you give Parker a nose, he'll win it. Now, what have you two got to say? Are you ready to go out there and do your job?"

Blue Eagle nodded. John spoke up.

"Yes, sir, I think I did let you and the team down last race. I wasn't in as good of shape, mentally or physically, as I should have been. I am now. I feel it. I believe we can win it."

"All right, then, let's all go home. Except you, Gannon. You stick around a minute."

When everyone had left the practice field, Coach Tiller walked with John toward the boy's home.

"I've been watching you and your friend closely. You're doing everything I've taught you to do, yet alarmingly, I get the feeling when you're running in competition, you act like Blue Eagle is going to win. When you're winning, you seem to be waiting; when Blue Eagle is winning, you work harder—a lot harder, it seems to me. That's what happened at the fair, wasn't it?"

John stopped suddenly and hurried his argument with his coach. "He had that race won, Coach. All he had to do was lean into the tape."

"That's not what I saw out there. What I saw was you taking it to Parker. You pulled ahead, and then you hit neutral. You didn't lean to the tape either. By the time your friend brought another step, Parker blew by both of you. It looked, in racing parlance, well, fixed. That's exactly the way it looked."

John put his head down and shuffled his feet a moment. Then he looked up at his coach. "To be truthful, Coach, I must have waited because I didn't lean either. I wanted Blue Eagle to win that race. It would mean more than anything in this town—"

"What are you talking about? What's going on with you two?"

John looked up at his coach and held his stare.

"It's not just me and Blue Eagle—it's about them. Nobody in this town cares one iota about those people across the river. They might as well be cattle penned up and left to die. That's exactly how Sherman felt. I read it at the library. 'Kill as many Indians as you can today. Then tomorrow you won't have as many to kill.' My friend, this son of a Mandan chief? He swims home or runs home every day. We found a way to get him into our school. I teach him vocabulary and language an hour every day. He's as smart as any kid in school, maybe smarter, and there's nothing out there in the wild that he doesn't know. Soon he faces the toughest test an Indian boy can face: the manhood test. I plan to take him to high school when I go to Kansas City." He paused a second or two.

"He needs to win, Coach. It will do a lot for this town, for our school, for my friend—not to mention all those people living out there in wigwams, who just a few years ago lost the biggest race they could ever lose—their land and their dignity."

"John, all you say is true, but if it were not true, none of us would even be here. You can't rewrite history, son. All that aside, what makes you think Blue Eagle can't beat you without your help? He's about equal to your speed, you know. And you said it yourself; he's a heck of an athlete. Look, I'm glad we're having this little talk, because this is precisely what I spoke about earlier. History will take care of itself, but runners run to win. If they don't, they are breaking all the rules of racing. Do you understand that?"

"Yes, sir. It's just something that hit me from the first day that we arrived here from Monmouth."

"Monmouth? You mean Monmouth, Illinois?"

"Yes, sir."

"Did you know Coach Stone?"

"Yes, sir. He coached our high school track team. He lived about four blocks from our house. He's quite a coach. I'd be surprised if he's still there, he's so good."

"We can talk about that later. Right now, you and your Indian friend had better huddle. If you don't, you've got no case at state. Runners who run there care about just one thing: winning. If you and Blue Eagle, each of you, don't want it for yourselves, then you're in trouble. You understand that, don't you?"

"Yes, sir. From here on, it will be that way. I promise you. I'll make sure Blue Eagle understands as well."

"You both had better get it right, because you have just one more shot at this level. That's all I'm going to say about it. You have the capability. It's up to you. Both of you. You go on home, now. It's getting late. See you Monday."

When John neared Chambers Bridge, he could see his friend there facing up the river.

He knew it was too late for a serious confrontation, if it led to that, so he jogged a third of the way across the bridge with Blue Eagle before turning back for home. He was no sooner in the front door when his father arrived. Tom spoke matter of factly to his family. Everyone recognized the mood and stood back, letting their father set the tone of the evening.

After everyone had washed themselves and stood around the table, John came in.

"I'm hungry as a bear," Tom said. Everyone took their seats. "Smells wonderful, Mother," Tom said. Everyone agreed with their dad, yet they were reserved. "How did you and the coach get on today?" Tom said, turning to John.

"He kind of thought we didn't want to win bad enough. I agreed with him."

"What happened?"

"We just messed up, pure and simple. We misjudged the finish—didn't lean, didn't finish hard enough. We weren't in shape." John got up from the table. "I have to go to the bathroom." He went in and threw some cold water on his face. When he came back to the table, banking was the topic.

Finally, Tom said, "Helen, this is the best pot roast you have ever cooked. What in the world is it?"

Helen smiled with that all-knowing look on her face and said, "Oh, some nice lamb shoulder that arrived just today." Tom Gannon made an awful expression.

"This is lamb?" he said.

"Indeed it is. Cooked just right, it's sweet and very tasty. Of course, the butcher and the chef both have to know their business," Helen exclaimed.

"Well, my dear, if you cook it this way, you can cook it any time you want to, can't she, Sallie?"

"Sir? Oh, yes, sir, she sure can," Sallie said. Then her eyes went back to her lap.

"What on earth are you doing over there, Sallie?"

Betty Jean spoke up before anyone could say a word. "She's drawing our pictures, Daddy. She is going to be an artist."

"Well, well! You must show it to us after dinner. Right now, let's finish our lamb before it cools out."

"Yes, sir," Sallie said, and put the artwork away.

"You asked about the bank, Helen. It's not appropriate to discuss it here at the table. Maybe later. Matter of fact, it's too personal to discuss, so let's talk about our track star. Go ahead, John. What happened?"

"Well, Blue Eagle and I got too cute out there. We had no plan to do it, but it looked like we were trying to tie each other and both win it. Coach Tiller thought so too and really let us have it. It was a costly lesson. I apologized to Coach quite a bit, but he laid the law down very hard to me, as I expected he would. I really had it coming. I promised him that it wouldn't happen again."

"How did your friend feel? Was he there with you?"

"No, sir. Coach held me back personally. He didn't pull any punches. I'll talk to Blue Eagle in the morning. If he has any problems, and he won't, he can go talk to Coach himself. When we get to state, it is going to be all for Chambers—nothing but running to win."

"Sounds like you and Coach had quite a talk. So, he's going to give you both one more opportunity, is he?"

"Yes, sir. Actually, it took a lot of stress off me. I was whipping myself about it. None of it made sense, and I knew that. It's just that James needs to win one big race very badly. Think what that would mean to all those people across the river. He would be their hero, especially to all those children over there."

"Those are some serious thoughts, John, but let's save that for another time. Right now let's look at the new artist in the family. What have you got to show us, Sallie?" Sallie retrieved her tablet and art pencil and showed everyone her sketch of their dining table with all the Gannon family sitting around it.

"It's just a quick sketch. It has to be filled in, shaded, and finished with highlights."

"Mother, come in here and at look what Sallie has drawn!" Tom yelled at the kitchen.

"Show him your other pictures," Betty Jean said. "She can really paint, Daddy."

Sallie looked at her little sister with her glowing eyes and smile, and said, "They are all sketches, not paintings."

"Hold them up where we can all see them."

Sallie obliged, starting at the beginning. "This is a group of kids at school during recess. This is Miss Rochelle reading some poems to us in class, and this one is my best. This is the track team getting ready to practice. That one is Coach Tiller lecturing the team."

"Let me see your tablet, Sallie."

"These are pretty remarkable, honey. Has your mother seen these?

"Yes, sir. Miss Rochelle has, too."

"That's impressive. Mother," Tom yelled toward the kitchen. "Have you seen what our Sallie has drawn?" He didn't wait for an answer. He looked at Sallie and said, your mother and I must talk to your teacher about these. There may be something we should be thinking about for your future. Some special school or another to be planned for."

Helen called John to help her; dessert pudding came to the table immediately. When everyone was cleaning their plates, a big noise came from the front door.

"Good Lord, what was that?" Before anyone could move, Betty Jean was at the door. She shrieked and jumped back, covering her mouth with both hands. "One looks dead," she said softly. Gannon went to the door immediately.

"He's hurt bad, Mister Gannon," one of the drifters said.

"How do you know who I am?" Gannon said.

"Daddy, I know those men. They hung around the train station. I thought you guys left town," John said to the men.

"Forget about that. What happened to him?" Tom Gannon asked.

"We're busted up something bad. Especially this er'en. That train boss knocked us both off the train. It w'rn't going no speed to tell of, but he busted Bob here a good'en and then pushed me hard right off'en the train. Bob's bad hurt. Can you stop his bleed'n? We ain't got no wher's else a go, Mister Gannon."

"Set him down right there on the porch, up against the wall," Gannon said. "John, get a pan of water and some old, clean sheets." Gannon cleaned his wounds. His hands and face had gashes, some quite deep. "His arm feels broken. John, run down to see if Doctor Allen is home. Ask him if he can come help us."

In twenty minutes, John returned.

"Doc Allen is changing; he'll be here in a few minutes. Five minutes later, the doctor arrived with his medical bag and adjusted most of what Tom Gannon had done.

"You did a pretty good job with … oh boy, this arm is broken badly. I'll have to reset it. Got any small, thin boards around here, Tom?"

"Just some heavy cedar shingles. John, go out to the wood shed and bring in a hand full so Doc can pick a couple of good ones for splints."

The whole family watched as Dr. Allen set the broken lower arm of the drifter.

"It's going to be several days before he can use his arm again. There's a shed out back of my office where you can stay until you get back on your feet again. Your friend can work for the city cleaning streets to earn a little money. Where are you men traveling to?"

"Goin' back to Pinto, 'bout a hunert mile due north. We ain't 'n no hurry."

Dr. Allen and the drifters walked down toward town.

"John, go help Doctor Allen do whatever he needs help with. Don't get involved with those hobos, and then hurry on back here. We'll have to wash up good before bedtime. No telling what those two might be carrying on them. Probably haven't bathed in weeks."

John was back in half an hour. "It will work out okay. There's a place for them to sleep. Water is nearby, and they can get some leftovers at the café—maybe do some work around town to earn a dollar or two … if they get cleaned up first," he added.

Soon the Gannons were bathed and off to bed.

"What a nightmare ending to a fine meal," Helen lamented.

"I know, honey, and it was a very special meal. I loved it."

The Gannons had no sooner put their heads on their pillows when Helen said, "Now what were you trying to tell me about the bank?"

Tom's mumble was barely audible. "You'll be all right. It's Chicago …"

"What in the world are you saying?" Helen asked. All she got for an answer was the beginning of a gentle snore and heavy breathing. She smiled as she pulled the sheet and bed cover over Tom's shoulders. She kissed him gently on the forehead, and soon they both were in another land.

The next week was an anticlimactic nightmare. It was the most anticipated event in the lives of the Chambers track team, and Nix was out sick, Baker was half ill, and Blue Eagle and John were "off their feed." Coach Tiller worked his runners hard and then gave them enough rest to run their best.

There was no doubt about who was the oldest, most gifted athlete out there running. Charlie Parker was not to be denied. He broke school records for sixteen and under and brought down the stadium of fans who came just to watch him crash through the tape.

Still, Blue Eagle and Gannon did well, beating out the other schools for second and third. Blue Eagle beat his friend by half a head, both straining hard at the tape. John was crushed that Parker put on such a show. He just wasn't prepared for such a blow-out performance by on older boy that he felt sure he could beat. Both boys went over to shake hands with Parker in spite of their feelings. Frederick Baker was disappointed as well. He placed a close third, behind two strong runners.

The ride back to Chambers that evening was long. Coach Tiller talked most of the way home, congratulating the team with enthusiasm.

"Good Lord! Just look at what you did. This was your first fair and your first state competition. You shouldn't hang your heads. You took three fine medals, and you ran against some of the best, if not the best in the state. And you are a year younger than Parker. So, no, sir! You got nothing but 'wanting it bad' hanging over you. That's a good position to be in. Why? Because you've got next year to look forward to. Parker? He moves on. He'll be running as a freshman in college in a couple more years, and it will be a different ball game. He's built for speed, though; soon he may be a real force around here in track.

"Hey! Since it's the end of the season, I was just wondering if we ought to stop by for some ice cream and soda to celebrate." That woke up the team.

"What a kick!" somebody shouted.

Chapter 24

Chicago Bound

The air around the Gannon house was akin to another planet. All conversations centered around the schedules of both ladies and Billy Jean. Sallie didn't lack for attention either, as Chicago School of Art was definitely on the menu. Their Saturday activities gave additional opportunity for everyone to back Sallie's efforts to show her sketches and possibly gain a future scholarship.

Finally it was Sunday noon, and the ladies gathered to board the zephyr for the Windy City. Half of Chambers was on hand to see Miss Rochelle, Helen, and the girls off for Chicago, wishing them all a big success.

Particularly noticeable was Fred Baker, Frederick's father, who called on Ruth Rochelle more frequently now. While Helen was gone, a Mrs. Easton would come clean the house and cook for Tom and John. The men, especially John, were already plotting what they might explore while the ladies were in Chicago.

Finally the last call was sounded, and two minutes later, Miss Rochelle, Helen, and the girls were at the windows, waving furiously as the zephyr gently pulled out of Chambers Station.

"Well, John, there goes the commander in chief and her crew. God speed!" Tom said.

"Gee, Dad, we have the house all to ourselves for, I guess, weeks. How long did Mom think they would be gone?"

"We don't know yet. Weeks perhaps, but it depends on how they fare in their auditions. All three of them. Sallie's schedule will be pretty predictable. We'll know in a week or two. I would not be surprised to see them staying on there for weeks, perhaps several months if they meet with success. It depends on their voices and their stage presence and how much they impress the music masters. Don't worry, though, you and I will be having our own fun."

As the Gannons walked to their car, John said, "I have the idea of asking Blue Eagle to come stay over one weekend pretty soon. What do you think, Dad?"

"Sure. If you wish. It would be a good opportunity for me to talk to him in a more relaxed atmosphere. Just let me know when. You better make sure he clears it with his chief."

"We wouldn't think of not checking, Dad. Certainly he wouldn't. Just like here with you and Mom. Perhaps life is even more strict in their family. While I'm an only son, Blue Eagle is a future chief. I get the feeling sometimes when we two are out of the city, they watch him like a hawk. Occasionally, I get the feeling that something is moving out in the woods or bushes, but I never see anyone. Blue said he feels the same way. He doesn't mention it often, but I see his reaction. Anyway, maybe the three of us can fish or just sit around and talk—cook up something."

Tom looked at his son. *He has grown a foot during these past two years. More mature, more mannered.* He raked his knuckles gently across the boy's jaw and said, "Don't you worry. We'll eat all the ice cream we want. Blue Eagle can join us. By the way, what does he eat? He may not even like ice cream, let alone our meat and potato diet."

"He talks about drying fish a lot, so I'm sure they like fish. I would guess squash and vegetables, things like that. Roast meats, too. We'll make out," John said. "It will be interesting to see his reaction in our house. I think he will do fine. You know, from the way he talks, their lodge is big. They smoke fish inside during the winter, and I've heard him talk about during the old days, in really cold weather up there in Minnesota, they even kept some of their horses inside the lodge to protect them."

"I've heard of that," Tom said. "When you live with Mother Nature, no matter if it's in the woods, the plain, or in a cave, you have to use whatever facilities you have. Anyway, you tell him your dad said he is always welcome here."

"Thanks, Dad. You know, when you're around us, Blue never takes his eyes off you. He seems fascinated. He watches your every move as if measuring how strong you are, how bright, if you can run fast. Want to race to the house?"

"You sly fox. I couldn't keep up with you. Especially since you're such a race horse for your track team. Anyway, who'd drive our car back?"

"I'll bet it would just follow along by itself," John joked. "You want me to drive home?"

"You'll be doing that soon enough. I'll take you out in the country and teach you in the next week or so."

"Yeah! That's a deal, Dad."

When the Gannons drove up near their house, Tom said, "Speak of the devil. What's he doing here?" Blue Eagle stood up on the front porch as the Gannons approached. He looked anxious.

"Mr. Gannon, we need help. My chief's wife is sick. She has fever. She's wringing wet with sweat. Can you come help us?"

"Sure I can. Be over there in ten minutes. But first let's see if the doctor can come with us. We really need him. Medicine is not really my specialty. Get in the car, and we'll go find Doctor Allen."

As Tom drove the boys near town, John pointed off to his right. "Isn't that Doc going in Hickerson's store? Sure looks like him."

"You may be right, son. I'll pull up here while you go look." Both boys ran in the store and came out with Doctor Allen. Tom pulled out immediately to cross the river, the shortest approach to Huron Island where the Eagles lived. Blue Eagle explained the problem as they drove.

When they reached the canoe, near a big willow across the river, Blue Eagle said, "It'll be best if I just take the doctor with me. My chief gets worried if a lot of people come around the house. You know—our experiences with trappers bringing us diseases long ago, but he worries. That's why he took our group out of Minnesota."

"Sure, I understand. You and Doc go ahead. We'll wait here for Doctor Allen to come back. You, too, if you wish."

In twenty minutes, Doctor Allen reappeared and crossed by canoe to the car. He was shaking his head side to side as he approached.

"She is about gone, poor woman. It's her heart. It's racing like crazy and is very weak. Not a thing I could do. She won't make it until morning. James said to tell you thank you for helping them, and he'd be with his chief for a while. That is quite a place. Much bigger than it looks. He has her confined in sort of a sweat lodge area. She looked pretty scared to me. I gave her some laudanum to make her more comfortable."

Soon they were letting Doctor Allen off at his home and driving back to the Gannon house. They saw Mrs. Easton through the windows as they drove up. Dinner would be ready as soon as they washed themselves.

Soon after the men settled down to eat, John spoke.

"I guess that means Blue Eagle is going to be up country for a while. I wonder if they will put her up on a tree platform or in the mound up country. I wonder—"

"Johnny, eat your food and relax. We'll find out about your twin after a while."

"That's just it, Dad. Don't you see? Some men are going to come down and take her away. Either that, or Blue Eagle and his chief are going to put her in their canoe and row upriver. No telling when—"

"John, I'm trying to tell you. There's more to life than you and Blue Eagle. You two have become too darn close at times. The next thing I know, you—"

"Dad, it isn't just friendship. You spent two or three hours recently reading and explaining their history to all of us. I haven't forgotten that—nor the fact that here we are, right now, right in the middle of it. Besides, almost every day since the first Fourth of July, when we first landed in Chambers, I see Blue Eagle as the best thing that could have happened to me out here. We do so many interesting things together. We learn so much. Other kids? They have jobs to do at ranches or at their store. Blue is on the move all the time, fishing, exploring, helping his father lay in food, curing fish, building things together. I think I just see him as not only a good friend, but as a project. He's coming with me, you know."

"Coming with you? Where are you off to?" Tom asked softly.

"You know, when I go away to Uncle Will's and Aunt Martha's to High School. I can hardly wait. Sometimes I wish it would be tomorrow."

"You want to know something, young man? You are what I call a pistol. Your mind is winning your race. You're rushing the days ahead of yourself before they even arrive. Now here is how your problem is going to play out. Chief Grey Eagle and your friend are going to take Mrs. Eagle upriver and bury her. They may be up there several days in ceremony. They usually take that long. Frankly, I think they will make a place and bury her up there on the plateau with the Mandan Tribe. Then they will return to Huron Island, before you can bat an eye. You and Blue Eagle will be fishing or racing before you know it.

"Look! How about looking after your dad for just tonight. My back is killing me, and if I could get my hand back there, I would claw my own hide off to stop the itching. I'm going to have Ms. Easton fix a tub of bath water so I can soak and wash up. When I call for you, I'd like you to do two things. Take a sponge of warm, soapy water to thoroughly clean my back, and then after I'm dried and toweled down, I'll call you back to put mineral oil on my shoulders and back to see if that will quiet the itching. Okay?"

"Yes, sir. I'll be out here reading my book. This is some history book. When you went to school, did you ever read how England almost took over France? They fought for over a hundred years."

"Well there you are, my boy. Your evening is secure. Do you think you can scrub your daddy's back and explain European history at the same time?" Tom said with a wink.

"Would there be ice cream in a deal like that? I could really stop the itching and stuff. They say white of egg works well, too."

"Come on now. Be serious. Egg white, indeed. I'll call you shortly. Ask Mrs. Nelson to look for some creamy, mild soap for my back."

"All right, sir." Then he said, "Oh, I saw some the other day. I got some for Mother. It's in the second drawer in the hallway cabinet, near the towels."

A good half-hour passed as John fast-read his history to get the gist of his lesson. Then he reread several parts that interested him.

"Ready on the right?"

"Right is ready, sir," John called back. He soaked the sponge in warm water and gently worked it over his father's back. He looked at his dad's broad shoulders as if seeing them for the first time. "How come your shoulders are so broad? I never notice that before. And mine are nowhere near that big."

"That's because you are not a Gannon yet. When you celebrate your twenty-first birthday, you likely will be a chip off the old block, as they say. Then you will be a Gannon. When the girls start bothering you too much, when all your Saturday nights are booked, you will have arrived."

"Goodnight, Mr. Gannon, good—oh, there's somebody at the door."

"Mr. Gannon, there's a boy out here asking for John. Shall, I let him in?"

"I'll be right out, Ms. Easton." John's mouth fell open when he saw it was Blue Eagle. "How did you get here?" he asked his friend. "Come on in. I'm helping my father with his sore back. What happened?"

"I can't stay long. My chief is very upset. We lost his wife soon after the doctor left. She spit up some yellow fluid, and then she just quietly put her head down and died."

"I am so sorry," Tom and John said simultaneously.

"I just came over to let you know I can't fish with you tomorrow. We'll be back late tomorrow or the next day. My chief isn't ready to spend much time up there with our people just yet. They will bury her up there on the butte."

"Come on back. My dad has a skin itch. I'm putting some oil on it for him."

"Buffalo grease is good for that, Mr. Gannon."

Both Tom and John broke out in a big smile.

"I know, Blue Eagle. But it's a bit powerful for me. We're not used to the odor yet. Pull up a chair. John will be out in a minute, and you two can talk."

John finished his job and left his father. "Come on over to the dining table and tell me about your chief. Is he okay? I mean, does he look real upset with grief?"

"I think so, but he will be all right. He is a very strong man."

"Stay a minute. Dad will be dressed shortly, and we are going to take you down to the store with us. Want to guess for what?"

"I know. You mention it often. No thanks, I have to run back. I don't want to leave my chief alone with her very long. You know … that's why he sent me away—so he could be alone with her. Okay then, I'll come with you and then run home."

John smiled, put his left hand on his friend's shoulder, and said, "I'm sorry about your mother, James. I wish I had a chance to know her."

Blue Eagle nodded and lowered his eyes. Then he said, "Soon after I get back, I have to start my training. Five miles a day walking, then ten."

"I can do that with you," John said quickly.

"Okay with me."

"What's okay with you boys? You both look okay to me," Tom said as he entered the room, smiling, dressed in clean clothes.

"Dad, can we go for ice cream now and take Blue with us? Then he has to get back home."

When the men reached Hickerson's store, they selected their ice cream and said good-bye to Blue Eagle, wishing him well once again.

"I'll come over when I get back," Blue Eagle said, waving, running toward the bridge.

John became absorbed by history and several interesting books that had been given to him to read. Tom Gannon brought home more and more work. They had their pleasantries at meals and chores and then resumed their interests. Tom seemed especially interested of late in the workings of a rancher that he knew well, traveling out of town one day to follow up on questions that kept recurring lately. Things still did not add up. In his mind, the monies involved were too great, too important to the bank's very existence. Yet, he wasn't a banker, a real banker with vast experience in finance. So, why was he so concerned?

Maybe he was over his head in applying logic to the matter—or was he? It kept coming back, like a circling coyote approaching a wounded bird. Then he would put it aside to address new matters that lay before him. Jim Bowers discussed bank business more and more, complimenting Tom on his progress, but there was always a common thread that lead back to the same ranch, the same questionable set of circumstances that permeated his mind regarding the history of the bank, unwritten history. He would sit on it, he said to himself, and keep his eyes open for any clues. They would show one day. He felt certain about it. "Look," he told himself, "you are not a detective, and you aren't on any legal assignment. Just do your job, smile, and be affable. That's it—case closed."

Two days later, hardly ten in the morning, Gannon looked up from his papers to see a familiar face walk by. The rancher saw Gannon but continued straight back to Jim Bowers' office. Tom heard their greetings and the door being closed. Nothing unusual about that. Customers did that all the time. Except this customer was Hetzel Cramer, one of the four gunmen out on the Charles Randel ranch. Cramer, Tom found out by reading loan papers extensively, was the half-brother of the very guy that concerned Gannon since their first meeting. Lots of pieces missing in this puzzle. He decided to just sit tight and collect them one at a time.

When Cramer walked past Tom's desk again, Tom was talking with a lady friend who was enquiring about Helen, Ruth, and the girls.

"Thanks for coming in, Mr. Cramer," Tom said as he smiled toward the rancher. Cramer held up his left arm, looking straight ahead, and continued out of the bank.

"I've never seen that man smile," the lady said to Tom. "I sometimes wonder about people like that. Do they ever enjoy life at all?"

"Good question, ma'am. I'll tell Helen and Ruth that you asked for them when I write to them."

It had been five days since Blue Eagle had been upriver to White Rock Point with the Mandan Tribe. When John reached home that day, Mrs. Easton spoke to him immediately.

"Your Indian friend came by. Says to tell you he'll see you tomorrow morning down by the bridge to fish awhile."

The next day, John saw Blue Eagle sitting on the old gnarled willow near the bridge on the town side of the Brule, now their usual meeting spot.

"Hey, how'd it go?" John asked as he approached his friend.

"It was a big ceremony. My chief said it would be. Even Grey Fox and some of his Dakota elders came by before we left and stood on the riverbank in front of our lodge, chanting and wishing us well. Up country there? It lasted forever. I never saw anything like that before. The Dance of Death, speeches, and more talks. Anyway, it's over. The tribe is sending my chief a woman to help us and I guess to be his woman. She looked very young to me. She smiled at me when no one looked. I smiled back, but then I looked away. She is supposed to be my chief's woman, and that's it. Look, I really don't want to fish. I need to take this bull boat across the river. Come with me. Then we can go directly up the meadow near Hagerty Woods and talk."

John told Blue Eagle all about his mother and the ladies and their Chicago adventures. Their auditions were meeting with quite a bit of success, and Betty Jean was a big story with everybody. Sallie was due for her interviews soon, and they were thrilled at the city sights they were taking in. According to them, Chicago was it.

"It's big, isn't it?" Blue Eagle said.

"No, it is huge!" John replied, arching his eyebrows and smiling ear to ear. "You can't imagine how big it is. You would think it's bigger than Hagerty Woods but with giant, tall-to-the-sky buildings. We call them skyscrapers."

"I know. You showed me pictures of them at the library."

"That's true. I did. One thing about being there, though, is how those immense buildings smother you. It can be claustrophobic. That's one of our study words, remember? But you get used to it quickly enough, according to most people. Same as a city boy walking out into the middle of Hagerty Woods. It engulfs you at first, and then you accept it for what it is. It's a beauty!"

"I must see it someday," James said.

"I hope … wait. Do you hear that? That wailing someplace?" John asked.

"I've heard it many times," Blue Eagle said. "It's far out there in the woods."

"Dang! I've never heard anything like that. That's a human making that noise. No wolf howls like that, and he's hurting," John said. "Let's go out there sometime. Maybe we can help him."

Blue Eagle look at his friend for a long minute before he spoke. It was that same look that John knew from the past.

As he rose to his feet, he said, "Come on. I have to get home. We'll talk some more tomorrow."

John followed a few yards behind Blue Eagle as they ran down the gentle slope of the green meadow that abutted the river. Off to the right lay the train trestle and highway bridge, and beyond was the Dakota Reservation with its hustle and bustle of children playing. When they reached Blue Eagle's path to his island home, he turned and waved.

"See you tomorrow?"

"In the afternoon, say, about three—on this side of the river."

As Gannon jogged across the Chambers Bridge to his home, the piercing, mournful cry deep in Hagerty Woods ran with him, with every step of his stride.

When John walked into his house, his father was sitting at the dining table reading a letter. Mrs. Easton was about to leave for the day. Dinner was just beginning to be served—beef chuck pot roast, small red potatoes, broccoli, and tomato salad. The men were ravenous, as usual.

"Your mother wrote us a six-page letter—small pages, but written front and back. Even a small note from Sallie and Betty J. Boy, are they having a great Chicago adventure. Go wash up, and I'll let you read it for yourself."

After John came to the table, Mrs. Easton tidied up and said good-bye. John put the letter down and began eating—starved, as usual.

"Look at our teenager eat. What did you guys do?"

"Run all day. We did quite a bit." He thought to ask his father about Hagerty Woods but decided against it at the last minute. "She really is a good cook, isn't she, Dad? And I'm hungry as a bear."

"At your age, everything well-cooked tastes and smells like a banquet. Our family, as you'll see in the letter, is really having a ball. I am so glad the girls went with them. The thrill of the big city and all that it offers, plus their coming-out party for their talents. I'm so proud of them all for taking this opportunity." Tom paused a moment and then continued, looking his son directly in the eyes. "See, son, everything is working out. Actually, it is much better than we thought. Opportunities sometimes are best taken advantage of when all the stars are lined up for you. Your mother and I have often argued about this very point. It keeps coming back. As you well know, she and I have covered this ground many times, but finally this looks like it is working out perfectly. I sure hope so, anyway. Maybe it will produce something special. At least they will find out once and for all."

John, while reading his mother's letter, nodded his approval to his father's statements and tried to imagine the amazing events that were unfolding in his family. *Now that they have found some success coming their way, where is it all going?* he asked himself.

"You know, Dad, I have another year in Chambers School. My sisters have a few years more. I don't like leaving all of you here yet, but I have to, don't I?"

"Finish this job, and then we will talk about your future, son. Your career likely will be in the big city. Probably New York. Now that's a handful, my boy. Quite a handful. When you get there, run up a flag at the mayor's mansion. You will be working and living in one of the most exciting cities in the world, at a time in this country's history that may very well be beyond belief. Just don't forget where you came from."

"And who brought me," John added.

"Well, that's right. Who brought you. That's good thinking, even for a track star." Tom smiled. "You know, John, times are changing so fast, and we are experiencing that right here in Chambers. This whole country is about to startle everybody. By the time you graduate college, time will be at the speed of light compared to my days growing up in Monmouth, fishing the Mississippi, hunting the woods there, my apprenticeship in carpentry and plumbing. Even later, during my other adventures. They are historic, to be sure, but the way this country is humming with industry, inventions, bold manufacturing, and with shipping all over the world, it's dazzling. You will be right in the middle of that after college. You'll be living it while you're writing about it."

John looked serious. "And what about you, Papa. What will you and Mother do?"

"Oh, we won't be sitting still. We have sewer plants to put in to clean up this fantastic Brule. Run for mayor, I suppose. Isn't that what bankers do? Run for mayor?"

John walked a few steps toward his dad. Then he ran and hugged him tightly.

"Well, isn't this something. My explorer son being so affectionate. You get an A+."

Just as suddenly, John released his father and stepped back a few feet.

"Dad, I was just thinking. Would you be okay … I mean if Blue Eagle and I took a small trip … like an overnight trip out someplace?"

"Like what? What kind of trip? Is this your idea?"

"Well, we haven't discussed it, but you know … I think I told you, Blue Eagle has his Manhood trials coming up pretty soon. That's ten days out in the wild. He has taken it on himself to start practicing in a few days. Short trips, then longer ones. It's not going to be easy. I'd like to go with him on these shorter trials. We likely would be out one, maybe two nights on at least one of those trips."

"Do you really think you would like that?"

"Yes, sir. When will I ever get to do something like that again? Maybe never!"

"If it were just you, alone out here in this frontier country, I'd say no. But with Blue Eagle, with what he knows and has practiced all of his life, well, it might be a fine opportunity to get out there in nature and experience it. Study the plants and trees. Find out what it's all about."

"Thanks, Dad. I love you for that. You know what I mean. I appreciate your confidence."

"When are you thinking of taking off?"

"Oh, in the next week or so."

"All right then, just let me know."

"Okay, Dad. I wanted you to be comfortable about it. Will you be okay?"

"Will I be okay? You think your dad's a tenderfoot?" Tom joked.

John smiled a warm smile at his dad. "I have the best daddy in the world."

"What if I had said no? Would my rating be so high?"

John came right back with, "Higher! By 1/64th an inch."

"We had better get to bed before all this horse manure covers us up."

"Goodnight, Dad."

"Goodnight, sport. By the way, tomorrow I'll introduce you to my hunting knife."

"Really? That's fantastic. Blue Eagle carries one. Now I'll have my own hunting knife. Goodnight, Dad. See you at breakfast."

Chapter 25

Hagerty Woods

When John Gannon reached Chambers Bridge the next afternoon, he was surprised to find his friend waiting in the bull boat. As John settled in the skin, Blue Eagle guided the round vessel along the shadows of the railroad pylons until they reached the far shore. They hid the bull boat in a thick stand of button willows. It was close to four p.m.

The boys walked slowly up the slope of the valley to the huge black walnut tree at the edge of Hagerty Woods. They sat talking and looking back at the small town of Chambers, which stretched out along the wide expanse of the Brule River to the left of the Chambers Bridge and railroad trestle.

Spring had come late this year, and the fading sun of May sent long shadows across the pristine waters. The raging torrents of spring had dissipated to almost normal. As the river moved silently, soon joining the Missouri in its long journey to the sea, the sturgeon, pike, and other fish prepared for spawning. Some schools could already be seen massing, thrashing acres of the river's surface in vast gatherings. Sharp grey and white earth highlighted the far embankment below the town of Chambers, mingling with the bright sheen of green buffalo grasses and willows. The crystal waters sparkled in the gentle curve of the Brule as it stretched beyond the town and meandered onward as far as the eye could see.

This had become the favorite rendezvous for John and James Blue Eagle as they discussed their lives and daily plans. They sat, as always, watching the far-off ant-like movements of horsemen, cars, and wagons near town. The faint, distant dimples upon the river's surface—some the final leap of feeding pike; the swift dive of the black-backed swallow in pursuit of gnats; the graceful, trailing feathers of the scissortail in its slow flight, hovering just above waving grass heads in the meadow to flush out insects for its family—all brought sights and sounds for these observers to tuck away in memory.

Now and then, the fish eagle—the latest arrival to the Chambers valley—brought both of the observers to their feet. Her shrill, eerie cries broke the silence of her kingdom as she soared, stooped at breathtaking speed, and struck with unfailing deftness a hapless fish near the Brule's surface. Then she adjusted the head of the fish to fly it head forward to her nest in some yet undiscovered snag or giant tree.

Sometimes the boys had long, somber talks about the Mandan, the reservation upon the white, striated, rock-marked butte where they settled, the mysterious status of the Grey Eagle family out on Huron Island, the Gannons, their school's future, and more frequently now, the lingering tensions between the Indians and whites. Now, just since yesterday, John looked at his friend with apprehension. They sat closer to the woods than ever before. Finally, John spoke up.

"Hear that? There it is again. I've made up my mind. When the sun gets to the top of that tree." He turned, pointing behind them. "Then I'm going in, with or without you. I'm not going to sit here any longer and do nothing. What do you say? We can be out of there in an hour, James."

Blue Eagle tore off a long, green stem of Johnson grass and bit into its sweet fibers. It was unlike him to be stranded on that end of a question. He leaned back on both hands that extended behind him. John curled in one leg and sat on his foot, waiting for an answer. Then he looked at the sun again. Blue Eagle cocked his head slightly away from his friend, his brow caught up in a deep furrow. Finally, he turned to John and said, "You mean you would go in to those woods—you who used to fear water like white death? You would go in those woods alone? Now who is the crazy one?"

John nodded his head up and down confidently. "When the sun hits that tree top. I figure it will be about five o'clock. If I move quickly, I should be able to get to the middle of the woods, or wherever that howling is coming from, before six. Those woods aren't that deep, according to my father. Maybe a section of land." He paused a minute. "It doesn't get dark until 7:30 or 8:00. I wish you would come with me, Blue. We'd be out before dark, and I could still make it home by my deadline."

Blue Eagle stood up and faced Hagerty woods. Then he replied sternly. "Ever since I can remember, my people have told stories about these woods. Have you ever seen that, big red-haired devil who lives out there? And that dog. Ever see that big, white devil-dog he has with him? They go into town sometimes. Don't you see them? That dog's got teeth big as a panther's. And that long, white, pointed nose! That thing just stares a hole right through you. They say beware of a dog that doesn't wag his tail. That is that dog exactly—he never wags," Blue Eagle warned. He was more disturbed than John had ever seen him. "I'll tell you, those cries out there are not human."

"They sure sound like it to me," John said. "And he's in pain and anguish. We hear it almost every time we come out here. It cries out for help—and no one is lifting a finger to help."

Blue Eagle exploded, "You're crazy. That's what you are. Don't you see? That's the trickery of it. It's the same moan all the time. It just lures you out to him," the Indian said, eyes blazing with excitement. "Two of our men thought just as you do—three years ago. They went in there looking for that thing. None of our men were stronger; none were as quick. Neither came back. Two days later, Crazy Dog and two men went in looking for them. They found Hoda, the youngest one, beyond the edge of the woods, out a distance. His throat was ripped out, and teeth marks were all over his body."

The Indian stood erect and looked at John gravely. "No one ever walks out of those woods. No one. If you are bound to go in there, then you go alone. I have too much at stake with my chief." He looked down and kicked a clump of grass. "I can't risk everything. Not just yet. My chief will move back upriver before long. I have to be ready to go with him. I think—"

John looked at the sun as it was just hitting the top of his marker tree on the horizon. He wheeled and ran without further argument across the final yards of the meadow to Hagerty Woods. He ran in straight on, determined.

"Go in downwind!" Blue Eagle yelled after his friend. "Don't let that white devil-dog get sight of you!" he finished his thought, audible only to himself, as John vanished from sight. "He'll rip you apart."

Blue Eagle turned from the woods and ran down the meadow slope to the bull boat, only to turn and charge back up the slope to the edge of Hagerty Woods. He stood frustrated, facing the hardwood undergrowth for a long time, listening to the silence that pierced his ears. Flush with anger, he slowly retreated halfway down the meadow slope, seating himself facing the river. He saw the white streaking head of the eagle as she dove to the river in a rare effort of missing her strike. The boy rose up out of the grass, cupped his hands about his mouth, sucking in all the air of the meadow that his lungs would hold, and sent across the Brule the giant bird's shrill cry—more loudly than he had ever known.

Dodging and bending to evade hanging tree branches, Gannon ran at a steady pace into the woods, using the sun as best as he could to guide him to his destination. He guessed he was half of a mile below the Hagerty house, and somehow he would arrive at the source of the agony that cried out to him. The forest thinned out into a clearing, and then a heavy thicket lay off to his right as he ran among the giant virgin forest and its progeny of saplings—a dark and dank surrounding that must have begun a century before. Huge white oak intermingled with red oak and hard woods, some nut bearing, yet John found clearance enough to run steadily in the dense maze.

Suddenly, as the boy worked his way cautiously to his left, he was stopped in midstride by a piercing growl. A dense thicket on his right parted as if cut with a knife. In the void stood an angry black sow surrounded by tiny, grunting piglets that huddled closely for their mother's protection. The sow's beady red eyes, the long menacing tusks, the pointed ears, all bent low before her massive shoulders, told of a mother ready to fight. She was four hundred pounds of savage fury.

With his heart pounding in his ears like kettle drums, John instinctively froze by a large tree. He held her stare, but his side vision looked for nearby large saplings that he might use to escape in case she charged. He knew he would have perhaps two seconds to climb to safety if he were put to the test. John estimated their distance—no more than sixty feet at most.

The sow's eyes wild, she stood motionless like a bird dog on point. Then, seeing that the boy was no threat to her family, she grunted a few signals to the piglets, and they all folded into the bushes from which they came.

John sank back in relief against the big oak just behind him. Several seconds passed. He watched the bushes as he eased away from the big explosion that never came. His heart still pounding, he continued his mission.

As John moved on through the grey forest, a late afternoon wind set the tall boughs of the intermingling spruce to a rhythmic moan. Here and there, limbs of oak trees creaked as they swayed, rubbing against one another, and evening birds began searching for roosting sites. As John ran on, quietly as possible, he passed a fallen log covered with decaying limbs. A swamp rabbit jumped two feet into the air directly in front of him and then bounded away. The boy stopped to dislodge his heart from his mouth and somehow settle the pounding in his chest. Here the mosquitoes swarmed unmercifully around his head and back. John jerked a small branch with heavy leaves from a nearby bush and swatted them away as he ran toward the light that grew brighter not far ahead.

Soon the grey woods yielded to thinning growth and the late sun. He was running against time. The trees thinned even more just ahead, and the undergrowth gave way to an old field, which had lay fallow, perhaps for years. Grasses, both brown from winter and green from new growth, almost head high to the boy, surrounded a weathered log cabin some 150 yards from the woods where John paused to survey his surroundings. In that moment came the pitiful cry that he knew so well, except now the low groan built up into a great agony, climaxing with a sharp scream of furry. Over and over it came, filling the woods to its borders, more frightening than anything the boy had ever heard.

A quiet moment, and then another, more distant noise came from the far right where the field met the timber's edge. John could just make out a man carrying a bucket. A huge dog strained on its leash. As the man with the big, white pit bull dog neared the cabin, the wailing stopped. John checked the wind direction as Blue Eagle warned him to do. He was downwind, and he stayed well camouflaged. John crept quietly through the tall grasses for a better view, moving to within fifty yards of the cabin.

Hagerty, a tall, slender man with a great shock of red hair, switched the dog's leash to his left hand as he approached the cabin, which now lay in silence.

"Back! Back!" Hagerty yelled as he approached the low front porch of logs placed side by side. He struggled to maintain control of his dog. He removed a coiled whip from his left shoulder and sent it cracking in the air, more for show and noise. Then Hagerty bent down to his bucket, took out some items, and pitched them where they could be reached through the bars on the door, leaving immediately as he finished.

John, mouth agape, heart pounding, crept closer to the cabin as soon as the man retraced his steps and disappeared into the far woods. The boy remained crouched over as he parted the tall grass, making his way just short of the front porch. When he was ten yards away, John saw the old rough-hewed pine structure. The heavy oak door frame swung on three thick, handmade hinges and five full-height iron bars. A window of iron bars, barely a yard square, added scant more light. Otherwise, there was little visibility inside the cabin.

As John crept near the front door, straining his eyes to peer deeper into the dark cabin to see the thing that had drawn him there, he shielded his eyes, moving to barely a foot from the iron bars. He stood there, eyes straining to block out the outside light, searching in vain through the dark interior of the cabin. Total silence fell upon the place. The boy's ears rang, his heart raced, and the stench was nearly overpowering. With sweaty hands, John took hold of the iron bars, putting his face up to the cold metal.

Almost simultaneously, amid a huge growl, a great fist came crashing down on him through the bars, sending the boy flying backward off the porch and onto the grass.

As John pulled himself to his feet and faced the cabin, his vision blurred, he uttered in disbelief, "My good God."

Step after slow step brought him near the door, near the massive, gnarled, outstretched hand, fingers curling and uncurling tightly at the middle knuckle; near the deep set eyes, aflame with torment and rage; nearer still to the huge shoulders and the great shock of red hair. A shocking, pitiful figure to a boy in his fourteenth year. As John searched for answers, there was no doubt the man was a Hagerty. Perhaps in his early forties. A son? A brother?

A calm fell over the boy. His safety no longer in danger, John nodded his head up and down as one would speak to calm a wild animal. Slowly he moved nearer the man. John spoke softly. He held out his hand in a gesture of friendship as if he were trained to do so. Softly, still nodding, he said over and over, "Friend, I'm John; I'm your friend." Finally, the man lowered his arm. He ceased growling, and the two looked at each other as Gannon continued speaking softly.

Realizing that he had little time, John felt he must leave this man something before he left. He rummaged his pockets, but all that he had was a piece of rock candy. He showed it to his friend, gently pitching it to where Hagerty could reach it. Then he slowly withdrew, smiling, hand raised.

John looked back from the edge of the grass, waived his hand in a small gesture of good-bye, and said, "I'll be back soon, I hope." He waved again and disappeared into the field. At the edge of the woods, he turned one more time and waved to the man. He could barely make out the figure of Hagerty still standing at the cabin front door.

As John raced ahead, deeper and deeper into the greying forest, emblazoned dreamlike before the boy was the man with the great shock of red hair and the long grasping hand calling out to him for help.

Finally, the crying wail came, pouring out over the woodlands in wolf-like clarity. It stopped the boy instantly, for this time it was a different cry. In that moment, it became a new race. It was the starting gun that sent him off the mark with power and fluid motion in a race with time. This time, he conquered the woods, setting a new record in his own diary. Though wracked with undergrowth and tree limbs that tore his clothing and skin, nothing blocked his path. He ran without fear, with a power that seemingly could not record such spent energy. Though forest leaves scattered from his driving legs, his memory of it would be that his feet never touched the earth.

He would wonder in races to come if this was the race, this Hagerty Woods thing, that he had to run to discover at such an early age the richest reward in life.

Chapter 26

Going Home

As John cleared Hagerty Woods, his brain numbed. Getting home before dark drove him onward. In near darkness, he ran down the hill of the meadow toward the Brule River. A dark figure suddenly rose up out of the grass, causing the boy to shriek with fright and leap in a different direction.

"Hey, it's me!" Blue Eagle shouted. "It's me."

"Thank God," John gasped, clutching his heart. "I just about crapped in my pants."

"Damn! You're all torn up."

"A few limbs got me. Come on, I have to get home."

"A few limbs? You look like a mountain lion chewed on you. Come on, I'll jog with you. It won't take long."

Blue Eagle looked at his friend as they ran. "Darn, John! You've got slashes all over your face and neck. Did that dog get after you?"

"No, he was on a leash. Dang, he is a fright. A person wouldn't last long in a battle with that thing. No wonder Mr. Hagerty keeps him on a leash with a chain attached to the collar."

"Come on, we've got to stop at the river a minute to wash your face and neck. You look like you've been tortured. We can't let your father see you roughed up like this."

After a few quick splashes of cool water from the river, Blue Eagle ran with his friend to the front door of his home. As they were saying good-bye, Tom Gannon opened the front door. He was about to say something funny to his son, but his jaw dropped as he saw the exhaustion and anguish on John's face.

"My God, son, what happened to you? You're almost shredded in those clothes, and my Lord … what did you boys get into? Your face and neck are a mess. Your eyes okay? Come on. Let's get you cleaned up and get something on those cuts. I'll go get Doc Allen later to have a look at you."

Gannon led his son by the arm to the back wash bench. Mrs. Easton had left early.

"Get out of those clothes, and let's check these wounds." A hundred questions were starting to pour out of Gannon when John interrupted him.

"Dad, I'm just a bit exhausted. All the running is beginning to catch up with me."

"Of course. Here, sit in this straight chair." Gannon reached for a soft sponge. "If this weren't so serious, it would almost be comical. You look like someone took a cat of nine tails to you. Those clothes are ready to be burned, unless you want to frame them." While Gannon spoke, he gently cleaned John's wounds with the mild soap, soft sponge, and water.

"That feels so soothing, yet it burns a lot," John said.

"Yep. That's the nature of scratches and cuts. Look at this. Hold still now. Look—you ran through a briar patch. Why did you do that? Something chasing you?" Before John could say a word, Gannon addressed him, even more determined.

"I can't imagine where you have been to get torn up like this. Want to tell me about it, or must I wait?

"You're going to find out sooner or later, so I may as well tell you now," John said, and he preceded to tell his father the entire episode. He reached the point where he left the sow and piglets and came to the field that housed the Hagerty man, when a knock came at the front door.

"Who could be wanting us at this early hour? It's dinner time," Gannon said as he walked to the door.

"Doc! How did you know about my son?"

"His Indian friend saw me on the street and said I should go up right away with some medicine for deep scratches. He sure is a fine boy. Bright as a tack."

"Well, he is that. Come on back, Doctor Allen. John is back here. I was just bathing his wounds when you knocked. He's been running through the woods, and I'm afraid the woods weren't too kind to him."

"Good Lord, John, you must have had a grizzly after you to sustain all of this. Couldn't you find a tree to climb? Look at these big ones; they're pretty deep. You are going to be sore as the devil tomorrow. Here are a couple of briars left in you. How are you under that underwear? I see your drawers are torn in a several spots."

John turned around as the doctor motioned him to do so. There were only minor spots on his buttocks, but they needed attention.

Tom spoke up. "When you get into Hagerty Woods and start running like he did, most anything can happen."

"Hagerty Woods? You sure picked a friendly spot to take a run. Pretty spooky out there, I hear." Doctor Allen continued putting salve on John's wounds for a minute and then looked up at Tom Gannon and said, "I've been after Hagerty for years to stop trying to do the impossible … caring for his son. They have a professionally run home with a hospital organization right up there in Pierre, but he won't hear of it. Says it's his own problem, and he will take care of it. What I'm afraid of is, as he gets older and older, the problem is going to get out of hand."

"Dad, would you go to Mr. Hagerty's with me in a few days when I get better? You might be able to talk him into letting you fix up a place in his upstairs. Get that poor man out there in that cabin. He's all alone out there. It would save him all those trips out there as well."

Doc looked up at Tom and said, "Well, sir, what do you say to that, Mr. Gannon? What do you say to that kind of good advice?"

"He's always thinking about others, always has."

"Tell you what, John, when you get your battle scars all healed, you and I will take a trip out to see Mr. Hagerty. While we're there, I'll find an excuse to get upstairs to see what kind of a facility he already has. You know, he doesn't leave his son out in that cabin in the cold of winter. Of course, all this is between the three of us for now. Okay with you, Doc?"

"Yep, sounds like a victory in the making. Then Hagerty will only have to worry about things getting out of control at home. Of course that's one of the reasons he keeps ole Rex with him. His son is scared to death of that dog. And who wouldn't be? He's bad as a bear."

Doc continued turning the boy around, examining him and dressing his wounds. "A few of these are going to take bandages for two or three days, maybe longer. And, I hate to tell you men this, we do have a major problem here. No salve in the world is going to take care of those scratches there on your pistol." The men and the boy, caught up in being a man at that moment, had a good laugh. "I was deliberating about how much of it we should amputate, but then, seeing as how you're the only Gannon son I see around here ..." Doc looked up at Tom and winked. "I guess we can just leave it to Mother Nature. Or John can doctor it himself. How does that sound, John?"

"Sounds great to me." John laughed. "It's hardly enough there to fool with anyway." Then everyone did get a good laugh.

"Tom, this tiger sounds rested already. Got any chores he can do while you and I visit?" Doc asked.

"Oh, fifty or a hundred pushups each day for a week for going into Hagerty Woods alone. But John and I will work on that one shortly."

When Doctor Allen left, John told his father the rest of his adventure, but he had no memory of getting any of his wounds. They concluded with John giving himself the remaining chore of taking a sponge bath and dressing for dinner.

Tom Gannon analyzed his son with two thoughts. Hadn't he done exactly the same thing when he was a boy—perhaps even more dangerous? Yet if anything happened to this boy, especially while Helen and the girls were in Chicago, he would never forgive himself. "Little son of a gun," Tom said through a veiled smile as he went to the kitchen. He was suddenly ravenous, and he imagined that the tiger in the other room was even more so.

When John came out to the dining table, all dressed in fresh clothes, hair combed, Tom looked at his son and smiled. "That's more like it. Going out on a date?"

"Yes, sir. I think her name is Miss Mattress."

"At least you have a sense of humor."

"All this for me?" John said, waving his hand at the table of food.

"Mrs. Easton said she hoped that you would share a crumb or two with your poor old father, especially because he works so hard putting food on the table, scrubs your wounds, and occasionally loves you," Tom said, grinning.

"Oh, that Mrs. Easton is one smart lady. I'll have to hug her neck when she comes in tomorrow," John said.

"Now, you were about to tell me how it came to pass that you went in those woods by yourself."

"Actually, Dad, now that it's all over, I wonder about that myself. Blue Eagle's people have nothing good to say about Hagerty Woods. They've lost people in there before. Believe me, Dad, Blue Eagle has more guts than any kid I know, but he wasn't about to go in there with me. Maybe it's just as well. I wouldn't have had the experiences that I had, and maybe both of us learned something from them. I wasn't trying to be brave or anything. I just made a judgment and ran in there. Those howls were just getting to me every time we sat out there and talked. It is such an ideal place—the top of the meadow, I mean. To sit there and discuss things. The view of the Brule, the town, the bridges—it's very special. Even the reservation off to the south. Maybe this was the one time that Blue was to say no. Maybe it was some test for just me, alone. Maybe—"

"John, listen to me, son. By all accounts, that was some adventure for a boy your age. As tough as it was at times, you have to admit, a lot of things went your way. Call it luck, call it skill or instinct. Some of those things could have gone very badly for you. Even for an experienced man. I shouldn't tell you that deep down I'm proud of you and your survival instincts. I shouldn't tell you that I've done more daring things. I shouldn't tell you how concerned you make your family, now that you're sprouting your wings like those eagles out there—and I do mean the feathered ones. There are some important life lessons that you're learning every day. If I don't get anything else across to you, remember this: helping your fellow man is one of the most noble attributes that we humans have, especially in a small town or community where most every citizen is like a friend.

"Here is the crux of the matter. You—all of us, really—have to pick and choose. You size up a situation, and you act or you walk away. If you try to be a savior to the world, you won't have much of a professional life. You'll become the rescue dog wherever you go. So, what do you do? You use your God-given talents, your brains. Slow down a bit; think about the situation. Solicit help in some cases and then act. Case in point: if you had asked me or asked Doc, and I'm sure there are others, you would have found out that Mr. Hagerty's son out there in the field is not news around town. That unfortunate man is middle-aged. The whole town is aware of their situation. What I am saying is that you did a noble thing trying to help. And who knows? Maybe your efforts will pay off in the long run. Just be careful about putting your life on the line. Think, then think some more if you have time, and then act. That's the smart way to tackle tough situations. That make sense to you?"

"Yes, sir. I guess I just got caught up in such a surprise by Blue Eagle not standing with me on this; he always has in the past. If a bear attacked me, he would jump in between us to fight it. He's not afraid of anything except those woods. I just didn't understand. And that poor man out there calling—"

"You see, John, that's exactly my advice to my young son: you deal with the situation; don't let situations push you into taking action without a plan. Even a quick plan. Think about things. Some things call for an instant reaction. Those are rare, hopefully. Sometimes that's how heroes are born. But a couple of minutes, sometimes much longer, normally won't make a difference in our actions, and it could save your life. So, mark it down. Use this lesson.

"While we are on this subject, now is a good time to bring up something you asked about the other day. Where are you and Blue Eagle going on his warm-up walks for his trials?"

"We haven't discussed that yet, Dad. I imagine we will just take off one day, walk a few miles somewhere, and return. It's not an overnight thing."

"Even so, wherever you two go, I'm not so worried. Both of you together can avoid a lot of possible trouble that might come your way. Just remember what we just talked about. Think about your actions. Think about your safety. Think about your family as well as your friend."

"Dad, didn't we just cover this?"

"Doubling down doesn't hurt once in a while. Just take care of yourself, sport."

"I will, Dad." After a long pause, he said, "When do you think we could go see Mr. Hagerty? I don't want to miss Blue Eagle's warm-ups."

"Two days hence. How's that? Gives you time to stay at home tomorrow and gain back your strength. I'll ask our chef to fix you a steak, and the next day, we'll go out to the Hagerty place. It'll be regarding bank business—just for a good cover."

The morning of the third day, the Gannons got up at seven, had breakfast, and dropped by the bank to pick up some papers.

"Good God, Tom, why in the world are you wasting your time with Hagerty? He hasn't done business here in years. And everybody in town talks about him and that son of his—and don't forget that pit bull he keeps. He'll rip you apart. Then you'll be half a banker," he added.

"My son and I have business out there. I'm going to bring you a customer back with us. We'll be gone no more than half a day."

"Just be careful," Bowers cautioned.

"That's the lecture I just gave my son. Good advice, though," Tom said.

The Gannons pulled up in front of Hagerty's house. It was quiet. No dog, no Hagerty.

"They must be out. Look! Isn't that them coming through the back garden?"

"Just sit still and let him come to us. When he secures that dog, we'll know what to do. Seth! I never knew his first name. I pulled out some old papers. Must be five years old."

"Hellooo!" Gannon shouted as the man and the dog drew within earshot. "Tom Gannon here. Could we visit a few minutes? My son likes your dog."

"My dog? Ha! Rex ain't much for youngsters. As matter of fact, he ain't much for anybody beyond me and … me and my family. You and the boy come on in. I'll wave from the door when I get Rex chained."

When everyone settled down in the living room. Tom quickly opened the conversation. "I'm just calling on folks I don't know very well. I'm sure you know that I'm a banker, but I doubt that you know about my other talents. I'm also a master carpenter and a master plumber."

"Do tell!" Hagerty exclaimed.

"Usually every home owner has something they need from me. Mind if we look around? My vice president here has sharp eyes, as well."

"Help yourself. Nothing's been done to this place in ages. I never seem to have time. Just don't make a mistake and go out on the back porch. Rex won't like that."

Tom and his son quickly inspected the ground floor, made some notes about the kitchen and the wash water drain, and then spoke to the host. "Mind if we look upstairs?"

"I'd rather you didn't, Mr. Gannon. It's a mess up there, and I don't want to think about that right now."

"Mr. Hagerty, my son accidently visited your son a few days ago. We know your circumstances very well. I'd like to help you secure your house if you'll allow me to, sir."

With some hesitation and chin rubbing, Hagerty, nodded his okay and said, "Just watch your step up there. It needs a cleaning real bad."

"John and I are real good at that—aren't we, John?"

"Yes, sir, Mr. Hagerty. We really are. We can tidy up pretty fast."

"Don't say I didn't warn you," Hagerty said.

When the Gannons reached the top of the stairs, the smell told them that bones and probably rotting garbage needed to be cleared in a hurry. A good sweeping and mopping were badly needed, and security certainly was a huge problem.

"John, get a pail and broom from Mr. Hagerty and start clearing this attic of all this debris." Gannon opened a window for some ventilation and then took out a pad and started sketching. A good framework already existed, so that was a big help. He likely could get some iron bars—no, he would use two by fours. Face the two-inch side to the room and hall for strength. It certainly would look more like a home than a jail for the poor man.

In half an hour, John had cleared the attic and started mopping. Mr. Hagerty appeared shortly thereafter and said, "My Lord. What a difference. What a difference." He stood there shaking his head and then retreated to his living room.

When the Gannons came down, they saw Hagerty wiping his eyes. "There's just one problem with this. I have almost nothing to pay for all this."

"Pay? Mr. Hagerty—Seth, if you don't mind. You know I'm Tom and this is my son, John."

John shook hands with Mr. Hagerty, who immediately looked at Tom and said, "Come sit a few minutes."

When they were settled, Hagerty looked seriously at Gannon and continued. "Now why don't you quit beating around the bush with all this attention and caring for an old rancher and fess up. Just who in the heck are you? People don't come calling around here and straighten up my whole house without some big scheme."

Gannon looked at the rancher a moment and then turned and spoke softly to his son. "John, why don't you tell Mr. Hagerty?"

"I sit over across the river next to your woods a lot, Mr. Hagerty. My friend and I. We sit and talk, and every time we do, your son sends out a howling distress call. So, the other day, I went looking for him."

"Good God! You went in those woods by yourself?" Hagerty asked.

"Yes, sir. I saw you and your dog come through the field and leave some things for him. When you were out of sight, I went out to the cabin to see him. He gave me quite a welcome, too. See this place on my forehead?"

"That's the reason we are out here, Seth," Gannon interrupted. "We don't know your circumstances, but we really came to see if we could help with your son. You know, winter follows summer as sure as anything, and you'll have to make other arrangements for your son then. Why not right now. As John told me last night, it'll save you a lot of trouble of going out there in the field every day.

"I expect it will cost a hundred dollars or so for materials. You can repay that any time you can. If you can't, then who's to know. As far as my son and I, well, we came out to help a neighbor who needs help—didn't we, John?"

"Yes, sir," John said. Then he spoke to their host. "Mr. Haggerty, I talked to your son for a few minutes when I was out there to see who he was. He quieted down a lot. We could help you get him home in no time—couldn't we, Dad? What, in a week or two?"

"I'd say a week to ten days easily," Tom replied.

"How could I repay you? You have some work around your house that I could help with? Maybe clean up your yard, or anything like that? Things you hate to do yourself?"

"We'd hate it if you came fishing with us sometimes." John smiled.

"Look, Mr. Gannon—"

"Tom's the name, and as I said, this is John."

"All right then. All I can say is no one in this town offered to do things for me before. Ever."

"Aw! They're just afraid of Rex. Everybody in town talks about you two. I've never heard them say one bad word about you. Getting back to your repayment offer. I'm also out here on bank business. You can help the most by a good recommendation to other folks around here, or when you find gold out back someplace. Now when can I have some lumber brought in? I must tell you I can only work on the weekend, as I'm at the bank during the week. My helper can work, too—can't you, John. You might even bring Blue Eagle along if he can get off on a Saturday."

"I don't know, Dad. You won't see Blue anywhere close to Rex. All his people are deathly afraid of that dog. I'll invite him though."

"Send the lumber anytime, Tom. Just stack it on the front porch."

"Okay then. We'll see you next Saturday. I'll get the lumber brought in Wednesday or Thursday."

On the way home, Gannon looked at his son and said, "There you are, son. Just look what you accomplished. Your first really big, good deed."

"This is something, Dad. I'll be really glad when we get Harold home with his Dad.

"Harold? How do you know his name is Harold?"

"I saw it on a stack of old letters up in the attic."

When the Gannons got home, Mrs. Easton had their food about ready. They went to the back and washed for dinner. John sat beside his father, thoughts running across his mind. Then he looked over at his dad, putting his right elbow against that of his father. As their eyes met, the boy smiled and said, "You know something, Dad? You're a pistol."

Tom Gannon, mouth shut to hold the food that he was chewing, started shaking with laughter. When he recovered, he said, "I guess we have room for two in one house, don't we?"

"Yes, sir. So, since we're a pair now, don't you think I should run into town to Hickerson's store as soon as we're finished eating?"

"I felt that one was coming."

"Chocolate?"

"Suit yourself. Just don't open it until you get home."

After licking the last chocolate from their spoons, the Gannon men settled down to Helen's last letter and speculated about all the fun the ladies were having in Chicago—their upcoming meetings, perhaps some auditions, and the museums and other sights that they were seeing.

"The first time you see a big city, a special sight, well, son, those moments can never be repeated. They are unique, one of a kind."

"Dad, what would we do?"

Tom looked up from the letter. "What do you mean? Do what?"

"What would we do if they have to stay on in Chicago? Would we get to go there?"

Tom Gannon shot a glance over to his son that would stop a clock. "Down, boy, down! You better get to bed, son. And guess who is going to beat you to slumber land?"

The following Saturday, both Tom and John were working at the Hagerty house by eight in the morning. After a short break for lunch, they were back at it. Tom had measured well, and the upstairs room was taking shape quickly. It was spotless. There was no sawdust, as the lumber was being cut outside the house. The room was ten by fifteen feet. It had a nice single bed and a toilet through the floor with collections below the flooring. Light at night would be by lantern only when the father came up after dark and left it sitting for short periods on a small, secure platform that Gannon built, which was across the walkway, about five feet across from Harold's room, well out of reach of his long arms.

When Seth Hagerty came up for final inspection the following Saturday, he just stood there shaking his head from side to side. His eyes teared up, but he held back any outward emotions. "I don't know how I will ever be able to repay your kindness, Tom. You people make me cry, you are so thoughtful."

"When can we go get him, Mr. Hagerty? Next Saturday?" John asked.

"Absolutely. Next Saturday it is," Hagerty replied, smiling from ear to ear at the boy. Then he grew solemn. "I just had a horrible thought. What if Harold doesn't like it and starts raising all kinds of hell? He's had fits like that before. On second thought, I guess it doesn't really matter where he is when that happens. I'd imagine he will be happy as a boy."

"I'm going to come visit him some—at least in the beginning if that's all right with you, Mr. Hagerty," John said.

"Sure, anytime you want to, John. From what you say, he might like that a lot. Might make a difference."

"We'll see," Tom said. "Well, we better head on home. I brought home some work from the bank."

Hagerty disappeared a moment and then came to the front porch with Rex, leash held short for control. He rubbed the big dog's head as he said good-bye to the visitors. As the Gannons drove away, Hagerty said to his dog, "I just wanted you to get their odors, boy. You have some new friends. You won't find many like them."

The following Saturday morning, Tom and John Gannon pulled up in front of the Hagerty house. They stayed in the car until Seth Hagerty came out to greet them, but this time, he held Rex by a short leash until they reached the car.

"You can come on in. You'll be all right. I just want to introduce you so Rex will know you're friends. We'll all walk up to the field together.

When we return with Harold, maybe Harold and John can walk ahead of us, and we can follow along right behind them with the dog."

When Tom and John got out of the car, they slowly came around to Seth and Rex.

"Now, John, lesson number one: until you get real acquainted with Rex, the first thing you watch for is his tail. A dog's tail in the air means he is not in an attack mode. If his tail is down, you better beware; he might be about to chew your arm off. Call his name. Talk to him. If you get a good reaction, then you're making some progress toward friendship. I'll be in full control of him at all times. Still, be cautious. When we're all together, give him room; he's always on guard duty. John, when we release Harold, let's try you walking beside him and up front of us. If anything goes wrong—and it won't—don't worry about Harold. He's petrified of old Rex here, so he's not about to get out of control.

"When I've brought him home in the past, he walked in front of me calm as you please. He would go right up to his room when we got home. We're safe as long as I've got Rex."

With Rex straining at his leash, the men walked to the cabin in less than half an hour. It was quiet when they reached the old cabin in the field. When they approached the front door, there was no sign of Harold.

"John, here's the key. Open her up. Harold, we're going home. Come on out, son. These are your friends."

Harold finally saw that it was his young friend at the door and came out on the log porch cautiously, shrinking away from the dog.

"Okay, let's go home," Hagerty said.

Harold got wild eyed. He was incoherent, but he talked wildly. When Seth motioned to the field toward home, Harold turned and started out. John soon caught up to him, and Hagerty held Rex right behind them. After a few steps, John walked closer and closer to Harold until they were nearly side by side. John reached up and took the crazy man by the hand. Instantly, Harold went into hysterical, joyful laughter, all the while skipping and swinging their arms to and fro.

John looked up at Harold's big smile, just visible through his long, flowing red hair. As they moved forward, they alternately ran in circles and skipped until they reached the edge of the woods. Harold grew somber and stopped.

John pointed forward and said, "Home. Let's go home."

"Hooome," Harold said, grinning widely, and pointed forward.

"Home," John repeated. "We are going home for good."

When they reached the house, Harold, with John still in hand, ran up to the front steps and stopped, unsure of himself and his predicament.

John quickly moved in front of the tall, gaunt man with the wild red hair and reached out his hand, saying, "Come on, Harold, you're home."

Harold took two steps to reach the porch and then turned to look at the black car parked out front. His expression was childlike as he pointed to the Buick and said, "Car."

John reassured him, "Yes. My car. Come on in the house. I want to show you." The boy led Harold inside, and Harold went without hesitation up to his room. John was immediately behind him.

"Your new home." Harold, stood there trying to puzzle out the newness and what it all meant. "See your new bed?" John said, pointing to the bed.

Harold went slowly over to the bed. Stood there for over a minute, and then he threw back all the covers and lay down, facing the wall. "Home."

"Bye, Harold. I'll be back to see you," John said loudly as he and his dad retreated to the living room. Haggerty locked Harold's door and came downstairs. He grabbed a dish towel and buried his face in it.

"John, don't forget the food in the car," Tom said.

"Yes, sir. I'll go get it." When John bound down the front steps into the yard, he suddenly stopped dead in his tracks. Rex was sitting beside the car. Without missing a step into that path of sudden danger, John picked up a stick and waved it for Rex to see. "Here, boy, go fetch! Go fetch. Get ready—here it goes." John threw the stick well away from the car. Rex started for it but stopped halfway and ran back to the car. He sat and waited for the boy. John instinctively kept talking excitedly to the dog, looking directly at him while approaching at an angle to reach the driver's door. John spoke with enthusiasm. "Want something to eat, boy? Come on, let's get something to eat."

John opened the front door, and Rex leaped upward into the driver's seat. John slammed the door immediately. His pants were all wet in front, and his heart was pounding like a sledgehammer. When he looked up to call for help, he saw Mr. Hagerty on the front porch with a rifle at the ready. Hagerty ran to the dog immediately in time to pull Rex away from the food basket.

"I think you made a friend there, son, but good Lord, that was dangerous."

"I know. I'm shaking like a leaf."

"You all right, son?" Gannon asked.

"Yes, sir. A little shaken, I guess."

Hagerty secured the dog and handed the food basket to Gannon. "All is well that ends well," Hagerty said as he got out of the car, Rex standing on hind legs, straining on a leash, begging for some fried chicken.

"That chicken probably saved my life," John said.

"I'll tell you this much, you certainly had the right instincts about your situation," Tom said. "We didn't even realize that Rex was out there until we heard you talking to him. You did just the right things. Thank the Lord for the chicken basket."

"Amen," Seth said. "I can't imagine how in the world that dog got loose. That's the first time ever, far as I know."

"Well, heck, he knows a good meal when he smells one."

"You all wait up a minute. I'll be right back," Hagerty said as he took Rex inside and returned in time to say good-bye. "I don't know how I can repay you both. If you ever need anything for a family, or for anybody else for that matter, I want you to come to me first."

Tom nodded and said, "We'll be seeing you, Seth. I hope things go well for you and your son."

The Gannons drove home mostly in silence until Tom took a quick look at his son, sitting in total exhaustion, and said, touching the boy's knee with his right hand, "I can't tell you how proud of you I was for the way you handled that dog and your situation. Talking to him constantly, yes—but who would have thought of trying to lure him away from the car with a stick? He almost went for it, too."

"Dad, could we go see Harold in a day or two? You know, he's filthy. Maybe I could help Mr. Hagerty give him a bath. Get some clean clothes on him."

"Absolutely. If you want to do that, absolutely. Harold will like that." After a short while, Tom continued, "There is one thing you want to keep in mind, John. We don't really know how bad Harold's mind is. A person in that state can sometimes be dangerous. He's strong as an ox if you haven't noticed. He could, well … he could hurt a fellow mighty quick without really intending to … or if he did intend to. Just relax, but don't take any big chances, okay? Especially until we know more about him. I recommend that you don't visit them too frequently. You have your own life to live. Go out once a week for two or three weeks and then tell them you can only visit with them once in a while … if that's what you want to do."

John nodded.

"When we get home in a few minutes, we both are going to need a bath after handling Harold and the dog. We smell pretty raunchy."

The transformation of Harold over the next three weeks was amazing. He was happier, he continually wanted out of his room, and his appetite doubled. According to Hagerty, when the Gannons come to visit, Harold lit up like a Christmas tree. What was amazing, too, was that he and Rex started to become friends. Rex seemed to like the company.

The transformation in Hagerty's life soon spread around town—like any small town—and people saw the difference in Seth's face. He came to town more frequently, sometimes without the dog. He kept himself better and was actually friendly.

Now, instead of going out into the valley, Blue Eagle and John did their practice walks by walking the four and a half miles out to visit the Hagerty men. That was a good nine-mile hike with a good-deed visit thrown in to boot. After two trips, they ran a mile and then walked a mile. The boys' stamina showed improvement almost immediately.

John said to his friend one day as they walked home, "Coach is going to be impressed when we tell him this. It's our road work. You know, like boxers or long-distance runners do."

"And it gets me ready for my test," Blue Eagle said.

"Any news about when it will be?"

"No. The Mandan don't give their sons much notice. They come one day and tell you it will be the next morning. They will make it a little extra tough for me because I'm a chief's son. I expect that. They don't even let you know where they are taking you. The morning of the trials, four of five men will show up, pick me up, and take me out some place. I will find out the location when I get out there. Likely, I will not even know the place or how to get home.

"I do know this much: I am to wear a shirt, long pants, and shoes. That's it. It is up to me to get home, without help from anyone, within ten days. If I accept help from anyone, I will be disqualified. That's why it is so important to know the plants around here. Many are good to eat, and some are poisonous. The valley is filled with everything you can think of.

"Next Saturday morning, real early, like first light, I am going to try another five miler out in the Valley of the Moon. I'll rest awhile, then come on back home. I think that is the most likely place that they will pick for me. It's a personal thing. Make it hard as possible for the chief's son. You can just see them laughing about it every night. I don't care though. It is what I have to do."

After a brief pause, Blue Eagle looked at John once more. "You want to go out this Saturday with me? Might be your last chance before I vanish into the mountains."

"Nothing's going to happen to you, Little Chief. You know why?"

"Why, pale face? Speak up."

"Because you're a bad-ass kid. And you probably taste like a stink-bug. No decent bear or panther would dare take a bite out of your butt." Both boys looked at each other and starting laughing.

"You're probably right, Hagerty Woods. So, what about Saturday?"

"Sure, I'll go. I don't want you to get lost out there and get your chief's new wife all worked up in a lather—her little new son, lost to the wolves."

Blue Eagle walked slowly toward his friend with mean written all over his face, sending John into laughter. "Don't hit me. Don't hit me again."

"Come on, let's jog some more. You're getting silly," Blue Eagle said. After a quarter of a mile, the boys settled to a brisk walk. "It's all over town, what you did for Mr. Hagerty's son. I told my chief that I thought I was pretty tough, but I couldn't begin to do what you did.

Run through those woods alone, make contact, and run through them again.

"My chief just shook his head. He told me that you were also very lucky no big animal was on the prowl for food. They see you running, and their instinct is that you're dinner."

"Here's my bridge to Hickerson's store. You know, where we buy ice cream and groceries. See you next Saturday—first light, the big willow, my side of the river."

John waved good-bye to Blue Eagle, jogged across the bridge, and walked the remaining distance home.

On Wednesday, with darkness nearing, the Gannons were enjoying dinner when a loud knock came at the front door. It was Blue Eagle.

"Can you come, Mr. Gannon? There's been a fire out at Mr. Hagerty's house. I thought I could see a lot of smoke coming from that direction, so I climbed the big plains tree near our house. Sure looks like they're in trouble. I ran as hard as I could to get here."

Gannon and his son were getting ready to go even as Blue Eagle was giving them the news. The three men headed for the Buick. Tom drove past Doctor Allen's office, in case he was needed quickly. They all drove quickly to the Hagerty's.

"My Lord!" Tom exclaimed as they drove up in front of Haggerty's place. The upper half was mostly gone. The house was smoldering badly as all but a few small flames were spent.

"There he is, at the side of the house, with … looks like the son … and the dog."

Seth Hagerty was quiet, but his eyes were as red as coals of fire.

"No need to hurry," Hagerty said as the men got out of the car. "I hope you can help my dog. He's burned badly. It's too late for poor Harold. Looks like a broken neck."

"What happened to his hair?" John asked.

"Oh, my God! He was a fireball when he dove out that window up there."

"Seth, what in the world happened?" Gannon asked.

"I've asked myself that a dozen times, Tom. I just don't know how it could have happened. All I know is that somehow he did the impossible. He knocked that lantern down, which, as you well know, he couldn't reach. I had taken Harold up to his room. I set the lantern on the stand, well out of his reach, and locked his door. Then I heard a big noise out at the barn. It was still light enough, so I went out to check. The barn door was flapping around in the breeze, so I locked it, looked around a minute—probably some varmint. Saw nothing and started back.

"I heard a scream and looked up, and my house was going up in flames. Rex tried like hell to get Harold out. Time and again, he ran up those stairs only to come back down. The fire got bigger and bigger, and there was no way I could get to Harold. He was screaming his head off, poor devil, and I was yelling at the top of my lungs. Finally I saw what we had to do; it was just a hope. I ran outside and called Harold to the window. I yelled for him to jump out the window. A split second later, he came crashing through that little window up there head first. He was just one big fireball of solid flames. I just froze here in awe as he came crashing down.

"The screaming didn't stop until he hit the ground with a terrible thud. I never got the fire on him put out. Just look at his neck. It's solid black with blood where it broke. Thank God it was instant except … except for that awful fire on him."

Gannon said to John, "You boys don't want to see this. Stand over there by the car." Tom herded them over there to make sure they moved quickly. "Doc will take care of this situation, but I'm afraid poor Harold is gone," Haggerty said. "His neck is a mess. Maybe Doc can save Rex. Now don't move from this car. Understand?"

"Yes, sir," John said as he and Blue Eagle leaned on the front fenders of the Buick and strained to see what was taking place.

"Nothing I can do for your son, Mr. Hagerty," Doctor Allen said, looking at Seth.

"I knew that before you got here. Nobody could help him. Poor Harold. Now he won't have to live in misery anymore. It's just a shame. We were just beginning to get him settled down a bit. But that's life for you."

"Here, Seth, hold your dog. He just might grab my arm if I put some salve on those terrible burns. Good Lord! He's seriously burned. Look! All the hair is burned off the top of his head and his back as well. It will take a few weeks for him to heal, but we can patch him up pretty good. Gonna leave burn scars, though."

"Doc, you've got to save my dog. He's all I got left now."

"Here, Seth, you dab this salve on him gently with the cloth. He's gonna whimper, but he'll let you do it. I'm just not too sure he'll sit still with me helping him."

After fifteen minutes of taking care of Rex's burn wounds, the big pit bull became as gentle as a lamb, at least around the men. He moved over closer to Hagerty for reassurance, whining and looking up at his master. Hagerty talked gently to his dog, trying to reassure him that he would be okay.

"So, what shall we do here? We need the sheriff. Look; somebody's coming. Think I see a couple of riders coming up the road."

It was the sheriff and his deputy. After a lot of questions, Sheriff Smith declared Harold dead. The sheriff started talking about sending Harold to town.

"Sheriff, I want to keep my son right here. Just help me take him out to the barn. My dog and I will sit up with him all night. Mr. Gannon, if you would, could you bring a few men here tomorrow morning about nine, and we'll have a private service up there a ways by that big birch tree in the edge of the field."

"Absolutely, I'll see to it as soon as I get home. Okay with you, Sheriff?"

"Sure. We can all pitch in and dig a good deep grave, and we'll give your son a nice burial service. Is there anything we can put under Harold so we can move him?"

"Sure, a tarp—down at the barn."

"John, you boys run down to the barn and see if you can find it."

They were back in minutes with the tarp. They eased it under Harold's burnt body and rolled him over one time. The smell of burnt flesh hung heavy in the air. John almost threw up. He and Blue Eagle stepped backward several feet.

"Anything to sleep on down there until we can make other arrangements for you, Mr. Hagerty?"

"Plenty of room. I'll be living down there for a while—Rex and me—at least until I make plans."

The men grabbed hold of the tarpaulin and moved Harold's badly burned body to the shelter of the barn.

"You and your dog will be okay? Or should I send some men out here to help you stand watch, Mr. Hagerty?"

"Of course not. Rex and me, we'll be fine."

The next morning, Tom Gannon, accompanied by his son, made all the rounds again to make sure a dozen or more people showed up to bury Harold Hagerty. Helen's friend, the Methodist minister, delivered a fine standard service, personalizing it with Harold's name several times. Finally it was done. Tom Gannon sent out a stone carver to make a small headstone. Several people in Chambers went by from time to time to check on Hagerty. Doc Allen came regularly to medicate Rex, who didn't even bark at him anymore. Hagerty, though, could not take a step without Rex walking right by his side, virtually pressing against his leg.

At dinner on the day of Harold's burial, John was very quiet. Tom looked at his son and said, "I know, it hurts to lose someone you know, especially after you just rescued him, so to speak. Don't ever think it was anyone's fault, because it wasn't. It was a freak accident; nothing more, nothing less. We did the best we could, and Harold found a lot of happiness because of our efforts, even if it was for such a short time. Now, don't you make anything else out of it, you hear me?"

"Yes, sir. I'll be all right, Dad. It's just that it's so sad—poor Harold having to jump, all on fire like that. He could have had some good years ahead, the way we fixed up his room."

"Well, son, that's true, but we have to let it go. It's done, past. But we can do one more thing. In a day or two, I'll start making the rounds in town and start rebuilding Mr. Hagerty's house. The bank should be the first one to get this drive going. Hickerson, Tiller, and several other storeowners will likely help."

John said, "Mr. Hagerty will be overcome. I'll help carry lumber. Maybe Blue Eagle and Frederick Baker can also. That will be some project."

"Good! You come sleep in my room tonight. You have the little bed in there. If it's not comfortable, you can sleep in my big bed with me. I might talk and snore a bit. But at least you will have company."

When the Gannon men turned in that night, they had scarcely settled down when John spoke.

"Dad?"

"Yeah?"

"If I never get a chance to tell you again, I just want you to know how proud I am to be your son."

Tom Gannon had to clear his throat before he finally spoke. "Well, by golly!" Then he put his right fist up against his son's cheek and gently clipped his jaw in that little personal way that the two of them had developed lately.

"Someday, son, I just hope all of your sons feel exactly the same about you." Gannon cleared his throat again as he said, "I wonder if Mother and the girls are singing in the bright lights tonight."

Chapter 27

Tom Gannon's Dilemma

The bank was brisk with business since opening. Finally Tom Gannon had time to sort through the mail and plan the rest of the projects that would fill his day. Deep in the stack was a very interesting letter. He had seen these letters being circulated among banks before, especially if a robbery had been committed within the last several months.

"Wells Fargo. Pierre." None had ever come from there since he became a banker.

Interesting, very interesting. "Be alert to any bank notes, especially hundred-dollar bills in a series DE 866 ending in 6, 8, and 900s. These bills are marked with light blue checkmarks in the lower right-hand corner of each bill. Contact Wells Fargo immediately."

Gannon checked the teller's cash, and interestingly, the bank had at least seven bills fitting the warning in the letter he just read. He pulled the bills immediately, made note of the serials numbers, subtracting the money from the teller's opening money. He pinned the bills to the letter and presented everything to Jim Bowers, the bank owner.

"Where did you get this?" Bowers asked, pointing to the letter.

"It's addressed to me by name. Came in this morning's mail."

"But why? Have you been doing something besides loan work?"

"I just do whatever is at hand. Whatever I can do to make life easier for you. If anything interesting pops up, you're the first to know."

"Tom, there's more to it than that. Wells Fargo has their own security force. Sheriffs, cops, investigators—the works. Now this letter would never be addressed to a loan officer. Never. So what's the deal here?"

Gannon looked Bowers directly in the eye. "I have no idea why this letter is addressed to me. Maybe they sent it to all loan officers—who knows. But I do have one very interesting clue. I visited several ranchers when I first went to work for you, to meet them, encourage them to come in and do some business with the bank. Some of that seems to be paying off. Also when I returned to the bank from visiting the Randel ranch last year, I was not exactly enchanted with his people. You know, his gunmen. Why does an honest rancher need four gunmen around his house? That's a mystery to me, especially if they give me bum information on how to get to a neighbor's ranch. And especially if that rancher worked here at one time—the same one who was 'accidentally' killed in a crossfire when he was out deer hunting. Shot by Randel's men."

"You know something, Tom, I respect your talents. Here, pull up a chair. We might as well settle this right now before you get yourself shot or before you screw things up around here. You would have to know a lot of history around these parts, particularly in regard to the money flow here at my bank. As you can understand, when I take on a new employee, I take a person's character at face value. You are no exception. Wells Fargo came back with a triple-A rating on Tom Gannon. I look at you, your actions, what you've done with your life, etc., and I see in you far more than a teller or a loan officer. You could run this bank tomorrow if you had to.

"Kick that door too. No telling who can hear me talking. Thanks. Now just sit and listen. I'm only telling you this because you already have found out too much about our situation. Very few people in town know this, and you are about to become one of those few. When I opened this bank in 1899, I didn't have much money. I did have a reputation. Money came in slowly at first, the cattle drives added quite a bit, and then just when I needed it most, a rancher came in here with quite a bit of money. I almost kissed his boots, I was so pleased. Long story short—he saved my bank. I was busted. Made some bad loans and investments, and I was literally ready to throw in the towel. That was five, maybe six years ago.

"Everything was fine for two or three years, and then I started getting notices like this one, but without any serial numbers on the notice. Look, Tom, I'll be straight with you. You are feeling your way along here, and I can see how cautious you are. I know that you went to Pierre, I know you went to district headquarters of Wells Fargo. Both were bad news for me. Fargo detectives have been out to my house at night—twice. The thieves have an insider at Pierre. Even I can figure that one out. The detectives don't know who just yet, but they will. They are good at their business." Gannon interrupted.

"So, why aren't they out at Randel's ranch checking out that bunch? They look and act like they're right in the middle of something."

"To an outsider, it might appear that way," Bowers continued. "Take those four gunman out at Randel's. Federal agents, I'm told. Take Randel's brother, Hetzel—retired ranger from down in Texas. Who's behind all this passing hot money? That's what we, or rather Fargo agents, perhaps all of us, hope to find out pretty soon. See those eight marked bills you picked out this morning? They are not from the same batch. I see them coming in here from all over. All the stores in town change money for everyone. Ultimately, most bills come right here to my bank. Do I have your word that none of this will be mentioned by letter or word of mouth by you to anyone? Absolutely no one. Do I have your handshake on that, Tom?"

"Absolutely." The men shook hands firmly. "What about you, Jim? What if you are the big man behind all of this, passing off money for a lot of crooks?" Gannon said with a straight face.

"Oh sure. I see you know me real well." There was a long pause. "You can't be serious."

"Am I smiling or laughing? New family in town. Looks like just the right people you need. You befriend them, hire them. Wait for an opportune time—set them up," Gannon explained.

"My oh my! You've been reading a lot of crime stories."

"This is not a blame game, not in the least," Gannon said. "What I'm saying is that in a big equation like this, it's logical that there are many pieces to the puzzle. You know a lot about me, but you don't really know me, not just yet. And I know hardly anything about Jim Bowers. Owns a bank in Chambers. Has a beautiful, charming wife who can entertain and cook with the best. So we are part of that puzzle, all of us. Of course we are innocent until we are proven otherwise. Just like you're a good friend of mine until you tell me otherwise. So, now, those federal agents out there with Randel, you ever check out their ID?"

"No. But the next time one of them comes in the bank, I intend to."

"Jim, outside of an ex-ranger, the only men that I have ever seen who strap on guns like those around the Randel ranch don't wear them slung that low, don't dress the way those men dress. I may be wrong, and I sure hope that I am, but you and I both need to keep our eyes open around that bunch. Even Randel. He seems real, yet there's an underlying current there.

"Something doesn't quite fit; a piece is missing when you talk to him. Don't forget, I spent a couple of hours with him at his home. He should have been like any good host—relaxed. He wasn't. His eyes. His body. All wound up inside, it looked to me."

"Tom, I can see how those things make you suspicious. What if I told you why Randel needs those four gunmen out on his ranch. You notice that he has no money in our bank? A lot of ranchers keep their money in jars. But it takes a mighty big jar to support a ranch and four bodyguards, which is what those men are. What I found out is—don't ever repeat this, even in your dreams. If you told it around, in no time at all, you would be a target, and your family would not be safe."

"Family? Out here?" Tom asked.

"Don't write off anything out here when you're dealing with crooks. It is especially true regarding this 'free' money that is floating around all over the state. If you can take this in, listen to this. Three years ago, according to Randel, he saw some riders way in back of his property. Sounds like where he and you saw those wolves chasing some deer. Randel went over there the next day but saw nothing unusual. Two month later, the rains came and exposed some packages near a big rock just up from the creek. He got his brother and went over to investigate. They pulled up out of that hole a stash big enough to start up five banks. No one knows where it is now but Randel, his brother, and Wells."

"So, why don't they just give it back to Wells Fargo?"

"It's bigger than that. Three to five murders were involved from California to Arizona to South Dakota. They want the crooks to return to collect their loot. Then this whole thing will be settled in court—if any of them survive capture."

"Jim, how do you come to know all this?"

"It's simple. I'm a banker. Crooks like to keep money in banks, as well as rob them. Some do. Others like to bury it for ten or twenty years and wait. People die, people forget. Then the crooks make their move. You just never know when. The real crooks could be doing time right now."

"You just passed the final exam. Unless you're a mighty fine actor. There is just one major difficulty, though."

After a small pause, Bowers asked, "Which is?"

"Could you and Mildred come to dinner shortly, when Helen and the women return from Chicago with their war stories?'"

"Why you sly ole detective. I can tell you this. I sure know somebody who can answer that question instantly. Any rough ideas?"

"About three weeks. I'm guessing now. Soon as summer ends. The key is, of course, unless they all get enslaved with can't-refuse contracts to hang on for an extended stay to dazzle the living daylights out of the Chicago opera crowd."

"As we break, two words: mum and discretion—absolute discretion. Tell no one until this is settled, not even our families. Got it?"

"Got it!" Gannon said. "See you in the morning."

"Goodnight!"

John saw his dad coming up the walk and greeted him at the front door. The boy's smile faded. "Dad, you sure look tired. Rough day?

"Not too bad," Gannon fudged, "not too bad. How about you?"

"I'm pretty rested. Hungry though."

"Oh, that's a big surprise," he said, winking at his son. "I am a bit whacked. I'm going to get a short soak, clean up for dinner. Which is?"

"Yummy! We have fried rattlesnake and collard greens."

"Yeah, I know. Same ole stuff every night! Seriously?"

"Mrs. Easton said, 'We're going to exploit your daddy tonight like no other, with a big plate of fresh chicken and dumpling and hot biscuits."

"If I had two sons like you, my boy, I would have to send one back to Monmouth. This town would simply be overrun with brilliance and finesse."

"Finesse! Oh, you are my kind of dad. *Star Bulletin*, page one!"

Gannon, chuckled, shaking his head, and left for a bath.

"Dad, when you're finished, call me, and I'll come rub your neck and put mineral oil on your back if you still need it."

"My, my, my! Where is my second son?"

"Likely he's sampling the chicken and dumplings," John answered.

Minutes later, John grinned as he heard "Oooos" and "Ahhhhs" out of his father settling down to his warm tub.

Sometime later, John yelled, "Dad! I hear you snoring." No answer. John went to the back porch to see his dad sitting in the round bathtub, neck bent forward, snoring loudly.

"Hey, Mister! You need assistance!" John yelled, bringing his father upright.

"Well, you better get to work on these tired shoulders. I'm sure not going to last long in this warm bath."

John took the soapy sponge and washed his father's back. When he had rinsed the soap off, he started a gentle neck and shoulder massage.

"Oh my God. Don't ever stop," Gannon urged.

"Lots of tension in these shoulder muscles, Dad. You know something. My daddy has powerful shoulders. Do you think I will be far behind?"

"Oh, you have time to burn, son. It's going to take you another two weeks at least."

Afterward, when John finished putting mineral oil on his dad's back, he held a bath towel for his father to dry himself, saying, "Here, Master Tom, your bath towel, sir."

"You are spoiling your daddy something fierce, you know."

"Oh, not completely. I haven't run down for the ice cream yet."

"You devil!. Thanks, sport. See you at the table."

Chapter 28

Dead Teller's Ranch Revisited

Early on the following Saturday, Tom Gannon offered to take Stanley Jones, a real estate agent, out to the Kyle Whorton ranch. On the way driving there, Gannon, as was his habit with new acquaintances, talked mostly in casual interview fashion, sizing up his visitor with each answer to his question in his personable manner. In the end, he concluded that Mr. Jones could be a real estate agent as he claimed, or he could easily be a detective for Wells Fargo. He decided to play it straight and cater to real estate questions, but at the same time, be relaxed yet guarded. Smile, play dumb, and see what happens. After all, detective work was not his specialty, and he did not want to arouse suspicions in case Jones had ulterior motives.

When Gannon drew near Whorton ranch, he pointed off in the distance to his right. "That's the Randel ranch," he said.

"Their property adjoin Whorton's?" Jones asked.

"Most certainly. You do know that Randel has one of the most scenic ranches around this area. I suspect that he coveted the smaller Whorton ranch simply as 'empire building,' but he may have recognized it for what it is: a fine piece of real estate. After all, it does follow a certain creek out to a very picturesque hill country."

"This creek, what is it called?"

"Well," Gannon said, noticing the special interest in either water or some unknown factor, "I really don't recall hearing the name spoken when I was last out here. Mind you, I am seeing the Whorton house for the first time, just as you are. I may buy the ranch right out from under you, if you aren't careful, Mr. Jones," Gannon said with a sly smile and wink.

"Oh, slicker things than that have happened in real estate, Mr. Gannon."

"Tom's my name, Stanley. Call me Tom."

As Gannon neared the Whorton ranch, the creek just beyond the ranch house became visible. The rolling hills swept up beyond in a way that immediately gave cause for admiration. Both men saw it and reacted favorably with expressions of "Oh, beautiful. Beautiful."

Tom parked in front of the small, natural colored, wood ranch house, and the two men entered when Tom unlocked the front door. It was quaint. Nice wide stone and fire-brick fireplace with kettle hooks for hanging cooking pots. An attractive brick hearth extended a safe distance into the living room. It had an open kitchen flowing into the dining room to add a spacious feeling, leading to two of the three bedrooms. A center dog trot divided the house.

"Small, but nice for a small family," Stanley said. "Let's see the back porch." As the men walked to the open porch, the scene engulfed them.

"Oh, well," Tom said. "Look at this sight. Now I know why Whorton bought this place. You won't get tired of looking at this view when you've settled down from a long day's work. And look at this big, bricked water well on the back porch. Fine oak wash bench, too."

"Well, well, I will certainly agree with you on that. Very pleasant indeed. Care to walk out a ways with me, Mr. Gannon—uh, Tom?"

"Sure. I'm with you. Allow me to lead the way."

"Let's follow along the creek toward that big rock way up there."

"I should tell you, Stanley, a few weeks ago when I visited the Randel ranch, we saw a pack of wolves chasing a deer right up into that area you're talking about. I don't have my rifle with me, and something tells me we would be smart not to get too far out in that area. Besides, your land, as I understand it, ends two or three hundred yards this side of that rock."

"You mean that rock is not part of this property?"

"As I understand it, that rock is on Randel's land, or across from it. Of course, I haven't seen the Whorton ranch all plotted out as yet. Randel led me to believe it was his property. Why? What's so special about that big old rock?"

"Oh, it's such an attractive landmark. Maybe I just like big rocks." Stanley turned and looked at Gannon in a serious, meaningful way. "How far would you say it is from the house?"

Before Tom could answer, the crack of rifle and pistol shots filled the air.

"Damn! Who's doing all the shooting?" Stanley asked.

"I don't know. Maybe … look—there they are. You can just make out the men way to the right of the big rock." More shots filled the air.

"Oh. I get it now. Those are Randel's men out there for target practice. He keeps a pretty large crew on hand for work and I guess personal protection. I saw them the other day out here," Gannon said.

"Hell, they'll scare the wolves with all that shooting," Stanley said, smiling wryly.

"Are you any good with firearms?" Gannon asked.

"I shoot a bit."

Gannon spoke excitedly for a moment and concluded with, "I should have brought my pistols. I have a matched pair of target pistols, and we could have joined in the fun. Though that might not be too smart of an idea. Those gentlemen might think we were shooting back at them and aim a few rounds this way instead of the creek."

Gannon started to bring up the hunting incident that took the life of the former owner of the house, but he decided against it.

"So the owner was shot dead in a hunting accident?" Stanley said.

"Do you read minds? I was just thinking of that very thing. Come on, let's take a quick look at something that caught my eye over by the creek. We'll talk along the way," Gannon said.

By the time the men reached the creek, Gannon had finished telling about the hunting accident.

"That's pretty much the story that I've heard, except some people in Chambers seem to have their doubts about the coincidence of why it happened—what with the experience of the hunters and the numbers of them opposite the teller that unfortunate day."

As Gannon and Jones came upon the creek, Jones lagged behind, tying his shoes.

Gannon's eyes caught the strange paper trash that lined the creek bank for a long distance. He instantly reacted, backtracking toward his guest.

"Stanley, I just realized it's later than I thought. I have to get back to relieve the boss on some critical business."

Tom walked him back to the house, talking about how he would be glad to join Jones another day if he needed additional time to make his decision about the property. See it a second time. "Good idea before making a purchase such as this property."

As the men walked toward the house, a sudden *whir* sound stopped them in their tracks as a covey of prairie chickens flushed from the tall grass just ahead of them. Both men jumped back a step, startled from the noise so abrupt and close.

At that moment, a burst of shots rang out in unison from up beyond the big rock on Randel's ranch.

"Sounds like an invasion."

"Or San Juan Hill," Gannon replied, managing a grin.

When Gannon let Stanley Jones off in town, he hurried on to the bank. No Bowers. The Bank was closed … early it seemed. Gannon drove immediately to the Bowers' residence, calling his boss out on the front porch. After a lengthy discussion, they agreed that first thing the next morning they would go to the sheriff's office. They would need him for more than one reason if what Gannon saw at the Whorton ranch creek was indeed real. Judging from Bowers' face, Gannon wondered if they were being smart going out there with just the three of them.

The following morning, Tom Gannon tried to make small talk to his son for a while before dashing off to the bank. Jim Bowers was noticeably nervous as they left for Sheriff Blocker's office. The men talked a good half-hour before departing for Whorton ranch, leaving the deputy sheriff behind once he finished breakfast next door.

When Gannon and Bowers pulled up in front of Whorton ranch, almost immediately they could hear Sheriff Blocker's horse a short distant behind them. Gannon led the three men out to the creek, some one hundred yards behind the house. Gannon was first to reach the sight that attracted so much interest yesterday.

"Well, gentlemen. It looks like somebody beat us to it. It's been cleaned up. Gone."

"Are you sure you saw what you claimed you saw? After all, you didn't go down there and bring out a sample."

"Now what the hell would you do, Sheriff, if you were out here with a stranger and saw what I described to both of you three times already," Gannon said impatiently.

"I'm sure you're right," Blocker said, adjusting his hat and his gun belt. "Let's go down in the ravine and have a look. Maybe whoever cleaned up this site missed some of it. Wild water can deposit things in weird places. Let's go up and down this stream, but don't go anywhere near Randel's place just yet."

Tom was first down in the ravine. The creek was down almost to normal level from the recent flood waters, which left drifts of small limbs and numerous grass clumps scattered up and down the banks of the creek.

"Look at this!" Tom said, trying to keep his voice down low. "This is exactly what I was talking about. And that looks like another package up ahead sticking out of that pile of drift."

For the next fifteen minutes, the three men kicked and examined every pile of drift, even the small ones, netting out a handsome pile of wrapped money. Especially well-wrapped money. Tied with special binding and special glue, no doubt.

"This is enough. Let's get this money into town and see what we've got." They secured the sack of money in the floorboard of the backseat, the sheriff sitting with it while Bowers sat up front. Gannon eased the Buick down the road toward Chambers.

When they rounded the heavily wooded turn near the entry road to the Randel ranch, they came face to face with Randel and four horsemen riding slowly in the road toward the Buick. Both parties came to a halt just twenty yards from each other, the horsemen blocking the road.

Randel sat near the middle, appearing very secure in his all-black outfit. The men all wore colt .45s and appeared all-business. Randel spoke first.

"Good morning, gentlemen. Going into town with some of my property, are you? I'm afraid I can't let you do that. Oh, I thought that was you, Sheriff. Just toss my bag of stuff you collected on the creek down on the ground there and drive on your way. That's it. Small request. No charges filed, understand."

Sheriff Blocker said to Gannon, "Cover me on the left. Let's both open our front doors and stand behind them. Ready, open." The doors opened slowly as the two men got out, standing behind them as shields.

"Rancher, you are already in trouble enough for blocking the law from its duty, now you want to lay claim to stolen money. What kind of a jerk do you think I take you for? Can you identify this stolen money you claim is yours? This stolen money that showed up on Kyle Whorton's ranch.

"What kind of bills are these, and how are they secured in that they weathered all this water? Oh, by the way, rancher, if that *is* your line of business, looks like that pack of wolves finally caught up with that stag deer. Ate some of him and dug a big hole across from your property and buried him—right beside a big pile of neatly wrapped one-hundred-dollar bills. Old money, too. And specially wrapped, just like a bank would wrap it for distribution to other banks. Interesting! And you say it all belongs to you. My! My! What will a jury make of that?"

"Very cute, Sheriff. Now throw out that bag of my money. Right now. One, two—"

"Randel, look behind you. You've got Wells Fargo company."

"Oldest game on the range—"

"Drop it up there, Randel. Game is over," came a stern voice behind Randel and his men. All of the Randel riders made a break for it and headed toward the Randel ranch house. Gannon nicked one rider, and the Fargo people nicked two others before Randel and the fourth rider gave up.

"See you men in town," Sheriff Blocker yelled to the Randel riders. "Good job, men. Let's go see what this is all about. Let's take this stuff to the bank. Okay, Jim? You can lock it up better than I can. Also, tomorrow I'll bring some men back out here and search downstream some more. That storm may have things scattered for a mile. I'm not forgetting Randel's house and barn either. That barn looks mighty interesting. That may be the real jackpot."

At the bank, Gannon and Bakers' hands were trembling like leaves in a March breeze. After washing up, they settled down and tempered their anxiety. "This money is old," the sheriff said. Maybe forty or fifty years old. No telling. And I doubt Randel knew where it was. Just some place near that rock. No one knew just how close to the creek it was. See, that creek ate away at the far bank day after day. In a month or two, it wouldn't have needed no wolves digging to set it up for the creek to work its magic. It would have just dug on in there and ripped out the whole stash all by its lonesome. Ain't that a good one for ya? Water and time and wolves. One hellofa combination if you ask me. So, did Randel know? If he did know, did he know before he bought that property twelve year ago? Or was he lingering on old wives' tales? We may find out pretty soon. Old Judge Collins, over in the capital there, is a tough old judge. He'll sort it all out. You can count on it."

The next week, Jim Bowers' tracers revealed that this money, nearly $300,000, did indeed come out of San Francisco forty-seven years ago, bound for Pierre, by stage coach, for the state banks. It got hijacked twenty miles southwest of where it was buried. The hijackers were later killed or went to prison, apparently dying there. Only rumors lingered. Now, with the find, a third of the total amount of the hijacked money had been accounted for. Over seven-hundred-thousand dollars was still missing.

Two weeks later, Gannon sold the Whorton ranch to Stanley Jones, pending the Randel trial and all of its ramifications, representing the Chambers bank and its owner. The startling news came a month after that crazy day when Gannon discovered money strewn in drifts all along the creek bank behind the Whorton ranch house.

John handed his dad the mail when Tom arrived home from work. One was a strange-looking envelope, perhaps from Helen and the girls. No, it was from Wells Fargo Bank in Pierre.

Dear Mr. Gannon,

You may have recently heard that at one time there was an ongoing, handsome reward for information leading to the recovery of the Fargo stage robbery of $1,000,000 in US government bills in hundred-dollar denominations. The reward was ultimately dropped after forty years had passed. However, your actions in discovering our money and your immediate action that led to the recovery of it has moved the principals of our bank to reward you with the enclosed check of $10,000 for your bravery and for the intelligent manner in which you faced the several criminals involved. In addition, if ever there is anything within reason that the Wells Fargo company can do for the Tom Gannon family, please do not hesitate to contact this office so that we may give it our full, respectful consideration.

Sincerely yours,

S/ Layton Frazier, President

Wells Fargo Bank
Pierre, South Dakota

The entire town of Chambers was abuzz with the details of Tom Gannon's suspicion and roundabout investigations as he made his banking visits with clients of the bank. Soon stories appeared in the news for miles around, even Monmouth, Illinois. Helen wrote immediately after she read the news in the *Chicago Sun* and made plans to bring everyone home for a break in their city routines.

When Tom arrived home from the bank on Wednesday, eight days after the episode at Whorton ranch, Betty Jean opened the front door amid loud greetings from the entire family. Ruth Rochelle was among them. Everyone laughed and talked at the same time. Hugs and kisses filled the room.

"We're taking you back to Chicago with us, Daddy," Billy Jean said as she wrapped her arms around Tom's legs and looked up at him with her laughing eyes and big smile. She buried her body into that of her father's and moved her little shoulders from side to side as if to rock him with her enthusiasm and love.

Helen rushed to her husband as Tom folded her in his arms, kissing her passionately. Finally, Ruth saw an opportune moment and excused herself to go.

"No, no. Stay and have lunch with us," Tom urged.

"Thank you, no. I have so many things to do. We go back in a few days, you know."

Finally, the Gannon family settled down. Sallie was very quiet, almost withdrawn, throughout all the excitement.

John, after all the warm greetings, said, "You all just barely caught us. Dad and I were just packing for a long trip up to Cypress Lake."

At lunch, stories flowed out of everyone simultaneously, and then in a quiet moment, John spoke up.

"Mom, I don't know whether to go to Chicago when you all return, or stay here and go out on long trial hikes with Blue Eagle. Likely, our first trip will be Saturday."

"Can't you two frontiersmen wait a day or two longer? We have to go back to Chicago Sunday. They have all of us booked on a terribly busy schedule. Wait until you hear what we have been up to."

When the Gannons awakened from a midafternoon nap, Helen and the girls were eager to tell the family about incredible Chicago. The first hour was all about sights, sounds, experiences—Chicago on parade. The next hour was all adventure in the metropolis.

"They absolutely had a fit over Betty Jean at the opera, the Light Opera Company, and Vaudeville talent tryouts. Betty Jean could not have been more relaxed and played up to the talent scouts like a professional. They were impressed to no end.

"Then we found out what they had in mind. The Opera Company wants us, both of us, me as a stand-in for contralto soprano, and Betty Jean as an active child singer in several operas. Light Opera promoters were very aggressive, wanted us to sign contracts right away, and Vaudeville could not wait to have us go to work for their shows. Finally, Sallie scored very high at the Chicago School of Art.

"So there you have it, and as you men can see, we have one big problem. What are we going to do about it? What is the family verdict?"

"Helen," Tom said. "I've been thinking about this very thing ever since you all left town. 'What if they make a big hit in Chicago? Then what? It has run through my mind virtually every day. Especially since receiving some of your letters. Look, Helen, you and the girls went to see if you had any real talent—talent that would excite big-time scouts. From what you tell me, you pretty much hit the jackpot.

"If you stay in Chicago, you have to be prepared for those expenses while you hone your skills and hopefully find some work as extras in shows, etc., waiting to catch that big break. Sounds like Sallie is all set at the art school. What happens if you sign with a company? They likely will hit the road some of the time. You have to be ready for that. Who will look after Sallie? How will Betty Jean and Sallie get an education? You will make sure that you and Betty Jean work with the same company or you don't work at all, right?

"And, finally, you do want to do this? You hopefully will be successful, but you also have options. Like time. You may find that this is what you want to do with the rest of your lives—or you may not. From what little I know, show business is not easy. You work on your skills every day, or you lose those skills very quickly.

"Then there's Betty Jean and her young age. What happens when she turns twelve or thirteen? Could be an attractive career looming or could be career descending. Could be exciting or could be 'this is getting to be a bore.'

"All that aside, I don't worry one moment about you, Helen. Show business can be tough back stage at times, no doubt, but I'm confident that you can handle that. When it comes to children, well—who's going to look after our precious girls after the curtain falls, every time it falls? Not to be underestimated as a real issue. Surely there are reliable chaperones for minors, but they must be checked out. People get busy. People can be untrustworthy. These are just some of the things that cross my mind. You, no doubt, will have your own criteria.

"As far as John and I are concerned, we're pretty self-reliant. John is about two minutes from busting out of this frontier town for Kansas City and a new life. He has family there, and he is taking friends with him. I'm not at all concerned about our son. His life is set for the next eight years of high school and college. Then he too will be off to see the world. Likely, the bright lights of New York.

"Those are my major concerns, but the real decision is up to you, Helen. Should you come back here or stay and see where your talents take you? That's a question for you to answer. I'll back you all the way, and I am not going to try to influence your career one bit. I want you to make up your own mind. Living a life of regrets is more gut-wrenching than knowing that you tried, and you either failed or you won. It's that simple in my book. So, think about it. Make your own decision. Whatever you choose, I'll back you 100 percent. We have the money to do it. If you want to talk more about it, we can spend as much time as necessary, but I rather imagine you have your answer already. Likely you are waiting for me."

Helen couldn't contain herself any longer. She rushed to embrace her husband.

"Oh, Tom Gannon, you are incredible—just incredible. I don't know how I can ever repay you, for this won't be easy for you. Or maybe it will. You are half-wilderness and half-city. You have so many projects going in this town that they'll keep you busy for the next ten years. And you must come to Chicago when we get settled and start working. So 'yes,' that is my answer. I want to do this, not only for myself, but for the girls. They are going to be fantastic achievers, Tom. Both of them. The School of Art is already talking about Sallie's art talent as if she's ready for an exhibit next month. And you should have seen grown men carrying on over Betty Jean Gannon. What a reception!"

Tom pulled his wife close to him and hugged her firmly. "Whoever said life would not have its thrills and its challenges. My dear, splitting up like this is not going to be easy for any of us, but I know we can succeed if anyone can." Then he looked down into the big brown eyes of his youngest daughter and said, "Well, princess, you have an adventure ahead of you. If you make it big time, John and I will get on the fastest zephyr to Chicago just to see you perform."

Night fell. One by one, the Gannons were in bed by ten p.m.

Tom took his wife in his arms and kissed her as if it were their wedding night. It was as it always was after an absence, an hour of passion for them both. Soon they too were deep in sleep.

The next day, Jim Bowers came over to Gannon's office soon after the bank settled down from its first group of early customers.

"I know you offered first, but Mildred insists that you and Helen and the children come to dinner Saturday night to celebrate. They are home so briefly that you sure don't want your wife working at entertaining."

The men talked at length, but mostly about what lay ahead when the Randel group came to trial. Would the trial be held in Chambers, or Pierre, or some unlikely place? It was anybody's guess. One thing was almost certain: both Gannon and his boss would have to be there to testify.

John walked on eggshells in the waiting. It was such an extravagant interruption, his family suddenly going off like skyrockets. Mother and sisters home with their Chicago adventures, Dad anointed as hero—and good Lord, why not? Excitement like this would be tumultuous behavior for any family in Chambers, yet it interfered. He had to be ready for something he had no control over. Even his mother noticed. John overheard her talking to his father about it. He heard his father's answer. "He's just anxious for his own adventures. He and his Indian friend have big plans that may come at any minute."

Saturday night, the Gannons settled in at the Bowers house, and everyone was consumed with Chicago and the found stage-coach money that had been missing all those years. Betty Jean stole the show when she sang a small, sad little ballad that she recently learned for one of her auditions in Chicago. Mildred interrupted Sallie's report on her drawings and art school prospects when dinner was announced.

"Chicken Pomodora with white wine sauce! Of course the alcohol is burned off in the cooking," Mildred announced.

The evening could not have been more successful, except for the Valley of the Moon—it never left John's mind. He followed all the conversations. He smiled and was courteous. Finally, Jim Bowers turned to John and pulled him in the discussion.

"John, we've all overpowered you. I hear you and your friend are going off soon to map the rest of the world."

John blushed through all of the laughter and said, "No, sir, just ten miles of it—on the moon." More hearty laughter.

"Well put, my boy. I was a bit like that myself when I was growing up. Always wanting to see what was over the next hill or the next river. Very exciting to a young man. Especially out here. Where is it exactly that you two are going?"

"It isn't my plan, sir, so I really can't say. It's a practice hike. Likely about ten miles. Could be out in the woods or could be the valley. We have several of these to practice before Blue Eagle gets his call for his big test. The elders of the tribe don't give a warning, and you don't even know where they're taking you. It's just that it will be more than a hundred-mile trek. You are allowed a knife, three days of food, and three days of water.

"This is our third, short trip coming up in a couple of days. I'm just doing this to keep Blue Eagle company, plus these short hikes are fun. I learn a lot, and it's good exercise. I checked the library. There just isn't that much written about the Mandan. The most interesting things are their earlier friendships with trappers years ago. Also the incredible dances the tribe does periodically to form bonds and unity. The notorious Buffalo Dance for one, where members of the Buffalo Bull Society show their bravery in a salute to the animal that keeps them alive, as I understand it."

Jim Bowers, as well as John's father, smiled. They continued looking at the boy, so he entertained them with his plans.

"The amazing thing about my friend is how fiercely loyal he is to his people and his culture. Many times, I ask him questions about his tribe, and he'll just look at me in a way that I know that I'm not going to get an answer. Then, again, he'll turn around and tell me intimate details about his lodge, his family life, and some of the problems their family faces.

"But certain customs, probably for only his people to know about, I get that look from him when I get too close with my questions. Then he'll counter with doing something together like fishing or boating in their bull boat. I couldn't swim a stroke when I first came here, but he had me swimming in ten minutes. We used to swim in the Brule every day. It was unbelievable fun. But our town has messed up the river with our toilets. The thing is, we whites are the only ones emptying our waste in the river."

"Well, son, there you did hit a sensitive spot. We are meeting on that very subject next week at City Hall. We may just call on you and your friend to come testify. The whole town is aware of our problem. I'm laying out a new plan. There's a new company that has developed a disposal plant that could be just what we are looking for. We might be on to something big for Chambers, something that will make a lot of big cities sit up and take notice. So, with that, we had better say goodnight to our incredible hosts and thank you for another great evening. Mildred, your dinner was amazing, as usual."

"Do you have to go back to Chicago Sunday, Helen?" Mildred asked as everyone stood up to leave.

"I'm afraid so, Mildred. We have a big schedule and are a bit on edge about our readiness, as you can imagine."

As the Gannons gradually moved to the front porch, the talks continued. Tom Bowers said to Gannon quietly, "When things settle down Monday morning at the bank, we'll talk some more about our future with the Fargo people."

Sunday was emotional as the Gannon ladies and Ruth Rochelle gathered for boarding the zephyr for Chicago. Their salutes and waves lingered for some time as the grand train slowly pulled out of Chambers.

"Well, sport, it's back to roughing it for the men. You're going to make it okay, aren't you?

"We'll be okay. Don't you think, Dad?"

"We should; we both have enough to keep us busy every day. Then, there's all that fishing you're going to get me involved in. Don't forget that."

"If the town lets you clean up the river, we can fish every day."

Tom looked at his son. His maturity over the past year bordered on amazing. He couldn't have been more pleased.

"When do you two think you'll tackle your next big trek?"

"I expect it any day now. Blue is talking to his chief. I gather that they're trying to out-guess whether it will be the Valley of the Moon, which is the most dangerous, or beyond Cypress Lake. Yet that's no picnic. You know, it's not like he's Crazy Dog's age. Still, he's older than most thirteen-year-old Mandan boys who have to do this."

"John, from what you tell me about your friend, he should do just fine. He knows his business out there, and we'll just have to let him do his job."

As they approached the Gannon home, Tom laid his hand on his son's shoulder and said,

"I'll bet it's leftovers for us. Whatever, I'll see you in an hour or so. I have some papers to prepare for Monday before we eat."

"I'm going to stroll down to the bridge, Dad. I'll be back before you finish."

John had not been on the river bridge ten minutes when he heard a call. It was Blue Eagle tying his bull boat to the button willows near the shore below. The boys stood on the bridge and talked family. The clouds were thin on the horizon. Only an occasional car passed. Grey shadows settled upon the meadow that abutted the woodlands across the river. The late afternoon sun prepared to settle beyond Haggerty Woods.

"Any ideas about where you want to hike?" John asked his friend.

"Not yet. My chief is trying to help me and protect me at the same time. At least that's my feeling. As for me, I want to make it a tough hike."

"That means the Valley of the Moon," John said.

"That means the Valley," Blue Eagle agreed. "Wednesday, 6 a.m., from your side of the bridge."

"Okay then," John said as he wheeled around suddenly, starting for home. "See you then."

Blue Eagle held up his hand and jogged across the Brule.

When John opened the front door to his house, his father had just stepped into the dining room. "You're just in time. I could eat a moose."

Both Gannons waited on themselves and enjoyed the leftover cold beef and fruit salad. The cold cornbread and milk topped off their meal.

"Dad, I'm going to read awhile and then climb in bed. Things are brewing out on Huron Island, so I want to be in good shape for a tough hike. By the way, we leave early Wednesday morning. I still don't know where we're going, but you can bet it will be the valley; it's the hardest. Don't worry, Dad. We have our knives, and we plan to take live willow poles as staffs. They could come in handy. Makes a good weapon if we need it."

"If you two are bound to go out there, then I don't need to remind you to keep your eyes open. Be sure to wear long sleeves and a hat. The sun will punish you. I'm sure you both will be okay. Just stick together. Look out for one another."

"You know we will, Dad. Well, goodnight. See you in the morning."

"Goodnight, sport."

Chapter 29

Valley of the Moon

Blue Eagle smiled as he came off the bridge to meet his friend. He was amused by John's floppy, brown hat. The Indian wore a wide, red bandana around his forehead. His hair was fluffed up high, acting as a shield of sorts against the heat they would face come midday.

"That should keep you cool," Blue Eagle said.

"You're early. We have four minutes before—"

"We'll wish it were four hours earlier by the time we start coming back home. Even at this time of day, it's pretty warm. At noon, we'll really know what hot is. At least that's what my chief says. Even riding a horse out there, you have to guard against the heat. Walking is tougher. Running is losing in that heat."

"You know what I was thinking as I waited for you just now? Just getting out to the start of the valley is at least a mile and a half, two and a half before we really get into it," John said.

"I know. My chief and I talked about it yesterday. We can still get out there a few miles before we turn back. We may wind up covering more than ten miles. Likely fifteen. Are you up to that?"

"If I get tired, then I'll start running." John looked at Blue Eagle through a sly smile.

"You'll be running all right, when the buffalo herds and the rabid elephants get after you," the Indian said with a straight face.

John grinned and then spoke seriously. "I feel like trying for five miles out into the valley. And you?"

"We'll see. When the sun is directly over us, we'll turn around."

Civilization soon faded as they walked past the first point of plateau that blocked the view coming into the valley. John gasped. This was a real-life journey, not a nature picture book. The beauts and the towering, red limestone chimneys seemed to form around them a vast circle that extended as far as the eye could see. The valley floor was covered with small clumps of sand hills, scattered grasses, endless flatness, various plants, tiny and huge cacti.

This was no walk in the garden. It seemed to be both a picturesque landscape and a beacon of quiet danger. The boys tried to comprehend it. They smelled its power under the early morning sun. They nearly gasped at its beauty, and like a bee venturing into a dragon cup, they could not possibly see the hidden dangers. Yet, Blue Eagle was schooled in these matters in the classroom of his own lodge as well as real-life experiences. This, both boys felt, was knowledge enough to see them through any ordeal of the valley. Perhaps.

Red sentinel after red chimney ringed them as though the path forward was more velvet than sand, cooler than they were about to endure. They walked in silence, admiring the red-rock mountains carved by thousands of years of wind and rain. They marveled at the ghost-like figure, the flat rock on a tower, the pinnacle, the great arch to an imaginary cave, the flat plateau that once could have been a garden or field, and the starkness of their red beauty. Their power was breathtaking. You could reach out and touch them if you imagined hard enough. Yet they knew if a man walked for two or three days, he might reach the closest across from them—or he may still have miles of work ahead of him.

John looked at his friend with all the empathy he could muster.

"You mean to tell me they might take you blindfolded beyond these mountains way out there and drop you off on your own? How will you eat or drink when your three-day supply runs out?"

"That's expected of all of us, especially me. I'll get an extra day added to my miles as sure as we're out here walking." They moved on silently for a while, and then Blue Eagle spoke again. "What I'm looking for right now are signs of both food and water. I see a few plants that I can eat but little water yet. Way in the distance, there are trees. See them up close to that red-rock tower over there?"

"Yeah, but that's way out of your way, isn't it?"

"It might be the best route, though. If it provides water, out here it will also provide food. That's what my eyes have to tell me. Also, the temperature drops quickly when the sun falls over those mountains. And I mean it drops."

"Are you dressed okay?"

"I'm all right—if I get food. Without enough food, you can get in trouble out here. Very quickly. And you must have water. See that cactus over there? The tall one. That's a friend: water."

"Hey, we've been out here looking at this incredible, strange country for quite a while now. How far out do you suppose we are?"

Blue Eagle looked at the sun.

"About ten o'clock. We've been walking almost four hours. Doesn't seem possible, I know, but we've both been talking, looking. Distracted."

"I don't know about you, but I've been absorbed. Still, I know it will get hot, and we'll find the going a lot harder. You tired?" John asked.

"No. We won't likely start to get tired until four or six more hours. Then we'll know we've been on a good hike."

Soon the sun was near to overhead, and the heat became intense. John was appreciative of his floppy hat with the string under his chin to anchor it in any sudden breezes or dust devils.

"I think a few more minutes of—stand still!" Blue Eagle cautioned as his eyes looked straight ahead and a bit off to the right.

"What are you looking at? I don't see a thing. Oh, are you talking about that black dot out there?" John asked.

"Be quiet and stand still." Both the boys stood there motionless.

"What do you think it is, if it's anything at all?" John whispered.

"It's something all right, and it's coming this way. It's not grey, so it can only be one thing. Likely a young bear. No grizzlies around here, so it has to be a black bear," Blue Eagle said.

"Listen to me. When I say 'down,' lay on the ground quickly. Pull your knees up toward your chin. Lock both hands behind your head to protect yourself. Pull your elbows over your face and lock tight. Even if she claws at you, don't cry out and don't move. Don't use your staff; it likely will just make her angry. You don't want an angry bear on you. She should give up after investigating what we are. The only exception is, if she does attack us and starts chewing on us, then we have to fight for our lives. Use our staffs first. One of us in front of her, the other behind her. Try to confuse her. Try to move her on to something else. If she gets one of us down, then we use our knives. Try for the heart or lower back. To start, if she does come on up here, we hit the dirt and get into a ball. Let her decide. If she turns bad, starts chewing us, then that person yells, 'Get her.' We'll give it all we've got—that's all we can do. It's us or the bear.

"Just keep standing still. Do you think you can get in a ball real quick? Lock your hands behind your head?"

"Sure," John said.

"Stand still. I'll give the signal if I think we need to hit the dirt."

The boys stood like a fence post as the creature moved toward them. Soon it was evident that something was unusual about this animal. She had an irregular gate. A few minutes later, Blue Eagle spoke.

"Looks like she's been hurt. It's a young sow, and she's carrying something with one hand. Looks like a kill of some kind."

The boys stood there mesmerized by the sight of a bear just sixty feet away. She stood up and sniffed the air, holding something strange to her chest with one hand as she moved from side to side. Blue Eagle's eyes widened. Then he called out, "Shata. Shata," in a calming voice. I know this bear. We had her in camp as a young cub two years ago. See that white burst over her heart? It's different. It's got to be Shata.

Look at what she's got. Must be her dead cub. You can see the head of it hanging over her arm, and, and … look at that. Her hand is missing. She must have been trapped." He continued calling her name. She was confused, continuing to look from side to side, but she stood still. Then she walked right at them.

"Lay down quick."

John hit the dirt fast and rolled up into a ball. Blue Eagle stood there a minute and then took two quick steps to the right to lure the bear to him. Then he quickly hit the dirt. It didn't work. Shata chose John, who froze and waited. It would come any minute, just like the razor strap that his father held over his buttocks that day he was late getting home. *It will come. First the pain and then the blood. Any minute now.*

His heart raced like a pounding hammer. Shata sniffed him. She moaned. She smelled awful. She dropped the dead cub and tried to roll the boy over, raking his back with her sharp claws in the process. The pain brought a teeth-clenching grimace from John, but he lay frozen as his friend instructed. Both boys curled tightly, laying perfectly still. Then the bear groaned again. Suddenly she tried vigorously to roll John over, causing him to cry out. Blue Eagle grabbed his staff and hit the bear hard on the butt, yelling her name.

"Hit her nose, her legs—any place. Stay on that side." The bear knocked Blue Eagle down hard and was on him instantly as John closed on her, whacking her rump hard with his green willow staff, causing the bear to come back on him—mouth agape and angry, yowling, allowing Blue Eagle to spring up and lash into her back legs and rump.

This time, the bear decided to give in. She retreated a few yards and growled in a distressing moan, leaving the dead baby behind. The boys faced her. They stood apart just a few feet, half bent over, staffs at the ready in case she charged them again.

"Keep facing her. Step back slowly. Don't run. Whatever you do, stay beside me. Let her decide. Blue Eagle called her name softly as the boys slowly backed away. When they were several yards back, the bear sniffed the air, put her nose to the valley floor, and moved slowly to the cub. She sniffed it several times and then lay beside it and began to eat.

The boys kept backing away, slowly, steadily. By the time Shata finished eating her cub, the boys were fifty yards away, steadily backing up, waiting anxiously to see what the bear's next move would be. When she turned and starting her three-legged journey toward the green patch that lay toward the mountains, the boys gulped and almost sank to the ground.

They stopped and watched her every move, now in search of water. Finally, as Blue Eagle felt the danger pass, he motioned his friend to turn and walk toward home.

"Just walk naturally. Don't run." When the battered boys had walked a safe distance away from the bear scene, Blue Eagle continued.

"Stop here a minute and let me see your back. Man, she raked her claws into you good. These marks are pretty deep. We only have a little water, and we need that for drinking. Look! Here's what my tribe does when we have no water. It may help, and we need to clean up these wounds. It may sound crazy, but just do what I tell you." John looked at his friend quizzically, but he pretty much knew what was coming.

"Pull your shirt out and ease it up over your head so you won't get splattered. Get down on your hands and knees and lean a little away from me."

"You're going to pee on those wounds, right?"

"Yes, we have to get them cleaned up, and they say urine helps keep away infection."

"All right, have at if you think it will do any good. I'll go see the doctor when we get to town."

When they had finished cleaning up John's wounds with his friend's urine, the hot valley sun soon evaporated all the moisture. John put his ripped shirt back on and …

"My hat! I left my hat back there. It will just stay there. I'm sure not going back after it." Blue Eagle didn't say anything. He checked behind them to make sure that Shata was still on course toward the mountains.

"The urine made the burning wounds settle down quite a bit. How many claw marks are there? Feels like they're all over my back."

"Pretty much," Blue Eagle answered. "Maybe a dozen or so. You'll be sore for a while; that's for sure. You'll have some battle scars to show our class when you tell them you've been wrestling a bear out in the Valley of The Moon."

"I'm not thinking of that just yet. Are you sure she's out of sight?"

"I don't see any sign of her, so I think we can just keep walking."

The boys walked steadily in silence for quite a time, and then John asked, "Was that a rifle shot I heard?"

"Yes. Hunters got her, most likely. I hope so. She can't live like that."

"Our bear? You think it was our bear?" John asked.

"I sure hope so. She was in bad condition. That foot of hers! She may make it, or she might get a big infection. Looked like she gnawed it off herself to get out of a trap. She had a cub to feed. An animal will do anything to get back to her babies."

"She wouldn't live with just three legs to run on, would she?

"You never know," Blue Eagle said. "She would have a hard time running down game or defending herself from danger. Anyway, let's hope some hunters shot her. She was such a pretty young animal when I knew her upriver. Almost tame. She was just in no condition to remember me here. Or maybe she did just a little. Slowed her up. Might have helped us. We were lucky as hell."

The boys walked steadily onward. No one spoke for a few minutes.

"Can you imagine if you were out here alone? That would be a disaster! And you are going to be out here for ten days. How are you going to do that, James?"

"That's why we're out here practicing, so I can get in shape. I'm not nearly as worried about the daytime as I am about the cold nights. Then again, my people might decide at the last minute to carry me seventy-five miles beyond Cypress Lake. You just can't know for sure. I have no choice. Just train and be ready for wherever they take me. Deep down, though, I feel it will be out past those red-rock mountains behind us. Way beyond that far pinnacle sticking up out there. You can see a long way out here, but you can't begin to see a hundred miles."

An hour passed, and soon, two.

"You look tired; you doing okay?"

"Not real bad. My back hurts some every time I swing my arms. Scabbing over, no doubt. My legs are heavier than I thought they would be, but I'm going to make it okay."

"I'll talk to you a bit about my people. It's private. Just between you and me."

"That's all right with me. If we can't trust each other, then who can we trust?"

"You know where my people live, upriver on White Rock Point, but you know very little about our customs. When my chief led us out of Wyoming, I was just three or four years old. We had to find someplace safe. We found it here on the Brule. Things went well for a while, and then the boredom started driving everybody crazy. Sure, the men got to hunt now and then. We have plenty of ducks and geese to hunt, but the big game is gone. The buffalo was our life. The point gives our people great protection. There is only one entrance to our lodges—the lower side of point. We feel safe, but what good is that if there's nothing to do?

"The problems started with that. Then when Grey Eagle wanted our men to give up our annual Sky Flying and dance the Sun Dance without it, there was almost a revolt. 'Give up Sky Flying? Never! We can't do that. A warrior can't get into the Bull Buffalo Society without it.' It really caught my chief by surprise. There were days and days of negotiation. The senior men wouldn't budge. Wouldn't think of it. 'Give up that custom? Then what else will you think of for us to give up?' they all said. 'What else?'

“Grey Eagle complained that it was too barbaric, too dangerous to their health. Some men died after each ceremony. ‘Well’, they argued, ‘those people were weak. They weren’t men. Mandan men are Sky Flyers or we are nothing.’ They stood their ground no matter what my chief said. They had never defied him before with such hostility. He has always been their leader. Always respected. Finally, after several weeks, he told them he was going away with his family, and he would not be back until he received a sign—a blue eagle would come and build a nest at his new home. Then he would come back to talk again. He warned them of the dangers of this ancient ceremony and pointed out how they were the last of the Mandan Nation, how their numbers were falling. At this rate, they would soon be no more.

“Then he packed his things and took his woman and me to live on Huron Island. We’ve been there six years already. It’s a happy place for me, but I see it coming to an end. Last month, a huge eagle did come to our home. Built a nest on that big dead tree at the end of Huron Island. She is solid blue. ‘She is the sign,’ my chief says. Now he must plan to return to White Rock Point.”

They walked on mostly in silence. Perhaps a mile or more. John glanced at his friend from time to time. Nothing. Then he said, “Let’s stop here a moment.” He wiped his face and neck. Both boys relieved themselves.

“Do you have water left to drink,” Blue Eagle asked.

“A little.”

“Then swallow it. It does you no good on your hip.”

Then Blue Eagle added, “Do you understand what I’m telling you?”

“Very much,” John said. Your people are in a hell of a situation. I can only imagine how you and your chief must feel. Without knowing any part of your story, Blue, I have always looked at you in two ways. One is that you are my best friend. You’ve made Chambers a special place for me. An exciting place. Just look at all the things you’ve taught me—things we taught each other. And that's why I talked to your chief about your future."

"You talked ... when was that?"

"I went by and called out for you from the far shore near your lodge. Your dad—your chief came out, and when he yelled over to me that you were out training, I asked if I could come over. He turned and walked away toward the lodge. As I was leaving, he called me back. Then he came over in a canoe. He took me back to Huron Island and walked me down the short distance to the tip at the sandy beach, near the big dead tree. We stood for a while, and then we sat in the sand and continued talking. I told him again that next year I would be leaving for high school in Kansas City.

"I told him I wanted to come back a week or two afterward and get you. Take you back with me to school ... and beyond. He said, 'I expected that for some time. I have planned for that.' He complimented me in Indian and English, much of which I did not understand, but I thanked him. I told him that I would make sure that you graduated. That you would be a track star and bring honor to the school and to the Mandan people. He shook my hand and said that he would be very pleased. He said, 'That way, my son will marry, have a family, and go out into the world, carry on the Mandan Nation in the white world.'

"Then we walked back to the canoe. As he paddled me to shore, he said, 'Then it is done, Little Chief. It is done.' He made a faint smile. I thanked him as he climbed in the canoe. I was so sad for a while, I almost cried. Then I realized that all the good that will come to you will repay your chief's sacrifice a hundred times, if not a thousand. And you will live a rich life. Someday I think you will want to come back here and help build schools for your people, all of the Indians around here. It may be too late for most of the Mandan up there on the point, but there are two reservations sitting right here near us that are just waiting. It could be your final work in life, something your people will talk about the rest of their lives."

"And you, Little Chief? What are you going to be doing?"

"Same as you. High school, college, work. I will write. You will build tall buildings in New York and then you come back here and build schools."

Blue Eagle shook his head and walked on toward home.

"Wait up. Not so fast. One last look. Come here and see this." As the Indian returned to the same spot, John pointed to the great red butte closest to them. A gentle slope ran from the rich red wall of the chimney formation down to the valley floor. A few small trees stretched parallel before the thin strip of green that kissed the slope. "See that chimney there?" John pointed out the powerful image. "When you look at that sight, what do you see? What do you imagine was here long before us?"

"I see Indian scouts on horses in the valley below the chimney. I see soldiers riding out of the trees attacking them. What do you see?"

"I see a caravan of white settlers moving their wagons through that beautiful land in a long journey to California. I see many Indians on horses charging down on them from the trees where they were waiting."

The boys looked at each other, nodded and walked toward home. In a while, John spoke again.

"One day, I hope we come out here again, perhaps in a new car. We will show your family the place where we decided that you would walk out into a new world."

"One day, perhaps," Blue Eagle said.

When they reached town, Blue Eagle spotted Doctor Allen going into Hickerson's store. He insisted on dropping John off for treatment while Blue Eagle went to get John's father. Before they reached the store, however, Tom Gannon came down the road from his home and yelled to them to wait up. He was pretty anxious when he realized that his son was leaning on Blue Eagle a little for support. John was tired and ached all over. His face grew red and very warm.

Tom Gannon spoke and grew grim as he saw his son's shredded shirt and general condition.

"My Lord, son, what has happened to you? Let me see your back."

Doctor Allen saw them immediately as he came out of the grocery store. Realizing there was trouble, he rushed to them.

"Let's get him over to my office right away, Tom. You boys been out fighting wild cats, have you?"

"No. sir, a bear jumped us. She couldn't get me turned over, but she raked me pretty hard with her paw."

"That she did, young man," Doctor Allen said.

As everyone settled down in the doctor's office, Doctor Allen tried to ease John's shirt off to clean his wounds. Blue Eagle excused himself and hurried home to his family before they grew overly concerned.

"Oooh," Doctor Allen said. "Some of these are pretty nasty. We'll have to get them cleaned and dressed so this bear wrestler can go home to eat and rest up. Tom, get him some ice tea from the ice box. He must be dry as a desert weed."

As John turned the glass of tea up to swallow the whole thing, his father took it from him abruptly.

"Not all of it. You'll lose it all as soon as you drain the glass. Here, now; sip a bit at a time. Rest between sips," Tom said.

After Doctor Allen dampened John's wounds where the blood had coagulated, holding the shirt bondage, he was able to gently remove the cloth from the dozen or so wounds so he could clean them, apply some iodine and ointment, and then dress them individually.

"Tom, keep an eye on these wounds. If they get red around the edges, bring him back in here right away. Otherwise I'll see you in two days so we can apply new dressings."

"Doctor, can you stay here with John? I'll run get the car. That hill is pretty tough in his condition."

"No, Dad, I can make it. The tea gave me a good burst of energy. I didn't realize we ran out of water some distance before we reached town."

"Okay, then. If you think you're up to it, I'll walk you home. Thanks, Doc. See you in a few days. Let's see how you're walking this small hill, sport. You've been through quite a bit of excitement, not to mention a very long walk, which you are not used to at all."

"I know, Dad, we did stretch things out a bit, but I'm okay. I feel better now."

On the way home, John told his father all about what they had been through. How Blue Eagle laid out the whole battle plan when he spotted trouble approaching in the distance, the young female, perhaps two hundred pounds, her dead cub, her missing paw.

"Good Lord! You boys were mighty lucky. Still, your friend sure gave you some good advice. Probably saved you from a deadly mauling, even at the hands of a young bear. Sounds like she was in a daze from lack of food. Just no telling. Your curling up for protection and then using your poles to whip her was a darn good tactic. Two of you attacking like that caused her to back off. You were lucky again in that she had her dead cub to eat. She must have been unable to hunt. Probably starving. Desperate. Here's our door."

John was leaning on his dad a great deal by the time they reached the front door to their home. Tom stood his son up against the side of the house near the door. As he turned to open the door, he saw his son sinking from the corner of his eye. Tom barely reached the boy before he slid down the wall to the floor of the front porch. In a single motion, he hoisted his son to his shoulder and carried him into his big bedroom for the night. John was white as a sheet. Tom changed the boy's clothes and underwear into clean under garments for the night. In the morning, he would get a gentle bath and some solid food. Right now, he prepared a cup of broth and crackers. Later, perhaps a glass of milk would work well for his tender stomach.

Tom pulled up an easy chair. He put a damp cloth on John's forehead, seated himself beside his son, and checked him from time to time for temperature. John was simply spent. He slept soundly. His breathing was normal, so Tom, feeling his own need of nourishment, went to the kitchen to see what the cook had left them for dinner. Pot roast from the day before. It was on the stove and just the right warmth for eating. Green beans and fresh bread were ready. The bunt cake, seasoned throughout with black walnuts, looked inviting.

Shortly, Tom was back to check on his son. John was deep into sleep, so the father covered him lightly and brought in some papers to peruse before joining his son for some much needed sleep.

The next morning when John awoke, he ached in every joint. In the night, he instinctively lay on his side to keep off his wounds. He had never been this exhausted in his life. According to his father, he would learn from it. He would make it a point to stay in better condition. He grinned widely as he recalled his father's advice, given with a wink: "When you are out on a trek like that, it's better not to tangle with bears."

John saw his father off to work and settled down to read and take it easy. For every line he read, he replayed yesterday's adventure for half an hour. Over and over, it gripped him. Were he and his friend just lucky, or did they react skillfully to save their lives?

What lies ahead for Blue Eagle if his people chose this dangerous land to test his survival skills—sometimes fresh, sometimes hungry and weak? Finally he lay down with the thought constantly running through his mind. He counted the red chimneys as they loomed up out in the valley until they poked up through the clouds that engulfed them. A long, strung-out, herd of bison moved ever closer. A group of bears seemed to herd them. Bears grew closer to him as he lay on the valley floor tucked into a tight ball. A mother bear, whining, rocked him back and forth, trying to turn him over. He exploded upright to find himself caught in the gentle grip of his father.

"Wake up, son. You're mumbling in your sleep. Come on, let's have some lunch."

John rubbed his eyes to get fully awake. His father stood before him. Mrs. Eaton was bringing food to the table.

"Oh, Dad, I was really out of it. I was having a horrible dream of being trapped out there in the valley."

"You really were in the middle of it. You were rolled up in a tight knot. I shook you several times, but all I got out of you was a groan. Take a minute to wake up and then go wash your hands and face. We'll have lunch together. Mrs. Eaton has made some nice sandwiches and tea."

Soon Tom and his son were seated at the table eating. John's head was still dull from sleep, and his stomach both growled and slept at the same time. Soon, after a swallow of cold ice tea, he started to eat a bit, his body more relaxed.

"You were a lot more tired, I should say exhausted, than you thought you were. How many miles did you men walk?"

"We set out to cover about ten miles, but it's two miles from the bridge just to get into the valley. Then we walked until about noon, the best I could tell. Blue Eagle was our clock. The thing was, we lost some time when she, our bear, was first spotted way out toward the mountains. Blue advised us to stand our ground. This took a while. Seemed like forever. It also took a lot of energy out of us, at least me. He's in a lot better condition than I am, that's for sure. He came through this quite well, I thought. Of course he didn't get mauled."

"We'll have to watch those claw marks carefully. When we finish lunch, let's remove your shirt to see how you're holding up. If any infection starts to get hold of you, we'll go back to see Doctor Allen right away. You stick around the house. Don't take off any place. Let your friend come here, if he wishes."

The men finished their lunch. Tom checked his watch, but he knew that thirty minutes had already past. He stood up as he finished wiping his mouth with a napkin. He looked at his son and put his hand on the boy's shoulder. As John looked up, his father said, "I'm proud of you for the way you handled yourself out there with that bear. That was pretty impressive. Pretty scary, too. I'm just thankful you got home with only a back full of claw marks, bad as they are. Still, it could have been so much worse—for both of you.

"Just take it easy and get rested. You need it. Your wounds looked okay just now. We'll check them again when I get home from work. By the way, we'll keep this to ourselves. Your mother would go off like a skyrocket if we told her. We'll tell her when they come home on their next trip."

Chapter 30

"Detective" Gannon

John Gannon had long since recovered from his Valley of the Moon trek; now he and Blue Eagle ran with the wind. They fished, sat below Haggerty Woods, looking at the Brule, talked about the problems in their lives, and enjoyed many river trips out in the bull boat. John was beginning to learn how to pull the oar through the water, curling it accurately to move the round craft forward, gaining a certain satisfaction out of his new skill. They spoke of Cypress Lake, but John sensed he should not press the subject. *The timing doesn't feel right. Not just yet,* he thought. Blue Eagle's solemn face told him, "Forget it for now; let it unfold naturally."

By midweek, there were some new men in town—a lot of new men. Almost immediately, Tom Gannon asked Jim Bowers if he had any news. Then they came to the bank. Three at first, and then three more. There were at least a half-dozen more moving about town. They had not been in the bank long when Jim Bowers came to the door and asked Gannon to step inside his office. The men introduced themselves as detectives from Wells Fargo. They closed the door and spent the morning discussing the details of Tom's experience out at the Kyle Whorton ranch. It seemed they were almost in cross-examining mode with any person who was involved.

During the questioning of Gannon, they asked twice, "Did you ever hear mentioned, or do you know anything about the name Rockbarn?"

"I know that name from one of our bank files, I can say for certain. It belongs to a rancher named Randel. Yes, I'm sure it's his file. There is a sheet of paper in his folder that's titled Rockbarn. Rather strange, as I recall, as there was very little on the page, yet there it was in a folder titled Important Papers, commonly used for deeds of trust, titles, etc."

"We would like to see that file."

"Sure. Just me give me a minute." Tom produced the Randel file, but there was no such letter or pamphlet in it. As he searched, one of the detectives said, "Is this the paper?" The detective showed it to Gannon.

"Yes, that's it. What's all the fuss about this?"

"You tell us, Mr. Gannon."

"Means absolutely nothing to me," Gannon said. "The first time I saw it was right after that so-called shootout Randel had with us, when he blocked the road from the sheriff and me as we tried to return to town last week. Just out of curiosity, I examined Randel's files to see if anything interesting showed up. That paper you're holding is strange. *What's the significance of it?* I thought. There is so little printed on it. What really piqued my interest is the title Rockbarn. Is it a man's name, a court case, a place? Or maybe it's a code. Strange."

"Anything else, Mr. Gannon?"

"My opinion? Well, gentlemen, I look at it this way. As a banker, I first want to know if any of his loans are in jeopardy, and secondly, does it have anything to do with my client's honesty or status as a good client. As a citizen and relatively new banker, I want to know why have I been suspicious of Randel and his ranch-hand bodyguards ever since my first visit to his ranch. Four, guns-slung-low men on the front porch when a lone banker drives up to say hello? Doesn't make sense! And now we know why. We just don't know how deeply involved he is in this case."

The questioning continued. The lead Fargo detective spoke.

"Tell us, Mr. Gannon, what were you doing out at the Whorton ranch in the first place?"

"It's my job to be out there. Whorton was killed in a hunting accident, but we—the bank, that is—have rights to a good chunk of his property. I have to know my client's property. I was right next door calling on Randel's ranch, so I thought it prudent use of my time to take a look. Perhaps fifteen minutes was the extent of it. The next week, I showed the property to a Mr. Jones, a realtor. It was the day after a big rain. When I walked ahead of Jones toward the creek, that's when I saw bundles of money strewn all along the creek bank in drifts everywhere.

"I rushed Jones out of there before he saw the same thing and got the sheriff and Jim Bowers involved. We went out there the next morning. We found and returned over $300,000 to Wells Fargo, as I'm sure you know. I might add, I risked my life in doing so."

"We appreciate that, Mr. Gannon. We really do. Let me ask you this. If you had one guess as to what Rockbarn meant, what would your guess be?"

"I naturally wonder about puzzles like that. My best guess is, since there's a huge rock out by the creek near the Randel house, and since he has an old barn nearby, I would be prone to examine both extra careful. Of course. the rain and the raging creek already produced a huge stash. You seem to think there's much more, so I would tackle both those locations thoroughly."

"Thanks, Mr. Gannon. That's all for now. Just don't leave town. We've got a lot of work ahead of us. By the way, I see that you have an impressive record. It's good to see a man like you get so much done so early in life."

Gannon nodded his head in recognition and went to his office. The men went into Bowers' office and closed the door.

Clients drifted in now and then until noon. Tom skipped lunch and worked at his desk. When the detectives left, nodding as they did so,

Tom went into Jim Bowers' office. There was little more to say, except that the detectives would go through both Randel's and Whorton's houses with fine-tooth combs. Likely they would search the barn and the grounds thoroughly, as well.

The Wells Fargo men left seven days later empty-handed.

"I guess we can show the properties if we have buyers?" Tom asked Jim Bowers.

"Not for sixty days. We're still tied up with Jones. I just don't want us to get more complicated in this. Not that we would, but we have no real way of knowing the future of this case. It's old as Methuselah, and it's big."

"It's just that darn Rockbarn paper that gets me," Tom said. "It's bound to have a meaning. You know it does. Why else would it be in a folder marked for important papers?"

"Say, what are you and your son doing Wednesday? Come down to dinner about 6:30. Tell John he can tell us his valley story."

"We'd be delighted, Jim, and John will certainly entertain you to no end. You can count on it."

When Gannon got home, John was still out, so he strolled downtown. Everybody in Chambers stopped him for information about all the Fargo people blanketing the town.

"Not much to tell. No one knows much of anything. Maybe they found out all they wanted to know and went home." When Gannon started into Hickerson's store, he came face to face with his son, on his way home with milk.

"What! No ice cream for your poor ole daddy?" Tom said with a wry smile.

"I got milk instead, Dad. Do you want some ice cream?"

"No, I came for writing ink for the house. We're about out. Hold up. I'll walk you home."

They walked home mostly in silence. John knew something was up. His father was stiff, more formal. Finally, John broke the silence.

"All those men in town. Everybody I meet asks me about them, everywhere I turn. Is the bank in some kind of trouble? People ask that."

"Don't you worry about it, son. Just tell them you don't know a thing—and you really don't, do you?"

"No, sir. I just tell them we don't talk business at home."

"That's a good answer. Just stick with that. You know how natural it is when people see something extraordinary happening in their environment—they want answers. So just tell them, 'Beats me! I haven't heard a thing.'"

"Dad?"

"Yeah? What's up?"

"Do you think it will be okay if Baker, Blue Eagle, and I go up to Cypress Lake? You're awfully busy right now. We would stay one night. I'm just asking, but I really don't think that Blue Eagle is thrilled about the idea. He gets all tensed up when I mention that lake. What do you think?" John asked as they reached their front door.

Mrs. Eaton had left early, but the freshly cooked Chicken Fricassee that was on top of the stove smelled like heaven itself. Tom lifted the lid on the ovenware pot and took a deep breath.

"Smell that? Boy, you want to leave victuals like this for Cypress Lake? You go ahead and rough it. I'm staying right here in the comfort of home."

Tom smiled a big teaser at his son.

"We better get washed up and dig in before all that great smell wears off. Are you hungry?"

"Yes, sir. I could eat the whole pot and lick the lid."

"You won't get a chance. Your daddy is just hungry enough to shoulder you out of way. Oh, you can lick the lid if you wish, but that Fricassee will have to go on two plates. Think you can handle that?"

"I'll have to, won't I?"

The men sat and enjoyed the dinner. John glanced at his dad now and then and knew that this was quiet time. Time to eat. Let things sort themselves out. The chicken simply fell off the bone. It seemed fitting to just sit and enjoy the moment with each other. But John soon thought of something special to say about his daddy, his new pal.

"I was especially glad to see you at the store a bit ago."

"Why? Was it an ice-cream play or are you still avoiding bears?" Tom joked.

"No, I just noticed you were a little taut. Something felt good, a special treat, walking home with you. It's so different now. Different from Monmouth when I used to get into little troubles so much. Here we have no ladies to get in our hair. Just us. I could even scrub your back after a while or tell you my story again."

Tom, a bit taken aback, put his fork down and looked at his son a moment to catch the pleasant expression on his face. He choked a bit. Then he said, "Well, what a nice thing for a son to say. I see my boy is growing up right before my very eyes. The next thing I know, you'll be off to the big city."

"Dad, are we okay? I mean we aren't in any kind of trouble, are we?"

"We sure aren't. We're good as gold. And, furthermore, we'll stay that way. You and I have a lot of fishing to do before you sail out of here for Kansas City. But, for tonight, I've got work, and you've got a good book. You still on *Alexander the Great*?"

"No, sir. I finished that three days ago. I'm starting a writing course. Just a short thing, but it's good advice. When I get to high school, there will be a school paper or journal. If not, I'll start one. Track won't take up all my time. Then, too, I have to get Blue Eagle settled in. Living in a big city will take some adjusting for me, but imagine what will it like be for him. He is very quick, even with strange things. But a big school? A new crowd of kids? Rich kids, poor kids? It's going to be a real adjustment for him."

"No doubt it will be. But guess what?" Gannon said as he arose and walked to the cupboard to cut two servings of Bundt cake. "If you'll clear the table, I'll allow you one piece of lemon cake to give you some extra energy." Then he added, "You'll have the time of your life in Kansas City. Your friend, as well. That's where you'll grow up, mature, become a man. Your track is going to be even more fun than you can imagine. More challenging, more competitive, more work—but exciting. Tell you what, sport. I'm going for my bath. If you'll clean up here, I'll yell for you to scrub down my back. Then we can both hit the homework."

The next morning, Tom shook his son vigorously before he could awaken the boy.

"Let's get some breakfast, son. Your dad has lots to do today."

In the office, Gannon found his boss pacing, hand on his bowed chin. Tom had never seen him so tense.

"Ah, Tom. Come in the office a minute. I've been up all night with this Fargo thing. You know, if they prove that money Randel lent me to start my bank is, well, tainted, no telling where this will lead to. Certainly in their minds."

"How were you to know? I'm sure you just thought you were working with a rancher who likes to hang onto his money. Yet, that money is pretty strange. They may say you should have examined it, questioned it. Maybe not. Did you question it, Jim?"

"I was so damn eager to get that money, Tom, it could have been tinted pink, and I wouldn't have known the difference. Not a bit of difference. It saved my ass. That's all the wisdom I could shine on it."

"Then, there you are. You're not a detective. You were dying to get your bank opened for business, and … and where did the money go? It's not in circulation, is it?"

"A small fraction of it is, but most of it is in the vault. I never had to use it."

"If I were in your shoes, Jim, I'd get those Fargo men back in here. Explain the whole thing. They can't hold that against you. But that's stolen money you can't use. If it were me, I'd get hold of Fargo right now. What keeps pressing my mind is that confounded Rockbarn paper. As sure as we are in the same room together, that word Rockbarn is the key to the last part of this puzzle. Figure that out, and we find the money. What did he say—$700,000 is still out there someplace? If it's all right with you, Jim, I'll take the sheriff and go look at Randel's place again. Particularly that barn."

"I'd like to come with you. Let's wait two days for the weekend. We'll make a search party out of it. Maybe get a half-dozen handpicked men in town to go out with us to make a real search of the place."

"Sounds good. With that many men probing the ground, we have a good chance to really find out if there's a treasure trove buried out there or not."

The sheriff showed up with eight men, making eleven probers to cover the ground. It seemed like an ideal plan. That is, if only life worked that simply. Putting that much money in the ground required not only a good hiding place but a clever way to camouflage the bounty.

The men arrived at Randel's barn shortly before nine Saturday morning and started probing three feet down with long, sharp rods. By noon, they had systematically covered ten yards from and completely around the barn. Now they would probe the inside of the barn, which meant they had to first move thirty or forty bales of hay to one side of the barn, probe, and then move them to the other side to probe the remaining area. Three bales of hay sat up near the front door. That's the spot Tom Gannon chose. He moved the three bales and drove his rod down two feet where he heard a definite "thud" that sounded like wood.

"Hey, Jim. Come listen to this. Get some shovels over here. This sounds interesting. We may just have something." Everyone in the barn rushed over to see what they envisioned as the big pay-off. Shovels of earth flew as four men simultaneously dug a hole about four feet square.

There it was. A wooden box, just as Gannon reasoned it would be. It proved to be a heavy, wood and metal trunk, perhaps more intended for clothes and personal ware than anything else. The men hoisted the box out to level ground where everyone anxiously waited to see the contents.

Jim Bowers stepped forward as if to open it, but Gannon already had the job done.

Everyone gasped at once, and then Gannon said, "This is a trunk of money, but it isn't what we're looking for. This is new money. As Jim told me long ago, Randel never kept his money in the bank, so this must be his private cash. Sure sounds reasonable, unless he's a bigger thief than we know him to be."

Then Sheriff Blocker took over. "Let's get a seal on this trunk. It's got to be counted and reported when we get it to the bank vault." Then Blocker looked up at Jim Bowers and said,

"If we can use your vault again, Jim, it would be appreciated. We've got to get Fargo involved in this again. Leave the trunk right there for the time being and finish probing the rest of the barn."

An hour and a quarter later, nothing new was discovered. Everyone seemed to focus on Gannon. He started this whole search party. Now what? Gannon stepped outside the barn, wiping the sweat from his forehead on his shirt sleeve. He drew out his handkerchief and wiped the salty liquid from his eyes. As Gannon returned the handkerchief to his back pocket, he was looking away from the barn. The one o'clock sun beamed brightly and reflected off the roof of the Whorton ranch just across the field. He pulled out the Rockbarn paper again and mulled over it a minute as if to find a new inspiration. His eyes glanced back to the Whorton ranch. Then he turned to Jim Baker.

"Jim, I just got a hunch. While the men rest a minute, come with me over to Whorton's place. We'll need two men with shovels."

When the men pulled up at the back of the Whorton barn, Gannon jumped out of the Buick and trotted over to the back of the corner facing Randel's ranch. A huge grin came over his face. He turned and motioned for Jim and the men to hurry over to the barn.

"Come look at this," Tom urged everyone. As the men drew close, Gannon pointed to the corner of the barn. "Look what they used as a building block for this barn. What you men are looking at, if memory serves me well, is a tip of an iceberg. How do I know? I've been in this barn when I showed the realtor not long ago. I thought this was quite interesting—a rock, a big rock for a building block. Why not use it? But it takes up a bit of room inside. Come around to the front. I'll show you."

The men followed Gannon to the front of the barn, opened the double doors for light, and went deep into the far left corner of the structure. "And there it is, gentlemen. There is the rock, and we are in the barn. If my hunch is right, we are about to find out what the devil Rockbarn, means. It's either a hoax or Wells Fargo is about to get their money back. One thing is for sure. We have a darn big rock anchoring this building. Wait right here, and I'll drive over for the men."

A half-hour of probing and speculating revealed little except what felt like more rock. The men started to tire and get discouraged, but Tom Gannon wouldn't let it go.

"We might be right on top of it. This has to be the clue right here. See this area here, just away from the round boulder there? From what I feel when I probe, it seems flat and doesn't fall away like a round boulder would. Doesn't seem to be part of that cornerstone rock."

"What are you getting at, Tom? Rock is rock," Bowers said.

"Things aren't always what they seem. Why is this area under me not round? Why would it be flat? These are boulders around here. I know you men are tired, but this just might be what we're looking for."

Three men picked up shovels and started to dig. A fourth joined them.

"Give me an eight foot square," Tom said. "Feels like it's nearly three feet down. A large, flat rock. I'm sure of it."

The men dug, slowly at first and then faster as they neared the thing Gannon was so excited about. It was big. As the men removed the earth from what appeared to be a sand-stone slab, it became evident that Gannon was right.

"This sure is a slab of rock. Maybe six or eight feet," Bowers said.

"Dig to the edges, men. Let's see what we've got," Gannon urged.

"Man, this is some slab all right. That is a big daddy. Whoever put this thing here rolled it on logs. They sure didn't pick it up and place it here," Bowers said.

"Let's dig around the edges, men. Make sure we uncover it completely," Gannon urged. "See, it's sandstone all right. Look at the sediment ridges. That came out of the creek bank."

"But what's it doing here?"

"I'll tell you what it's doing," Gannon said. "It's Rockbarn. Sure as we are standing here, you men are looking at the prize."

"Ah, come on, Tom. You mean some stage coach robbers shot up the stage and buried all that money here in the barn?"

"No, that's not possible. Look at this barn; it's not that old. What they did was bury money near two rocks: the one on Randel's ranch and this one. So, according to that piece of paper with Rockbarn written on it, the first barn here where we're standing could have been a little thing way back then. Whoever built this barn just used this same site to build a bigger barn. Dig out the edges over at the far end, men. Let's get this thing exposed."

"Watch out!" someone yelled, as the big slab dropped half a foot at the far end near the barn anchor-rock.

Gannon yelled, "Tap that far end with the end of your shovel, Sam. Hit it hard. Jump back!"

The big rock moved some, and then—crash! It fell through the earth for three or four feet, revealing a large trench that it had covered. The men stood speechless at the spectacle. Dust flew. When it settled well enough to see, it was apparent that they were looking at an extended pit full of boxes. Someone yelled, "Good God, look at that."

A shout went up, became contagious, and then quieted.

"This is it. This is it. You are so right, Tom."

Tom Gannon stood looking down into the huge pit. He was already a step ahead of everybody else. *This pit has to be protected. It has to be guarded until Wells Fargo can come in and take charge. This is 'found' stolen money. Who will take it out of the pit? Who will count it? It ought to be public. If this is the stage-coach money, then it definitely belongs to Wells Fargo.* These were not new thoughts flooding Gannon's mind. He had tossed them about for days.

"Sheriff, you've got a job on your hands. I suggest half a dozen of us stand guard out here until we get the Fargo people onsite to supervise everything.

Jim Bowers said, "Look, you can see better now that the dust has settled. Sure looks like it might be packaged money from here. Tom, you want to go in and check it out?"

"No, sir, I suggest—and, Sheriff, I hope you're with me on this—that no one goes down in that pit until Fargo gets here. That is not a hand full of change down there. This is huge. Another thing. Starting right now. We need a six-man guard on this thing. We also need back-up in case all of our activity out here probing didn't go unnoticed. Just to be safe, Sheriff, I suggest you put three or four good men with rifles out there in the woods under cover. No fires, no light of any kind."

"What are you getting at, Gannon? We don't need a darn army to do this job. All we need is three or four men," Sheriff Blocker said.

"You might," Gannon said. "Then again, when word gets out, and it will, the whole town is going to come out and will want to look at this. I suggest we play it safe. Men with rifles. That hill over there on the other side of the creek? I once saw a half-dozen men riding that direction when I was out here visiting with Randel. Who are they? What were they after? It's stuck in my craw ever since."

"Sheriff, Tom has some good points. His training in the past sure comes to fore right here. You might want to listen to his advice."

"Under the circumstances," Blocker said, "I guess you both are right. All right then. Men, any weapons among us?" One, two hands went up. "I'm three. Tom, if you and Mr. Bowers will drive into town, there are eight rifles in my office gun racks. Tell the deputy I said to give you five of them to bring back. Three for inside the barn and two for the woods. We have to move to beat dark. I'll go in town with you and notify the Fargo people."

"I'll bring my own guns as well," Gannon added. "I imagine we could eat a whole cow as soon as some of this excitement dies down, so I'll bring back something we can eat out of a can. That will keep us until morning."

"Keep us? You staying out here all night, Tom?"

"Why not? We don't want more people involved in this than necessary. Wells Fargo people will be here by morning, maybe even tonight. They could if they wanted to. In the meantime, we don't want any strangers drifting in here."

The next morning, three trucks of Wells Fargo agents swarmed the woods and barn. They were arrogant and anything but a pleasure to be around. They took over the barn site like an army boot-camp drill, ordering everybody around, and removing them from the area.

Jim Bowers confronted Delong Melton, the lead agent, and set matters straight. Finally the locals were treated decently enough as they backed away from the buried treasure.

After assessing the situation thoroughly enough, Captain Melton assigned two men to scale down into the trench, cautioning them to not disturb the huge rock in its precarious condition perched squarely on one of the boxes of money. The two agents dusted off an adjacent box. After some struggle with it, they were able to dig around the edges enough to free one of them for examination. They eased it out of its nest and hoisted it up over their heads to eager hands above the pit. Agents pried the lid off the box with little effort. The thin metal trunk was soft from decay, easily falling apart as it was handled. Everyone gasped at the sight of the money even though the top layer was heavily rust colored from the rotting metal trunk. Jim Mason lifted up several stacks of large bills and examined them only for a brief time before he broke out in a small grin.

"No doubt about this money. The age, the serial numbers—no doubt about it." He motioned for Jim Bowers to come closely, and the two men spoke softly.

Tom Gannon moved closer and called out to Bowers, who held him off for a moment with a hand wave. Then he waved for Tom to step up.

"Captain Melton, I want you to meet Tom Gannon, my friend and my bank's vice president." As the two men shook hands firmly, Bowers continued.

"It was Mr. Gannon here who engineered this whole search and discovery. You can thank him for figuring out how we came to be standing here hovering over all this stolen money. We've been working out here diligently since early yesterday morning—not just looking, but poking the earth systematically with these long rods. Not just blindly, mind you, but, as I say, systematically working under Tom's direction."

Captain Melton put on a thin smile as he turned to Gannon. "Mr. Gannon, my personal thanks to you for your fine work. This is no small feat. How did you figure out this puzzle?"

Tom Gannon showed the captain the Rockbarn paper.

"Ever since I first found this paper in Randel's bank records, it has been a thorn in my side. After we thoroughly examined Randel's barn and the area around it, finding only his personal money stash, I suddenly recalled the unusual rock that holds one corner of this barn off the ground. We probed the hell out of things in this vicinity all afternoon. When I hit that flat rock there, I got very excited, because there was no reason for a flat rock that size to be next to that boulder. The rest of the story is right there in front of you. You're looking at it."

"Mr. Gannon, you are a good man. I wish some of my men had your kind of inquisitiveness. Maybe we could have saved you and all your friends here a lot of bother.

Regardless, in my report to our president, you will be named for your leadership and for your acumen for this incredible recovery of our money. I want you to be part of the counting process when we get these rotten boxes transported to Mr. Bowers' bank. Can't be more—"

"I can help you with that," Gannon interrupted. "The post office has lots of mailbags laying around. I'll take a couple of men and borrow what we need to sack up this money and get it to the bank. Will that work, Sheriff? Since I'm a deputy at the moment?"

"Use my name if you want," Sheriff Blocker said.

Gannon soon returned with enough mail sacks to baggage the money. When he walked up to the trench, removing the money suddenly took on new meaning. The big rock slab sat balanced on one trunk of money. Was it stable? If the men started removing money from the other crates, would they be in danger of being crushed? It was hard to guess the safety involved, but they couldn't put men down in that pit unless it was safe.

Tom approached the Fargo captain. "Captain we may well have a bad situation on hand. That big rock looks stable. It's pretty straight up and leaning pretty squarely against the far wall of the trench, but what happens if the support of the other trunks of money is removed? I strongly suggest that we rope it and anchor it. The only thing is, a rope won't hold that kind of weight. That thing will go whichever way it wants to go if it loses balance. Maybe we could put one man down there to work. Break up a crate with a shovel and fill a mail sack with the money. Put a rope on that man and be ready to pull him out in a hurry if that slab moves at all."

"Sounds like a good plan. You an engineer, Mr. Gannon?"

"Tom Gannon's my name. Call me Tom. No, I'm no engineer. I'm a master carpenter and plumber. I fix things. I also think about safety. Things that look safe sometimes aren't. A man in that trench won't stand a chance if that boulder sudden slides toward him. What really should be done is to trench that boulder out of there. Fall it on logs and roll it out. We can't touch the trunks of money it sits on. Tons of weight on those two trunks. Your call, Captain. You're in charge."

Captain Melton wasted no time seeing through the problem. He choose to load out the sacked money that lay next to the trunks that the giant slab held prisoner. First, one man on a rope tested the safety of bursting up a rotted metal trunk of money, sacking it, and hoisting it to eager hands above ground. Then, two men worked in the trench. Everybody kept a steady eye on the big slab at the end of the trench. Finally, six large trunks of money were hoisted up to Melton and his men. Surprisingly, the money looked in pretty good condition. Finally, when the last man was out of the trench, it was evident that the rock did in fact claim two trunks of money.

"Shovel some dirt on those trunks down there, men. We don't want anyone to be tempted to disturb that rock. We have a good story right here. I'll let Pierre worry about moving that boulder out of the trench. Let's load up these twelve sacks and take them to Mr. Bowers' bank. Cut some heavy-leafed brush and fill up that trench. Stick some around that rock jutting up out of the trench."

In another half-hour, the rescue caravan moved out slowly toward Chambers and Bowers' bank. They had no sooner arrived at the bank when a crowd started assembling.

Jim Bowers closed the bank, shutting out curiosity seekers. Nevertheless, word spread, and soon the entire town knew Tom Gannon had once again made a name for himself.

Captain Melton selected four of his agents to help him, Jim Bowers, and Tom Gannon open each bag, make the count, list it, witness it, and number each sack. When the tally was in, it totaled $701,000. Everyone stood around talking about the money, the recovery of it. Finally, Melton turned to Jim Bowers and Tom Gannon.

"Gentlemen, I can't thank you enough for the remarkable way in which you ferreted out the location of this money, especially you, Tom. As I said earlier, your name will be the primary name in my story to the main office. I feel sure you will hear from them shortly. This is some story. The press will be on it in short order. This money has been hidden all these years, and no one has come up with the answer before Mr. Gannon came along. Don't be surprised if you hear from others about your work, Tom. Jim, if we can leave the money here in your bank vault, our people will be along shortly to haul it to Pierre. They may even put it on display. If so, Tom, you likely will get an invitation to come to Pierre to pose with the money. No guarantees, understand, but this is an unparalleled recovery of a historic robbery."

Captain Melton shook hands with Jim and Tom and joined his men outside to await word from headquarters in Pierre. Tom Gannon went home to lunch and to check on John. The bank being closed, Jim Bowers went home for lunch as well. By then, half of Chambers had gathered near the bank to learn about the exciting events that had unfolded in this tiny town.

"Dad!" John shouted. "I was looking all over for you until I heard people talking in town. What happened out there?"

"Oh, your daddy figured out where all the money was hidden. Then we had to dig it up. It was quite an ordeal."

Gannon spent the entire lunch telling his son a capsuled version of what happened, promising a full accounting this evening. Chambers was a constant hum for the rest of the day. Three days later, just as Captain Melton predicted, Wells Fargo requested Tom Gannon, Jim Bowers, and Sheriff Blocker to come to Pierre to meet with the president of Fargo. There were many pictures taken of the men with the stacks of money in a safe room, but the one that made the front pages was a very casual "hunter and kill" pose by Tom Gannon with his right foot placed upon the beginning of the pyramid of money in the safe room. The article was entitled: "Bank Loan Officer Bags Stash."

Then there was another picture of Gannon, Jim Bowers, and Sheriff Blocker. A third picture had Clay Mercer, president of Wells Fargo, congratulating a smiling Tom Gannon. With money in the hole, so to speak, it was decided to declare the Whorton ranch, the huge rock slab, and the trench that held the treasure not-to-be-photographed until Fargo could remove the giant rock, the guardian and protector of the last two trunks of money, perhaps another one hundred thousand dollars. The bank did not wait long. They posted guards at the site as well as in the woods nearby. They hired twenty men in town to dig—exactly as Tom

Gannon suggested—a long, gentle upgrade from the rock slab base in the trench, extending under the barn to the outside.

Then, as all this digging was taking place, it revealed the true footing of the massive slab. It happened to be uneven on the end that rested on the trunks of money.

An idea became clear to Gannon as the men dug. He immediately discussed the issue with the Fargo supervisors who were charged with running the project. Gannon reasoned that if the men extended the trench length by two or three feet at the opposite end, where the trunks of money had been vacated, they might be able to pull the rock until it fell toward that newly enlarged part of the trench.

Several people agreed that it was worth a try. It just might free up the money under the slab so it could be removed without danger, thereby saving many man-hours of digging a long trench to remove the huge rock.

When the trench was lengthened a few feet, the men encircled the rock with a long rope. One powerful tug pulled the off-balanced rock over into the trench with a gentle thud in the soft dirt, exactly as Gannon had envisioned. A hurried glance told them the money might now be free.

Two men were lowered into the trench near the two trunks of money. Sure enough, the trunks were free from the stone slab and ready to be harvested.

Loud shouts went up from the men, looking at Gannon and holding up their fists and hats. The money filled four more mailbags. It was then that more pictures were allowed: the giant slab, already photographed standing straight up in the trench; the slab laying down in the trench itself; and men digging and sacking the money. It told the story perfectly.

One of the workers yelled, "Tom, what are you gonna do with this rock when you get it home?" It brought about much laughter and endless wisecracks.

Gannon yelled back, "I'm gonna put it on top of my Buick and drive it to Pierre… if you men will load it for me."

When the boisterous laughter died down, the Fargo men and Chambers locals drove to town. People lined the street like a parade. The smiles on the men in trucks and cars told everybody that the money recovery was a big success.

Gannon's Buick got the most applause as the news of his leadership in uncovering the money preceded the caravan back to town. He was treated like a hero.

Jim Bowers opened the bank, and the men moved the four sacks of money to the bank to be counted, listed, and bags numbered. Three hundred thousand dollars even.

"Fantastic!" several men kept repeating.

"Not to be believed."

"Buried over sixty years," others said.

"That fills out the one million dollars that Wells Fargo claimed was the original robbery," Bowers said. "Looks like we found it all. What an undertaking."

Then Bowers looked directly at Tom Gannon and said, "When I hired Tom Gannon a couple of years ago, little did I know the town was getting a fine detective in the deal. So, officially, I want you to know that you're looking at the new vice president of my bank."

When the cheering subsided, Gannon looked at his boss, his friend, and said, "What can I say, Jim? Thank you very much. I really do appreciate the promotion. Does that mean half the money is mine?"

When the laughing died down, Jim Bowers said, "Didn't I tell you, Tom? You get exactly the same amount as I do: a big zero! But look at the entertainment you've had in this adventure. It's not over yet. You'll be called to Pierre again very soon—no doubt about it."

Everyone applauded loudly. The crowd milled about, talking and speculating. John and Blue Eagle worked their way up through the crowd. John was grinning from ear to ear as they came near Tom Gannon.

"Hi, son. I see you and James heard the news."

"I sure did. Can we go home and eat soon? Blue and I have been running a lot. We're starved."

"You boys go home and eat. I'll be along after a while. We still have some business to take care of here. I may be late getting home."

Two days later, Gannon and Bowers got word from Wells Fargo that both of them were invited a second time to come to Pierre. The money had already been transported to Fargo headquarters in Pierre. Tom drove Jim and Mildred Bowers and John to Pierre the following day.

There was a big reception at the bank headquarters. The money was on display in the lobby for all to see. It was placed in the middle of the floor, encased in heavy glass for easy visibility. People filed past in a single line to see what a million dollars looked like up close. News people and their photographers entertained everyone for most of an hour. Then Layton Frasier, president and chief executive of Fargo, spoke at length on the cleverness and the bravery that Tom Gannon exercised in figuring out where the long-lost money was buried and how to recover it. He thanked everybody who participated in the effort, commending Chambers as well.

Finally, Delong Melton, president of operations of Wells Fargo was introduced. He asked for both Jim Bowers and Tom Gannon to come to the podium. He proceeded to lay lavish praise on Tom Gannon for the professional manner he conducted himself in every phase of recovering the bank's money. He mentioned that more conversations would be forthcoming in the days ahead. Then he congratulated Jim Bowers for having the good sense to hire such a fine executive. Finally, he looked at Gannon and asked if he would like to comment on the occasion.

Tom Gannon was not shy. He looked at the crowd, and then at Jim Bowers, ending with Delong Melton.

"Thank you, Mr. Melton. I feel sure that you don't know my background, so let me explain that two years ago when I moved my family here from Illinois, I expected to ply my master carpenter and plumber skills in helping to build Chambers. I had not the faintest dream I'd be helping Mr. Jim Bowers build his bank. I like puzzles, I suppose, so being in the right place at the right time put me in a unique position to help solve the million-dollar puzzle, so to speak. I'll leave it at that. I'm sure the press will entertain you in the paper tomorrow with all the details. By the way, this is my son John." Tom motioned for John from out of the front of the crowd, put his arm around his shoulder, and introduced him properly.

"I should tell you, Mr. Gannon, if in the future, you ever need anything special—you know, such as a job as a Wells Fargo special agent—come see me. Can you start in the morning?"

The crowd responded with much laughter and clapped their hands.

Gannon, quick in his reaction, said, "In the morning, sir? I'm not busy right now—if I may be so bold." This brought more laughter and a quick reaction from Jim Bowers.

"Now just a minute, Tom. Didn't I just make you an officer of the bank? You better tell the gentleman thank you for the compliment and come drive us all home."

The photographers rushed in, taking pictures of the bank brass, Gannon, and one or two included Mildred Bowers and John Gannon with his dad's hand on his shoulder. He never felt so proud to be with his father, a picture he would replay in his mind throughout his life.

Music from the band drifted in from outside the bank. As the photos and interviews wound down, Mr. Melton's secretary invited Tom and his associates to dinner. They talked about it a minute and then thought it prudent to accept the offer. Both men knew very well that such opportunities did not come along as casual as a wind.

The trip back to Chambers was warm and friendly. The Bowers had become good friends, not just an employer.

"Well, it certainly has been an interesting day," Bowers said. "One you can recall for all of your days, Tom. When you drive into a strange town with your family, beware of other gentlemen offering you an invitation to come to dinner right off the street. It might change your whole life."

"Boy oh boy! I should say! I certainly will be on the lookout for men like that in the future. Can you imagine? Outside of John and I building Mr. Haggerty a room for his poor son, and then helping rebuild his house after it burned, I haven't done a week's carpenter work in the two years since we landed here. Should I hold 'em and play these, or draw a couple?" Gannon joked.

"I'm sure you already have the answer to that one. What do you think, John? You are very quiet back there."

No answer.

"He's sound asleep!" Mildred said.

"I'm awake. I'm just being comfortable," John said.

"I only wish that Helen could have been here with us. What do you here from her, Tom?" Mildred asked.

"We had a long letter last week detailing all their escapades. Helen and Ruth Rochelle are making great strides studying and singing. They have fine prospects. They just need a good break. Betty Jean's performances are getting a lot of attention. The Vaudeville people all want her and her mother to do a mother-daughter act. I just shake my head in wonderment about what could be their prospects. Sallie's drawings and painting are coming along fine, also. I just wish they had all been here to share in this excitement. Just as well, I guess. Too many of us to get in one car for this trip." A long silence ensued, and then Mildred spoke.

"I know you will be glad to get them home. It's got to be lonely for you and John there by yourselves. Of course you both don't want for projects to keep you busy."

They drove on as Gannon speculated about the Rockbarn paper, the key that enabled him to unlock the puzzle. Soon they were driving up in front of the Bowers' home.

"Thanks, Tom. Again, I'm real proud of what you accomplished out there. You've been amazing. You sure impressed a lot of people these last few days. See you in the morning, and we'll talk about the other money—your new salary." The Bowers waved goodnight and walked in the house.

"Are we home, Daddy?" John said as they left the Bowers' house.

"Almost, son. Short drive. Just up the hill."

When they got home, Tom said, "We better get to bed, sport. We've had a lot of excitement today."

"Dad, I just wanted to tell you, when you were up there talking with those bank men, I just wanted to jump up there and hug your neck." Tom turned to face his son. He saw through clouded eyes that his boy was no skinny teenager anymore. He was filling out, putting on just the right amount of weight.

He smiled at the young man, and said, "You old fisherman, you. Nothing wrong with getting that hug right now."

And the young man did.

"What did Mr. Bowers call you? Vice president? Does that mean we're different now?"

"It means you and your daddy had better hit the hay before this night catches up with us. Try to be home early tomorrow. I have things to talk about with you. Goodnight, sport," Gannon called out as he climbed into bed. There was no answer, and soon the Gannon house was asleep.

Chapter 31

Chambers crossroads

Saturday breakfast following the Pierre trip was quiet. John saw in his father's face expressions of a man turning over many ideas that pressed him.

"You want to go down to the river with me in a bit?" John asked softly.

"I could use a walk. How did you know?"

John smiled slightly and said, "You were chewing your food differently."

"I'll tell you what. No homework, no projects. Let's walk down to the big willow near the bridge where you and Blue Eagle like to fish. If he should be there, we'll say hello, take our leave, and you can take me to the spot where you two sit at the top of the meadow at the edge of Hagerty Woods."

"That's a great idea, Dad."

"Tank up with water, son. We may be awhile."

Soon the Gannon men, as Tom liked to refer to them now, walked leisurely past the entrance to Main Street, down a small incline, and then down the path that led to the Brule River. As they walked along the river's edge, John could not help but stop his dad to look at the water.

"Look at this, Dad. This is what Blue Eagle and I see every time we're on the river. When we first came here, this river was pure and beautiful as deep down as you could see. Every day we were in the water was like a holiday. But now, just look at it. Look at the filth. Here comes some now," John said, pointing out sewer drainage into the river. "Can't we do something about this, Dad?"

"We're very close right now. We meet again next Wednesday. I've already presented the solution to the city council, and they all agree that we need to stop dumping into our river; it's just a matter of expense. A sewage system costs a lot of money. Every city on a river or lake seems to do what we do. Put their garbage and sewage in the water. The very water everyone drinks and bathes in. Of course something needs to be done," Gannon explained. "The only way to get something like this through the council is to get them to agree to a bond issue or a sizeable bank loan … hmmm! There's an idea. Just might be something to explore there."

"What, Dad?"

"Let's talk about that later, son. Right now, look—here is your big willow. No Blue Eagle. Just look at that old knurled tree. Half its bark is missing in spots. No telling how old that old gentleman is. Fifty or sixty years would be my guess."

"I like the way it grows right out over the river so we can sit on it and fish. Also, it's nice and cool underneath all those weeping branches. The fish seem to like it, too. We usually catch some good ones right out there where the small limbs dip down into the water."

"You fish under the bridge, too, don't you? I seem to recall that you caught some really nice bass near the trestle pylons."

"Yes, sir. Come on, I'll show you. Just up ahead." As the men drew near the bridge, John pointed out the button willows that grew out into the river for nearly twenty feet. "That's where Blue Eagle hides the bull boat. He swims and then wades ashore to fish or just to meet me.

"Come on up to the bridge. We spend some time up there, watching the river and the reservation just downriver. The sun sets right over there usually. Sometimes the sky catches on fire, it's so bright. Sometimes I think of you and me in the square the day we left Monmouth—that blazing sun, our good-bye to that town."

"When I first saw a sunset here, John, I was not even grown. Just passing through. The sunset that day would knock your socks off, it was so beautiful. As I told you and your mother before, that's what drew me back here to live. I doubt there are many places like this in the whole country. Come on, let's walk the bridge. I'll bet I can pick out the very spot where you and Blue Eagle sit up there at the edge of the woods."

The men walked the bridge pretty much in silence until they were parallel with Huron Island. They looked over at Blue Eagle's home, but they didn't comment. When they reached the lower part of the of the hill that led up to Haggerty Woods, Gannon pointed straight ahead and just to the left. The highway curved off to the right of the bridge.

"Right up there in front of that big spruce tree. I'll bet you sit right about there," Gannon said, pointing. John smiled at his dad.

"That's exactly where we sit. It's the best place. You can see everything from up there." As they climbed the rising hill toward Hagerty Woods, John spoke excitedly. "That's where I went into Hagerty Woods that day." He talked extensively about the incident, explaining, proudly now, how it all unfolded and how Blue Eagle waited directly below in the middle of the meadow, sitting in front of some tall grass.

The men stopped near the wood line in front of the magnificent old spruce tree. "Man oh man!" Gannon exclaimed. "You boys have some view from up here. What a sight! Straight down the bridge almost—the Brule, Huron Island, the entire length of town strung out to the left. Look! Even the Dakota Reservation off to the right. And you guys have this all to yourselves. Reminds me of a giant playhouse high up in a big oak tree when we were boys. The feeling, I mean. It's exciting up here."

"Now you know where to find us. Just out of whistle distance, so you'd have to drive across the river to fetch us."

"John, look at that. Do you see what's happening? You have history in the making right before your very eyes. Not too exciting. Just worth noting. Wagons and teams of horses and mules mixing in with automobiles. It's like a tiny part of a giant change-over. A bit of real history. They say that in the next ten, twenty years, we won't believe what will take place in this country. Families are coming off the farm with the fury of a big bass striking your line, bending your pole double. Our country industrializing! The growth will be as exciting as landing that big fish. You'll be right in the middle of it. Living it, writing about it. By the time you finish college and head east, your feet will be running out from under you. New York City, likely. I was there only once—an incredible place. You'll find people there from all over the world, and it's filled with nothing but exciting opportunities."

"Why didn't you stay there, Dad?"

"Oh, I was on my way to see Sault Saint Marie. About then, Teddy Roosevelt needed some help in Cuba, so, being young and adventurous, I thought I'd join up. I was already a good shot with a rifle, so they took me right away. My advice to you, John, is don't do crazy, impulsive things. You have an exciting life ahead of you. Get your education and pick good, solid friends. In time, choose a pretty lady, one who likes you just as much as you like her. Make sure you know her well, first."

Tom's voice trailed off a bit. He tried to change the subject, but his son interrupted.

"Dad, are they coming back? They've been gone a long time. Now they're going to Europe?"

"You've been reading my letters."

"Yes, sir, I couldn't help it. You left it open there on the table. Now I know why you skipped over some of the pages in Mom's last letter. How can they do that? Just pick up and leave us? My sisters are still little girls. Suppose something were to happen? What's Mom going to do? How are they going to support themselves? They should be here with us."

"Whoa! Whoa! You're getting into a deep hole. That makes two of us. We both want them home. We want our family together so we can be a family. I feel that way too, but you have to understand that careers sometimes grab you by the ear and pull you in a direction you never dreamed of. That's why Mother's letter was so long. She wanted to come home for a while, but the big boss says, 'It's either your career or your home. Now which is it going to be?' They went to Chicago to find out if they had any talent. It looks like they found out that they all have talent, especially your mother and the girls."

The men stood up and brushed their britches, leaving this magical scene as they walked to the Chambers Bridge.

"Look over there. All those Indian children playing their kickball game. Are those the children you set up for English classes?"

"Yes, sir. I turned it over to one of the bigger boys, Trig. Remember?"

"Another thing, John. It's way too early to talk about what ifs. We'll just wait and see how things play out. I'm sure your mother just hasn't reached a point in life where she can make definite plans. She knows you and I are having a great time. Your school, my work. Our big, raucous social life here on the Brule. Why, heck, we can go fishing any day we please." John looked up at his father just in time to catch his grin. "Wait until she hears about our great Wells Fargo treasure hunt!" Tom continued.

"Wait until she hears another woman lives at our house occasionally."

Tom stopped their walk abruptly.

"What are you talking about?"

"It's all over town. A lot of people are talking about it."

"For crying out loud. The only woman that comes to our house is Mrs. Eaton. Do you suppose … Now isn't that just like a small town. You better set some people straight when you hear talk like that. No one has been at our house but you, me, and Mrs. Eaton, and that's the way it's going to be. No more, no less."

"Even Blue Eagle says he can get you—"

"Hold it right there, young man. I know what you're going to say. You tell your friend, 'Thank you, no.' We have different laws than his.

Anyway, we are in a prohibitive zone here. Your dad will give you advice on women, not the other way around."

"I just don't understand why Mom had to pick up and leave us. What's in Chicago? Some old shows, that all."

Suddenly Tom understood the real reason for this conversation. He hadn't realized his son resented his mother leaving that much. A growing boy really does miss his mother. When they reached the middle of the Brule, Gannon stopped John and turned him to face out over the Brule.

"We have two big jobs here, you and me. We have to make our river clear and pure again, and you, sport, have to influence your friend to come back here someday and get those children out there on the reservation into schools and colleges." Then he turned to face his son directly, speaking in a calm, fatherly voice. "You have to be a big boy just like your daddy. We have to let our women go find out if they have real talent. We may never see them again, or they may be home frequently. Or when you hightail it out of here to conquer Kansas City, why, who knows where I will go. I have options, too, you know. I may stay here in God's country, or I may just pick up and join your mother in Chicago."

"That's not what I'm worried about, Dad. I thought her letter stunk."

"You read that part too? Then you must have read the letter before that one."

"I'm sorry, I did. I wanted to read the news from my mother! I wish I hadn't read that part. I wish I hadn't read it at all. That's why I've been out so much. I haven't been with James that much. I think he's up with his people or some place."

"I wish you had told me," Tom said. "I thought something was different about you. Don't feel the need to hold back from your daddy, sport. I'm not here just to buy you ice cream. Sometimes we stub our toes and need a rub, sometimes we run through a briar patch and get a butt full of briars and scratches. Families that care about family look out for one another. I'm always here for you. You know that."

"But what about Mother? What about you? What are you going to do when I go off to high school?"

"John—look at me, son. I told you not to worry about what ifs. Your daddy has been well tested long before now. He's a pretty resilient old bird. Besides, your job is taking care of John boy. You need to toughen him up a bit. Keep all your good stuff, but toughen him up some. You do that with your mind and your heart, not just one of them. Put yourself in that equation a bit more than you normally do. That will pull you through the tough times. Be thankful you are blessed with good brains and a loving, solid family."

John's expression changed more to anger than tears as he blurted out, "She's not being very solid right now, is she?" Tom took his son firmly by both shoulders with his strong hands.

"Come on, son, we're getting a bit out of control. I don't like some of these things any better than you. But, you know what? Your mother is a strong woman. She can take care of herself. She's in a different world right now. People in the theater act differently. They sometimes are led off on tangents before they realize that particular direction is not part of their dream. Who knows? Your mother may come blowing in here with all kinds of news. She wants to see you as much as you want to see her. It's never been any different."

The men walked in silence until they crossed the bridge.

"Look," Tom said. "Is that your friend down there fishing at the big willow?"

"It's an Indian boy, but he looks different than James," John said.

When the Gannons got closer, the Indian boy saw them looking his way, so he raised his right hand in a greeting. As the Gannons drew closer, Tom spoke first.

"Are you catching anything, young man?"

"A few. They won't bite much for another hour." The Gannons were standing there frozen, mouth agape, looking at the new boy's face, trying not to show the shock.

"I see you like my mask. Everybody makes a fuss over it. Even my horse. I tell everyone how I was trampled by wild horses up in Wyoming. It's always a good story. A half-mask is unique, don't you think?"

"It's fantastic. Do you know Blue Eagle?" John asked.

"Do I know Blue Eagle? And you must be his best friend … with your father?"

The Gannons drew close and shook hands.

"I live with Blue Eagle and his chief now. For the time being! Just long enough to pull body and soul together, so to speak. How fortunate to run into Blue's best friends so casually like this. My name is Creature, my adopted name. My Indian name is too long, but it means He Runs with the Wind."

"Where did you learn such impeccable English?" John asked.

"From the great man who made my mask. My father, actually. We trapped. He died suddenly last year, so I followed the river. You know, the Missouri. Then I heard about Blue Eagle here on the Brule. I hope to get out of this mask one day, but I'm told I will have to travel many miles. Some place called Kansas City, where they have such doctors. Actually, a dental surgery school. I need them badly. You men want to see?"

Before either of them could speak, Creature removed the mask that covered his mouth and half of his face. The Gannons were stunned.

"It's a show stopper, isn't it?" Creature said. "Might as well settle the curiosity right away. Knocks out all the questions. Have you seen cleft palates before?"

John shook his head, and his father said, "Only once. That was in a hospital in Chicago. Long ago. John, why don't you ask our new friend to come home with us to dinner."

Not waiting a moment to make up his mind, Creature said, "Oh, how kind, Mr. Gannon. Would you ask me another time? I must get home soon and help Blue Eagle and his chief. I really must go now." Creature reached for his string of fish.

"Ask Blue Eagle if you two can come Wednesday. We have fried chicken on Wednesday. You'll both like that."

"You bet I will. We'll let you know. Good-bye. Nice meeting you both."

"What do you say to that, John Gannon? Where in God's name did that boy come from? The language he uses. His perfect diction. And his face, his personality. What an anomaly. One thing is for certain, he is very bright. We will have to get to know him better. A lot better. If you ever are sad about your lot in life, son, just think of that boy. What a father he must have had. What a life they must have had together, to learn and overcome. We have to know more about their story."

"Dad, I'm going to be sick. Can we go? Feels like it may settle now."

"We're not that far now. Can you hold out, sport?"

As the Gannons strode across their front porch and reached out for the doorknob, it suddenly opened. Sallie and Betty Jean jumped out, shouting in unison, "Surprise!"

"Oh, you two precious cherubs. My singing cherubs. Where are my hugs?" Both the girls hugged their daddy tightly as Helen came in, only to be engulfed by John. Then she strode over to her husband, who met her halfway with one outstretched arm to sweep her up into his arms and smother her with kisses.

"You singers, what devils you are. How long have you been here?"

"Less than an hour, perhaps. We are trying to get unwound from the trip. Ruth went on home. Frederick Baker met us at the station and brought us here."

"Fred Baker! What do you know about that. Good for him. He's a good man, and Ruth sure deserves somebody great to look after her."

"We thought you would be in Europe by now. How long do we have together?"

"I wish forever, but darn it, we have to start back on Thursday evening's 9:00 o'clock train. So there we are—five days."

"I suppose you saw all the drama in the paper about our recover of the money from the ancient stage-coach robbery."

"Our recovery? The Chicago papers made it to look like Tom Gannon, 'Rough Rider,' did it all by his lonesome."

"Hardly. But that's what sells newspapers. 'Pump it up and blow it out.' It was actually a sizeable effort by a lot of us at times. I sort of ferreted it out, a coded piece of paper. Then, it was dig, dig, and dig some more by a dozen of our men."

"But what about all the shooting? The paper made it out to be a real shootout."

"There was a bit of shooting just before we hit the jackpot. A couple of crooks took some lead in their shoulders. Several of us were shooting."

"Can you all eat? That empty vessel sitting over there, now fainting a fall-over on his teenage side, is ravenous."

"Sure. We haven't had much solid food for hours. Mrs. Eaton was kind enough to stay and fix additional food. We'll have plenty to eat, and it will taste like a banquet."

Tom swept his wife up in his arms and kissed her passionately again before setting here free. The girls giggled. Then everyone took their seats at the table.

"That's the best roast beef stew I've smelled in years."

"I agree, Helen. Of course. we will have to eat John's share. He is fast asleep on the couch."

"Oh no!" John pushed back as he sprang off the couch. "You are not leaving me out of dinner. By the way, is anyone singing for her supper or does that come later?"

Betty Jean piped up, "I thought you would do it, John."

"I would, but I'm too shy—and way too hungry."

After dinner, as the conversation subsided, John grew serious.

"Mom, after you all go to Europe, when are you coming back home?" Tom looked at Helen and back at John.

Helen wasn't quite prepared for that question so early, but she tackled it anyway.

"Good question, John. Do you miss us that much?"

"Well, it's just that we aren't a family anymore. It gets kind of strange. I thought that I would be the one to be leaving, and here we are ... we're all leaving but Dad. He might turn this place into a bawdy house."

"Good Lord, John, where on earth did you learn that word?" Helen asked.

"I heard one of the men in town talk about Stutz Hotel, that it used to have one upstairs."

"When you graduate next May, do you suppose Uncle Will and Aunt Martha will want you to move in with them then or will you stay here for that summer?" Helen asked, changing the subject.

"There's talk of my spending the summer with them. Uncle Will needs help at his new laundry. You know, the one in the West Bottoms down near the river was damaged so badly by the recent flood, he is building a new one," John said. Then he continued addressing his mother. "It just doesn't seem right. All of us picking up and leaving Dad here by himself."

Without batting an eye, Helen looked at her husband as she said, "I guess the rest of the Gannons will just have to move to Chicago, don't you think?"

Tom picked right up on the sly remarks, not knowing if they were meant in jest or if some filtered message was being thrown out. "I don't know, Helen. Chicago is such a little ole jerk-water town. Heck, they don't even have a sewer system there. Everybody just flushes out into Lake Erie—that is, when the rivers aren't flooding town. How can a growing boy and a grown man move into a town with such a big stinking lake that you can't even fish out of? What do you think, Sallie?"

"We're going to Europe next month. Mom says I may go to Paris to study art."

Tom looked at his family around the table and then at Betty Jean.

"What say you, Betty Jean? I hear you have a fantastic part in a big show."

"Yes, but ... but ..."

"What, darling?

The changed expression on Helen's face set the tone.

"I just don't like our boss. He ... he takes liberties. He grabs himself in front of us."

"Sounds like a nice wholesome group. How old are you now, darling? Nine?"

"I'll be ten this year. I'm already getting ... getting breasts."

"So you are, love. You're growing up before our eyes. You're going to require different dresses right away. You talk to your mother about this?"

"We're talking about it. When we do our duets, I'm all in costumes, and at home I wear casuals most of the time."

"I can imagine. Well, if you all will excuse me, I have some business down at the bank. I'll be back in an hour or so." Gannon walked out into the night, passing the bank, passing the willows, on to the bridge. John followed not far behind. Soon the man was in the middle of Chambers Bridge, stopped, facing downstream toward the Dakota Reservation. Twilight danced on the water. The last vestiges of running games and distant children filled the air around the wiggi-ups and great lodges. Somewhere among those structures, a chief struggled with similar leadership problems—problems not of a family, but of a people.

John Gannon saw his father from the other side of the highway, a safe distance away to remain neutral, nonintrusive. He already knew; a man needs room to breathe. Fresh air to fill his lungs, river dampness to cool the forehead, a moon, such as that one there on a fresh new slant, just hitting the stilled water. A man seeking direction needs space. John watched his father on the far side, bent with elbows on the waist-high concrete guardian that ran the length of the bridge, looking deeply out over the beauty and the calm of the Brule River. Noisy night birds were settling down in their evening shelters among the cloister of high-leafed branches, chattering lowly as if to reassure one another in this safe haven. It was a sound infinitely familiar to the man and more lately to the boy.

Scarcely fifteen minutes passed before Tom Gannon gave up the solitude of the river, heading home with measured steps. John turned back as well. Gannon didn't notice his son at first, not until he saw the boy waiting at the end of the bridge.

"I thought that was you. What brings you out here? Afraid I didn't know the way?"

John went right to the heart of it.

"Do you think the girls are in any real danger, Dad?"

"You can't tell from a distance, son. It's something your mother and I will talk about. I know the kinds of people one can run into in the theater business. Your mother is no amateur. She can take care of herself, but as you just heard slip out from little innocent Betty Jean, mother can't be with her constantly when she herself is busy performing. She's got to have a guardian, one who can keep a close eye on your sister and protect her whenever necessary, under all conditions.

"A life can be ruined pretty quickly. You are barely old enough for me to even discuss this with. A big city like Chicago is a great place. Great opportunities exist like no place else in the country. It can be a launching pad for great talent. I can't see that it's worth it, but your mother is convinced that she and the kids are on the verge of breaking out of their mold into something important. Who can say? I dragged your mother and all of you children out here with Helen practically kicking and screaming. If ever there was a time to let your mother go chase her own dreams, this is it. Only time will tell if they have the work ethic to develop into something special—if they can provide enough safety while doing it.

"Look, son, you stay out of this discussion, this tug of war. It concerns you, but yet it doesn't. You're going to be leaving home in less than a year most likely. You have to leave your parents' concerns to themselves. Your mother and I will work out our problems. You'll see. I told Helen several months ago that the time was right for the three of them to go see for themselves if they have professional talent worth talking about or if it's just a dream. Things changed. Betty Jean and Sallie both blossomed with new talents that we had no indication of before. So, we'll see. You support your family like a good son. Your mother and I will work out the details, okay?"

"Okay, Dad. I just wanted you to know I'm with you. I love Mother and my sisters very much. Like you said, I'll have to wait."

"Good lad. What do you say, let's stop into Hickerson's for some ice cream? Make them think that's what we went out for. You know, men of the house have to put on a show, right?"

John smiled and said, "Chocolate and strawberry?"

When the men walked into the house holding up ice cream, everyone's faces lifted. They asked why it took so long to get ice cream.

"Oh, John met a pretty girl at the store. That took a while," Gannon said.

"Come on, take a seat," Tom continued. "Sallie and John are dishing up ice cream."

"Two kinds?" Betty Jean wanted to know.

"Just for you, darling; it takes two kinds for a power-singer like you. By the way, tell us what you and your mother sing together. Opera, ballads, or what?"

"We sing ballads and folk songs over at the Orpheus, but at the Opera Company, we sang, 'O Solo Mio', and *Aida* sometime. Mama sings the big parts. I sing a few lines and act a little bit. The audience likes us a lot. We get lots of applause, Daddy."

"I can imagine, darling. You two are unique, you know. I know your mother wears her hair up in ball behind her head, and giant earrings, but what do you wear?"

"I wear—oh! Chocolate and strawberry," she answered as Sallie served her a bowl of ice cream.

"You wear chocolate and strawberry?" The family erupted in laughter.

Betty Jean, being used to this sort of family banter, came right back with, "Yes, but I don't offer a bit to the audience." More laughter.

"Sallie is doing real well in art school," Helen said. "Tell them about your last work, Sallie."

"Mr. Offit gave us several assignments to choose from for a sketching assignment, so I chose the zephyr in Grand Central Station with passengers in their dress clothes. He liked that very much. So did my class. Most all of them gave me an E for excellent. I also sketched a sailboat on Lake Erie. I drew several small sailboats behind the large one. Each sail showed full wind pushing the masts. The big sailboat was tacking left." She stopped abruptly because everyone was looking at her intently.

"That sounds very impressive, Sallie," Tom said. "I hear you and your class will have an exhibition shortly."

"Yes, sir, about two weeks. I really like my school, and the students are really different from Chambers. They're more … sophisticated, more educated, I guess—just different. I already have quite a few friends there."

"All boys!" John said with his usual grin.

"No, there's three or four girls, actually. But the boys are cute. I like all of them." Everyone at the table laughed for a moment, and then Helen said, "You should see some of her drawings. Some very complex, with lots of detail—especially the skyscrapers. She drew an insurance headquarters building, and right beside it she placed a one-story cutaway of the lobby. Mr. Offit suggested it. It's quite dramatic."

"Sounds like John and I will be able to retire and come to Chicago."

"And live with us," Betty Jean said. "You should see our house. It's an old mansion, Mama said, and it's fun. We have a big wraparound porch, big rooms, and the lobby is fantastic."

The conversation lasted another hour, but John was only mildly interested in it. Chicago just wasn't appealing to him right now. He had everything he could possibly wish for right there in Chambers. All roads out of Chambers pointed to Kansas City in his mind, yet he was happy to hear these fascinating reports about his family. Finally, John spoke up.

"How did my teacher like Chicago, Mother?"

"Ruth? She liked it a great deal, except she has big commitments and interests back here now. She is first and foremost a dedicated school teacher. Chambers is a unique school.

There aren't many schools like it left in the entire country. She knows every student very well. She follows each one all the way through until graduation. You don't have that opportunity in any other setting. It's very rewarding. Then too, she seems to have a serious personal reason for returning to Chambers."

Tom spoke right up. "I can guess who that is. Looks like a good match. As I said, Fred is a fine gentleman from what little I know of him and his son. What do you think, John?"

"You know what, Dad. Fred is not Mr. Baker's son. He told me all about the big talk he had with his step-father after you and I left that day. You can't imagine how that boy changed after that happened. Everybody in school likes him now. He used to be such a bully. Now he runs on our track team and—oh, I just remembered. I'm supposed to work up a fishing trip with him. That Cypress Lake trip. Remember, Dad?"

Tom smiled and nodded. "You'll make it up," he replied.

"Oh, another subject," John said. "You ladies can't imagine all the excitement around here just these last few days. Dad busted up a bunch of bad ranchers while just wearing his underpants, and he found a one million dollars in lost treasure by just kicking over a big rock." The whole table erupted with laughter. Tom Gannon went over to John, put a hammer lock around his neck, and mussed his hair with a knuckled fist, while Betty Jean squealed with her high-pitched voice.

"This dinner is hereby declared over, *finis*," Tom said. "We can all go into the living room while John helps his sisters clear the table. Mother and I need to talk. Don't we, Mother." Helen nodded her consent, and she and Tom went, hand in hand, into their bedroom and closed the door.

John and his sisters cleared the table, putting the dishes to soak for easy washing later. Sallie spoke up.

"You are so funny, John Gannon. When did you start talking like that?"

"Just today. Just to entertain you two city slickers. See, you have your gangstas in Chicago, and we have our crooked cowpokes. Both made from a common thread, I imagine."

Sallie and Betty Jean smiled. They seemed impressed with their big brother. In such a short time, he had changed. They all three had. John said, "Come on, ladies, let's do these dishes. Surprise Mom and Dad. We get spoiled rotten by Mrs. Eaton. Boy, can she cook and keep house. This place is spotless. I don't dare leave my socks or underwear on the floor. She'd yank my ear off." Betty Jean smiled and looked happily at her brother's every move to see what else he would tell them.

"I joked when I was telling all the things about Dad just now, but for real, it was no small thing what he did on both of those occasions."

"What! That stuff in the newspapers? I saw it," Sallie said, "but Mother didn't tell us too much about it. She just talked to our teacher and then told us that we were going home.

What did Dad do anyway?"

"Oh, he just shot a crook in the shoulder in a gun fight, that's all. Then a few days later, he figured out where all money was that had been hidden for the last sixty years, and he had a bunch of men from Chambers dig up a two-ton rock to get to the money. You should have been with us in Pierre. Daddy was treated like he just hung the moon.

They treated him like a real hero. He was, too. The entire town of Chambers just swarmed around him like bees around their nest."

The girls stood there, solemn, mouths partly open. Sallie said, "You're just making up a bunch of stuff, aren't you?"

"Don't you read the papers? We kept copies. I'll dig them out and show you. I'm not lying. Everything I said doesn't begin to tell you what our daddy did around here. Mr. Bowers down at the bank even made Dad the vice president of the bank."

"Gollleee!" Sallie said. "That's exciting."

"Now what's this mess all about with Betty Jean and that crazy pervert?" John pushed the issue that Betty Jean had brought up.

"I don't know. Mother said she'd take care of it. I guess she did. We have a new man to work with lately. He treats us fine. He's a bit hard to work with, but he seems fair with everyone on stage. He's pretty plain looking, but when he smiles, he could melt a rock."

"Mama said just treat him like everyone else. He has pretty blue eyes. We like him so far," Betty Jean said. She had grown up a bit, too.

"That story upset our daddy quite a bit when you told it. I wish you had been able to finish it. You know, he's pretty worried about you two living in Chicago. Here, let's leave these dishes to air dry and go sit out in the living room."

When they were settled in easy chairs, Sallie asked, "What have you and Blue Eagle been doing since we've been gone?"

"Not much." John's eyes twinkled, seeing an opening to have more fun with his sisters, taking a stance of worry and deep thought.

"We drug a nine-and-a-half-foot gator out of the river early one evening, and when I jumped in the water to grab his tail, a twelve-foot python grabbed Blue Eagles' feet and nearly drowned him. Would too, if his chief hadn't come along and helped out."

The girls squealed with laughter. Betty Jean said, "You're just making this crap up, aren't you?"

"Crap? Oh boy! Wait until your daddy hears about your refined Chicago language. He's going to yank you out of school and put you down at the bank where he can keep a close eye on you. No fooling, don't use language like that around here."

"Mom says it. We hear it on stage all the time—sometimes worse."

"You're home now, little sister, and by the way, you didn't even sing for us at dinner."

Soon everyone was yawning. John heard Sallie tell Betty Jean, after they said goodnight, "It's good to be home again." John yelled goodnight to his parents and closed his bedroom door. The family excitement tired him. Most of all, he was glad to know the outcome of his sister's bizarre situation. It also told him something about his mother's strength and resolve.

The Gannon house fell silent. Outside, the crickets set up a cacophony of their own symphonic sounds. John wondered if his dad knew the outcome of Betty Jean's story that so disturbed him. Soon, he belonged to the refreshing world of sleep … His zephyr pulled slowly out of Chambers, wheels churning at first and then pounding the rails seamlessly. Proudly, he sat by his father, whose strong right hand held a giant steel mallet, knowing confidently that their Chicago destination was a matter of defending the family. The rails smoked from speed. The rhythm of an angry engine's song overpowered all sound—until his dreams changed to red stone mountains releasing myriad small, three-legged, black bears rushing out onto the valley floor, caught in a giant, whirling dust storm.

Chapter 32

Ghosts of Cypress Lake

The Chambers ladies had returned to Chicago after several truly great dinners with the Bowers and other families who were anxious to have the news about the their latest adventures in opera and show business. Blue Eagle was away with his chief, likely up at White Rock Point with the Mandan. A blue eagle had come to the chief's island home. Now it was time to talk about the chief and his family returning to take charge of the tribe. *It is not unusual for Blue Eagle to accompany his chief on such a journey,* John Gannon thought as he walked down the trail along the Brule, but there he was, fishing at the willows that Monday morning.

"They're just not biting this morning. I've only caught one little bass, so I put him back to grow. Let's go to the library and read. There may be some new magazine issues that have come in. Might be some natives with bare breasts or just plain naked."

John looked at his friend with suspicious eyes. He never talked that way. "I am speechless at such bizarre language from such a refined Indian chief's son. What have you been eating to make you so sex-driven?" John asked.

"I suppose it's just that being-by-myself- business. You know how I am when I have no one to fish with."

"Look," John said. "Remember my wanting to go up to Cypress Lake? Let's go out and see Fred Baker. Maybe we can get him some time off to take us up there. If necessary, we could help him do a day's worth of chores when we get back. Mr. Baker is dating our teacher now, so he just might be amenable to letting Fred loose for a couple of days."

"John, I just don't feel right about going to Cypress Lake. I'll walk out to Fred's ranch with you, but don't plan on my going with you. I told you before how I felt. That's it. Sorry, Little Chief, but come on, I need another good walk. It's nearly five miles out to Fred's, so we better get going."

"James, I just don't feel right about going up there without you coming with us. It's fun with Fred, but it's not the same. You've got me so concerned about that place, it just seems funny if you're not with us." Blue Eagle just looked straight ahead, eyes downward.

The boys walked on at a steady pace, and it took a little over an hour to get to Fred Baker's house. They found Fred out back.

"I was going up to Red Deer Point to visit my dad. Come on, walk up there with me," Fred said.

It was an interesting little cemetery. Round, white rocks, laid out in a nine by twelve foot rectangle on a sloping hill at the edge of the woods, headed up by a large burr oak tree that grew acorns the size of bantam hen eggs. John and James stood there quietly with Frederick, who talked about how the cemetery came to be. "Every time I come up here, I get choked up a bit just remembering all the details that Fred, my adopted dad, told me. Their close friendship and all, it's just an unbelievable story. Even today, when I replay it in my mind sometimes. Me, so young, right in the middle of things;—I just break out bawling."

The boys soon headed back down to Fred's house. John tried to be cheerful.

"Tell you what, Fred. You and I never did get to Cypress Lake. What do you say to going this coming Saturday morning and coming back Sunday. Just a camp out. We'll fish for our supper and breakfast. We can travel light, eat what we catch."

"That would be great, except I have a lot of work to do."

"I'll come back Monday and help you. Maybe Blue can, too."

"Sorry, men, don't count on me. That lake is not for me, but you two go enjoy yourselves. Monday, I have work to do that won't wait."

All the way home, Blue Eagle talked about every subject on earth except Cypress Lake. John finally turned to him and said, "Guess what? I've got great news. Our city council approved Dad's sewage disposal plan. He presented it to them and spent almost two hours explaining how it worked and what it cost. That means that within six months, the plant will be in operation and ready to take on customers. It will be mandatory, of course, and finally, Blue, we will get our clean river back. I might even take you swimming with me." John smiled.

"You still know how to swim, pale face?"

"Like a fish. Once I swam eight or ten yards," he joked.

"How about the bull boat? Think you can paddle it without all that mess in the river to slow you down?"

"Like a river guide," John said with a straight face and menacing eyes.

The boys stopped joking and walked in silence for a few minutes. Then the Indian spoke.

"When you and Baker get up to the lake, sometimes there's a canoe near the main camping grounds. Look for it; it might be hard to see with brush on it. If you find it, take it and go out a short distance and fish. You'll catch all the fish you can eat in no time. If there is no canoe, you can fish from the shore—provided you watch your step. Whatever you do, don't be tempted to wade out in shallow water and fish. You can't see well in that water. Even from the water's edge, look down into the water for a sunken log that moves a little bit. If you see one, move back in a hurry."

"Snakes?" John asked.

"Lots of snakes. Some mean, some harmless. Just last month, some of the Dakota took a gator out of there that measured over eight feet long. He was a bull. A gator like that can stalk you if you're busy fishing or get trapped wading around. Just stay out of that water."

"Isn't it a beautiful place?"

"Very. Beautiful—and dangerous if you aren't alert. Some of the shallows have quicksand. You won't even know it until you get trapped in it. Carry a long pole at all times. And watch where you step. Some snakes look so much like the dead grass and leaves they lie in that it's difficult to spot them unless they move. So just be careful."

"Darn. Just my kind of lake."

"It is. You won't believe your eyes at first. It's just that with all the incredible beauty, it can turn around and kick your butt," Blue Eagle said. "Just enjoy the place, but watch what you are doing. When you leave, leave it just as it is. No trash, no mess. Make doubly sure the fire is out."

"Sounds like I hear my mama calling me."

"I just don't want you to get up there and find out the hard way—you or Fred."

"Sounds like we need a good Indian guide. If you think of one, let me know. We don't intend to go deep into the lake. I just want to see those big cypress trees with moss hanging down from every tree limb, like I hear people talk about. The fishing and the sunset thrown in, it should be something special." After a short silence, John said, "My dad says to ask you how cypress trees and alligators came to be located in this part of the country. We have pretty cold winters."

"Our people talk about the Miccosukee tribe and their gator wrestling. They could have brought gators up this far. Somebody sure did. But those cypress trees? Who knows that answer? We think they are spiritual trees. Likely that's why our burial grounds are in there. It's all too spooky to me. I've never seen them before, so I can't say—except how does anything get anyplace? Maybe they are just a water oak tree."

Friday, John stayed the night at Fred Baker's house. The boys packed that night. Right after breakfast, Fred's dad went into Chambers for supplies and checked on Ruth Rochelle's house. Fred saddled up Tony, his big, sleek, black gelding with the star forehead, and the two explorers rode him at a walking pace, sometimes in a steady gallop for short periods.

In the hour and a half it took to reach the site, they watched Haggerty Woods give way to a long, ancient field and then small timber with some Spanish moss hanging from lower limbs. Finally they saw the change in the structure of the land and in the trees that lay before them. They were lighter in color and the facade of the forest more sculpted. As they got closer, the huge cypress stood like sentinels guarding a strange lake. Just yards away, the high grasses of the field gave way to an atmosphere that emitted a sweet freshness, lightly damp and cool, fresh like a new meadow, yet extravagant as new cloth. To John it was more refreshing than he could imagine. The tree line made a sharp bend straight forward, as both water and land allowed, and led them to a crude camping site just at water's edge. Old charred bits of wood lay in cold ashes. Thirty feet further was the entry into a new kingdom, as both boys came to call it.

"Look how the cypress grow bigger deeper in from the shore."

"I know," Baker said. 'I've been here before—remember?"

John stood silently looking at the power of these giants, just standing there in their shrouds of Spanish moss, perfectly still at the moment. Out in the water a little way, the boys studied the inverse funnel shape of the cypress trunks, with roots reaching out in all directions to anchor the big giants. Nodules, or knees, many a foot and half high, reached upward. Some from below water. Some forming the shapes of elf-like creatures, tiny ghosts of varying heights.

John and Fred removed their gear from Tony, tying the horse to a small tree near the campsite, and then ventured cautiously down to the waters' edge. John put his right arm out to prevent Fred from going too close.

"Look into the water for a grey sunken log."

"Yeah, I know. My dad told me what to watch for."

When both boys thought it safe to do so, they quickly gathered wood from a nearby dead tree, taking great care to watch the ground for any snakes that may lay hidden underneath or near old, rotting limbs.

"Fred. Come here and look at this."

Fred ran to John, and when he saw the perfectly coiled, dark grey snake that lay in the grass sunning, he gasped.

"Thank God you didn't put your foot near that baby."

Baker clubbed it then ran it down, smashing its head with a sharp blow from his long pole. He scooped it up on his pole and brought it near John for a closer look.

"It's a blunt-tailed water moccasin. That would be my guess," Baker said. "See his blunt tail, his rustic color. Smells like musk. Darn, look at these fangs! He's not deadly, according to my dad, but you would be laid up for a month if that guy tied into you. What shall we do with him?"

"Eat him," John replied with a grin.

"Yeah, well, I'll let you do that, John Boy. You gonna cook him or eat him raw?"

"What should we do with this thing?" John asked.

"Let's toss him out there in the water," Baker said as he scooped him up with his long pole. Both boys walked down to the water with the snake on Fred's pole. As he came near the water, Fred flipped the snake well out into the lake, which erupted like a water buffalo breaking water. Something large took the snake in its mouth in one gulp.

"My God! What the devil was that?" John yelled.

"That, my friend, is something we don't want to be near. Especially out there. Damn! Did you see the size of that thing? Of course, you can't tell for sure how big he is, but one thing is for sure, with a head on him like that, he ain't small."

John looked at that scene in silence for a long moment. Then he said in a grim tone, jesting, "There goes our snake dinner."

"Come on," Fred urged, "let's rig our fishing lines. We've got to catch super."

"Tell you what, Fred. See that canoe over there in the bushes to the right? Hook your pole over the bow and bring it around where we can get it. I'll get our hooks ready."

"Oh no you don't," Fred said. "You go get some more firewood while I pull up the boat. Take your stick and beat the grass in front of you."

"Come here, Fred!" John yelled as he made his way near the dead tree again. "Come look at this."

"Hold on," Fred yelled as he repositioned the boat. When he reached his friend, his eyes popped out. "Holy shit! It's a twin. Kill that thing and let's get going. It'll be dark before we get any fish in camp."

John stayed well back from the water moccasin as it coiled up, tongue lashing out, testing the air to determine the size of his foe. John raised his pole like a spear, launched it, and got a solid strike on the snake's head, killing it. He stretched it out and scooped it up on the pole near the snake's midsection, still writhing, and walked it to the lakeside.

"An exact twin," Baker said. "Looks thicker than the first one. Probably a mating pair. They frequently run in pairs."

John tossed the snake out into the lake. It was still out there, belly up, as the boys poled the cypress flat-bottom boat out to where fish were feeding. They baited their hooks with earthworms. They used short fishing poles that lay on the ground near camp. John yelled out,

"Got one!" After playing the fish a minute, he hauled him up into the boat.

"A two pounder," he said. "This one is barely a keeper."

"Fish on," Bake yelled excitedly. Pole bending, he worked the fish up to the boat and grabbed its open mouth, landing it in the boat.

"Wow, nice," John said. "He'll make three and a half pounds, easily. That's it for tonight then. Let's clean these two rascals and roast them when the fire burns down to coals."

"You sound like a good scout," Fred grinned.

"Oh, heck yes, just got back from San Juan Hill," John said with a straight face.

"You out there with your dad?" Fred asked.

"Naw! He just came along to cover me in the big charges."

"Boy, you have some imagination for a city boy."

"Hey, these coals are about ready. Give me your fish stick." John turned both sticks of fish for a few minutes. Here, you better cook your own; it's too heavy for my left hand."

Soon the campers were smacking their lips over the best bass they had ever tasted.

Just before dark moved in, they built a fire near the water entrance and made their scant bed of an old quilt and a tarpaulin positioned between the two fires. Tony was tethered to a four-inch sapling just a few yards away. Soon the fires were faint glowing coals. The stars were brighter than John had ever seen them. The Milky Way was just visible over the treetops. Tiny, green frog peepers were all out in force. Deep "burrup" calls could be heard all along the shore of this incredible lake. As the boys prepared to settle down for sleep, they stoked the fire to foot-high flames and added more wood that would last a few hours.

As the campers lay out on top of their bed talking about their life, a deep, thunderous bellow sounded out in the middle of the water—then a fainter, more distant call came from deep in the lake. The master of Cypress Lake had just announced himself.

As Tony stood resting his weight on three legs, keeping watch over the camp, the men drifted off to sleep. Near midnight, a piercing scream just overhead from a nearby tree limb melded the two boys into one body.

"What the hell was that?

"A screech owl," Baker said, as he unwound his friend from himself.

"Damn," John said. "I just about lost my water. As matter of fact, I did a bit."

They settled back on their quilt when the small owl sent out another grating screech—an operatic high C mixed with grinding cement and a squealing freight train—in full break.

"That's the dangest sound I ever heard from a tree alligator," John said.

"Yeah! And he can fly, too."

The explorers lay there gazing at the zillions of stars and constellations until they grew more tired by the minute. The cool night air grew heavier, much like the eyes of the campers stretched out beside the smoldering camp fire.

Scarcely an hour had passed when a distant scream of a woman carried out over the cypress swamp. Then another.

"Don't tell me that's what I think it is," John said.

"Afraid so. Dad said he thought they were hunted out."

"I know wolves don't like water, but what are panthers afraid of?" John asked.

"Guns and maybe dogs. Did you bring any? I didn't either."

When first light hit camp, the men were awake. They broke camp, and Fred led Tony to a spot of grass nearby, putting the reins over his neck and allowing the black beauty to graze freely during the next two hours.

"You just going to leave him there? You're not tying him?"

"No. He'll come when I call him."

"You take the front. I'll pole," Fred said. "I want a closer look at that big tree just ahead in that small open-water patch."

Morning sounds came on a cool, gentle breeze. Light reflected grey off the large cypress forest as Baker eased the flat-bottom boat to the entry of open water, slowing the craft to a stop to take in the beauty.

Directly ahead, just fifty yards away, lay the ghost of Cypress Lake antiquity. The huge base of the tree flared out at least fifteen feet back-to-front where she touched the water. Snake-like sub-roots at the trunk, twice the size of a man's arm, twisted and spiraled downward, slopping into the water in search of rich decaying peat that lay just a few feet beneath the lake surface.

Hollow, thin-barked nodules, knees, grew skyward from major root systems, adding a bizarre finish to the grace and beauty of this ancient, mysterious giant. Spanish moss strands hung in varying lengths, now placid in the early light. The ring of cypress trees that circled this lone sentinel in the open water caught the morning light, emitting an irregular grey texture to the forest from the dangling moss flashing to the eyes in the first viewing. The boys sat in silence. Finally John said, "What an incredible tree. No wonder it stands alone out there. I'll bet it's 150 years old." Baker quickly corrected him.

"Dad says three to four hundred years old, according to people who know these things. Sadly, this whole lake is likely to be gone in a few years. Water gets lower every year. It will be just as weird a conclusion as it was a beginning. Dad says more weird things than this lake exist in this world, so we are not going to scratch our heads over its existence. Let's enjoy it."

In a few minutes, John suggested that they explore straight ahead, but Baker quickly cautioned, "Do you know where we are? Do you know the way back?"

"Sure. We go right back there." John turned and looked behind him. It already looked new to him. *Is that really the direction?* he questioned himself.

"Using your sense of direction sometimes works well, but out here, you can't afford to lose your bearings. Look at the sun. Where will it be in two, three hours—whatever you plan to be out here. Now look for your guide markers. In this case—just for us, just for this trip—it's the big giant ahead of us. Looks distinct from here, doesn't it? Thing is you won't be looking at it from here. We will be on the other side of it or to the right of it or to the left. You will see several waterways to choose from. Take the wrong one and you could wind up hopelessly lost. If that big gator doesn't come after you, the bugs will eat you alive."

"What are you getting at? What do you suggest?" John said.

"We need to mark our way. Sight reading is good, but you need more. Read the sun. Read the lichen and bark moss on the trees. Note their colors at the time of year you're here. First, memorize this waterway entrance. Here, let's row out a bit more. Now, look all around you. This is our route. Memorize it. Look for a big tree, but look all around and compare."

"Damn! You sound just like Blue Eagle," John said. "Where did you learn all this stuff?"

"My dad is pretty good out in the water. It's similar to land in many ways. He and I have camped out here a couple of times. He's a great teacher. I got lost as hell out here once, but he was with me to correct our course. You take note of things because I'm going to have you guide us back. I'll row most of the time, but you will guide us, okay?"

"Sure, but explain that bark thing a little bit. I don't get that."

After a short lecture, John seemed satisfied. He looked at things much differently there forward, keener eye to the detail, enjoying the beauty that lay around them. Fred guided their craft easily through the water trails for several hundred yards before facing another open waterway. Almost immediately, he quieted the poling of the boat, allowing the boys to drink in the beauty that lay before them. A field of green water lilies, tens of hundreds of them, each crowned in large white blossoms, surrounded two specimen American bald cypress trees. Here and there, fish fed freely, leaping out of the water to complete a lunge for smaller prey, disturbing the carpet of lilies only momentarily. Here and there, a dozen shad jumped furiously to get away from more powerful, large bass. Sometimes a school of yearling bass. Sometimes two and three pounders.

"This is one of the prettiest sights that my father showed me," Baker said. "We came back near sunset to see the sun blazing down over those treetops and light up these lily pads like diamonds on a green cloth. You've never in your life seen anything quite as spellbinding as in that short time we spent here. While we idled here, Dad said, 'Son, if you ever had bad feelings about any person, you could release it all right here in God's world.' I told him, 'That's the same feeling I get right now.' How he found the way back in the dark was a mystery to me, yet it seemed like a road home to him. He and his best friend, my real dad, use to haunt these waters often, fishing and hunting. It's a vision I have now and then about this place. I feel their presence out here."

The friends sat there in the open water field of lilies, drinking in its grandeur, and then Fred asked for the paddle to get across the deeper water. They skirted the lilies, just at their edges. A blue gill jumped in the boat. John admired the hand-size fish as he held its gills and then eased it down in the water to its safe haven, watching it dart for the lily pads.

"Mark these trees," Baker said. "The big, dead limb in that tree on the left? Study their limbs. There may be others around here nearly like them. So, coming back, we swing to the left. Look back at them now; mark it down. Close your eyes; set the scene. That's what my dad taught me. It works. Let's try one more slip through the trees and one more open hole. They are all a little bit different. Gee, look out there on that tiny island near the two trees."

"That's a small alligator," John said.

"Sure is, and where there are little ones, there usually are big ones," Fred replied. "You will know them when you see a large snout and a pair eyes floating in the water—or coming toward you if he wants to say hello."

"I just as soon we leave that big guy to himself," John said.

Baker used his long pole again and guided them through a long, narrow waterway to another open pond. Though smaller than the one they just left, it was even more spectacular. The same beautiful lilies, but they encompassed a lone cypress.

"Dad said this guy is three to four hundred years old," Baker said.

"Darn! It's breathtaking if ever a tree was," John said, in awe. "Another ghost. That's two huge monster trees."

The explorers sat there enjoying the beauty of this primal paradise. The sun played on the green of the lilies in their full bloom. From a different angle now, the greys and greens were lighter than before. A light breeze moved long strands of moss, some still in bloom with light yellow stems that jutted from each green one, tens of which attached themselves in irregular patterns that made up a strand of Spanish moss.

"Look at the dense group of long strands of moss hanging near the top branches," John said as he pointed to the big tree. "There must be a ton of moss on that guy. What a beautiful thing. Oh, I wish Sallie could come out here and paint some of these scenes. She would have a fit just in seeing them. Look—look—look! What is that bird?" John asked as he pointed to a big cypress. "He has a red head, or at least a red beak. Look at the size of his feet. Look how he just walks on top of those lily pads."

The men watched the graceful red-headed gallinule race across the lily pads, stop, keeping its balance perfectly as it flipped up a lily pad with its beak for a juicy tidbit, and then move on to other prospects. A red-leafed tupelo tree grew nearby, dwarfed by the lone eighty-foot-tall cypress. Its red leaves barely protruded through the heavy cloth of Spanish moss that draped it, some thick strands hanging down eight and ten feet in length.

John pointed it out to his friend.

"If ever there was a tree out here that you would call the Old Ghost, that bald cypress right there fills the bill."

"That's exactly what Dad calls it, the Old Ghost. Look at the knees growing up around the base. It looks like a group of little men, fairy like. Those knees are very thin, and when we cut into one of them, they were hollow. Speaking of Dad, we have to get both our dads and camp out here this fall. As the season changes, the cypress canopy takes on a beautiful orange-red. You have to see it. The woods are really fantastic, all colored in God's glory."

"Okay, that's our next project," Gannon said. "Dad will love it. He hasn't been up here yet. Maybe we can get in a distant sneak at the Indian burial grounds. You know, the tree platforms. I know it's very special to the Indians and all that, still, I'd like to see them at a good distance away."

"We can talk about it, but I'll tell you now, it's quite a row from here," Baker said. "Dad and I made that trip once. I was only about ten or eleven. We didn't intrude; stopped about a hundred yards away, but we could see one or two old platforms. Moss hanging down from them, too. Strange place."

"Yeah, Blue Eagle would not like it if he knew we went in there. Since we are such good friends, I have to respect his feelings. The tribes think of it as sacred, only for them, and only at certain times do they enter that grove of trees."

"Just one more thing to point out right here. See that water trail to the right of those lilies up ahead? Look at it closely on top of that water. There is not one lily growing on that water—just green, weird-looking moss in the water. My dad cautioned me never to go in that water lane. He said it's filled with floating island trees, and they move with the wind, making it almost impossible to find your way out of there," Baker said. "I hate to give this up, John, but by the time we ease our way back to camp, catch our breakfast, and cook the fish, it'll be time to head out home. Are there any worms alive in that can?"

"Yeah, they're all wadded up in a ball, but they're okay."

The men enjoyed the moss-laden woods, the far-flung white and pink lilies, and blooming grasses that bordered the water around small islands that had been built up over eons of time. Baker steadily rowed, winding through the woods and ponds, back toward camp. Periodically, Baker quizzed Gannon on their guide markings.

"Now here is the last big pond with twin trees. Which way from here?"

John pointed off to an angling right turn through a narrow path that led into the long, shaded waterway that pointed back to camp.

"I see fish churning the water up ahead. Let's see if we can be as lucky as yesterday and catch a couple of nice ones. I'm really hungry," Baker said.

"You're hungry? I'm starved."

As they settled down near a dead snag of tree, Fred suddenly poled the boat to a halt not three feet before they would have hit a dead tree.

"Look at that. Tap that snag with your pole, Baker said.

"Why? I don't see … holy mackerel," John yelled out. "Three more feet, and he would be in the boat with me."

John taped the dead snag and grimaced as a five-foot-long, black water moccasin fell from four feet up on the dead tree into the water, slithering away in a small wake. After the excitement, John tied the boat to the tree and passed the worms down to Baker for his hook.

They fished a few minutes, moving their hooks around to different places, and then John threw his line over near a nearby snag. Instantly, he got a hard strike and pulled in a nice bass.

"Fine fish," Baker said. "Looks like a twin to your catch yesterday."

After several more minutes, John yelled out, "I got a good one here. Get ready."

"Play him, don't let him get away," Baker encouraged.

In three or four hard runs, the fish tired.

"Grab his lip when I get him up," John said.

"Boy oh boy! This is a nice fish," Baker said as he reached down in the mouth of the fish with his right thumb, first finger underneath the fish's lip, and hauled him into the boat. "Really nice bass. I guess five and half or six pounds. What do you think?"

John nodded agreement as Fred long-poled the boat toward shore. As they landed at camp, John said, "Why don't you put my smaller fish back in the lake, and let's eat the big bass. He's plenty for both of us. You want to clean him, Fred? I'll get the fire going and build up a good bed of coals."

In half an hour, John had two forked sticks with long, thick fillets on each, and in no time at all, the hungry campers had beautifully roasted bass—too hot to handle at first, but shortly, as the fish cooled, they gobbled down the fresh, sweet fish.

"Darn, I sort of wished we had kept the other one, too."

"What are you, a teenager?"

"Heck no, I'm John Ravenous Teenager," John replied.

The men drained the remaining water in their water skins into their mouths and set about dousing the fire with lake water.

"What are we riding home? I don't see Tony," John said.

"I see him out there a ways. Watch this," Fred said as he turned and, with thumb and little finger tips to his lips, sent a shrill whistle out into the woods. Tony jerked his head up immediately and walked slowly toward camp with his tail heisted in the air.

"He's busy at the moment." Fred grinned and then yelled, "Come on, boy." Up trotted Tony right on cue.

The reddish-haired Baker, now a foot taller than his friend, mounted the horse first, freed up the stirrup on John's side, and pulled his friend up by his arm. As they trotted down the trail toward home, John looked back at the moss-covered cypress giants thrusting up out of an amazing natural lake that had housed this forest for hundreds of years. He could not help but think that he had just added another notch to his belt—an experience that he would proudly share one day soon with his father.

Chapter 33

Golden Summer—Bronze Fall

The two friends stood near the center of Chambers Bridge. Blue Eagle listened intently to John's stories of the Gannon-Baker trip to Cypress Lake. The snakes, the gators, the fishing, the screech owl, and the distant panther … all the details came out.

"You're writing a book already," James commented. John smiled and went right on, having a good time amusing his friend. Then he stopped and faced the Brule.

The purple martins climbed and dove, pursuing and gobbling up vast numbers of insects in the late afternoon. The Dakota children downriver laughed and yelled as they played kickball. John thought he saw Trig out there among them. They all were growing, just as he and Blue Eagle were sprouting up.

"My last summer in Chambers," John said. "We both are going to miss this place."

"What do you mean 'both'?" James said.

"What have we been talking about for the past six months, Blue? We have to break out of here. We're going to Kansas City to high school. That's where the pretty girls are. That's where the hot-shot track team is. That's where all these new words you've been learning are going to mean something. When those Center High School girls hear you speak, you're going to turn heads. Every cute, young thing in a Kansas City skirt will be panting to date you. You won't even be able to study at night just wondering, *Which one shall I ask out?*"

"I told you, pale face, don't count on my going to some foreign town. My place is here. I need to be with my father up at the point to organize our people. I keep telling you this. You aren't listening."

John looked out over the river, pointing to the Dakota.

"Those kids down there need you a lot worse than your people. You need to think about the future. Your future, my future, all of our futures require education first and then going on the biggest hunting trip of our lives: a career. That's why your chief agreed with me. 'Yes, I want you to take my son with you. He will come back one day, strong, prepared. Then he will be ready to lead,' he said. We've talked about this before, James.

"I'll be going to Kansas City as soon we graduate next May. Track will be our ticket. I've thought about this a dozen times. They likely have an all-white school with an all-white track team. They are going to take one look at your speed and be thrilled to death to put you on that Center High School track team. They might even be so hard up for good runners that they will take me as well. And that's the easy part." John grew silent a minute and looked across the river.

"What do you mean 'easy part'?"

"You know the white mentality, 'Give 'em an inch, and they'll take a mile; bring one of them in here, and ten will show up the next week.'"

"So why should I go … if they don't want me?"

"Once they see you run, they'll forget all about the blue feather in your hair. That's the easy part that I spoke about. Incidentally, Dad and I ran into your new friend the other day, the boy with the mask. As soon as I get our track coach all hot and lathered up about wanting you so he has an edge with his track team, well, that will be the time for me to approach him about Boy that Runs with the Wind. All coaches want to win. Winning it all? No goal is bigger than that. If Creature is what I hear he is, heck! We likely could take them to state."

"What do you do, lie awake at night and dream up these schemes?"

"We call it planning ahead. You will be thinking ahead, making big plans before you know it. Uncle Will says he would love to have us stay at his house. He and Aunt Martha have a big back porch that's screened in. We'll winterize it when cold weather begins. There's plenty of room for all three of us. They even have a huge tree house their son built before he moved on to college over in Kansas. Look, Blue, after Coach sees you and me run, I'll let it be known that we have one more weapon, and only one more, who can put all of us to shame. Not just with track but in other sports as well. Athletes like Creature are good at anything. They even have rope climbing, swimming, and baseball there at Center. Can you imagine the impact we'll make in that school? It also gives me a chance to begin writing. They don't even have a yearbook as yet, so that's a big project. They need representation in the *Gazette*. That's a huge opportunity for me. I dare say, Kansas City is not ready for that—not ready for us. But I'll tell you, Blue, you are going to have the time of your life there. All while you are getting ready for Carlyle."

"Come on, John. Stop it! What the hell have you been dreaming? I have to get back here to help my chief. We have responsibilities up there at the point. Those people up there are it. Don't you understand? There are no more of us. We are damn near extinct. This is my chance to help our people. They need a leader."

"You are 100 percent right. But when you go back up there, you are going to run the place. You *will* be that leader. And you don't have to be chief to do that. What you do need is an education. You need to know how the white world works. You've got to come back here and get schools built, get all the kids around here educated. You've got three groups of Indians here. Don't you see? They will never be more than they are now without schools—American schools. Even college. You can do that, James. Your father thinks so, too. He thinks just as I do. He'll kick your ass halfway to Kansas City if you even think about staying here."

The young men stood there looking at each other and then faced the Brule. Finally, John said, "James, Kansas City is the way out. Get ready." As he stepped around Blue Eagle, he added, "But first we have to train our ass off for this year's track team. We're going to state." John jabbed his friend on the shoulder and jogged toward home. For the first time in his life, James Blue Eagle stood alone in the middle of the bridge, befuddled by all the dreams his crazy white friend threw at him. It was like a quaking marsh, mushy and unstable.

Finally, the Indian cupped his hands about his mouth and yelled loudly after his friend, "Tomorrow … the library." Then he turned in a quick spin and dashed across the bridge toward his lodge on Huron Island.

When John walked in the front door, his father was sitting at the table with a letter in his hand. His face was solemn as he greeted his son.

"Hi. What's new with you?" Tom asked.

"The usual. I keep challenging Blue Eagle about getting ready for Kansas City, and he always acts like he's not going, like he's going to stay with his father and go upriver to the point."

"Well, keep working on him, but don't overdo it. Let's hope he comes around okay."

"We got a letter from Mom?"

"Yes. They are going to Europe on a tour. That's the nature of show business. I wish they could just get a house to perform in and settle down. Betty Jean is a wonderful, very flexible girl, and she will have an incredible experience. That's just the problem, though. She will be a huge responsibility for your mother."

"We can't worry about her then, can we?" John asked.

"No, that's your mother's job."

John went over to his father and stood next to him. As he put his hand on his daddy's shoulder, he smiled and said, "May I read it?"

John took the letter as it was offered and sat close by at the end of the table. He read it quickly, reread parts, and frowned slightly, moving his head a bit side to side.

"They aren't coming home, are they? They won't even be here for my graduation. What a pisser."

"Learning some new language, aren't we."

"It's just that they aren't even on the first team, and they're taking off on a long tour away from us. Don't we count for something with them?" John asked his Dad.

"I know. I know just how you feel, son. The fact is your mother at least went along with my idea of moving us all out here to God's country. It was no small thing for her, John. Your mother's got a great deal of talent, and she either has to stay here with us and forgo any opportunity to develop those talents, or she has to go where the opportunities are. That's Chicago or another big city, including off-season tours to Europe. That's the way it works out, pure and simple.

"You and me? Well, we aren't exactly bored to death, are we. Look, you are going to be doing the same thing very shortly. I agree; it's very hard on her family, those of us left at home waiting. It's just that way for all families with different dreams. We just happen to fall into that category. We, you and I, we're just gonna have to let it all play itself out. And it will; you'll see."

"I just can't get it out of my mind. We're a family. We need to be together," John said.

"I know, son. But it can't be both ways. Things happen in life. They may not even go to Europe. Things get cancelled all the time. Don't think that Mother doesn't care about you and me, care about your graduation, etc., because I know your mother. She cares very much. You just have to be patient."

John leaned over the table and looked into father's eyes, "Who's going to take care of you while we're all gone? You're going to be very lonely around here. They are three; I'll have a family with me. Why don't you come to Kansas City with me, Dad? They have banks."

"Johnny, me boy, we better stop talking like this; you are going to make your daddy cry. What do you say we give it a rest. Okay?"

"Okay, Dad. I'm going to go lie down awhile."

"All right. Just for twenty or thirty minutes though. I want to hear some more about your Cypress Lake trip."

"Okay, Dad," John said as he got up and walked to his bedroom.

When Tom awakened his son a half an hour later, John was face down on the bed, lying on folded arms. Tom saw his red eyes. He started to muss his son's hair a bit, but he didn't.

"I've got the chicken and dumplings on warm. You love that dish. Wash your face and straighten up your hair. I'll wait for you at the table."

The dinner was subdued. Even so, John managed to be lively enough in his description of the wildlife he and Baker had encountered in their Cypress Lake adventure.

"I want to go up there with you one day, Dad. It's an unbelievable place to be in. Just sitting out on the water among some of those big cypress—moss covered all over them, some isolated giants that you can't take your eyes off of. Boy, that's a sight to see. Baker's dad has taken him up there two or three times before. He really knew his way around that place. He is very safety oriented, too. We even heard a panther scream a long ways away—way in the night."

"You two really had a great experience. I'm pleased for you, son. Now, you're one up on your dad."

"It had a certain excitement being up there, just the two of us boys. Out there on our own, nobody to look out for us except ourselves. Makes you more alert," John said. "Let's make it a point to go up there together before next spring is over. I have to pack shortly after that."

"Sounds like a great trip," Tom said, smiling at his son, neither agreeing or disagreeing. If it happened it would be beautiful, yet somehow, it seemed remote in his vision. All he could see at the moment was the skyline of Chicago, a family on a puppet string performing on the big stage, the master puppeteer in a tall, silk hat hovering over his wife and daughter performing in Verdi's opera, *Il Trovatore.*

"Dad," John said in a soft voice, "we better get some sleep."

"You go ahead, son. I need to work out a few things for tomorrow."

John came around the table to his father's side and spoke as he put his hand on his dad's shoulder. As Tom looked up in a faint smile, his son grazed his chin lightly with a closed fist. "Don't stay up long, Dad," the boy said, and left for bed. John looked back before closing his door to see something new in a man he had always imagined possessed the strength of a goliath—a father peering out into the night, sorting through the chips of life.

At breakfast the next morning, Mrs. Eaton cooked coddled eggs, hot biscuits, and coffee. Both men were alive with hunger and made short work of their food.

"When you get off from work, Dad, let's go for a long walk. Maybe we can go over and visit Chief Red Hawk. He'd like it if you came over. You could tell him about the new sewer system, how the city is going to clean up the river."

"Why, you rascal, you. How did you know I was just thinking about those people? That's a deal. I should be home by five."

John waited until six, and his father still had not showed up. He walked down the hill a bit. Tom met him halfway, walking quickly to meet his son.

"Sorry, sport, the boss wanted to discuss some business. We still have a lot of light. Let's go get that walk. Maybe just across the river and back. We'll have to visit the Dakota another time. Maybe Saturday, okay?"

"Sure. I'll be at the library most of the day. Blue Eagle and I are working on a history project. I'm making sure he's not going to have any difficulty getting into high school."

When the Gannons got home from their walk, a fat letter from Rome had arrived. Helen, Ruth, and Betty Jean were having an exciting time working in a summer opera company and visiting the Coliseum, the Forum, Moses in Chains, climbing to the dome of the St. Peter's Cathedral, and … "oh what exciting food." There were more pages; there was more news.

"Here the women are having a big Roman adventure." Tom held back three pages written front and back.

"They're going to be there all summer, aren't they?" John asked.

"You can't blame them, son. When you're in an exciting country, you owe it to yourself to see as much as you can. You may never get that chance again. Betty Jean is old enough now to absorb it very well. So there we are, sport. We are free to go out dancing with the girls every night." Tom looked at his son with a certain grin that John had come to know as a father joking with his son.

"I think when they finally do get home, we ought to lock them up for a week or so. Just let them know that the party is over," John said with a serious face.

"Not a bad idea, but then again, you know what I said about careers. You either run with your dreams or you raise your family. Rarely can you do both. All I can tell you is a repeat of what we discussed before: patience … we have to be patient."

"What if they don't come back? What if they—"

"John, I know what you're thinking. I told you before. You and I will just have to go fishing and find our own projects to occupy our time. If the women get a singing career going, well, who knows the answer? We'll cross that bridge down the line, okay? Now, you have to do your part. Focus on your future. You have track to develop. That's going to take more time than you think. Have you and your team picked out a place to train? You have a lot of summer left. Is the team going to do any training? Talk to Coach Tiller. He probably has a complete regimen for you guys."

"I'll tell you something else you and I can do, Dad. We can set out some special hooks down at the willows and the bridge. I've seen some big fish hanging around there. You just get a glimpse of them when they come up to the surface now and then to get air. One hangs out under the big willow that overhangs the river. Also, when Blue and I are out in the bull boat, we see some big guys down deep. You couldn't see them if they didn't move about slightly, sometimes flashing their white bellies."

"Where are you going to get a hook big enough to handle a fish like that. You're talking forty or fifty pounds, aren't you?"

"At least that heavy," John said. "How about we get Mr. Sorsby to make two or three for us when he has time at his smithy shop?"

"You have a good idea there. Go down and see what he says."

The next week, John and his dad were eagerly scouting the Brule for suitable green limbs that would hold a big fish. The big willow out over the water was definitely a prospect. The other two places, one to the right and one down near the bridge pylons, had fine young willow saplings that would counter the demands made by a big, river cat fighting for its life. The give and take of the willows would soon wear down the efforts of any big fish, even a ninety pounder.

Mr. Sorsby forged several big fish hooks to order and handed them over to young Gannon with a smile.

"What are you fishermen after? Water buffalo?"

"Shhhh," John said, first finger to his lips. "That's exactly what we are after, sir. Water buffalo. There aren't many of those left in our river, but my dad and I know exactly where they hang out," John said, grinning big.

"I'll bring you some fish steaks for your trouble," he continued. "These hooks are big enough for monsters. Thanks, Mr. Sorsby. Get ready for a fish fry."

Sorsby grinned and waved good-bye, and John rushed home to try to match up some rope-size line that would support such a challenge. The Gannons had only one suitable rope, and it was doubtful. *Not long enough*, John thought. *Maybe Teel Hardware. They have everything.* John dashed off to town. He was soon back home with a roll of two-hundred-pound test rope that surely would do the job. He had taken a hook with him to make sure his selection would thread through the hook's big eye. Then it hit him. *It's going to take more than a knot to hold a big fish—a really big fish.* He was stumped for an answer, so he put it aside and waited for his father to come home from the bank.

"Your rope is a bit awkward for a fisherman's knot, but try a square knot. You know how to tie that knot?"

"Sure. Fred showed me when you and I visited them, remember?"

After John tied the square knot, his father examined it, pulled it taut, and handed it back to his son, saying, "Just to make sure, get some bailing wire from the shed and wind it around the loose end of the rope tightly, just above the square. No fish will pull that apart. Now then, sport, what are you going to use for bait? A big fish's gonna want more than a wad of earthworms."

"What about liver?" John asked, as his dad stood there pondering the big hook.

"Tell you what. Run down to the store and buy four small chickens. Fryers should do the job. See if the butcher has any outdated ones. We're going to put them out in the sun anyway to let them ripen good. That will take two days, maybe three."

John grimaced and then was off in a trot to Hickerson's store. He was back shortly with a package, calling his dad to come out front. He was standing there holding his nose, pointing to the sack on the ground.

"Darn, those are ripe. Put them in a pail and tie them up high on a tree limb. Old Brown Toes out back will have a fit to get at them if he can reach them."

The Gannons let the pail sit out for another day, stinking the area up unbelievably, sending Brown Toes into a frenzy circling around and looking up at the bucket. John was amused to no end watching him. Finally he called his father over.

"Dad, come look at this."

Tom grinned from ear to ear as he looked through the kitchen window with his son.

"I guess you could call that the Brown Toe Waltz. When Ruth comes back, she can teach it at school. You better get washed up really good. Wash your hands two or three times with soap. You don't want those germs on you. Salmonella will wipe you out. Wash your wrists too, or any place else that you might have touched."

"It's a good thing we're eating out, Dad. Oh, did I tell you Mrs. Eaton couldn't come to fix dinner? She thinks she'll be back in the morning."

During an early dinner at the Stone, John announced with authority, "I'm sure not having any chicken tonight—maybe never after smelling that stuff we fixed for fishing."

The Gannons walked down to the river to check their line positions for their set hooks just to make sure they were happy with them. They both agreed on four positions, as they had an extra line. Then John suggested a walk across the river bridge. He felt elated about spending this time with his father. Gannon looked at his son, head slightly turned away.

"You keep tallying up every month. You're going to catch me before you know it."

John smiled. A few cars passed. A wagon rolled slowly past them, the rancher waving as he passed. The games down the river echoed out over the bridge. The split-tailed swallows were out in force, diving for gnats.

"I've got to get back in shape with my running. I feel the rust in my legs. Blue Eagle and I are going to go all out this year. We have a good chance to go to state."

"What does Coach Tiller say?" Tom asked.

"I saw him in town just yesterday. He seems really excited to get the season started again. Dad, we're really lucky to have him for a coach. He gets along so well with everyone, and vice versa. He's a fine coach."

"You work harder for a coach like that. I imagine you're going to start your strength-building program, from what I understand about track. It's just like any other sport. Being in perfect shape gives you the opportunities to win. Don't slack off on that one," Gannon urged.

"Heck no. Blue Eagle and I have been talking about it. Even before track starts, we will start lifting some light weights, working on different parts of the body, and doing our sprints. We've staked out a good place for the two of us to run sprints down here by the river.

"Down by the river? You run with your fishing pole in hand," Tom joked.

John came right back with, "No, sir. We carry our long staffs like up at Round Pond. I just hope it won't stir up the fish too much, all that foot pounding on the ground."

"You know, you've put on a pound or two. Think that's going to slow you down?" Tom asked.

"I hope not. We're all getting bigger. Blue Eagle is really filling out. He gets more exercise than I do. He swims almost every day, over on his side of the Brule. The water is clean over there. The Indians don't foul up the river like we do. I told him about your putting in the new sewer system. His face just beamed. I imagine he has told all of his people by now. I just hope that's the end of the problem. It would be great to be able to swim again over here where we fish. A lot of kids would swim with us."

"I've got good news for you, son. The engineers are making great progress. They think they'll have that equipment up and running one or two months early."

"Gollleee!" John yelled. "What a great day that will be. Then you and I have to go around and make sure every house and business that dumps in the river gets hooked up. Have you seen all the trench-digging that's going on downtown? Will they hook up our house, too?" John asked.

"Everybody gets hooked up. There will be plumbers coming in from as far away as Chicago, no doubt. I'm just glad one of them is not your dad. Nasty work, that particular project."

"Dad, let's swing back to the last tree near the bridge. That water looks really deep. We need a good bait set out here. Want to bet that's our biggest fish."

"They might fool you, son. Sometimes they feed deep; sometimes shallow. We'll set a line deep down there near the bridge and over at the big willow. Then we can go shallow at the other two spots."

As dark began closing out the next day, John and his dad took the ripe chicken, pail and all, to the river.

"Dad, this bait is God awful! Do we have to use this stuff?"

"To a catfish, son, this sun-ripe chicken is chocolate and strawberry ice cream rolled into one. Let's just see if I'm right when we come back at midnight, though it might take till morning."

When the Gannons arrived at half past twelve, a hunter's moon completed half its journey in the sky. It was nicely dark. Their coal oil lanterns gave good light. As they approached the first hook, John yelled out.

"Dad, look at that willow go! It's under water, and our fish is really pulling. Look at it go!"

"I can see. He's not tired out just yet. We'll give him some more time. Let's check the others." As they approached the big willow, it was quiet. John walked out on the big trunk to double-check. Suddenly, the limb anchoring the line tugged with a fury.

"We've got one, Dad. Feels like a big one. Boy, I can't move him much."

"See if you can ease him up near the surface. Let's get a look at that baby," Gannon urged.

"Yeah, well, he seems to have other ideas. He's just holding his ground. Either that or he's hung up down there, and there's not much for him to hang up on. Not many places that have dead trees, especially along here. He's just a big stout fish."

"Be careful and back out of there, John. Hold on to those limbs and—"

"Dad, this old willow tree is like our living room. I'm here almost every day, remember."

"Well, come on back. I want to take a look at that line," Gannon said.

When Gannon walked halfway out on the tree, he almost lost his balance, catching a limb with his left hand just in time. John stifled a loud giggle with his left hand over his mouth. His eyes told the whole story: *Be careful, Dad. Ease out on that tree slowly. Grab that limb ...* But he thought better of having that much fun with his father just yet.

Tom Gannon, holding a sturdy, upright limb with one hand, bent down and grabbed the nearby limb that held the line. He couldn't budge the line. He pulled harder, but the line still would not move—or did it?

"There's something on here, all right, but it's either hung up on something or is too big for me to budge. I think we have a big fish here, son." He pulled, and then he pulled hard.

The line gave a half-foot and then two. Then it came up readily. The head of something big came to the surface, Tom's eyes widened, and he yelled, "Look at this!" John looked hard, but the angle of light was too bad for him to see anything. He worked his way out on the old willow again until he reached his father. Tom held the line taut as the fish moved out away from shore and surfaced just fifteen feet from the fishermen. It was a roll-over surface, the fish's wake, but Gannon and his son clearly saw it. A monster catfish.

"Gollleee!" John yelled. "Pull him in, Dad."

"Yeah, well, this fellow is big. We have a ninety or hundred pounder here. He still has some fight left in him. There is no man-handling this baby. He could take a while, son. I'll see if I can get him up to the surface again."

Slowly, Tom started pulling the line with a strong effort. The big cat just sat there. Came up just a few inches, producing very little slack line.

"Come here, John, I want you to feel this fish. Can you slide under my arms and get up in front of me? I want you to feel this monster. We'll both pull him up."

John eased up around and under his dad's position, stopping where Tom could share the line with him.

"You pull the line from below my hands. We'll both work on him, maybe he will tire some more." Up he came, one foot, then two. Then he just sat there.

"He's strong as a bull. We have a lot of work to do here to tire out this baby. Let's pull up hard, and maybe he'll come up to meet us."

The line grew slack, and the men gathered the line quickly in a teamwork effort as the excitement grew. The big catfish rose to the top in a hurry, long enough for the men to get a wild-eyed view of the monster fish, mouth agape, long, thin whiskers on each side, only to flip its tail and sound straight to the bottom. The line flew through their hands, from wet, noodle-like to taut, and back to wet-noodle flimsy, filling the fishermen with awe and disappointment.

"Damn it! He got off," Gannon said, and both he and John pulled up the loose line.

"Look!" John yelled. He straightened out the hook. "My big hook! How did he do that, Dad? It was forged just yesterday, and it was darn big."

"Son, we had a real monster there. Did you get a good look at him? His head was at least two feet wide. We had a big fish on our line. A big fish. I'm sure he went well over a hundred pounds. No doubt about it. We might have landed him had we waited until morning, let him tire himself out working against that bending willow limb. Too bad!"

The boy and the man stood there looking down into the water as if the monstrous cat would resurface. The disturbed water smoothed out as new, clear water moved slowly under their tree.

"Darn the luck. That's a shame. We nearly had him, didn't we."

"I just don't see how he could straighten out my hook," John said, shaking his head.

"He was one powerful fish. I'll tell you one thing—he's going to have a mighty sore lip tomorrow. Too bad, too bad. Well, let's climb out of here and see what's down near the bridge," Tom said. "With any luck, maybe we'll catch his mate."

As they approached the line anchored on a small willow tree between the button willows and the railroad trestle, they both spotted the tree shaking and bending toward the river.

"Oh boy," John yelled. "We got another one. Look at him pull. I hope we tied the line well enough."

"Looks good to me," Tom said as the fishermen rushed up to test the line.

"He's deep, also. Shall we try to pull him in?" John asked.

"Let's see the resistance," Tom said, taking hold of the line with a strong pulling motion. "This one feels a bit smaller, but he will weigh in nicely. Let's not risk losing both of them. We'll let that willow wear him down until morning. We'll come back about first light and see if we can talk him into going home with us."

John smiled at his dad and nodded agreement.

"Are catfish that big good to eat, Dad?"

"To tell the truth, these are way too big. The best frying steaks are from a six to nine pounder. They're tender, and they've got great taste."

"So, what do we do with it if we do land a monster?" John asked.

"Haul him into town, weigh him and take a picture, bring him back, and release him. That would be my plan. How do you feel? Get yourself pictured beside a monster catfish, right in the *Pierre Bulletin*."

John looked up at his grinning dad and smiled pleasantly. "I'd like that," John said. "Snap his picture and turn him loose."

Day was barely breaking the next morning when the Gannons arrived. They landed a twenty-six-pound fish on the first line, and then a nine-pound fighter on the second. The third line, at the big willow, was taken in during the midnight struggle. Now the men walked quickly to the final line, hoping their big fish was still there—tired or not. The tree wasn't moving, but the moment the line was touched, the tree bent almost double.

"He's still on, Dad. Let's both haul him in, if he'll let us."

"We have to keep him out of those button willows, work him over toward the pylons, but not too close. He likely is hanging over the drop-off out there, at least on the edge of it. See where the water turns dark out there? The depth changes dramatically. Looks sharp and deep," Tom said. "I think we can land this fish if we take it easy," Tom added. The long line suddenly changed direction, moving gently toward the surface.

"There he is, Dad! See him?"

"Of course I do. He's a big gentleman, too. Looks like we may have him. He looks like most of the fight is just about gone." The fish made one final attempt to free himself, but it was a weak run.

"Pull him steadily. Walk him well up on shore. Boy, he's almost as big as our monster at the willow last night. Not quite, but he's a big one." In the excitement of the catch, the fish was suddenly given some slack in the line as it was at river's edge. It twisted double, flipped its tail in one last surge, and dropped free of the line in the shallow water. Tom Gannon sprang over the fish between it and freedom. He grabbed the big cat by both its gills, causing the huge fish to lash its tail desperately as Gannon struggled to slowly drag it well up on the grass away from the river's edge.

"Just look at this guy, John. He is a beauty. I'll bet he'll go sixty pounds. Man, is he powerful, even after being exhausted." Tom lowered the fish gently to the grass. "Tell you what, son. Trot up to Doc's office. He has a camera. If he can spare the time, ask him to come take a photo of us with our fish. Bring a scale, too."

John turned and ran up the trail toward Main Street. Soon Doctor Allen and John were back with camera and scales.

"Sixty-seven pounds!" John yelled out.

"Man, that's one more beautiful fish," Doc Allen said. "What do you intend to do with him?"

"Thought we'd photo him and then put him back."

"What about those people out there?" Doc said, pointing to the Dakota Reservation.

"Good thought, but the Indians get their share easily enough. Besides, this fellow would be a bit on the tough side."

"Yeah, you're right about that," Doc agreed. "Let's get a couple more pictures just to be sure." The fisherman posed with the fish between them, and then Doc took a picture of Tom and John holding the catch between them.

"That's the one to send to the *Pierre Bulletin*," Doc said.

"Good story, too: 'Chambers Boy with Monster Cat,'" Tom replied.

And that's exactly how it appeared in the paper. The whole town chided the Gannons for not parading their big fish all through town, but the real story in the paper was "the one that got away." John told that story very well to a reporter while Gannon looked on admiringly. Later, John and Blue Eagle would have their own story of using the bull boat as a huge cork in wearing down and landing their own monster, weighing in at sixty-two and a quarter pounds, a battle that lasted six and a half hours up and down the Chambers side of the Brule River. That one they took to Blue Eagle's home for processing for winter stores.

The following Wednesday, John and Tom Gannon gathered around the dining room table as Tom opened a fat envelope from Venice. Enclosed, with all their news, was an Italian paper giving much praise to Helen and Betty Jean Gannon, the American mother and daughter team, for singing in the Venice Opera House with a summer opera company. The letter went on at length about staying in the nearby hotel, La Fenice, where all the opera people stay, their trips through endless canals with a special gondolier, and two hours of touring St. Mark's, followed by coffee at a quaint restaurant overlooking a sea of people and pigeons on the vast square abutting St. Mark's Cathedral. The elegant plaza tower was directly in front of them. Fine shops surrounded the square, providing endless browsing and entertainment.

John studied the newspaper over and over. He wondered about the excitement his family was having. Deep down, he was quite happy for them, yet envious of them in a way even he didn't understand. He hoped he would someday follow in their steps, traveling Europe with his camera and pen. Italy would certainly call first. The history, the art, the architecture! The room fell quiet as he looked up at his father, just putting aside the last page of a long letter.

"Good news, Dad?" John asked.

"Oh, they're having a great time of it. They are being fussed over quite a bit. Well, there. You have the article in your hand. The Italians love family, so when a mother and daughter go on stage, the audience is ready to receive. Then, when they hear your mama and sister open up in beautiful voice, they erupt with applause. The promoter wants to expand their tour there, meaning they will perform in Italy all summer. From Milano up north to the boot. Probably as far down as Leche. Theirs is not a big-time opera company, understand, but exciting nevertheless. And, they could easily get an important break by some agent noticing their skills.

"How do you know Italy so well?" John asked.

"Oh, it was once a dream I had, years ago."

"Was I with you? In your dream, I mean."

"Afraid not, sport. That was long before I met your mother. By the way, from her letter, looks like they will be home by October. Let us hope."

John smiled faintly. After a pause, he asked, "May I read it?"

"Here is most of it. These two pages are personal."

"Those are the ones I want to read," John said quickly, grinning.

"I know; young devils are geared that way. Hard cheese, ole boy."

John read the letter with more pleasure than prior musings. He felt some of the joy his family expressed. He could see each one of them: enjoying the sights of ancient Rome, especially climbing inside the dome to the top of St. Peter's, the incredible cathedral in Milano, Betty Jean climbing to the top of that one also, and in the cathedral in Leche. It was there that they came upon a padre lecturing twenty squirming boys in pews on the value of being Christians and what would happen to good little boys, but more so, what would become of them if they were bad boys—all the while being helpfully supervised through the watchful eyes of a young man of twenty with a fifteen-foot cane pole that rapped on any boy's head that might be seen nodding-off. *"A more squirming bunch of eight-year-olds are not to be witnessed anywhere,"* Helen wrote.

"Throughout our visits to churches and cathedrals, the beauty of architecture and the unbelievable materials and workmanship are something a master carpenter would die to see, especially you, my love."

The boy smiled as he read the personal reference to his father, himself, and the love his mother sent. At that moment, he felt a small rush in feelings of love pulse through his whole body.

"They are really having a good time, aren't they, Dad? Dad!" Tom raised his nodding head and smiled, his eyes glazed over.

"Your dad's tired. Tough day with the money changers," he said.

Summer moved as summers will. No fish was safe from the apt skills with which John and Blue Eagle trolled the Brule. They piled up fish for James's chief, helping to clean them and ladder them on racks for drying in the sun. They camped out more than one night on the sandbar at the base of Huron Island, in sight of the tall, dead snag where the young blue eagle came to build her nest. The chicks were now grown, flying on to hunt and raise their own families. On two occasions, the boys took fish to the chief of the Dakota, who accepted the gifts graciously, once walking with the boys back to the bridge as he continued on to some matter not readily understood.

Monday, Wednesday, and Friday, the boys spent two hours at the library. Their vocabularies were expanding beyond their grade level, and John often complimented James on his progress, many times with funny remarks.

"Serrated knife? Serrated? Now you are my kind of Injin. What say we ask them to let us skip a grade next year?" Or, "Damn, Skin, you're going to be teaching me words before the moon gets half full again." Or, "Holy wiggi-up! Redskin swift learner! If you aren't careful, people are going to accuse you of being white."

Blue Eagle had long since become accustomed to such friendly banter, for deep down he knew that now he could basically hold his own in English, and he even taught his friend a few words in Mandan and Assiniboine.

"You know why these words stick so well," James said to John, "it's because when you and I have worked them half to death, my chief wants to hear them when I get home. He knows most of them quite well, but now and then he hears omnipotent, onomatopoeia, or slang such as pisser, and he grills me until I wind up teaching my teacher. When I told him what pisser meant yesterday, do you know what he came right back with?"

"No, what?"

"We were sitting straddle-legged there in the lodge like two big-shot chieftains, and he said, 'Pisser: I piss, you piss, we all piss.' I fell backward and laughed until my gut split. My chief never cracked a smile. I'll never know if he was joking with me, which he never has before, or if he was Indian-chief serious. He looked at me lying there, holding my belly from laughter, got up and went to the other end of the lodge. When I calmed down, I went down there, sat near him, and said, 'My friend John said to ask you if you if you would go with me and John and his father to visit Chief Grey Fox over at his lodge.' He said yes, but first he would have to send word to the chief that we're coming."

"Why did you say that to him? Now we have a project on our hands."

"I know, but I had to say something important or he would have thought his only son was getting out of control."

"Well I guess we could talk about war canoes and things like that. Maybe figure out where they can get just the right kind of tree to build one. There are none on the reservation."

The following week, they started swimming almost every day. John improved his overhand stroke rapidly and became a good swimmer by the end of summer. Blue Eagle said John would never attract a squaw with his slovenly style, but his speed would pass.

John retorted that he didn't need to be graceful; it drew such a crowd of young girls. Then he switched to more important things: track.

"Starting Monday, let's get started on a running program that will get us in decent shape so that when Coach Tiller gets his barbs in us, we will be halfway ready. You know he is going to work our butts off. We all have one thing in mind: state. No telling who we will run against. Could be somebody with Charlie Parker's speed. We won't know until we get out in some of those county fair meets. Those will be our first clues. I wish your friend Creature could run on our team. We would sweep everything if he's really as good as you say he is. How in the world did he come by such talents, anyway? He was in the woods all his life, wasn't he?"

"I don't know that much about him yet. He did say that he started running by racing his pet fawn in the clearings and through the woods. As the fawn grew older, of course, Creature couldn't catch him. He mentioned climbing a lot. Seems like gathering Muscadine grapes that grew in tall trees, his favorite wild fruit, helped. Huge vines—forty and fifty feet high. Then sometimes he *had* to climb pretty fast to get away from wolves."

"I can't wait for us to spend some time with him. In your wildest dreams, can you imagine a fifteen-year-old boy coming out of a life in the forest speaking English, German, Italian, and French? Plus two Indian dialects. What in the world was a man as educated as his father thinking becoming a trapper? Did Creature show you his face yet?"

"Just once. I nearly fell into the river. That night I went outside the lodge to pee, but I really went outside to pray."

"He looked that bad?"

"No! He looked worse. If a charging buffalo stepped on his mouth, it would not be this bad. At the end of my prayer, I kept going. A long prayer. First, for my own face, and then to Him for sending him to us. To my chief and me."

"He also came to us, James. To us. That boy is miles ahead of any boy his age. His attitude is unbelievable. He is going to make high school people sit up and take notice. They likely will graduate him in a year. I'll be willing to bet his education level is above senior class just as he stands.

"Regardless, my Uncle Will said they have a fine dental surgical school in Kansas City. Let's hope and pray they can help restore his face. Besides that, we all have jobs waiting for us there. Uncle Will just lost his big laundry business to flood waters. He needs help rebuilding it and then running the new plant. I'll be going there first. At the beginning of next summer, right after graduation. It occurred to me that you and I have to talk. Not only is a big class going to be strange to both of us, there are other things that are new. Society, expectations, hygiene, eating habits. We live out here in the woods, Blue. We can strip naked and go swimming most any place in this river, and no one would think twice about it. When we live in close quarters with family and friends, especially at school, a different code of conduct is expected of us. Cleanliness, body odor—really a lack of odor, social behavior, clothes, and on and on."

"You mean I can dress like this?" Blue Eagle said, grinning.

"Well, you know what I mean. Clean blue jeans and shirt for school, a jacket for dress up. Nice restaurants, church, certain affairs, etc. You've seen the pictures. You know what I mean. I hope you like taking a shower every day. I'll have to get used to it myself. Keep your hair braided. That should be fine. I'll invite you home with me for dinner several times pretty soon and just before we make the move. White eating behavior is different from Indian eating, so to speak. Not a thing difficult about it. It's just different, that's all. Nothing to worry about. No sucking your fingers at the table, and no farting or belching either."

"Are you implying there is civility lacking amongst my people?"

"Not at all, sir, just amongst thee and me. We both have to shape up. We get pretty loose out here on the river. And you had better get used to wearing jockey shorts. We can't have you go flopping around campus like you're swimming the Brule. Not only will the girls' eyes go out of focus, but the lady teachers are liable to lose focus altogether."

Blue Eagle almost blushed and started laughing without making a noise. Then he said,

"Why, I wouldn't want to miss my big chances for getting acquainted with the ladies of Kansas City. 'Why, here, ma'am, I'll show you—we do take precautions.' Then I'll fake lifting my front flap by grabbing it and quickly lifting my hand without it."

Blue Eagle howled with laughter as John said, "Boy, you are going to be a big hit on campus, and I mean big. If not big-in-jail. Listen, we are going to start dressing in jeans this fall. I'll order yours when I order mine in late August. First we have to go get your sizes, but not until it's almost time to leave. We're both growing so fast, we'll change sizes by then."

"That's it, then? That's my final exam?" Blue Eagle said, grinning.

"Those are the questions. No rush on the answers. Oh, there is one other little nettle in our society. I've rarely seen you pick your nose in public, yet you don't carry a handkerchief."

"That is true, pale face. Indian doesn't hark and spit in public for other people to step in and track into their houses, and Indian doesn't carry little white rags to save his snot in and take home. Only backward people do things of that order," Blue Eagle said through a veiled smirk and twinkling eyes.

"You are so right, sir. Gawd! How white you are destined to be, noble savage."

"Destined? How misguided, your inferences to a cultured people, to the few of us who have not been vanquished by the dreaded white man's pox."

"We better quit this crap, James. You are getting too factual. Regardless, we start training in the fall: schoolwork, track, and social graces. How's that, Big Chief?"

"First, pale-face community has to stop doing number two in our river. Then we talk. Seriously," Blue Eagle said in a mocking Indian tone.

"Guess what? That is exactly the subject we will take over to Chief Grey Fox. He will be ecstatic when he hears what my father has to report. See all the earth flying out of the ditches in town? Deep ditches, miles of pipe. We are getting a sewer system, my friend. It's coming. It's finally coming."

As John arrived home that afternoon, Tom Gannon was sitting in his easy chair in the living room looking over the mail.

"Come on in, son. You're just in time to get a small geography lesson of Italy. Our family has been singing all over the country. Well, at least in several big cities. I'll let you read it in a moment, as you are mentioned several times. They've been there a month already. Looks like three or four more weeks of touring will just about be the extent of it.

"Seems as though Betty Jean gave your mother a bit of a scare. They were out for a gondola ride late at night. Since other people were singing up and down the canals, Mother and Betty Jean starting singing as well. Betty Jean decided to change positions in the gondola, fell in the boat, and hurt her arm pretty badly, carrying on performing nevertheless. People were hanging out hotel and apartment windows joining in the singing. They were singing 'O Solo Mio,' of course.

"Normally people who carry on in that fashion have had a glass or two of nice wine with their dorado fish dinner. That's the great treat there for their evening meal. Right out of the Mediterranean to your plate, the same day. Must be incredible. Most all the restaurants there in Venice have outdoor tables under awnings. They ate at the Martini, very near the Venezia Opera House. Tomorrow, they are going to Tarranto, a naval training town way down in the boot of Italy. Old and colorful.

Then to Leche and back to Naples. Oh, and looks like they will be home in two more months. How about that, son?"

John took the letter as his father handed it to him to read.

"I know they are having the time of their lives, but I would rather wait until I'm grown to see such incredible sights. As a matter of fact, I hope one day you and I can see it together, Dad. Even if it's just Rome, Florence, and Venice for starters."

"Mr. Mason was talking to some customers the other day about Italy. He says, 'Once you visit Rome, see all the great churches, cathedrals, and antiquities, you will return over and over again.'"

"That's what I would like to do," John said. "I'll meet you in some big port like Seattle or San Francisco, even New York to take off, and no one will hear from us for months."

Gannon looked at his son, hearing an old familiar dream that stroked the deepest files in his mind, touching the pleasures of it. Old as it was, hearing it again afresh from his son enhanced the pleasure of it.

"Shall I start packing now?" John asked.

"Right after dinner," Tom replied. "But for tonight, you aren't getting dorado. Our channel catfish, however, is every bit as good."

"Blue Eagle and I brought some home earlier, skinned and cleaned them. We even had enough for Mrs. Eaton to take several good cross-section steaks home to her family."

The cool night brought heavy sleep to the Gannon house. Sometime during the night, amid the twitching of heavy eyelids, John floated out in billowing mist amid gentle waves on the Bay of Venice. Cascading lights from ancient villas were the candles of the night. His gondolier smiled, handing the young man a large dorado fish. A beautiful, young girl pulled alongside in a decorated gondola, waved, and disappeared. At dinner at Antico Martini's, he sat at a splendid table waiting for his father to join him. He was shocked to see Blue Eagle and his chief a few tables away, aware yet unaware of the moment. Then his table drifted out to sea among song and verse of a small armada—a regatta of a thousand decorated boats, led by three Mandan war canoes.

At breakfast, his father commented, "What happened to you last night? You talked all night."

"I hope it was a dream; all the same, I feel as though I rowed every canal in Venice. I'm still at the Martini waiting for you to come to dinner."

Tom smiled widely and tapped his son's shoulder as he headed out the front door for work, turning back with a suggestion.

"You and your friend go sit under the big walnut tree across the river and organize your day. We have a lot of planning of our own for our family's reunion. In the meantime, I'll be in the sewer, so to speak."

As Tom Gannon worked two jobs—helping oversee the sewer installation being the second—John and James Blue Eagle entertained themselves reading two novels, *Panama Canal* and *The San Francisco Earthquake*, doing word-building exercises, and taking more long hikes. The summer faded into a crisp fall. The edge of Haggerty Woods across the Brule took on a special brilliance of orange, yellow, green, and crimson. The giant black walnut, its branches so long they cascaded halfway to the ground, was easily the cornerstone in the middle of the front line of those woodlands. Almost yellow now, everyone who passed that way, even from the bridge, stopped a moment to pay homage to that incredible, ancient giant.

"Do the Indians extol the beauty of such a sight?" John wanted to know from his friend.

He got such a ridiculous look from Blue Eagle that he changed the subject.

"It's almost criminal for them to keep you waiting like this. A test of nerves," John said as he and Blue Eagle walked closer to the middle of the Chambers Bridge.

"I think it will come at the end of spring. They won't come for me in the winter because they have their own ceremonies up there at White Rock Point. Some of that is what my chief talks against. The so-called

Flying during the Bull Buffalo Ceremony. It isn't enough that we have so few men left to keep our tribe growing, but to define manhood in such a barbaric act as fastening hooks into a warrior's naked breastplates and then hoisting the half-dazed, half-conscious man into the air by rope is right out of the dark ages. But tell it to these men. 'You take from me' is the first thing thrown in your face.

"If they don't do something pretty soon about my Mandan Test, then I … I sometimes think, *Why am I even bothering with this?* Even though it is part of us, ever since we became a tribe. It's as common as eating, or making babies, to make us stronger. Here I am, moving out of this way of life into the white world. Into what you call civilization, a new beginning, so that I can return and help my people follow my path. For what reason?

"But look at the concept; it's daunting. One against hundreds. Yet, many of our children are bright. They have to be molded. That's why my chief pushes me out the door. 'Go get yourself educated,' he says, and he is right. He respects your friendship with me far more than you can imagine. He still shakes his head when he says you were sent. Recall the evening, that Fourth of July? You came back to check on Crazy Dog. He says, 'No white boy would do that in a million moons. Look at him now. All the things he teaches you are about your future. A friend so strong is not just a friend. He's a brother. He is the way for you. Perhaps for us, for he does for you what I can't begin to do.'

"Then you know what he did? He got up from the campfire where we sat in counsel, came over to me, and put an arm lock on me—our handshake—that startled the pee out of me. I thought he never would break the grip. All he said was, 'The Blue Eagle nests. Now it's up to you.' He walked out of the lodge to the sandbar at the tip of our island. He chanted in prayer until the moon passed overhead. He never talked to me like that—ever. Just like he was vanishing from this earth. He's saying, 'Here's the banner; take it home.' It was my longest night. I could see myself on that sandbar, an anointing, and I don't yet have the words."

"I think you do, James. I think you found them tonight. The fact that you can now tell me about your family's drama is proof enough," John said. "Starting in September, it's all about winning. School and track first. Get Crazy Dog in it with you. Pick out as many promising young boys and girls as possible to push to the front. When you come back here in a few years, they will be ready. That's what your father expects of you. Just look how far you've come, James, and that's nothing compared to Kansas City and Carlyle. You are about to catch a fish that won't even fit in this river."

Chapter 34

The Last Year

The Gannon ladies returned right on schedule. The late summer sun was as warm as their Chambers welcome. Frederick Baker accompanied his dad to the Chambers Station, meeting Tom and John Gannon as they drove up. The Masons and others from town had friends arriving, so it would be a nice welcome for Helen and the girls as well as Ruth Rochelle. It was no longer a secret around town that Fred Baker had serious designs on Ruth Rochelle. Perhaps this was the overriding factor, at least with the teacher, that brought the party home—and likely the glue that was needed to make it permanent. The Gannon men certainly hoped so. Fred Baker was certain about it. In his mind, he and Ruth would announce their engagement and marriage within a week.

The zephyr soon arrived, discharging over a dozen passengers. Betty Jean raced ahead of the crowd, screaming, "Daddy!" When she was near enough, she launched herself into Gannon's arms and delivered her hugs and kisses. Then she went to John as Tom and Helen found each other's eager embrace. Their deep kisses suddenly bridged their long absence in the warmth of the moment.

Almost immediately, they were at the car waving good-bye to Ruth and the Bakers as they drove home. Betty Jean bubbled over with stories, while Sallie smiled and remained reserved, confident of her place in the family.

All three travelers stretched, laughed, and everyone talked at the same time.

"All of you must be stiff and weary," Tom said. "Go wash your faces while John and I bring in the luggage." The luggage rack on top of the Buick was filled and overflowing.

"Take a good look at this, son," Tom said with a wink. "This is how the ladies travel. Note it. File it away."

When Tom finished taking Helen's bags into the bedroom, Helen, having refreshed herself with cool water, followed behind him. Tom held the door open a bit and yelled to the children, "John, you and the girls go get ice cream. We are napping." Tom turned, took his wife firmly in his arms, and kissed her in a way that she knew she was home again. He closed the door and pulled Helen over to the bed and slid under her as he pulled her gently toward him. "I thought you never would get home."

"I thought so, too," Helen replied as she kissed him fully and with a renewed passion. He unbuttoned her blouse at the neck and kissed her there, gently at first, and then passionately as he rolled on top of Helen. He looked into her eyes and stroked the hair from Helen's forehead, kissing her again and again—gently, vigorously, gently.

"Let's get out of these clothes and get comfortable."

"Here, unbutton me in back," Helen said. They lay side by side.

"Now, this is more like it," Tom said as mounting passion raced through his body. He caressed and kissed his wife down to the navel and back again. Their mouth kisses increased as their bodies became one. Helen arose to lay on top of her husband, started to speak, but Tom gently put his hand over her mouth, removed it, and pulled her down into a strong embrace and kiss. He rose to the top and fashioned himself into eternal bliss that ebbed and flowed until the lights shuddered vigorously, flushing their bodies and searing their minds with joy. The calm that ensued was a release that cascaded head to toe. Hearts still pounding wildly, singing, total bliss. They lay there in exhaustion and in peaceful exhilaration. Finally, Tom said, "I think we both can say, 'Mrs. Gannon is home.'"

"I should say so. Shall we just stay in this room for a while?" Helen said as she ran her fingers across Tom's face and lips, pressing her warm body against his.

"Certainly, but not over a week," Tom said. "I have to go shuffle money."

"That ole bank can wait. I'll go down there and serenade your customers; you can stay home and rest."

"That's just the ticket. I'll notify Jim Bowers right away." Tom grinned. "I hear the kids returning. Oh, I don't know if I can get up, but I guess one must."

"We'll get the hang of it again in a day or two."

"We better, or I'll perish," Tom said.

"Well, well," Tom said, putting on a good show as he and Helen greeted their family in the dining room. "You got two flavors, I suppose."

"We sure did: strawberry and vanilla," Betty Jean said with enthusiasm.

The family settled down at the table while Helen and Sallie served the evening meal that was still warm in the stove.

"Oh, that Mrs. Eaton. She's done it again. Chops and mashed with hot biscuits. And a nice salad of greens. She certainly is a winner, dear."

The room grew silent as the Gannon family ate heartily with a trencherman's gusto. Soon the ice cream came out. John assisted in takeaway, returning with three-layer coconut cake and two small round balls of ice cream servings alongside it, one of each flavor.

"Oh, yummy," Betty Jean said. "Guess what kind we had in Italy."

"I can't imagine," Tom said with a smile.

"Gelato! Every day, gelato. All over Italy. And guess the flavor."

"Why chocolate and strawberry, of course," John said.

"No, almost never. We had hazelnut. Fantastic hazelnut gelato. It will make your eyes roll right out of focus," Betty Jean said with a big grin.

"I can only imagine," Tom said. "You children get to clean up. Your mother and I have things to talk over before bedtime. Don't stay up beyond another hour. You ladies get to sleep in tomorrow. Goodnight."

Fall, with its cool days and nights, set the stage for dinner parties. At first, it was for the return of the Gannon ladies, and then it fell back on common ritual. No matter the celebration, Helen and sometimes her daughter were asked to sing. Usually they obliged with little fanfare, enlivening the evenings and solidifying their friendships. Now and then, Helen would beg off and allow Betty Jean to sing one or two songs. Once she sang four short pieces and drew vigorous applause.

Friends started asking about their futures. What did their Chicago trip point to? "Is there a career there?" they asked. "Are you going to follow through?" Indeed, there were lots of questions, but no concrete answers just yet. Both Helen and Tom left it that way.

School was in full swing. Ruth Rochelle collected several new recordings in Chicago and signed up for additional new records by mail as they became available. The schoolhouse was filled with music most of the time, spilling over into the yard during recess. In the beginning, the classes were absorbed by tales of Italy, many of which came from the demonstrative BJ, as Billy Jean was beginning to be called by her friends. Sometimes she made things up as a joke.

"Italy's known for its food—gelato. Particular hazelnut. Just when the machine stopped turning, but not the next day." Sometimes she called attention to her sister.

"Sallie, my famous artist sister, didn't get to go to Italy, so I told Mama that we have to go again and take Sallie with us." Then she added, "John, too—if he's good and doesn't gargle from his finger bowl." This caused raucous laughter and boys punching John's shoulders until Mrs. Rochelle stepped in.

Then BJ continued, "Oh, you are all invited to Sallie's art exhibit, coming soon downtown. I'll post you. You should know also, and please excuse same, if John and Blue Eagle show up with any of their big ole slimy catfish, they are both going to have to sing." She was right out of vaudeville with her storytelling and not in the least inhibited.

Track season was getting much attention. Coach T. had the boys meeting after school four days a week, and they had workout assignments for one day on the weekend. Conditioning was the main thrust at this time. Coach seemed extra enthusiastic as he introduced new drills.

They had no weights, so they improvised: custom pushups, squats, duck waddling, ending with giant springs forward, difficult combinations of pushups and squats, twenty-yard sprints, laps around the playground field.

On their tenth day, the boys could feel their muscles taking on shape and tone. Soon they were bursting out in forty-yard dashes. John was rather lethargic, very disappointed in his own time, but he took some pride in noticing how well Blue Eagle was performing. It gave him incentive to work harder. Baker looked much stronger than during the year before.

Coach Tiller noticed it too, taking every opportunity to point out little things that James and Frederick could do to improve even more. Then he turned to John and said, "You picked up a few pounds, John. You need to lay off the ice cream and sweets a lot. Fill up on carbohydrates and water. Hit the exercises hard, but don't overdo it. You are way off your mark at the starting line. The push off is key to getting your time down. Stomp the devil out of the ground with your left foot, and then push with all the power you have with your right leg. See if that works better for you."

John practiced at home and sometimes with Blue Eagle down at the trail along the big willow tree. They placed quite well in the county fair, winning two of three events with both gold and silver. That picked up the team's spirit. Baker, now the sandy-headed, barrel-chested, long-legged, two-twenty entry, improved steadily. He won bronze medals earlier, in their first meet. Then he brought home the bronze in the tri-state, where Blue Eagle took gold, and John won bronze in the one hundred.

Three weeks later, the whole town of Chambers grew excited. Chambers School track team was going to state. Coach T. grew more elated with each meet, bringing the team along steadily, pumping them up, pushing just enough to get them ready and keep them at their peak.

There it was, Pierre. The big stadium. A good crowd from Chambers followed their team and yelled out their support among ribbon and balloon decorations. Even Blue Eagle, always the calmest of the lot, grew tense. In the warm ups, there were three heats, with eight schools qualifying. Only James, John, and Fred Baker represented Chambers. Chambers was selected for the second heat. The mystery: who would unleash an unknown dark horse to spoil everyone's dream?

All three Chambers runners came off the line with quickness and sterling form, ruined by a false start—Baskin School jumped the gun. A second start sent the runners out twelve abreast on the straightaway. Blue Eagle was in the middle of the pack, with John just a stride behind, grimacing, arms and legs churning in perfect unison. Baskin School led all runners until the last twenty yards when James and John fought through the field and finished first and third, Blue Eagle taking gold. The excitement was tremendous. The runners celebrated in jumps and yells and then circled back to the middle of the crowd. John waved to his family and his coach, and then he found Blue Eagle for a victory lap in front of the crowd before heading back to the medal presentation.

The ride back to Chambers was short and delirious. Coach T. had to calm the boys down several times in order to keep the car safely on the road. First and third! A first for everyone: the coach, the boys, and Chambers.

Finally! Chambers was on the map. Every paper in South Dakota knew about Chambers, giving John Gannon a special surge of adrenalin.

"Blue Eagle, the fastest runner in South Dakota." The runners rubbed Blue Eagle's head and punched his shoulders. Finally, Coach pulled into town and eased along Main Street to the front of Hickerson's store. Closed! "Looks like a rain check, boys. Meet me here tomorrow, twelve noon, and we will celebrate with the town." Then Coach T. drove up the hill to the Gannon house. Tom Gannon drove up right behind them. Everyone got out of their cars, straining to see who was on the front porch in the grey of dusk.

Blue Eagle recognized his chief immediately and walked over to him quickly to get his special, double arm-lock congratulations. Then everyone congratulated the chief and his son. For a moment, the chief was disarmed by all the warm attention. From the shadows at the edge of the house came another Indian who strode with purpose to Blue Eagle. No one had seen Crazy Dog in months, but there he was with as near a smile as he would allow.

"Indian ran a great race," he said to Blue Eagle, but his eyes and manner told James far more. "Get ready, they're coming soon," he said to the boy.

Chief Grey Eagle spoke to Tom Gannon in a firm, soft tone, "It is true, my son won, but your son showed the way. I won't forget. Soon the river will run clean again. All the children will swim once more. Thanks to your son, we will have a regatta. Thanks to you, it will be in clear waters." Gannon smiled, nodding his thanks as the Indians left for Huron Island.

Inside the Gannon house, everyone wanted to see John's medal. Afterward, he put it with his medal collection on top of a vanity table near his bedroom door. His mother and his sisters gave him several big hugs.

"Now, if everyone will excuse me, I can't wait for a hot bath," John said. The Gannons sat and talked about how hard John trained for these races, how important tonight's state contest really was. Bit by bit, they came to realize that his planning and persistence won the day, putting

Chambers on the map. The Chambers one-room schoolhouse danced off its blocks as much was made over John's initiatives.

The new sewer system was by far the big event of late, but for tonight, there were gold and bronze medals to fill the town with pride and celebrations. The fact that it reached out across the river to the Dakota was not lost on this changing frontier town.

When John emerged from his bath in his underwear, Betty Jean shrieked in a near high-C voice, "Eeeek—a naked man."

"Hardly," John said. "I'm just cooling down."

"We had a man run through backstage in his jock strap one night after rehearsals," Betty Jean said.

"That's the one we want to hear about, B.J. Tell us all about it," John said.

"All right, you two, that's enough of that. Take your seats, and I'll serve dinner—right after John finds his pants," Helen said. "Then, if all of you are in the mood, Betty Jean and I will entertain you with a song after we finish dinner."

The fall gave way to winter. John was now fifteen. Ruth Rochelle was even more effervescent, as she married the happy rancher, Fred Baker.

The Christmas holidays were special. Helen and Mildred Bowers engineered a reading of Charles Dickens's *A Christmas Carol.* After the reading Helen said, "Of course, if you cooked a goose like that today, it would not be fit to eat." Then she pointed out all the details, ending with the menu being served in a few minutes. Ruth's spectacular Christmas dinner included roast goose, dressing of cornbread, minced oysters, minced goose innards, and sage; mashed chestnuts combined with whipped potatoes; green beans and homemade fruitcakes. That was followed by Helen's incredible eggnog mousse made with twelve whipped egg yolks and gelatin, served with heated vanilla, apricot, and brandy sauce. "Tiny Tim's Christmas came in a distant second!" Helen exclaimed enthusiastically.

School was never more serious for John and Blue Eagle. By now, they were working in one of the back rooms of the library. John had an agenda every day that seemed strangely maddening to Blue Eagle. *Why is he in such a hurry?* he thought. Yet, in time, James got the point. It was better to be over prepared to ensure meeting their goals.

"When we go to the big city, we don't want to be weak in any area that we face. Math, history, science—all of it. If anything, we want to be out in front in every class that we take, understand? These words we've been working on, they are the links. We put it all together, and everyone is going to look up to us, not at us. We will be the drivers. If anyone has a problem with us, they can meet us in the classroom or on the track. We'll be ready, smiling, and set. When the questions are asked in class, we want to be there with quick hands. Actually, I think what we will bring to Center, in time, will win us some good friends. If not, they have a problem—not us."

So, they marched through English drills, vocabulary building, and more Spanish and French, using the books' guides to pronunciation. Blue Eagle's keen mind allowed them to cover lessons quickly. John grew more confident and happy with each drill. He was proud of their progress, walking a bit taller.

Still, deep down, as John gazed at his friend's brown skin, he knew from experience that social battles ahead would have to be overcome, for the face of prejudice has too many friends.

Chapter 35

Kansas City Zephyr

John Gannon had been awake since first light crept into his bedroom. His suitcase packed, he rummaged through it for a book. Then for over an hour, he stood in his backyard beyond old Brown Toes' house, at the bluff's edge, focused on the Brule.

This was the last day. Still there was no sign of Blue Eagle. He promised to come, so night after night for the past three days, John had waited, occasionally climbing down the rope ladder to check the secret ledge twelve feet directly over the bluff's edge where they sometimes met. Yet, each night, nothing. Then he would give it up for reading and sleep.

Something was wrong. He was either bound and gagged someplace, flying in ceremony, or in a ten-day battle to survive his manhood test. Morning brought the bright dawn, finding John still searching. Leaning back against a large plains tree, he faced the sun that lit up the Brule River and the meadow that met Hagerty Woods, beyond it. It was a June sun—clean, crisp, and brilliant, sending shafts of yellow light cutting through the cottonwood and river birch to play upon the heavy mist of the Brule's warm surface.

The boy folded his arms, shifted his body, and looked downriver to the bridge. He smiled at the white speck, his one-room school, that had been his day-life these past three years. "He would never forget it, just as he would never forget Miss Rochelle, the teacher who filled them with knowledge, drove them, inspired them. She became a second mother to the entire class. Even more than his own mother, Miss Rochelle would always be a beacon that made him think, pushing him onward.

Hers were the eyes that danced with the spontaneity of class maneuvers. A teacher's teacher—sparkling one minute, soft the next, jewels among the long, black hair that curled about her high cheekbones. Her voice golden, always rich, commanding and then soft. A teacher of her time.

He saw her mouth, the cupid lips smiling one minute and then sternly barking out the assignments to each class in the big room. Each student receiving his orders personally, privately. The entire class room, the essence of a one-room school.

God! How lucky we were. There we grew up helping: the older children teaching the younger—single lessons, doubles from back to the front row. The room absorbed you, at first in a nightmare, and then as a gift in learning. The full gamut of English, Latin, beginning French, and math. Then history, poetry, literature, reading, and special subjects … like how to think, how to lead, how to obey. She brought us London, Dickens, Flaubert, Byron, Keats, and more.

She fought his cause to bring his Indian friend inside the school house. During and after school, she showered them with recordings of Brahms, Liszt, Tchaikovsky, Chopin, Schubert, Haydn, and others. James Blue Eagle covered his ears when he first heard Verdi and Puccini. Later, they captured his soul. Clearly, teaching was a passion with Miss Rochelle, and music was the spear that launched it, along with "her children," the students themselves.

The medal she delivered to him at his home was his treasure in his memory of her. And when she pulled him into her bosom yesterday to say good-bye, he melted, taking away a blurred vision. Her letter in his hand when he left her, he placed it in his book of Maupassant. That too she had given him for his leadership in class.

John looked back from the school to the foreground. The dirt road along the Brule twisted in and out of the cottonwood and birch and stopped on the granddaddy of them all—the gnarled old willow that extended out over the Brule, casting its weeping shadow, harboring a never-ending supply of bass and catfish. Occasionally, a pike cut through the clear waters. Two boys finding a friendship that bonded them for life.

In a fond moment, he saw himself and Blue Eagle racing against time with all their skills, always shoulder to shoulder, knees churning, arms pumping in rhythm, feet pounding the soft earth, chests almost falling to break the tape first. Afterward, they ran in tandem, silently, in the joy of winning. One, two, like fingers of a closed hand. Brothers, really, for neither of them had such. In this time and place, few were faster, few brighter. They won over the boys, they convinced the town, and they gave hope to the people across the river—though over there, there were no ribbons to be won, just the trophy of right and a mission to rescue.

He saw the final race, too, the state meet. He brooded about the outcome for a while, as the whole town did, but soon he came to realize that his friend simply ran a better race. The town? Well, they would have to get over it—the Indian won. They both brought pride and honor to Chambers. It wasn't just hanging in the trophy case; now it walked Main Street.

Finally John looked out to Huron Island, the earthen lodge of his friend and his chief. Soon it would be gone, reclaimed by the fishermen and picnickers of the town. Reclaimed by history, yet saved in memory, it would always anchor there when he needed to reach down deep and battle for right. A species foundering on the rock of extinction. Perhaps, but he felt good about intervening, perhaps more so than he gave himself credit.

One last time, he looked toward White Rock Point, with its strange white strip of rock molded horizontally along the center of its surface, jutting out to the edge of the Brule. A master painter's stroke of grace and beauty, visible as little more than a dot on the horizon from where he now stood.

Maybe the Mandan Test was called early. Perhaps the train station ... But there he gave it up and walked back in the house.

"You've been out there a long time," his mother said. "Saying goodbye?"

John nodded yes and smiled faintly.

"Are you completely packed?"

"Yes," he said, rather solemnly.

"Are you all right? You look a little faint."

"I'm okay, mother. It's just my stomach."

Helen looked at her son, waiting for more.

"It's taut."

"Maybe some coffee will help," she said. Helen filled the cup before him and placed the cream and sugar nearby. Neither spoke for several minutes.

"Did you see your father before he left for work? Oh, of course—I recall seeing him walking out your way."

John looked up from his plate, turning slightly to face his mother. The kitchen light caught the sheen in his light brown hair. He looked very smart in his new, beige Norfolk jacket.

"Dad and I have become much closer, almost like friends, since you and my sisters went to Chicago. Out there just now, he put his hand on my shoulder and said, 'Whatever you do, son, be a man. Be true to yourself. Always remember: in business, make friends, but question them all. Come home when you can, son.' He tried to say more, but his lip trembled a bit. He squeezed my shoulder hard and left. I shouted out, 'I love you, Dad,' but he was already closing the car door. Then he was gone. It was like being in the middle of the river in a boat without oars."

Helen had kept her back to her son as they spoke. Now she faced him with a smile.

"That's all right. He knows you love him, but I'll tell him again tonight exactly what you said, exactly how you felt. You look so handsome, so grown-up in your new jacket," she said affectionately.

She leaned over, taking both of his hands, and put them up to her warm cheeks. Then she added, "This is your big day, John. I can't believe it is here already, but it is. You know, when we first came out here, your father and I being so wide apart about living way out West, I used to look at you and think, *Take me out of all this, my son. Rescue your mother when you get that dream job.* Then everything changed. Chicago changed everything. I thought hard about staying there, developing the girls' careers there. But you know what? Molding the girls' careers here in Chambers if far more important. And my career will be right here. Miss Rochelle, I still call her that, Mrs. Baker now, and I will set up music schools and put on shows right here in Chambers. We have a lot to develop here, you know. Then, who knows. The girls can finish their high school in Pierre and maybe get scholarships in art and singing to take them off to their own dreams. Right now, my love, it's your show."

John stood up, looking directly at his mother. He loved her auburn hair, shoulder length, curved stylishly about her cheeks. Her white blouse and ruffles set her easily on stage—perhaps *Aida*, more likely *Tosca*. He loved her with his whole heart.

Their talk comforted him. He felt more secure. His family was not falling apart as it once appeared; they were stronger. He was leaving with some assurance now. He had a job on his hands. Fun. Intriguing.

Helen assembled breakfast as Sallie and Betty Jean rushed in to kiss John with premature good-byes. Brown sausage patties, eggs, toast, juice, and always the big pot of Gannon strong coffee, which the children milked down generously to their own taste.

Kansas City! It was all about Kansas City. "You write as soon as you get there. Tell Uncle Will and Aunt Martha we all send our love."

"Tell them to throw you in the river if you misbehave," Betty Jean said.

"You haven't forgotten anything, John?" Helen asked.

"No, ma'am."

The trip to the train station was all Mrs. Mason. She began immediately as everyone boarded her Buick.

"What a handsome young man you've become," she gushed. "Why, you are getting to be as big as your father. How much do you weigh? Oh, I know Mr. Gannon is proud of you. We all are, you know." Her words trailed off in the distance as they drove through town to the station.

John searched every storefront, every block, every street corner as they drove. He had something important to say to his friend. *He said he would come. Something has to be wrong.*

"Mr. Mason was telling your father yesterday at the bank, that he guessed the track team would just about fold up, now that you're gone and … and that boy …"

"Who is that, Mrs. Mason?" John baited her, trying not to show bad manners.

"That … that Eagle boy," she said, unable to say his full name.

"Oh, you mean James Blue Eagle. Oh yes, he put Chambers School on the map all by himself. The fastest ninth-grader in South Dakota, you know." He didn't wait for a reply, as his mother cautioned him with wagging finger and a stern look. But he continued.

"First Place! They put it right in the *Gazette*. 'Eagle, local Indian boy, wins gold medal, putting Chambers School on the map." Helen rolled her eyes in disbelief. "I took bronze. But you know, Blue Eagle just did a better job out there. He's simply the faster runner. Let's give him his due."

Helen thought she would suffocate; the air got so overheated. She quickly changed the subject. Smiling prettily, she said, "Oh, John, I almost forgot," and she talked until Mrs. Mason pulled into the parking area.

Everyone in town was at the small train station there on the edge of the prairie. The schedule, however, was delayed nearly an hour. Someone near them said that they thought Mr. Hartford had "robbed the bank—he had been in there so long." That was the meeting Tom had to attend.

During the long wait, John said good-bye twice to his family. He graciously thanked Mrs. Mason for driving them to the station. Then Mrs. Mason talked endlessly about what a fine man Tom Gannon is. "Why, he is practically mayor," she said. "He no doubt will be soon. Why, he's done so much for our town."

The time ticked down to the last minutes. John searched the crowd and the distant, open prairie. His heart sank, but he busied himself with moving his bag into position and making little conversations with his sisters. He looked at them and joked, "I'll send for you both as soon as I get settled. You'll have to canoe down the Missouri because no one has money to send two fine ladies by Pullman car." Both girls giggled. Betty Jean slapped John on his butt and told him how bad he was.

As the train pulled in, John said his last good-byes, straightened his shoulders, and climbed aboard the elegant zephyr for his first train ride. He positioned himself on the far side of the aisle, the prairie side, seeing the crowd as well as the open landscape of small cacti and scrub sage. He could still see his family quite well, waving his assurances now and then, but always searching—not only the crowd, but the prairie. John then looked afar. The scene was different. Several hundred yards away, an object, big as a pinhead perhaps, appeared. It wasn't there before, he thought, so he trapped it in his vision. *Are my eyes playing tricks? They sometimes do when you look constantly at a thing,* he thought. But no, this object grew. Then it grew some more.

Suddenly, John stood erect, bent slightly, and stared out the top of the window, being more clear than the bottom. His mouth parted, and his heart raced.

"Holy God," he whispered. Then everything fell into place.

"That's Crazy Dog's horse. He's right out of his manhood ceremony." Now up close, he could see the stallion had been ridden hard; he was wet at the flanks and heavy with foamy perspiration where the belly touched the hind quarters.

"Look! There's an Indian boy!" someone shouted, pointing out the window.

"My Lord," said the mustached, ruddy-faced man with her. "Looks like he's riding an Appaloosa."

"He is," John butted in. "It belongs to Crazy Horse, the chief." Then he turned back to the window. Blue Eagle pulled up thirty feet from where John sat. The dappled, white stallion, with bowed neck, flowing main, pranced to his left, away from the train. The Indian, sitting arrow-straight, looked ahead. Several more passengers on the prairie side of the train filled the windows.

"What is it?" several people asked. Then, all the passengers rushed to the windows, especially in the cars with direct vision of Blue Eagle and his mount.

John lifted his left hand to the window, palm facing out. His face broke into a wide grin as the rider moved closer to the train. Never had he seen his friend dressed out in the likes of this.

Blue Eagle wore tanned deer skin leggings to his knees, tan moccasins with designed beadwork, and a tan breech cloth bordered in blue bead work. A blue and white bandanna hung under his chin, rolled over his long braided hair, and a white wolf-tooth necklace hung to his chest. A thin, tall strip of porcupine quills adorned the center length of his head, and each cheek bone was scarlet red in triangular design that pointed the base of the middle of the nose. His beaded headband of red, white, and blue was crowned at the forehead with a round disc of horse hair painted in alternating red and tan wedges, its center a smaller disc of brightly colored beadwork. And hanging from the top of the right braid of hair was a single blue eagle feather.

There was no saddle. The only bridle was the voice, the vice-like knees, the rider's heels, and his strong hands in the stallion's flowing mane. Blue Eagle had all the excitement of Crazy Dog in formal ceremony. Suddenly the Indian's teeth flashed white through a yell, heels digging abruptly into the nervous stallion's flanks, sending them in an instant burst of speed halfway to the train—stopping just feet away from John's window. Their eyes never met.

Blue Eagle set the stallion back on his haunches. As the great stallion rose in the air, the Indian flattened, lay there, feet dug tightly into his mount's soft haunches. The stallion reared almost to tipping in the air.

The white stallion, spotted beautifully from shoulders to flanks with dark grey on shades of white, slashed the air with his black front feet. With bowed neck, nostrils flared below the wild eyes, he pranced for all to see.

Blue Eagle let go of the mane and slid down the stallion's back to the ground. A gasp came from the crowd. The moment the horse's front feet touched the ground, a swift running leap sent the Indian over the stallion's rear, astride the horse's back. At full charge, they left the embankment, pounding hooves sending small rocks crashing into the steel train cars. The Indian guided the stallion in a tight Apache-like circle near the train. He slid from the back of his mount to one side, disappearing from view except for a part of one leg and his hand. Then the boy reappeared only to disappear again on the other side of the horse, obscuring himself from the onlookers' view.

Still more applause came as the rider guided his mount in a larger circle. With hand in the horse's mane, he slid off the stallion's right side completely, bouncing from the ground in the same motion back to a sitting position, only to repeat the feat from the alternate side. The train passengers went wild. "It's like a rodeo out there!" someone yelled.

John's heart pounded as if he were the rider himself. In a lull, he suddenly remembered his family, wondering if they could see the performance. Amid all the excitement, he had not noticed that the station side of the train, where all the visitors had gathered, could see very little. They ran around in tight little bunches looking between cars, but saw bits and pieces of the show. Some looked under the train cars. A wry grin came over John's face when he spotted Mrs. Mason caught up in all the clamor. Then again, he thought, it might have been good for her to see his friend performing amazing feats that pleased so many people.

Blue Eagle stopped abruptly, dismounted, and removed his bandana. He tied it tightly over the stallion's eyes, as he saw the train was set for departure.

A steady drone of conversation engulfed the train as well as the station.

The trainmen yelled out, "All aboard!" The clamor increased. The trained slowly pulled out of the station, accompanied by the horse and mount.

When John remembered to search for his family, he barely caught a glimpse of his sisters waving furiously.

He responded as Betty Jean caught his eye. Everyone stayed at the windows as Blue Eagle showed no sign of quitting. The train gathered speed. Blue Eagle urged on the big stallion. As the zephyr gathered momentum, John looked back, his head pressed hard against the window. He could see the long, striated, distorted view of pounding black feet; the rider's flowing hair, his hand the whip; the pumping head of the powerful stallion, now running blind; surging onward with the flying white mane and forelock; the bright headband of the rider, and the stallion's long, white tail flowing in the wind.

Just as his friend drew even with the car, scarcely six feet away, John saw Blue Eagle face to face—his nose dilated, teeth glistening bright, lifting both hands to cup his mouth in a full scream of the eagle.

As rider and stallion reached the twenty-foot-high cliff of the Brule River, the cry of Blue Eagle as he plunged through air to water was lost in the deafening sounds of steam and steel as the zephyr raced over the trestle bridge to the open prairie.

John looked back in time to see horse and rider swimming to shore.

About the Author

Richard Ellison began writing in college—numerous articles, short stories, and poetry, followed by business papers, journals, and manuals.

He studied creative fiction writing at New York University in 1975 and 1976 under active novelist professors Sydney Offit and Sol Yurick.

After two careers spanning fifty years, in corporate New York and Dallas, he found the excitement of writing could wait no longer.

Born on a farm in northeast Texas, the Depression years, Ellison developed a keen relationship with nature, enjoying a lifetime of treks, fishing, music, the arts, sports, and travel.

Ellison's seven years of active military duty included US Navy 1945, Petty Officer, Commander in Chief Pacific Fleet Headquarters, WWII; US Air Force, Captain, Second Air Force, Strategic Air Command, 1951, Korean War.

After *Monmouth in the Morning*, two more exciting novels follow the Gannon family trilogy as Ellison watches each Gannon and their friends achieve the American Dream. Through wars and Industrial Revolution, they all take time to listen to the music.